EAGER TO PLEASE

JULIE PARSONS

EAGER TO PLEASE

MACMILLAN

First published in Ireland in 2000 by Town House and Country House, Dublin

First published in the United Kingdom 2001 by Macmillan
an imprint of Macmillan Publishers Ltd
25 Eccleston Place, London SW1W 9NF
Basingstoke and Oxford
Associated companies throughout the world
www.macmillan.com

ISBN 0 333 72990 0 (hardback)
ISBN 0 333 90509 1 (trade paperback)

1 3 5 7 9 8 6 4 2

A CIP catalogue record for this book is available from
the British Library.

Typeset by SetSystems Ltd, Saffron Walden, Essex
Printed and bound in Great Britain by
Mackays of Chatham plc, Chatham, Kent

For John,
for always and ever

ACKNOWLEDGEMENTS

My special thanks to:

John Lonergan, Governor of Mountjoy Prison; the prison officers, teachers and women I spoke to in the women's prison; the psychologists and probation officers who shared their insights with me; Donald Taylor Black and Veronica O'Mara of Poolbeg Productions; Mavis Arnold; Bernard Condon BL and Dr Kevin Strong; Gillian Hackett and Alistair Rumbold of the Irish National Sailing School; Peter Harvey of the *Liverpool Echo*; Sue Colley and John Stafford, Forest Enterprise, Kent. Alison Dye for all her wisdom, compassion and sense of humour. Renate Ahrens-Kramer, Sheila Barrett, Catherine Phil McCarthy, Cecilia McGovern and Joan O'Neill for their constructive criticism, good sense and friendship. Treasa Coady, Suzanne Baboneau, Beverley Cousins, Alice Mayhew and Nina Salter for their knowledge, experience and generous support.

EAGER TO
PLEASE

THE BEGINNING

SHE REMEMBERED THE way it was the first time she ever saw the prison. It was through the mesh that covered the windows of the van in which they brought her from the Four Courts that day all those years ago. It was winter. It was late afternoon, early evening. Rush hour in Dublin. It was dark. Or it should have been dark. Instead it was very bright everywhere. Shining white lights flooding the tarmacadam when the van stopped at the gate, so she could see out, and see the high cross and the gravestones set into the scraggy grass.

What's that? she asked the prison officer.

The tall well-built woman shrugged and said, *Kevin Barry. Monument to him.*

Who? She tried to think. *Who?*

You know, Kevin Barry, the hero of the War of Independence. He was hanged here and a load of others too. Against that wall.

She tried to stand up to get a better look, but the officer tugged at the chain that joined them at the wrist.

Where do you think you're going, eh? Sit down and mind yourself.

— 3 —

A snigger ran around the van. She looked at them all, the other women who'd made the short trip from the court to the prison. She had tried to sit away from them, to keep a distance between their tracksuits and trainers and her best black skirt and jacket, to keep the smoke from the cigarettes that drooped from their mouths and tattooed fingers away from her nostrils and eyes. But there was no distance in the van, no means to separate her and her shame from them.

And then the van began to move again, through the high metal gates, past the tall stone building that looked like a church, the cluster of portakabins at its side, and towards the metal cage that surrounded the entrance. It was interesting, she thought, remembering back, how quickly she had become used to the metal. It was everywhere. Steel, she supposed. A malleable alloy of iron and carbon was the way her architectural textbooks had described it, capable of being tempered to many different degrees of hardness. Incapable of rust. Beautiful too when used with glass the way her heroes, Le Corbusier and Frank Lloyd Wright, had employed it. To create palaces of light and space. Ugly now in this place of containment, where it couldn't be pulled apart and used as a weapon of defence or attack. Interesting too how she had adapted to all the hard surfaces. The tiled floors, the bars on the windows, the upright chairs, the wooden doors, three inches thick, decorated with locks and spyholes. Even the pad, as the padded cell was known, wasn't soft. Walls, floors covered with hard rubber. Nothing she could use to damage herself, or anyone else, that first night. After they had taken away her clothes and handed out her prison issue – a clean bra and pants, as if she needed them. A tracksuit, as if she ever wore one. A night-gown and a dressing gown, as if she didn't have her own, at home, lying across the bed, her own bed, that she had hoped she'd sleep in that night.

That she had hoped she'd sleep in that night. That she had been sure she'd come home to. That at the end of the trial the jury would believe her. That she hadn't done what the prosecution said. That she didn't take the 12-gauge shotgun and shoot him, first of all in the right thigh, severing the femoral artery so his blood pumped out on the floor. Then as he screamed and weakened and fell back that she didn't shoot him again, this time in the groin, tearing his genitals apart, so there was a lot more blood, spattering her clothes with small tear-shaped drops. And some of the jury, two, to be precise, believed her and not them. One of the women, older, pale-faced, wept as the foreman stood and delivered his verdict.

How do you find the defendant Rachel Kathleen Beckett? Guilty or not guilty of the murder of Martin Anthony Beckett?

Guilty, your honour, by a majority of ten to two.

And the sentence?

The judge with the ruddy face and flabby jowls leaned forward across the bench.

I have no choice in this case, when the verdict is guilty of murder, there is a mandatory sentence of life. And this I shall impose on you, Rachel Kathleen Beckett.

Life or death? Which began and which ended on

that cold November afternoon twelve years ago? She still could not decide.

Form P30. That was what it was called, the stiff piece of cardboard which was slotted into the outside of her cell door. Everyone had one. It stated registered number, name and religion. It stated when committed and for what sentence. And it gave the particulars of discharge, sentence expiration and earliest possible date of release, with a box beside for the day, the month and the year. The other women, those who weren't lifers, had numbers written in the boxes. But she didn't. Hers were blank. She stood and looked at the piece of cardboard, put up her hand to touch it, then pulled it from its slot and tore it into tiny pieces, shoving them into the pocket of her jeans. Behind her she heard the laughs, the taunts, the insults, and heard the shout of the officer she remembered from the van.

What do you think you're doing? Who do you think you are? As she grabbed her by the arm, pulled her into the office, dragged the pieces of cardboard from her pocket and said, *Here, you, Miss high and mighty. Think you're better than everyone else, do you? Think you can do what you like with prison property. Well, now, have another think while you put it all back together again.*

Handed her the roll of Sellotape, made her stay there in the stuffy little office, until the jigsaw was complete, then forced her back out on to the landing. The women lined up on either side, jeering and shouting as she walked up the first flight of stairs to her cell. She took the piece of cardboard and put it back where it had been. And looked down and away as the officer, Macken, that was her name, said loudly so that everyone else could hear, *You'd better start using your brains and using your education, Beckett, and finding out how best to please us. You'd better be bloody eager to please me, or else, Beckett, your life sentence is going to last a lot longer than anyone else's. Do you hear me now? Do I make myself plain?*

Pushed her into the cell, followed her and said, *It's a funny thing about time, isn't it? Right now it's standing still for you. The hands of the clock aren't moving at all. And they won't until you get your attitude straight. Do you hear me now? Do you read me loud and clear?*

She was right about that, Macken the bitch, as she was right about most things. It was such a long time, her first night and first day. Her first week, month, year. So long till Christmas, Easter, New Year. So long that she hardly noticed her daughter, Amy's birthday. And the anniversary of Martin's death. When all she wanted to do was stay in her cell, turn her face to the wall and weep. Because she missed him, because she had loved him. Because she had lost him and everything else.

She didn't remember much of any of that year, or the one after that or the one after that. Time passing had no meaning for her now. No meaning at all. The only thing that meant anything was the mood, the atmosphere, the feelings around her. Sometimes they were good. Most times they were bad. What was it all about, she wondered, these waves of tension that washed up and down the landings, dragging the women with them. She watched how they would congregate outside one cell or another, how huddles would take shape in the far corner of the exercise yard, in the laundry in the basement, or in the showers. They would turn to her when she approached, sometimes laughing, joking, their faces animated with an inner glee which frightened her with its excess. At other times they would turn on her, far too ready with their fists and feet. And their needles. Although they were much too careful of their precious spikes to waste them on an outsider like her. An outsider? Hardly. Not when she slept every night behind a locked door. When she woke every morning to the sound of a key. When her prison sentence drifted out in front of her like a piece of seaweed in mid-ocean as she lay in her bed in the dark and conjured up the sea beneath her. Felt the lift and surge of an Atlantic swell. Heard the rush of water beneath the keel, the breath of the wind on her face, the sudden lurch in her stomach as the boat heeled over, and she felt as if she would fall, tumble head first down through white water, green water, and into the blackness of the deep from which there was no way up. No way out. Not now. Not for her.

The Outside. What could it possibly be like, now, after all these years inside? She remembered how in the beginning she would try to stand as close as she could to the prison officers, so she could smell the freshness they brought with them every day. She tried to ask them what it was like outside, beyond the enclosing stone walls which leached out even the brightest colour. Was it raining, was it sunny, from which direction came the wind? She wanted to know in early summer if the dew was thick on the grass in the mornings, and in midwinter if they had to scrape the ice from their windscreens. In the beginning they shrugged off her questions, suspicious of her motives. But most of them softened, gradually, came to see that all she wanted was the raw material with which to imagine.

Most of them softened, and some even came to like her. She was different. She wasn't the same as the other women. They were in and out of here every few months, prison a respite from the demands of the street, a chance to rest and sleep and eat, maybe even go to school for a few months, catch up on a bit of the childhood that so many of them had missed.

They talked about her, some of the prison officers, and speculated why she had done what she did. But that kind of interest wasn't encouraged. The tall well-built woman who had brought her to the prison, Macken, Macken from the van as she called her, put it into words for the others.

You're kidding yourself if you think any of them are like us. They're not. They're different. They think differently, they act differently. None of us will ever end up here. Don't start getting into a 'there but for the grace of God' kind of mentality. And as far as Rachel Beckett goes, forget it. She killed her husband. She murdered her husband. She stood over him when he was drunk. She loaded his gun. She took off the safety catch. She aimed at him and she pulled the trigger. Twice. Stay away from her, I'm telling you all. And what's more, Macken said, *will she admit it? Will she take responsibility for it? For what she did. She'll no more do that than saw her way with a nail file through the bars out of here.*

And they turned from their cups of tea and watched her as she slouched with the others against the wall of the landing, her expression as blank and withdrawn as any one of the rest.

The exercise yard on a dull, blowy afternoon. The women, twenty, thirty of them, standing around, smoking, bored, idle. Gossiping, moaning, complaining. And Rachel, by herself, in the corner, reading. Then a voice began to sing a favourite song, a song of defiance. And soon another had joined her, and another and another, until there was a circle of women, arms linked, all singing. Throwing their voices out and up towards the windows of the men's prison next door.

Oh no, not I,
I will survive,
As long as I know how to love
I know I'll stay alive.

Waiting for the voices of the men. Roaring the chorus back at them.

I've got all my life to live,
I've got all my love to give . . .

Shadows seen against the windowpanes. Their words muffled by the iron mesh.

And I'll survive
I will survive.

The expressions on the women's faces. Joy, pleasure, exhilaration. The faces she was beginning to sort out and differentiate, assigning them names and histories. Patty, Tina, Lisa, Molly, Denise, Bridget, Theresa. Who now looked over to where she leaned against the wall, laughing out loud, clapping in time. Stamping her feet on the asphalt. Singing along with them.

And they held out their hands to her and sealed her into their circle. The vibrations shook her throat and diaphragm as she shouted as loudly as the rest. And they stamped and roared as one voice and swung their arms backwards and forwards, until the screws came through the meshed gates. Five, maybe six of them in a group, shouting at them.

Break it up.

Quieten it down.

Come on.

Inside now.

It's tea time.

And Rachel watched the way the women opened their circle, then closed it again around the screws, singing more and more loudly, while the men's faces pressed against the bars of the windows that looked down on them, singing too, chanting out the words, their voices low, resonant, ferocious, beautiful.

And the circle got tighter and tighter, pushing in closer, trapping the screws, so they began to twist and turn, this way and that, suddenly small and defenceless, just women like their prisoners, their uniforms meaning nothing, their fear plain to see. As the volume of the singing rose even louder and the chanting from the men above became less and less musical, more and more staccato.

She felt it there, for the first time on that dull, blowy afternoon in the exercise yard. The charge of energy when the group forms, becomes a mass and realizes its power. She watched the women's bodies. They were growing, changing shape, there in front of her. And the officers could see it too. They knew what was happening. They stepped this way and that, their faces pale, their attitude defensive. She could see the way they were trying to catch the attention of individuals, break them from the group, calling out their names.

Hey, Jackie, Tina, Molly. Hey, Theresa. Hey, I'm talking to you. Hey, calm it down. Break it up, or else.

Or else? Or else what, she wondered as she watched. These women were beyond *or else*. And everyone out there knew it. So she waited, tense and expectant, not sure what came next. Asking herself, What will I do? Where do I stand? Her hands clenching into fists, the muscles in her legs tightening.

And then, suddenly, it had ended, as quickly as it had begun. The women made the decision. They had had their fun. They knew there was nothing further to be gained, so they unlinked their arms and moved apart. They stopped singing and they walked quietly back inside. She smiled as she followed them indoors on that dull, blowy afternoon, hearing the jeers and catcalls of the men who watched. They wouldn't have walked away from it. They would have taken it to the limit. But they would have been beaten. This way, she thought, the women had it all. They'd flexed their muscles. They'd shown their power. And they'd do it again. Singly, collectively, one way or the other. It was always there. A choice. A possibility. Never to be forgotten. Ever.

She had asked to see the psychologist. She had faith then. Back at the beginning. Faith in her own kind. Reasonable people with education and understanding.

Why? The response was polite but disinterested.

I need help.

Really?

She had waited. They were short-staffed. There was a list. Her name was added to the bottom. The day came. She had prepared what she would say. She had practised the words, remembered the vocabulary.

Look, I shouldn't be here. I'm not violent or dangerous. This is a mistake. I didn't kill my husband. It wasn't me. Yes, we had a row. Yes, I was angry. But I didn't kill him. Please, don't you see? I'm not a psychopath, a sociopath, someone like that. Don't you see that I shouldn't be here?

The psychologist's report had stressed her state of denial, her inability to accept responsibility for her actions, her lack of remorse.

She waited to see what would happen. Time passed. She asked to see the Governor.

Surely, she said, *surely the psychologist has told you that I am innocent. That I didn't do this. That I shouldn't be here.*

Rachel. The Governor's voice was kind, concerned. *Rachel, I don't think you quite understand what this is all about. You have been tried by a court of law. You have been found guilty by a jury of your peers. You have been sentenced to life imprisonment. That is the only reality. Anything else is the stuff of dreams.*

It was a long time before she willingly went to see another expert. There were duty calls that had to be made. And sometimes they made her laugh, the students, sent on work experience or placement, so serious, so concerned. The do-gooders who thought they could relieve her burden of guilt. The priests and nuns who came to offer succour. She'd smile at them all and imagine the conversations they'd have when they went home.

You'll never guess who I met today.

Do you remember her?

Yes, that's right, the one who shot her husband.

Life sentence, that's what she got.

Nice? Oh, she's lovely. Very polite, well spoken. You'd never guess, ever.

It was boredom really that made her go the last time, and the recommendation from the others.

You should see this one, Rachel, they all said. *He's different. He's nice.*

He was older than the rest. Just doing a locum, he told her, filling in for a while, needed a few bob. He looked through her file. She watched him. He looked tired, ill. His clothes were shabby. He was a smoker, nicotine stains on his fingers, yellow marks on his teeth. He slowly turned over the pages, then he looked up and held her gaze.

The time has come, he said, *for you to admit your crime. You've been here for too long for your own good. Your sentence was reviewed after seven years by the Sentence Review Group. It was reviewed the following year and the year after that. They decided against probation. And do you know why?*

She nodded.

Of course you do. You're not stupid. But you're too clever to be here still. Next time you're looking in the mirror think about what you see. Think about the lines on your face, the grey in your hair and the wrinkles on your hands. Think for once about your future. Then ask to see the Governor. Tell him you're ready to accept responsibility for killing your husband. You're ready to admit your guilt and that you now feel genuine remorse. And as you say the words they will transform you. They will make you worthy of pity and redemption. And maybe not tomorrow or the next day or the next, but some day in the still-to-come, those words will release you. Now go away and think about what I have said.

The Governor had sent for her. Told her he had good news. That the Sentence Review Group had made a recommendation. She was to be made ready for temporary release. Or perhaps she should think of it as release on licence.

You understand, don't you, Rachel? Your life sentence will always remain. But if you behave yourself, follow the rules, you will be able to live once again as others. Well, almost as others.

She was to learn how to shop and cook, handle money, use public transport, pay bills, look after herself once again. That twelve years after surrendering her life to the institutions of the State, they had now decided to return it to her.

Did she want it? She lay on her bed at night, securely locked in, and let her eyes wander over the familiar marks on the walls and stains on the ceiling. She had been in this same cell for nine years, eleven months and two days. It was on the top landing, in the corner nearest the road. Not that she could see beyond the walls during the day. But at night it was different. At night she could see the lights of the airport, and the planes as they landed and took off. By day they were insignificant smudges, an occasional flash as sunlight glanced off a metal wing or superstructure. But at night she could follow with her eyes their lights as they rose through the air, up and up and up. And she could go with them. To London or New York. To Paris or Rome. To all those cities she had once visited, all those years ago. And she would summon up from her memory, the names of the streets, the buildings she had studied, analysed, wondered about, admired, and she could smell the air, feel the warmth of the sun on her arms, the light dazzling her eyes. Now she stood and went to the window, pushing it open through the bars as far as it would go. It was cold, but she didn't care. She raised her eyes to the blue-black sky. The moon was in its dying phase. She could clearly see the Copernicus crater and the crater named after Kepler. Martin had loved the moon. He had shown her through his binoculars the seas and craters and named them for her.

One of the things that fascinates me about it, he had said, *is the way it's always there, even during the day. You can't see it because of the light from the sun, but it's always out there, waiting till night comes, and then it can reveal its face again. It's the way a good surveillance officer should be. So carefully concealed and camouflaged that none of the people you're watching can see you, until you want them to.* He had said it to her in the days when he still talked to her, shared his work with her. Told her everything.

Jackie the probation officer, the one she had known the longest, said to her today, *You must have some friends, some family, someone you can re-establish contact with. You're going to need them now, when you're out. It's very hard to get by on your own. I know you've been lonely in here but loneliness on the outside is a completely different kettle of fish.*

Had she been lonely in here? She tried to remember, to compare the way she felt now with what had gone before. All around her she heard voices. Women's voices. She knew them all, their names, their ages, their crimes. She had sat with them in the dust of the yard and listened as they told the stories of their lives. She had told them stories too, the stories her mother had read to her when she was a child, which she in turn had passed on to her own daughter. The Princess and the Frog, the Twelve Dancing Princesses, Beauty and the Beast, Bluebeard, the Princess and the Pea. She watched how their faces softened and their eyes closed as they lolled against each other and dreamed. Now she heard them calling out through their windows to the men behind the grey walls of the prison across the yard. Brothers, boyfriends, husbands. Men she had come to know through the letters she had helped their women write. Puzzling over the words, fingers clumsy with biro or pencil.

Dear Johnny, I love you. I can't wait to get out of this kip and be with you again.

Dear Mikey, how's it going? Are you any better? Are you going to the hospital and taking your tablets like I told you?

Dear Pat, I'm sending you all my kisses and hugs. I miss you. Do you miss me?

Are you listening? The women shouted now. *Are you listening?*

Sometimes she felt like joining in, even though she had no one of her own behind the barred windows opposite. But sometimes she just wanted to hear the sound of her own voice, calling out, waiting for an answer.

Who would she call to now?

Are you listening, outside world? I'm coming back. Are you listening?

She had asked them if she could have a map of the city, the biggest they could find. The assistant chief officer, a middle-aged man called Dave Brady, brought one in from his car and held it out to her.

Here, Rachel, you can have this, he said and smiled. He had a lovely smile. Genuine and kind. He was a favourite with the women. They teased him and slagged him off. And he just shrugged and laughed, and let it roll all over his lanky frame and greying hair.

When she put the map's shiny cardboard cover to her nose, she could smell wax or polish, dust, a faint tinge of petrol. It was tacky, clinging to her fingers. She smelled again. Lollipop, maybe. Wine gums, possibly. Mr Brady was always talking about his kids. They were nearly grown up now. Two at university, and the oldest was working in Silicon Valley in California. So Mr Brady said. Rachel couldn't imagine a place with a name like that. She could barely imagine California. Or even Dublin, for that matter. Now.

That was why she wanted the map. She opened it out fully and stuck it to her wall with Blu-tack, pressing her thumb hard down, feeling the surface of the stiff paper smooth against the rough plaster beneath. Then she sat back on her bed and looked at it. Her whole life was contained within its boundaries. Everything of importance that had ever happened to her had happened within its confines. She stood up and peered at the criss-crossing rows of streets. She found the hospital where she was born, the house in which she had lived as a child. She picked out her school, the university where she had studied architecture, the crooked arms of the harbour at Dun Laoghaire where she had learned to sail. She saw the places she had gone with Martin, the church in which they had married, the arc of the cul-de-sac where once they had lived. Where he had died, and she had grieved for him.

For years now she had refused to think of what lay beyond the prison. She had imagined herself in a desert or a forest. Isolated, depopulated, living outside the limits of time and space. There was nothing real out there, especially since she had stopped going to see Amy. Even to think of her name made her feel sick. She pushed the memory back, deep down, hidden where it could do her no harm. And she looked again at the map and picked a red felt pen out of the jar on her little table. She began to mark the map with small round dots. Red was for everything connected with her punishment. She found the prison and outlined it first, then coloured it in so it was unmistakable. She picked out the Garda station in which she had been questioned, the Four Courts where she had been sentenced. She found the Department of Justice and the office of the Director of Public Prosecutions. Somewhere in those buildings were all the files that related to her and her case. She could imagine the filing cabinet and the buff-coloured folders. They had refused her leave to appeal. They had sentenced her to life. She wondered who they were, those men and women who had made all those decisions. Did they think about her now, remember who she was? She supposed they did not.

She picked up a ruler and drew neat lines between them all. Backwards and forwards across the city they zigzagged in bright red. Then she picked up another pen. This time it was blue. Amy's colour. The blue of her favourite dress, the one she was wearing the last time she saw her. Not the faded, washed-out blue of the shirts that the prison officers wore, or the dull blue of the sky above the prison roofs, filtered through the city's pollution. She marked the hospital where she had given birth to her. The house where they had lived. The house where Amy lived now with her foster-family. She found her schools too. The little national school where Rachel had taken her every morning for her first year, kissing her goodbye at the classroom door, waiting outside to take her home again at lunch-time. And she found the other schools Amy had attended. She had memorized the names that the probation officer had told her.

You have a right to be kept informed of your daughter's progress. You know that, don't you? We can arrange for you to see her outside, not in here. You know that, you do know that, Rachel?

But she had refused. She could not bear it. She had seen the way that Amy had begun to cling to the woman who was now waking her in the morning and putting her to bed at night. How could she compete with that daily contact?

I'm your mother, she had whispered in her daughter's crumpled ear those first few times that Amy had come to the prison to see her. She had held her on her knee and breathed in the sweetness of her child smell. Rested her cheek on Amy's fine brown hair. Kissed the little folds of softness around the nape of her neck. She wanted to take off all her daughter's clothes and look at her body. So she could remember. This was the way it once was, this was the way it was to be a mother. To be able to touch her, hold her, kiss her round belly, stroke the curve of her backbone. Memorize this child in her entirety, this child who had once been as much a part of Rachel as her own hand, arm, leg, breast, face.

In the past, that was. Not, she realized, despair knocking the breath from her body, not in the future.

I'm your mother, she had said, and Amy had nodded and sucked down hard on her thumb.

My mother, she had repeated, and said, *Come home, Mumma, come home with me now.* Her eyes had shifted to the door to the outside, and she had begun to fret, one hand twisting through her hair, her small body tensing, then wriggling with anxiety.

I want to go home. Now, she whined. *I don't like it here.*

She stamped her foot on the floor, the buckles of her sandals making a tiny ringing sound. New shoes, Rachel noticed, like the rest of Amy's clothes. She had outgrown the dresses, dungarees, sweaters, blouses, that Rachel had bought for her. Now she wore nothing that Rachel had chosen. She had shed the skin that Rachel had provided. And when time was up and the foster-mother came in to collect her, Amy lifted her arms and clutched at her heavy thighs. Rachel had met the woman's eyes over her daughter's head. They were kindly, concerned, loving. And they were winning.

Now she drew the straight, careful lines between them all. Somewhere out there she would have to find her own place. But there could be no rest for her until she had fulfilled the promise that she had made to herself that day when the judge had passed sentence.

This is not the way this will end. This is just the beginning. And no matter what happens, I will see this through. I will never let go.

*

She watched the woman with the grey hair and the thin face walk towards her through the crowd of lunchtime shoppers in the department store. She moved slowly and carefully as if she had just woken up and she wasn't quite sure that her body was as yet her own. She was wearing a white shirt and faded denim jeans, with a grey cardigan, unbuttoned and sagging from her shoulders. Her arms hung awkwardly at her sides and as Rachel watched she slid her hands up her forearms until they were grasping her upper arms just above the bend of the elbow. Then she stopped and closed her dark brown eyes. Her head drooped on to her chest. Her shoulders shook and sobs burst from her throat. She took three more steps forward, then leaned her ruined face against Rachel's in the full-length mirror in front of her. Rachel felt the cold glass against her cheek. She opened her eyes and looked at the woman she had become, trying to find herself in the reflection. Tears poured down her face. She turned to the younger woman standing beside her, who had reached out a hand to offer her comfort.

Please, Jackie, I've had enough. I want to go back. Now.

It was to be her big day. Her first day out. The first step in the re-socialization programme which the Sentence Review Group had recommended. She had been given a date, two weeks' notice.

Something to look forward to, Jackie had said cheerfully. She had bought her new clothes, paid for out of her 'grat', the savings Rachel had put together down through the years. A pair of grey trousers, straight-legged with a sharp crease down the front. And a grey jacket to match. Shoes too, real leather, slip-ons with a pointed toe and a neat heel. Rachel's feet felt huge in them. She tried walking up and down in her cell, hearing the little click as the leather soles met the tiled floor. She was used to runners, soft shoes that were silent, with plenty of room for toes. She tried on her clothes, gingerly, carefully, reluctant to shed her familiar prison wear.

Jackie had bought her make-up too.

Come on, Rachel. Try some of this. You remember how, I'm sure. Don't you?

She handed it all over in a small plastic bag, with a zip and blue flowers printed on the outside. Rachel sat at her desk with her pocket mirror propped up on top of her radio. She spread out the bag's contents. Foundation in a tube. Lipstick in a silver metal case. Mascara, eyeliner, brown eyeshadow. Even blusher, a dark rosy pink with a translucent shine. She rubbed the tip of her index finger across it, then smeared it on the back of her hand. It glowed and shone like skin after a day in the sun.

She picked up the tube and squeezed a pale brown worm-like twist of it on to her palm. She began to smooth it across her face. Up and over her forehead, down the centre of her nose and across her chin. She stretched up her throat so the skin was taut and smeared it over and around, from one distended tendon to the other. She wiped her fingers on a piece of toilet paper, then opened the little bottle of eyeliner. She dipped the fine brush that had come with it into the black liquid. She painted precisely around the outline of first her right eye, then her left. She unscrewed the mascara and swivelled the barrel, jerking out the stiff bristles. Her eyelashes lifted and separated as she coated them with a shiny black covering. She filled in the deep hollow between lid and socket with dark powder, so her eyes sank back into her head. Then she picked up the lipstick, turning it upside down to read its name. Crimson poppy, the label said. She twisted the silver barrel and the pointed nose cone of red poked out. She held the mirror carefully with her left hand. Her own lips looked palely back at her. She moistened them with her tongue. They gleamed now in the dull overhead light. She pressed them to the reflection in the mirror, feeling the cold glass push against her teeth. She hadn't kissed anyone else for years. Sucked and licked and teased with her tongue the hidden lips of other women in here. But she had never kissed their mouths. She did not want to look into their eyes or let them look into hers. She was keeping that for some other time. Now she drew the outline of her mouth with the thick red nib, then filled it in, rubbing the lipstick backwards and forwards, caking it thickly over her lips. She could smell its perfume and taste its synthetic sweetness.

Martin had hated her wearing lipstick. *You don't need it*, he had said to her. *You have a beautiful mouth without it. I like its paleness. I like the way, when I kiss you and kiss you, it gets darker and darker.*

She remembered the first time she had gone to his flat he had taken her into the bathroom and wiped the make-up from her with his face cloth. *Look*, he had said, showing her the smears of brown and red that stuck to its towelling ridges. *See how ugly it is. Look how much more beautiful you are without it.*

And he had bitten her lips, gently nipping the delicate skin between his front teeth so they had reddened, almost to purple. The colour of membranes suffused with blood. The special skin of dark and secret places.

Now she sat back and looked at the face in the mirror. It wasn't hers. She angled the glass so she could see her body. The grey jacket and trousers, the neat black shoes with the pointed toes and the small heel. A shiver of revulsion ran through her. She kicked the shoes from her feet, tearing at the wool which held her arms and legs tightly, ripping the clothes off and flinging them in a pile in the corner by the toilet. She pointed the mirror at her naked body, moving it up and down. Her ribs were clearly visible, her stomach, concave. The skin of her hips was ridged with silvery streaks, like satin frayed by the point of a scissors. Her breasts were as small as ever, but now they drooped and flattened, accentuating the bones of her sternum and upper chest. She ran her hand over her pubic hair. It curled around her fingers, clinging closely, as black as always. She squatted down and looked at her face again in the mirror. The skin of her body was pale, but above it loomed the fake brown of the make-up on her face, the black around her eyes, and the livid red of her mouth. She stood up and went to the basin in the corner. She ran her hands under the hot water and picked up the soap. She lathered it thickly, feeling the burn and sting as it crept into her eyes. She bent her face to the water, then lathered again, scrubbing with her fingers, until the water ran dark. Her breath came quickly. She buried her face in the rough surface of her towel, then picked up the mirror again. Smears of black still clung to her eyelashes, and faint traces of red marked the fine lines around her mouth. She whimpered and ran fresh, steaming water into the small basin, washing, rinsing and washing again, until her face was clean and pale.

As pale as the face she saw reflected in the side mirror of Jackie's car as they inched through the traffic towards the North Circular Road.

I can't do this, she said. *I can never do this again. I won't be able to leave the prison when the time comes. Please, Jackie, don't make me.*

And why won't you? The voice inside her asked. And the voice inside her answered. Because then I'll have to face what happened, and I'll have to find a way to make it right again. And now, after all these years, I don't think I can do it. Ever.

THE MIDDLE

CHAPTER ONE

IT WAS AN interesting case, the Rachel Beckett case,
Andrew Bowen thought as he got up from his desk
and walked across the corridor to the kitchen to make
the first of the day's cups of coffee. It was a rare event
in the mundane world of a probation officer to get a
lifer on your books. It had only happened twice before
in his career. And he'd never had to deal with a
woman. Of course he'd had women sitting here in his
office who'd killed. Quite a number of them. Killed
their husbands or boyfriends, killed their children. But
they had been judged to have killed on the spur of the
moment. Out of fear, in self-defence, responding to
aggression, reacting in anger or madness. Never the
way the prosecution said Rachel Beckett had killed.
Slowly, deliberately, precisely. With foreknowledge
and premeditation. And now the Department of Justice, in its wisdom, had decided that she had shown
due remorse and recognition of her crime and it was
time they let her out. On licence of course. And at
nine o'clock this morning, 10th May, she was coming
to see him.

Remorse, now there was an interesting concept.

From the Latin verb *remordere*, to bite again. A second bite of the cherry, a second chance. An opportunity to make good the bad that had been done in the past. Or was it? He had always wondered about instances of remorse. He thought of the energy that went into denying the crime that had been committed. The elaborate defence that was put together for the court, expert witnesses produced and paid for, tearful delivery of evidence, hand-on-heart denials of wrongdoing. And then, somehow or other, years later, after the reality of prison life had begun to sink in, along came Mr Remordere, fresh and bright, and new, and good as gold.

Please, sir, I didn't mean to do it.

Please, sir, I did it all right, but it was a mistake, an accident. I didn't want it to be like this.

Please, sir. OK, I admit it. I did it. I planned it. I thought it through, but let me out and I'll be good, I promise.

It was quiet in the kitchen at this early hour of the morning. He stood still for a moment and listened. He was alone. His other colleagues invariably drifted in a good hour after he had already made a start. They blamed their lateness on the traffic. He attributed his punctuality to the same traffic. He got up an hour and a half earlier to beat it, he said, and they all looked at him as if he had a screw loose. He didn't care. They could manage their days whatever way they chose. Nominally he was in charge, but they all knew what kind of a boss he was. Benign to the point of disinterest. And that was fine by everyone. An easy life, that's what they all wanted. And who was he to argue with that?

He filled a glass Cona jug with water, and tipped ground coffee, Colombian, his favourite, into a new paper filter. He lifted the jug high, then poured the water down in one smooth movement, quickly placing the empty container underneath. He waited, listening to the faint hum of the machine, then walked around the small pine table to look at the noticeboard beside the window. The soles of his shoes peeled off the lino underfoot with a satisfyingly sticky sound. He straightened the various notices pinned haphazardly into the cork. There was a lecture series on young offenders beginning soon in UCD. It was part of their extramural programme. Night courses for adults. He noticed his own name next to two of the sessions. 'Young Offenders – The Therapeutic Approach' and 'Young Offenders – Identification and Treatment'. Christ, he'd forgotten he'd agreed to take part. It would be awkward. He'd have to get someone in to sit with Clare. She didn't like it when he went out at night. She was happy enough on her own at home all day. Especially as he had washed her and fed her and left her with everything she could possibly need within arm's length before he went to work in the morning. But nighttimes were different, she was always telling him. She couldn't bear the dark on her own.

He sighed and felt that instant of release as he let go his breath. Just for a moment. He hadn't realized he had been holding it in, holding on to it, keeping everything locked up tight. And then he felt the tears that came so easily these days, filling his eyes, blurring his vision. He felt in his pocket for a tissue. He blew his nose. Don't start, he thought, just don't start the day like this. It was so important to keep it all under control. That was what was so good about coming into work early. It got him away from the house. And Clare. Her illness, her pain, her despair, and her death to come. How soon would that be, he wondered, as he wondered every day. Perhaps when he got home this evening he would find her curled into a ball, her muscles already in a state of rigor. She would have tried to phone him, tried to get help. But she wouldn't have realized that he had pulled out the telephone jack before he left, so there could be no help. From him or from anyone else. It would look like an accident, the inevitable consequence of the illness that had slowly destroyed her life over the last ten years. He knew how it would seem. He had thought it through. He had rehearsed what he would say. To the doctor, to the police. I can't understand it. She was fine when I left this morning. Well, as fine as anyone who has advanced multiple sclerosis can possibly be. She said she would phone if there was a problem, but she didn't. I was in the office most of the day, except for a couple of hours when I was in court. But Clare had my mobile number, and my secretary always knows where I am, and besides, if she couldn't get me she would have phoned for an ambulance. She knew what to do.

But it was too soon now. He knew that. Clare still had a way to go. She couldn't stand or move without help. He thought of all the medical terms that had become familiar to them both over the last ten years. Paraesthesia, abnormal sensations without external cause, pins and needles to the uninitiated. Propriasaesthesia, the inability to judge the position of the limbs in relation to the rest of the body. Retrobulbar neuritis, the inflammation of the optic nerve, causing her sight to fail, and the pain behind her eyes which was increasingly dominating her life. She now had no control over her bladder, and she was finding it hard to swallow, hard to cough, hard to clear her chest. What lay ahead? They both knew. She had asked the doctor to spell it out. Pneumonia would kill her eventually, that and the urinary tract infections which were already making her miserable. But when? For how much longer could they bear it?

The kitchen was alive with the smell of fresh coffee. He lifted the jug and poured himself a large mugful, adding milk from an opened carton in the small counter-top fridge. He walked back across the corridor to his office. He sat down and opened Rachel Beckett's file. He noted her date of birth, 31 August 1957. She was forty-two. His age. And now she was getting her second chance, while she was young enough still to enjoy it. He remembered what she had looked like all those years ago when she had been tried for the murder of her husband, convicted and sentenced to life in prison. He had seen her a number of times, on the front page of the newspaper, on television and in the Round Hall of the Four Courts, sitting with her daughter on her knee, her father by her side, waiting, waiting. He had been working in Mountjoy at the

time, in and out of the courts all day, and she had been
a curiosity. For everyone. She had been beautiful, he
remembered. Delicate was the word to describe her.
Such a contradiction between how she appeared and
what she did. So everyone said. He had looked into
Court Number Four during the trial, whenever he had
a spare few minutes. And, as luck would have it, he
was there when the jury returned, twenty-four hours
after they had first retired. They had taken their time,
been sequestered over night. It was a majority verdict,
he remembered, ten to two. He remembered it all so
well. One of the jurors was crying. But Rachel Beckett
didn't cry. She just said very clearly and distinctly, No,
I don't believe it. And then she was gone. Barely time
to say goodbye. Taken away by the prison officers.
Removed from the gaze of decent people.

A buzzer rang on his desk. He looked at his watch.
It was nine o'clock exactly. That was good. She hadn't
lost the ability to be punctual. He looked up at the
security monitor mounted on the wall in front of him.
There was a camera aimed at the front door. He
watched her as she waited to be let in. It was hard to
tell in the grainy black and white how she looked. But
her hair was different, he could see that much. And
the way she stood, her stance, her posture. He pushed
down the button. His secretary answered him.

'You can tell my first client to come up now,
Maggie,' he said.

He watched the monitor, the way she leaned forward to hear the voice that crackled from the intercom.
He saw her reach out and push the door. The camera

in the stairwell picked her up again. She was wearing a coat that looked too big for her and carrying a plastic bag in her hand. She looked ill and weak and out of place. 'It's your second chance, you stupid cow,' he said out loud as he heard her knock on his door. 'You've got yours, and I need mine.' And he stepped away from his desk and walked towards her.

CHAPTER TWO

HER BEDSIT MEASURED fourteen feet by twelve. She had paced it out. Fourteen by twelve was one hundred and sixty-eight square feet. She stood with her back to the wall and looked up at the ceiling. How high was it? She moved into the centre of the room, underneath the dangling light bulb, tilted her head, looked and judged. Fourteen foot six she thought. That would be about right for a house like this in Clarinda Park in Dun Laoghaire, mid-Victorian, built around 1860, three storeys at the front, four at the back. She compared it with her cell in the women's prison. She had measured that out too. Ten feet by nine feet. Ninety square feet in all. In which to sleep, eat, shit. A net gain now of seventy-eight feet. And that didn't include the bathroom next door, with lavatory, washbasin, an old-fashioned full-size freestanding bath with a shower attachment. And a lock on the door.

She put her hand in the pocket of her jeans and felt the satisfying weight of the bunch of keys that her landlord had given her that morning.

'Just don't lose them,' he said. 'I've lost count of the number of times I've had to have the lock on the front door changed, and it'll be added to your rent if it's you who's responsible. OK?'

She had just smiled at him. She had no intention of ever letting those keys out of her grasp. Now she held them in front of her and shook them gently. They jangled together, a gentle musical sound, not like the ugly clatter of the huge and heavy keys that had dominated her life for so many years. The first sound that woke her every morning at seven-thirty. One chamber of the double lock being opened on the cell door. The solid satisfying *thunk* as it slid smoothly back into its casing. The squeak of the screw's rubber-soled shoes on the polished lino of the landing. But the door still shut tight, unmoveable until breakfast time at eight, when the second lock would be opened and the door would be flung back, this time with a shout and a roar.

'Come on, ladies, get up, rise and shine. Shake a leg. Breakfast is waiting.'

The first time she had been punished. Lost all her privileges. No letters, no phone calls, no visits. The Governor had shaken his head at her, his expression a model of sorrow rather than anger. 'I'm surprised at you, Rachel.' His voice was so low that she had to lean forward to hear what he was saying. 'Very surprised. A woman of your education and advantages. What on earth came over you?'

It was simple really. It was rage and a scalding, overwhelming desire to hurt. Something she hadn't felt since she was a child, when the playground bullies had picked on her, or the teacher had treated her unfairly.

She had learned how to control her temper, how to channel it, dampen it down, hide it behind a cold, shuttered face. But not this time. Now she wanted to stop that stupid woman's mouth with her fist, close off her patronizing, holiday-camp repartee. What was it the others called them? Kangaroos, standing up on their hind legs, safe inside their blue uniforms, with their badges of rank, their bunches of keys, their camaraderie and banter. Rachel had never hit a woman before. She had balled her hand and smashed it into the screw's soft, ample solar plexus, knocked the wind out of her, so she began to gasp and sob, backing out of the cell, her face red, her legs crumpling beneath her in shock. The response had been swift and brutal. One of the other officers had grabbed her hair, twisting her head back. Another had snatched at her hands, pulling them behind her waist, both her small wrists jammed together in the grasp.

'Fucking little cow. Who do you think you are? Miss fuckin' high and mighty, is that it?'

She had been dumped in the pad and left there, while all around she heard the boos and whistles, the cheers and catcalls of the women who until now had laughed at her, whispered about her, mocked her, sneered at her. Now she was one of them. There was no doubt about it.

And now she was here, in this room on the top floor of an old house in Dun Laoghaire with something she hadn't had for twelve years. A view. And such a view. It was so beautiful that she was scared to move in case it turned out to be an illusion, or the kind of hallucination that came to her often when she woke out of a dream. The room's single window was a large three-sided bay, hung with sagging cotton curtains. The glass in the panes was smeared and cobwebs decorated each corner. She moved closer, slowly, pausing between each step. She closed her eyes for a moment, squeezing them tightly together so that bright worms of light wriggled across her eyelids. Then she opened them and gasped out loud at the sight. It was the sea, spreading to the horizon. It was a blue that made her cry out with joy. The blue of the hydrangeas that her mother had grown in a tub outside their front door, tinged with streaks of purple and mauve.

She took another step forward and turned her head first to the right and then to the left. On one side she could see across to the crocodile-shaped hill of Howth, on the other to the smooth walls of the stone quarry on the Dalkey side of Killiney Hill. Below her spread red-tiled roofs and the crowns of trees – chestnuts, sycamores, bright green now in early summer. She watched the traffic streaming down the hill, stopping at the lights at the bottom, and the pedestrians, straggling from one side of the road to the other, and she began to panic. She could never become like any of those people down there. She was fooling herself if she thought that she would ever be able to move among them as if she belonged, without feeling that she was being watched, spied upon, her every move and nuance of behaviour logged and noted.

It had been like that this morning as she had stood

outside the small office building just off George's Street, where she had gone to meet her new probation officer. She had been early. She had misjudged how long it would take her to walk the quarter mile from Clarinda Park to the town centre. How far, how long, how much time to take? So she had given herself plenty. In case the traffic might be heavy and it took a while to cross the road. In case the footpaths were crowded and she wasn't able to find the right way to manoeuvre around the person in front of her. In case, in case, in case. A thousand reasons why it could take her forever to make the short trip, and so she was early. At least ten minutes to wait before she needed to press the buzzer to announce her arrival. She stood outside the solid metal door and noticed the security camera angled, pointing directly at her. She looked up and away. She was familiar with cameras like these. They were all over the prison. To be ignored and disdained. But she wondered as she stood still, waiting, who was watching. In the prison she knew. She sometimes felt as if the cameras were two-way. When they looked at her she might as well have been looking back at them in their poky little guard room, the desk covered with piles of paperwork, mugs half filled with cold tea, cluttering up every surface. And the same officers, day after day, week after week, month and year after month and year, scanning the security monitors, flicking from camera to camera, as familiar to her now as her own family once had been.

She stood and waited until it was time to buzz and be admitted. A small plump woman appeared at the top of the steep staircase that led from street level. She introduced herself.

'Maggie Byrne, Mr Bowen's secretary. If you need anything at any time, you can always phone me,' she said, her soft white face crumpling with concern. Then she pointed to the door behind her. 'He's expecting you.' And she tapped on the brown veneered surface and pushed his door open.

In prison her probation officers had always been women. Pleasant, friendly, concerned. She had watched them come and go over the years. Played little games with them, seen how much she could get them to reveal about their lives outside the prison, until invariably they copped on and stopped. It didn't do to mix the personal with the professional. They had been warned.

'Don't let them know too much about you. It's not good practice. They are inside. You are outside. Keep it separate.'

But they let their guard slip with Rachel. She was different. She spoke their own language. And sometimes they forgot.

Andrew Bowen wouldn't forget, Rachel could see that immediately from the way he kept her standing while he flicked through the pile of paper on the desk in front of him. She stood still. She didn't move. She waited. And then he raised his head, looked straight at her and smiled. He gestured to the chair set at an angle to his large polished desk. She sat. He was very thin. The collar of his white shirt looked far too big for his neck. His fingers were long and slender. His hands moved constantly, rolling a pencil backwards and forwards as he spoke. His voice was soft, so she had to lean forward to hear what he was saying. She shifted uneasily in the chair. He was telling her what her new life was going to be like. There was work for her, a job in the dry-cleaner's in the big new shopping centre which had opened recently in the town. It would be simple and straightforward. She mustn't worry that too much would be expected of her. To begin with she would need to come and see him every week.

'And then,' he cleared his throat, 'if all is working out well, we can consider after a year or so reducing your visits to once a fortnight, eventually once a month. And then, who knows?' He paused, and rested the index finger of his left hand flat against his upper lip. 'Who knows, someone in your position is, of course, never entirely without supervision, but all going well, this can become more of an informal arrangement. A phone call every month or so, perhaps a visit every six months. Notification if you're planning to change your place of work, move flats or get involved in a relation-ship. That sort of thing. Who knows how it will work out for you in the future? But I'm sure we both want everything to go well, isn't that right, Rachel?'

She nodded dumbly, unable to speak, suddenly aware of the reality of her life through his eyes. She stood up. 'Thank you,' she said. 'Thank you, Mr Bowen, I'm sure it will all be perfectly all right.'

'Wait.' His voice was suddenly loud. 'Just before you go. Let me remind you of the conditions of your temporary release. So we have a clear understanding. So we know what's what.

'Number one. You will not associate with anyone who you knew in prison. Is that clear?

'Number two. You will make no attempt to communicate with anyone who was involved in any way with the victim of your crime. In particular any member of his family. Is that clear?

'Number three. You will remain within the law at all times. Failure to comply with these conditions will result in your detention and your immediate return to prison. Is that clear?

'And number four. You will respect your daughter's wishes. You will not attempt to make contact with her without her prior agreement. Understood?'

His words drummed in her head. Orders, commands, restrictions, limits. Her responsibility now. Her duty. She was trapped, filled with panic. She turned away before he finished speaking and walked quickly to the door. She opened it. The stairway lay before her, a dark tunnel. She ran, outside and along the main street, dodging people and cars, her heart pounding, her breath catching in her throat. She didn't stop until she was back inside her room, her precious bunch of keys locking the door behind her. Sweat drenched her body, dripping down between her breasts. The window lay before her, the view glowing in the morning sunshine. She backed slowly away from it and looked around. The room was far too big. It wouldn't do. She paced out the dimensions again. Ninety square feet.

All she needed. She began to move the furniture, the small single bed, the table and two chairs, the heavy wardrobe with the door that wouldn't shut, the book-case, the cupboard with her mug, plate and bowl, her knife, fork and spoon, her two saucepans and one frying pan. And the cardboard box that had come with her from the prison, that contained her scrapbook, her few photographs of Amy, of her mother and father, of Martin, and the folder of official letters she had accumulated. The records of her case.

Now she bent down and tugged at the large rectangular rug, grunting with the effort, the dust making her sneeze, until she had pulled it away from its neat centre position, and revealed floorboards, unpainted underneath where it usually lay. She pushed and shoved and hauled until everything was in the necessary space, ten feet by nine feet. The last thing she moved was her map, the one she had brought with her from the prison. She carefully pulled it from the wall and, kneeling on her bed, lined it up where she could touch it easily. Then she lay down. She had been about to go for a walk by the sea, perhaps as far as the little beach at Sandycove. Dig her toes into the fine white sand. Watch the mothers and their children playing in the gentle wavelets that lapped around her ankles. Remember the days when she had taken Amy by the hand and led her into the sea, held her floating body gently against her own. But now she couldn't go there. The thought of all that open space and the sea stretching off to the horizon made her skin crawl. Memories crowded against her closed eyelids, so she pressed her fingers hard against them until all was blackness.

She lay curled tightly into a ball until her breathing slowed. Then she reached up and touched the smooth, stiff paper of the map. She had added a few other places to it since she had left the prison. She had used a black felt pen. But now she was worn out. She pulled the sheet over her head. It was almost dark, like the nights in the prison. Almost dark but not quite.

CHAPTER THREE

TEN DAYS SINCE she had been released and still she woke at seven-thirty every morning. Listening, waiting, trying to understand the sounds that rose up through the floors of this old house. Nearly the same age as the prison, she thought, built with the same materials. Stone, wood, plaster. But the prison had a hard shell laid on top of it. Tiles, concrete, metal. Making it ring like a series of bells of different dimensions enclosed in an echo chamber.

She shifted cautiously underneath her nest of blankets, moving her arms and legs tentatively. It was so quiet she could hear nothing but her own breath and the whistle from the water tank above her head in the attic. Someone must be up, she thought. There were five other bedsits in the house. She had passed some of the other tenants going up and down the wide staircase. They all seemed to be young, much younger than she. Except for the elderly lady with the yapping mongrel who lived in the room across the landing, which looked out over the front door. There was a girl and boy in the room directly beneath her. She could hear the sound from their television and the music they played filtering up through the cracks in the floor-boards. She had woken suddenly two nights ago and heard voices raised. Shouts and screams, then silence and loud sobs. Later on there was laughter and the unmistakable climactic shriek of lovemaking. She had put her fingers in her ears and wrapped the blankets around her head, but even that didn't stop it. You didn't hear sounds like that in prison, she thought. The walls between the cells were too thick, and even though the doors were open most of the day, the women had perfected the art of the silent orgasm.

She had caught the smell of dope from the couple's room too. She had stopped on the landing, resting against the stained wallpaper, and savoured it. In prison she had her own regular supply. She was a reliable customer. She paid her dues and she was good for favours. Besides which she was different, special. She'd been in prison for as long as most of the regulars could remember. She'd watched them grow up, have children, fall in and out of love and in and out of relationships. She'd given them a shoulder to cry on and listened to their stories of beatings, of exploitation, of self-destruction.

'Write my letter for me, Rachel,' they'd say. 'Tell me what to say to my brief. Social welfare are going to take the kids away from my mother and put them in care. What'll I do? Tell me, Rachel,' they had pleaded. 'Give me the words to say.'

And she had told them what to do and how to do it, translating their language into the language of the hierarchy. She wondered how they all were now without her as she stood on the landing and smelled the couple's spliffs, and remembered the way the same smell had hung on the landings in the stale prison air. Then the door had opened and the girl had stuck her head out.

'What is it?' she said. 'Do you want something?'

'No.' Rachel shook her head, remembering the conditions of her probation. 'No, I was just feeling a bit tired. These stairs are a bit much.'

'Yeah, right.' The girl looked at her without curiosity and walked back inside, slamming the door.

She would be about Amy's age, Rachel thought. Seventeen, eighteen. But Amy wouldn't look like her with her pierced nose and naval, her hair in thick matted ringlets, her fingernails painted in different colours. Nor would Amy be living with her boyfriend in a cramped bedsit in a rundown house in Dun Laoghaire, getting by on social welfare and a bit of dealing on the side.

Or would she? Rachel walked slowly up the rest of the stairs, her bag of shopping a dead weight in her hand, the smell of the dry-cleaning chemicals clinging to her skin and hair. They gave off a strong, pungent smell, which disgusted her so much that she filled the bath with hot water and lay soaping herself until the skin on her fingers had risen into white ridges and a grey scum of soap floated around her.

It was nearly a year since she had last seen her daughter. It was the day before Amy's seventeenth birthday. Amy had made it clear that she didn't want a visit on the day itself. She had other plans, a party with her foster-family and her friends from school.

'And do you have a boyfriend?' Rachel had asked her.

Amy had shrugged. 'Maybe.'

'Is he nice?'

'What do you think?'

They had met in a neutral venue. A convent to the west of the city, virtually empty now except for the small group of elderly nuns who still clung on to the building and their traditions. Rachel had waited in the long, dark hall, pacing up and down on the cream and red tiles. She stared down at them as the minutes passed, as she placed each foot neatly in front of the other. Every tenth tile was decorated with a small black crucifix. The two officers who had come with her watched her carefully.

'What're you doing, Rachel, playing hopscotch?'

She didn't answer. She'd given up on conversation with screws. She no longer had anything to say to them.

When Amy and her foster-mother finally arrived, Rachel asked if they could go out into the garden.

'It's a bit cold, isn't it?' The foster-mother, Pat was her name, stepped forward protectively. 'Amy's just got over the flu.'

Mother and daughter sat in silence, facing each other across the polished mahogany table. Rachel put out her hand. As her fingers inched across the shiny wood Amy stood up.

'There's something I want to say to you.'

Rachel looked at her. Her hair had been fine and floppy, light brown, when she was small. Rachel had pulled it back into a little ponytail and tied it with a ribbon. Now she was very dark. Her hair was cropped like a boy's. It suited her. Her skin was dark too, but her eyes were a light grey, just like her father's.

Rachel waited. Amy cleared her throat and straightened her shoulders. She was small, but very straight and she looked very fit. Rachel had seen the photographs. Amy winning the one-hundred metres sprint at school. Amy winning the high jump. Amy taking part in the gym display. Amy running cross-country for her athletics club.

'I just want to tell you that I've decided— It's my decision, it has nothing to do with my mother,' she paused, 'with Pat or the social worker or anyone else. I have decided I don't want to see you any more.'

Rachel let her eyes drift past Amy's face to the French windows behind. They gave out onto a paved terrace with a small stone bird table. Blue tits were feeding. She noticed the way their little heads jerked up and down, watching, listening, alert for danger as she should have been.

'I'm sorry.' She heard her daughter's voice as if in the distance. 'I know this is painful for you. But I have to think of myself, and my future. After all,' she paused again and when she spoke her voice was high pitched, on the edge of hysteria, 'you only thought about yourself all those years ago. You didn't think about me, and what effect everything would have on my life, did you? How I would feel growing up with my mother in prison for killing my father. What that would be like for me. Did you? Did you?'

She had begun to cry, her face turning red, tears bursting from her eyes as they had, Rachel remembered, when she was small and she had stubbed her toe or scraped her knee or lost her favourite teddy. Rachel got up. She walked around the table and stood beside her daughter. She took her hand and turned it over. She kissed her palm and closed her fingers on it. Then she walked to the doors to the garden and opened them. The birds flew up in a panic as she approached, shouting their displeasure in loud clicks and whistles. Amy's foster-mother had been right, it was cold outside. Too cold. If Rachel had been a real mother herself she would have known and done the best for her child.

Her child. Amy was still her child. The first thought that came to her when she woke, the last that stayed with her until sleep. And nothing and no one could ever change that. She crawled slowly from beneath the blankets and began to dress. Today was her morning off. She had been told she need not come to work until one-thirty.

'Because it's late closing tonight, we're open until nine. I'll need you here until then. OK?' The woman in charge of the dry-cleaner's, the owner's wife, Rachel had quickly realized, looked her up and down.

'We'll be very busy. You'll be on your own. No skiving off for cups of coffee. I'll be in at nine to get the takings and to lock up. Do you hear me?' Rachel had heard her, loud and clear. She recognized her type. A bully. In the same mould as the bitch Macken in the prison. Her mouth tightening and drawing downwards, her hands balling themselves into fists as she spoke.

She looked at the clock on the mantelpiece. It was barely eight. She made tea and drank it quickly. The hot liquid scalded her mouth. She spat it out, and gulped down a glass of cold water. She couldn't get used to the tea she made herself. Prison tea was always lukewarm. Like the rest of the food. Cooled on the walk from the queue at the kitchen door to the cells where each prisoner ate on their own. Locked in. The heavy clang of metal on metal as the doors banged shut. Their Grace at mealtimes, their cue to lift their plastic knives and forks. She pulled on the clothes she had put out the night before. Leaving everything ready so she wouldn't have to make any choice in the morning. Denim jeans, a white cotton shirt, and a denim jacket. The same kind of clothes she had worn inside. Her uniform. Her security. She cleaned her teeth and brushed her hair. She put money in her pocket. She picked up the bunch of keys. She bent down and looked at the map. She traced her route with her finger. It would not be hard to find. But she needed to hurry. If she was to get to see Amy, she needed to hurry.

CHAPTER FOUR

THE BODY WAS lying where the tide had dumped it, on the tumble of rocks and seaweed between the bathing place known locally as the Forty Foot and the little slipway that was just past the Martello Tower. Jack Donnelly could smell it as he picked his way carefully over the slippery stones, jumping awkwardly across pools of stale saltwater. He could never understand how people could swim here. It was freezing, even at the height of summer, and as far as he was concerned it was dirty. Too close to the town. Even though gales regularly scoured the waves, he was of the opinion that all the wind did was to bring rubbish and filth back to shore rather than driving it out into the dreary grey of the Irish sea.

And that was precisely what had happened with the body that lay now at his feet. God knows where it went into the water, but wherever it was it couldn't escape the coastal pull. He took a clean handkerchief from his pocket and held it over his nose as he bent down to take a closer look. The smell hung in front of him like a nasty sea mist. He closed his finger and thumb tightly over his nostrils and tried not to gag as he knelt beside the dead man. It was a man, he had decided, although at first sight he hadn't been sure. Shoulder-length mousy hair was strewn across a face that bore the depredations of sea creatures. Parts of the cheeks and forehead had been completely eaten away, and, he saw with disgust, so also had the lips and the flesh beneath the chin. Christ, he hated doing this. He had no stomach any longer for the flesh-and-blood realities of his job. He was sick of it all.

He got to his feet, grunting slightly, feeling his breakfast writhe within his belly. Duffy, the uniformed guard, sniggered as he saw Jack's pallor.

'What do you reckon, drowning or something else?' he asked.

'Who do you think I am, a fucking psychic?' Jack moved away and turned his back on the body. 'Where's the pathologist? Will he be here soon?'

He walked away towards the little road that wound around the coast and perched on a large dry rock. From here he could see the body clearly. And now he was out of range of the smell, he could think better. Adult male, probably twenty to twenty-five, undernourished by the look of the skinny arms and legs that protruded from the torn shirt and trousers he was wearing. He'd noticed that the lad's fingernails were bitten to the quick, and that there was heavy bruising on his ribcage and on his shins. Could have been the beating the sea had given him, or could have been a beating of another kind. Whatever it was, he was sure the pathologist would tell him. And he'd tell him as well that there were needle marks on the pale, delicate skin on the inside of his arms, possibly in his groin too. Jack was sure he was a junkie. Even in death, after being in the sea, he had the look. It was unmistakable.

He sat and watched as the forensic team did their work. The morning passed slowly. It was lovely out here by the sea, he thought. Big houses, worth a fortune. Respectable families. Professionals. Well-brought-up kids. Loads of money. Not a bother in the world. They'd all be relieved that the body on the rocks had been washed in from the sea. That it was just a piece of flotsam like the plastic bottles and used condoms that fetched up on this shore and lay tangled in the seaweed until another high tide would release them again. They'd all be reassured that it wasn't one of their children, disturbing the quiet of these neat, comfortable roads where the same families had lived for years. He watched the cars that drove past, that slowed to a standstill as their occupants peered out at the white tarpaulin that had been put up over the dead boy. It would give them something to talk about over their pre-dinner drinks, he thought, then chided himself for his lack of generosity. Who was he to complain about the rich, he thought as he stood and stretched, lifting both arms above his head, pulling himself up to his full height, then turning his face towards the sea so the wind riffled through his thick, black hair. Wouldn't he give anything to be one of them? Living in a fancy house with a sea view and a new Merc or BMW parked in the drive. He'd never get it this way, he thought as he followed the body bag to the ambulance and watched the lads packing it away inside.

He'd have to do something drastic to get out of the debt that he'd accumulated over the last year and a half. It was really getting him down. Everything he owned and earned seemed to belong to Joan and the two kids. He didn't mind about the kids. He owed them. He loved them. They needed him. But Joan, she was a different story.

Still, there were others who were worse off. He was reminded of that later that afternoon as he sat waiting for Andrew Bowen in the bar of Walsh's pub just around the corner from Andrew's office. Little Joe Bloggs, who'd been swimming with the fishes, was, as Jack had predicted, a heroin addict. One of Dun Laoghaire's many. He'd been given the Probation Act the last time he was convicted of possession. What was the point in sending a minnow to Mountjoy, the judge seemed to think? Jack was in two minds. Of course there was no rehabilitation in prison. All the boy would have done was work out even more ingenious methods of getting hold of his gear and getting out of his tree. But on the other hand, removing the little bollocks from the area wouldn't have been a bad move either. Anyway, the deed had been done. And somehow little Joe Bloggs, identified by his fingerprints as Karl O'Hara, had ended up being half beaten to death, then dumped somewhere, the tidal experts reckoned, between the harbour walls and Dalkey Island. He had been alive when he hit the sea, his lungs were filled with saltwater. Jack hoped for his sake that he hadn't been conscious, although according to the pathologist he probably was. Conscious but in agony. Blows to the kidney, liver, three broken ribs, a badly crushed ankle, and a broken right arm. The poor kid had got a right going-over. He'd been in the water for three to four days, but his mother, when Jack had called to see her an hour ago, said she hadn't seen him for weeks. Jack had backed hurriedly out of her front door. The woman looked young, much younger than he'd have guessed for the mother of a twenty-year-old. Well dressed and made-up. As clean and neat as her house. She must have been dusting when Jack knocked on the door. There was a J-cloth in her hand the whole time he was speaking to her and it never stopped moving. Flicking invisible specks of dust from the polished dining-room table and chairs. Wiping tiny smudges and smears from the brass handles on the interior doors. He fought to suppress a giggle, winking surreptitiously at Tom Sweeney who was hanging back on the doorstep. She'd be a brilliant clean-up person after a job. Never miss a print.

But she'd absolutely nothing to tell them about her son.

'I haven't set eyes on him for months,' she said flatly. 'Not since he robbed the new TV and the microwave and the CD player. He even took all my Garth Brookes CDs. I could've killed the little bastard. So I kicked him out. Up until then I'd been making excuses for him, feeling sorry for him, trying to help him.'

Being a mother, Jack thought.

'But after that, I'd had it up to here.' She waved the cloth above her blonde head. 'His father always said I spoiled him. Gave him everything. Treated him different because he was the only boy. And the youngest. And the cutest.' She gestured towards the framed photos on the sideboard. Family groups. Mother with baby in arms, swathed in a crocheted christening robe. First communions and confirmations. Four blonde heads smiled. Three pretty little girls, and an equally pretty boy. She was right, Karl had been a cute little lad once.

She began to crumple then, her anger giving way to the sense of loss, which Jack knew had been waiting, probably for months, to be acknowledged. He offered to make tea, but she walked him to the front door and jerked it open.

'I've nothing more to say to you lot,' she said. 'If you did your job properly my Karl would be alive today. He'd be a normal, healthy, happy lad, with a job and a car and a girlfriend. It's all your fault. You don't give a toss about people like him. You can't be bothered. You're fucking useless. Now,' she stood back to let them pass, 'get out, get lost and leave me alone.'

She had a point. He knew in many ways she was dead right. He said as much to Andrew Bowen as they waited for their pints to settle.

'They don't want much, do they?' was Andrew's response. 'I suppose it would never cross her mind that her darling son should've tried taking a bit of responsibility for his own actions. I tried telling him often enough, the number of times he was in to see me. But it was like water off a bloody duck's back.'

Jack watched the head of his pint turn to cream

and waited for the moment when it was ready to drink. Andrew, he noticed, wasn't waiting. He had ordered a whiskey chaser and he had already drunk half of it. Jack picked up his glass. He raised it in salute before he put it to his lips.

'Sorry,' Andrew looked embarrassed, 'bad day today, I'm afraid.'

'Yeah?'

'Yeah.' Andrew's thin face sagged. He reached for the pint glass and picked it up. He took a long swallow and wiped the froth from his upper lip with the back of his hand. 'Well, to be honest, it's not the day itself that's bad. It's the going home part that's the real killer.'

'Could you not move her into a hospital or some kind of residential care, or something?'

'Oh, for God's sake, of course I couldn't.' Andrew's tone was exasperated. 'I couldn't. What would everyone think?'

'Do you care at this stage? "Everyone" isn't looking after her the way you do.'

'I couldn't do it to her, Jack. Her home is pretty much all she's got left now, and all her little routines. They're what keeps her going. Without them she'd give up.'

'And what keeps you going, eh?'

Andrew shrugged and picked up the whiskey glass. 'This, I suppose. This is a big help.' He drank and put it carefully down on the shiny tabletop. 'And . . .' He paused.

'And, yes, go on.' Jack's tone was curious.

'And, you know, "and". Do I have to spell it out?'

'You don't have to, but it might be interesting, might spice up the conversation a bit.' Jack smiled at him, watching a sudden flush spread across Andrew's face.

'Ah, go away with you. Leave it out. Leave a bloke with his private life. Let's just say that it's something to look forward to after a dull day at the office. Although, to change the subject,' Andrew held up his hands against Jack's protest, 'funnily enough something very interesting cropped up in the job today.'

'Yeah?' Jack raised an eyebrow. 'You don't say. You amaze me. Interesting, among that lot of no-hopers who parade past your desk every day. You could have fooled me.'

'My, oh, my.' Andrew sat back and folded his arms. 'Talk about me having a bad day, what's got into you?'

'Ach, you don't want to know.' Jack finished his drink and gestured to the barman for a refill.

'Wives, eh, former, present, something like that?'

'Let's not talk about it. It just depresses me. Come on. Tell me, interesting cases in the probation and welfare service. Surprise me.'

And he was surprised. Although looking back on it he shouldn't have been. A letter should have come from the Department of Justice, telling them that a prisoner of Rachel Beckett's standing was due for TR and was planning to live in their area. He would be very surprised if there hadn't been some kind of notification. It was standard procedure. And, after all, she wasn't just any common-or-garden husband killer.

Her husband was a guard. And not just any old guard but one who was very well known and highly regarded, from a family of guards. Been in Special Branch during the eighties when things up North were really bad. Done all kinds of surveillance, gone under-cover. Practically a hero. And when he'd been shot and she'd spun the line about the men who'd broken into the house and killed him, everyone believed her. To begin with. Until after the funeral anyway. Then it had all begun to unravel, her carefully stitched-together story.

Tell me again, Rachel, what time did this happen?

Describe to me again, Rachel, if you wouldn't mind, these men. What did they look like — height, weight, physical build, accents? What did they say to you? What did they say to Martin?

You were definitely on your own the whole time, were you not? Apart from the 'masked men', definitely on your own the whole time, is that what you're saying?

You and Martin, how were you getting on, Rachel? Was everything all right between you? Are you sure about that now?

And you're sure about these 'masked men', you don't want to tell us anything else?

Because we've found something. You see, you know you told us that they'd stolen Martin's gun, after they shot him with it. That they took it with them when they left. Well, you see, we've found it, wrapped in a plastic bag, dumped in a skip not half a mile from here.

And do you know what else we found in the same skip? A nightdress. And do you know what was all over it,

Rachel? Martin's blood. And do you know whose nightdress we think it was? We think it was yours.

And do you know what we found on the gun, we found fingerprints, and we'd really like to take your fingerprints if you wouldn't mind, just so we can eliminate you from our enquiries. Just so we can be sure. Sure that they're not yours. Because we've tested the gun and the shot that killed Martin. And, well, you see, you were definitely right about that. It did come from Martin's gun.

And so it had gone on. He remembered the details. His first case after he'd become a detective. A minor player, really, in the team. But somehow or other he'd been with Michael McLoughlin when they were called to the house. He'd seen the body. The blood all over the floor. The woman, frantic, handcuffed to the radiator beside him. And what he hadn't seen and heard for himself he'd heard from the guards who'd been in on the interrogation. From the informal sessions that took place over coffee and biscuits in her sitting room, with her daughter asleep on the sofa beside her, to the arrest and the formal questioning, conducted in an interview room in Stillorgan Garda station, in a room that would have stunk of fear, and stale cigarettes, and misery.

They'd celebrated for days after she'd been charged. Old Michael McLoughlin was her arresting officer. He was cock of the walk, in his element, at the time when he could still handle everything. The drink included.

'How does she look?' Jack asked, remembering how she had looked then.

Andrew shrugged. 'How does anyone look when they've been inside for that length of time?'

'I dunno. Think of Nelson Mandela. He looked bloody great when he got off Robbin Island. Don't they have a name for it? The sleeping-beauty syndrome, isn't that what they call it? All that routine life, no alcohol or drugs, plain food, plenty of outdoor exercise. I remember reading some article or other in one of the English papers. They reckoned that he was at least twenty years younger than his actual physical age.'

'Yeah, Jack, but there's one major difference between our Nelson and Rachel Beckett. He didn't have a guilty conscience. And he had three-quarters of the free world rooting for him. He had right and God and whatever else you choose to mention on his side. I'm afraid he was a one-off in that respect.'

'So she's not gorgeous any longer?'

'Depends what you mean by gorgeous. Her hair's grey now. She's very thin, almost frail. Her skin has that dried-up, bad-diet look about it. But, you know . . .' Andrew finished his second pint and raised his glass questioningly to Jack. Jack nodded. 'Give her a couple of months, sea air, sunshine . . .' His voice trailed off.

'Gorgeous' was the word Jack would have used about her back then. Some had been a bit more graphic, explicit. They'd all known her and fancied her at one time or another. She was old Gerry Jennings's daughter. His youngest, his one and only girl, his favourite. And they'd all been surprised when even Martin Beckett fell for her. Martin wasn't like that. He wasn't the kind to get involved.

'Do you remember at the trial, Jack, all that stuff about Martin's brother, Dan? Didn't she try and implicate him?'

None of them had believed a word of it. Michael McLoughlin had pooh-poohed it right from the start. He remembered him coming back into the station after he'd been with her in the house. After he'd confronted her with the shotgun and told her about the fingerprints, that they matched hers. He'd walked in and announced to the whole room that the woman had come up with another great story. She was blaming it all on the brother. And did she have a reason for her allegations? It would have made some sense if there'd been something going on between them. But she was adamant, they were just friends, nothing more.

So tell us, Rachel. Tell us again what really happened. You're backing off from your 'masked men' story, is that right? So, start from the beginning. You say that you and Martin had a row. What was it about? Nothing much, you say. He was drunk. He was often drunk these days. And when he got drunk he got violent. Is that your story now? Well, you were right about one thing. He was drunk all right. His blood alcohol level was five times over the legal limit.

So you were frightened what he was going to do, scared of him. So you phoned your brother-in-law to come and help. Why didn't you just leave yourself, just get up and go? The car was in the garage, you were a free woman. So why did you stay in the house with a man who you say was drunk and violent? Tell us, then, what happened next? Tell me about Dan Beckett.

'You went to the trial, didn't you, Andrew?'

Andrew's face was devoid of colour. He looked exhausted. He took off his glasses and rubbed the bridge of his nose. He gazed at his reflection, blurred, unfocused, in the mirror on the opposite wall. He knew he should go, that Clare would be waiting. But he couldn't face her. Not just yet.

'Hey, Bernie, same again,' he called to the barman. He glanced over at Jack who was slumped back against the padded upholstery, munching handfuls of dry-roasted peanuts. Andrew had known him one way or another for years. He'd watched his progress through the guards, followed his domestic ups and downs. He had to admit that Jack was looking pretty good these days, despite his moaning about the wife. He'd lost weight, got his black hair cut short in a kind of Brad Pitt look, and he no longer wore that beaten-puppy air which had hung around him in the months before he'd finally left home. He waited until the barman had dumped their drinks on the table, taken his money and retreated behind the counter, then said, 'The trial? Beckett's trial? Yeah, I was there for a bit of it.'

'What did you think of Dan Beckett?'

Andrew shrugged. 'He had an alibi. It was his mother, wasn't it? Didn't she say he was at home with her at the time? And I think the general feeling was that she'd be hardly likely to make up something like that to protect her son's killer. Even if the suspect was her other son.'

'Her adopted son, Andy. Don't forget that.'

'Yeah, so, her adopted son. Still the person who had

been accused. Surely above all she'd want justice, wouldn't she?'

'Even when it came out that they'd been having an affair. Rachel, her daughter-in-law, with Dan, her son?'

'But even you lot didn't believe that Dan was involved, did you? You didn't believe what she said about what happened. You never charged him with anything.'

'No, we didn't. We had him in for questioning, all right. I remember. His father came with him. Tony Beckett, another old-timer. I never knew him, but everyone else did. Half the lads in the station were working for his security company, on the quiet. Doing nixers here and there. So they all knew Dan too. They all had stories about Dan, how he was Tony's gofer. Drove him around everywhere in that big old black Merc. Bought him his Cuban cigars and his bottles of Bushmills. Took him to the golf club for his dinners and drove him home afterwards, old Tony snoring away in the back and Dan as sober as a judge. Also took him on his trips to the girls in the massage parlours that they did the security for.'

'You're kidding, massage parlours? At his age, lucky old sod.'

'Yep, the guys in Vice knew all about it. But mind you, they know all about the foibles and peccadilloes of half the pillars of this society. They've got some stories to tell. Anyway, so when Dan came in for questioning it was all backslapping and reminiscing. The good old days, the great rounds of golf. But they didn't get anything out of him anyway.'

'And the same thing at the trial too. He said that when he left the house, Martin was asleep on the couch. The jury believed him and they didn't believe her.'

'That's right, that's what it came down to. And what about you, what did you think? Then. And now, after you've met her, what do you think now?'

'What I think, Jack, is that I'm late. I'm going to finish this in double-quick time, and then I'm going home. That's what I think.' He picked up his pint and drank deeply. He put the empty glass down neatly on the beer mat, stood, picked up his briefcase, nodded, then walked to the door.

Poor fucker, Jack thought. What a life. Around him the bar was beginning to fill up. It was an odd place for a probation officer to drink, he thought, not for the first time. At a casual glance he could spot any number of Andrew's former and current clients. They'd all have been mates of poor dead Karl O'Hara. He'd be seeing a lot more of them in the days to come. His heart sank as he thought about it and remembered the state of the poor kid's body, and then remembered the way Martin Beckett had looked in death. It hadn't been a pretty sight. A huge wound in his groin. Half his abdomen blown away. A dreadful smell. Blood everywhere. Dried, dark, sticky.

But at least his face was untouched. They'd taken him home to his parents' house after the post-mortem and all the forensic formalities. There'd been a huge crowd to pay their respects. Jack had been nervous about approaching the coffin. But Martin looked fine.

Very pale, his fair hair slicked down over his forehead. His eyelids closed over his bright blue eyes. And she had been sitting beside him on an upright chair, silent, rigid with grief, he had thought. Jack had been part of the Garda escort to the church. He had liaised with Dan Beckett about the arrangements. The parents couldn't cope at all, they were so distraught. He'd always liked Dan somehow. He was much more easy-going than his brittle, difficult, ambitious younger brother. But then, Jack remembered how he'd pointed it out to Andy, they were only brothers by adoption. Not by blood. What difference does that make, he wondered as he finished his drink and wiped his salty, oily fingers on a piece of crumpled tissue. It must mean something. It must be significant. There must be a difference, in personality, in character as there is in looks. He stood up and put on his jacket. And then he wondered if Dan Beckett knew that after all these years his sister-in-law was free.

CHAPTER FIVE

IT HAD BEEN so cold, the day that Martin died. Early March, daffodils everywhere, glowing with the promise of spring sunshine still to come, but ice on the roads in the early mornings and a lowering grey sky which had been threatening snow all week. She remembered the chill in the air, how it had been, as she walked now along the road by the sea, towards the DART station. Today there was an easterly wind, so even though the May sun was warm on her face and hands, she could feel a shiver running up her spine, gooseflesh rising on the skin of her upper arms, her nipples tightening.

All that week, all those years ago. She remembered the red of Amy's cheeks as she hopped and skipped on the doorstep, waiting for Rachel to come outside to unlock the car door. She was going to stay the night with her friend from playschool. The child's name, Rachel remembered, was Lulu. Her parents were English. It was Lulu's birthday and her mother was going to take them to see a film. Which one was it? A Disney cartoon or something like *ET*? She couldn't remember, but she did remember how excited Amy had been. The child couldn't keep still. She had hopped and skipped up and down, swinging her patchwork bag from side to side. The one that Rachel had made her for Christmas, just big enough to hold her nightie, and her teddy, and her hairbrush and toothbrush.

'Come on, Mummy. Hurry up. I'm waiting, I'm waiting.' Rachel could hear Amy's voice, sing-song now as she repeated the same phrases over and over again, running backwards and forwards from the front door to the gate, while Rachel fiddled with the lock, checked in her bag that she had her purse and the letters she wanted to post, then remembered that Amy needed her woolly hat, and went back into the house to look for it. And all the while hearing Amy's voice.

'I'm waiting, I'm waiting. Come on, Mummy, silly Mummy, slow coach Mummy. I'm waiting, I'm waiting.'

But Amy needed her hat because she'd just had another ear infection. She hated wearing it. Rachel knew what she would say.

'No, Mummy, I don't like it, it makes my head itchy.'

But she'd have to insist, even if it meant putting up with tears and tantrums. Otherwise the cold wind would make her ears sore again.

And just as Rachel had finally got everything together and had closed the door and checked that she had locked it, she heard the phone ring. And she turned, hesitated, waited, wondered. Perhaps it was Martin? He had said he would phone last night but he didn't. He was away again. He was always away these days. This time it was Los Angeles. Some kind of international conference of forensic scientists, she thought that was what it was. She was angry. He'd said he'd phone and he hadn't. She was sure it was him now. She turned back to the door.

'Hold on, love, I won't be a minute. It might be Daddy, don't you want to say hallo to him?' And she had her keys out and unlocked the Chubb and then the Yale and pushed open the door and ran down the hall to the kitchen. And just as she reached it, just as she picked up the receiver, it stopped ringing, and there was nothing but the dial tone vibrating in her ear. And then another sound. Louder, terribly loud. A screech of brakes, like a sound effect from a TV movie, and a scream, and a thump. And another scream. A howl. And she turned. Could see down the hall, the front door open, the cold bright light falling on the polished floorboards, and outside the flagged path to the gate, the gate open, a car stopped just beyond. And now there was silence.

All that week it was so cold. She remembered that she never seemed able to get warm. Sitting in the ambulance beside Amy as they rushed her to hospital. She looked perfect. There was hardly a mark on her, a graze on her cheek and a small bruise above her right eye. And then Rachel heard the ambulance man swear beneath his breath and she saw Amy's face change colour, suddenly very pale, her breathing shallow and very fast. She began to whimper, looking up at her mother. She was frightened. Rachel saw the ambulance man reach for her wrist, feeling for her pulse. Quickly strapping the tight black band around her upper arm, listening with his stethoscope.

'What is it, what's happening to her?' Rachel's voice bounced off the shiny surfaces on the inside of the ambulance, competing with the high-pitched wail of the siren. He didn't answer. His fingers rested on Amy's wrist, then moved to feel for the pulse in her neck. And all the while the child's face grew whiter and whiter, until Rachel began to feel that she would disappear in front of her eyes.

So cold too sitting in the waiting room after they had taken Amy away, and every time the swing doors opened a blast of chilled air enveloped her and inched open the other doors, the ones that led into the emergency cubicles where she knew Amy was lying. And every time the doors creaked open she thought that someone was coming out to tell her Amy was all right, Amy was fine. It was nothing serious. But if that was so she would have been there, at her bedside, holding her hand, instead of waiting here in the cold. And then a young doctor was standing in front of her. There was blood on his green scrubs and dark circles under his eyes. She felt his hand on her shoulder as he told her that Amy's spleen had been ruptured. She was bleeding internally. They were going to have to oper- ate. She'd already lost a lot of blood. Would she sign the consent form? He handed her a piece of paper and a pen. Her hand shook as she wrote, and looking down she saw that she had used her maiden name, Jennings, she had called herself Rachel Jennings. She crossed it out quickly, put Beckett. How stupid of me, how silly, she said as she handed it back to him.

But already the young doctor had left, gone back through the heavy swing doors, the draught blowing just for a moment as Rachel tried to think. Where was Martin and how could she tell him?

And still so cold four days later, huddling in the garage, waiting for Martin to fall asleep, for the alcohol in his bloodstream to travel to his brain. Listening to the sound of his voice, shouting at her, screaming abuse. Waiting until there was silence, when she would know that he had lain down, his eyelids drooping, his body relaxing, that he had finally drifted off, so she could come back into the house and phone for help. But she couldn't be sure what he was doing in there. Every time she was just about to unlock the door that led into the kitchen she would hear a sound, a noise that might be him. She couldn't chance it. He had already hurt her. Punched her in the stomach, then kicked her as she lay on the ground, so that when she breathed in and out she felt as if one of her ribs was piercing her lungs. And as she had begun to crawl away he had tried to stamp on her ankle, but the sudden movement had upset his balance and he too had fallen. And as he lay on the ground, bellowing with anger, she had staggered to her feet and hurried into the kitchen, unlocking the connecting door into the garage, then hurriedly turning the key in the lock so when he followed behind her and hammered and banged the door would not budge.

She sat on the cement floor, huddled shivering against the lawnmower in the corner. Her feet were bare, her nightie pulled tightly around her knees. She had been in bed when he arrived home, trying to catch up on some of the sleep she had missed during those three days and nights when Amy had lain in intensive care, surrounded by tubes and wires and machines and blood had dripped from the bag on the stand into her arm. Rachel had been with her when she opened her eyes for the first time, asked for water, smiled, then slept again. And she had at last allowed herself to listen to the urgings of the nurses, to go home. She had crawled into bed and closed her eyes. And when she had opened them again Martin was standing beside her. She reached out her hand to him. But he stepped back and she saw the look on his face. The expression that she knew so well. That transformed him. Turned his face dark, pinched his lips, made the bright blue of his eyes a murky grey. Balled his hands into fists as he said, 'Blood? Whose blood? Not mine. It couldn't be mine.'

As he told her, explained very carefully to her as the doctor had explained it to him.

'So you're a blood donor, Mr Beckett. That's great. We really appreciate people like you. And you're O negative? Even better. We always need O negative. The universal blood group, as you know, of course. Compatible with practically every other blood type.' He looked down at Amy's chart. 'But your daughter, now she's group A. So her mother must be group A too, because A is always dominant. Did you know that?'

He smiled in that know-it-all way that doctors have.

'But you aren't, are you, Rachel? Remember how we were worried, all that stuff about rhesus negative and positive when you were pregnant. You remember, of course you remember. And we found out that you were O positive. Isn't that right? So there I was, sitting by Amy's bed, watching her and wondering, thinking about it all, wondering if it was the jet lag that was confusing me. So do you know what I did, Rachel? I made a phone call. I called my old friend Peter Browne – you remember Peter, the pathologist? And I said, I've a case that's worrying me. And I asked him about blood groups. And do you know what he said to me, Rachel?'

He leaned over and pulled her from the bed by her hair.

'My old friend Peter Browne, he said to me. Father O negative, mother O positive, child's blood group O. Child's blood group A, then either father or mother must be blood group A, because A is always dominant. Did you know that, Rachel? I bet you didn't.' He dragged her across the floor.

'So next time you're thinking about fucking around with someone else, watch your fucking blood group, do you hear me, you bitch?'

Now she heard him outside trying to open the metal roll-down door at the front of the garage. But she had locked that from the inside too. He banged a couple of times, but she knew he wouldn't want to make too much noise, that he wouldn't want to attract the attention of the neighbours in the quiet cul-de-sac where they had lived since they married six years ago. In the two-storey house with the red-tiled roof and the small garden at the front and the long stretch of lawn and shrubs at the back. The pond which she had dug herself and lined with thick black plastic and filled with oxygenating plants and water lilies and fish. And the beautiful conservatory that she had designed and which Daniel had built, that first year when she and Martin had just got married and Martin had been transferred to Letterkenny, to border duty.

She waited and waited until there was silence, then she opened the boot of the car and took out Martin's gun. He shouldn't leave it there, she was always telling him. It's dangerous. He of all people should know that. But he had laughed and said, 'Only when it's loaded, for God's sake. A gun without ammunition is as harmless as a dog without teeth. Didn't your father tell you that when he was teaching you to shoot?'

If she could just get to the cupboard in his study where he kept the cartridges. If she could just load the gun and keep him quiet and still, while she explained. While she told him what had happened. That it didn't matter. It would never happen again. It didn't mean anything. That they could have other children. That anyway he loved Amy and she loved him. He was her father, no matter what. If she could just keep him there, keep him still, hold him at bay, while she begged him to listen, begged him to forgive her. Waited for his expression to change. The way it always did, eventually. Whenever she had done something wrong, made a mistake, given him cause to be angry. Whenever she hadn't pleased him, she could always make him come round, eventually.

But he was awake when she crept from the garage, through the kitchen into the hall. Lying back on the sofa, in the sitting room, a glass of whiskey in his hand. And he called out to her, and laughed at her as she stood in front of him with the gun in her hands. And said, 'You stupid bitch, what do you think you're doing with that? You couldn't shoot me to save your life. Not you, a liar and a cheat and a coward. Come on, tell me. Who was it? Spit it out. I've a right to know. After all these years of playing daddy to a kid who isn't mine. Tell me.'

So she told him. Blurted it out. Thinking that somehow it would be better that it wasn't just anyone. That it was someone who he knew. Thinking that he might feel he could forgive her. He could accept what had happened. That it might be all right again. The way things used to be. But she had forgotten. For some reason she could never understand, she had forgotten the way he felt about Daniel.

'That bastard who calls himself my brother. You and him, together. Where? Here in this house? Here in my bed, in my room? Here, under this roof? My roof? You and him? Of all people. How could you? If I had known that he had touched you, you know, don't you, that I would never have touched you again. Ever.

You know, don't you, that he's literally a bastard, don't you? My mother told me about his mother. A fifteen-year-old somewhere in the sticks who got into trouble. But we know nothing about his father. Some lucky bollocks who had a bit of fun, then buggered off before he had to face the consequences. Just what I should have done with you, Rachel. I don't know what I was thinking about, marrying you. I must have been crazy.'

He reached out and took hold of the barrel of the gun, pulling it towards himself, pulling her with it.

'Here, let me give you a hand. Let me show you what to do with this. What I would do with this.'

They moved together, out of the kitchen, along the passage to the small room at the front of the house. His room, where he kept his books and his papers, his private possessions as he always said.

'Here.' He pulled open the top drawer of the desk. He took out a box of cartridges. He opened it. He jerked the gun from her grasp. He broke it open, pushed the cartridges into the chamber. He snapped it shut. He held it out to her.

'Here.' He smiled at her. 'Now, that's what I call a weapon.'

The cars were rushing past her now as she stood at the junction of Merrion Square and Clare Street. She tried to judge their distance but it was hopeless. For twelve years she had never looked further than the walls of the prison yard. Nothing within their confines moved at a speed that wasn't human. How to know how far a moving object was from her, how to determine its relative speed? She put one foot on to the road, then hesitated. Lurched forward, drew back. Remembered the sound of the car as it had hit Amy. And the elderly man who was driving, who had wept as he saw the child on the ground and kept on saying, over and over again, 'She just ran out in front of me, there was nothing I could do.'

Now Rachel hung back, waiting. There must be something wrong with the lights. They didn't change. All around her other pedestrians passed her out, passed her by. Occasionally someone would look back at her, curiously. She wanted to reach out and tug at a sleeve, a coat, ask for help. It was getting late. Amy would be walking down Leeson Street to school, any minute now. She had to make a move or else she'd miss her. And then she'd have to wait until she came out at lunchtime.

Tears dripped down her cheeks. She twisted and turned. How stupid she must look, she thought. A mad woman with grey hair and a grey face, making a fool of herself in a busy city street. The cars streamed past, then slowed and stopped. A buzzer sounded, a high-pitched shriek. The green man flashed up. She took a deep breath and ran, dodging through the traffic. She kept on running, holding her denim jacket, hearing her keys jangling together in her pocket. The laces from her runners flopped from side to side. She stared at her feet as she ran and saw shoes of all shapes and sizes pass by. Black leather, shiny, expensive. Buckles, decorative punching, heels stacked and stiletto. Toes squared off, narrow, tapered. Once she had worn shoes like these. Presents from Martin. Elegant, sophisticated. Now she saw herself reflected in a large mirror in the window of the chemist on the corner of Merrion Row, framed by photographs of beautiful women advertising make-up and perfume, and her own face, lined and drawn, staring out at her.

What had she done all those years ago on that cold day in March when Martin had died? She had thrown away her own life when she pointed the shotgun at him and pulled the trigger. Why had she done it? What had possessed her? The doorbell had rung as they moved together into the hall. She could see the shape of a man through the frosted glass.

'Oh,' Martin jerked his head dismissively, 'I see. You couldn't handle this on your own. You had to call in the cavalry. Well, what are you waiting for? Let the bastard in.'

She put her hand out to the lock. Hesitated. Heard Martin walk away towards the kitchen. Heard the sound of crockery and glass breaking. Turned back, saw that he was taking everything from the cupboards. Dropping the plates, the bowls, the dishes. Dropping them on to the tiled floor. Stamping on the shards of china and glass with his shoes. She turned and opened the door and stood back to let Daniel pass her by. She heard the shouts of anger, the screams of abuse. Heard the rage of years pour out from both of them. She walked into the sitting room, the gun in her hands. Heard her husband's voice, the disgust, the revulsion, the bitterness. Felt shame like she had never felt before. Heard him say, 'The cuckoo in the nest, a neat trick that one was, wasn't it? Laying your egg in another man's basket, getting that man to raise your foundling chick for you. Pretty fucking neat. But then you know all about that, don't you, Daniel, or whatever your name really is? Do you realize,' and here he paused and looked towards Rachel, 'do you realize just how much you owe this family? If my mother hadn't been so desperate for a baby and she hadn't convinced my father that any old leftover bit of rubbish was worth it, what would have happened to you, I wonder? Answer me that if you can. Well, I think we all know, don't we? You'd have been brought up in that children's home, wouldn't you? The one where the priests beat the little boys, bugger them when they're bold and turn them into little perverts. And what kind of a future would you have had?'

She looked at Daniel. He was very pale and very still.

'And you took it all, didn't you? Took it and threw it back in their faces. Always trouble. Never did what you were told. Nearly broke my mother's heart with the way you behaved.'

'Stop it, Martin. Stop it.' She had found her voice at last.

'Stop it? I haven't even started.' He turned towards her and moved closer. 'Never at home. Couldn't mix with decent people. Found your own kind. That gang of joyriders you hung out with, who drove into that woman and child, out for a walk on a fine summer's evening, left them for dead, wasn't that what you did?'

'No, Martin, stop, please stop!' she screamed at him.

'Why should I? You didn't stop, did you? You unbelievable, disgusting little bitch. How could you sleep with him, when you know the way I feel about him? And then passing that kid off on me. I should have realized she wasn't mine. She's the image of him, isn't she?'

'Don't.' Daniel had moved too. Moved closer. 'Just don't.'

'Don't what, Danny boy? Don't you tell me what to do. I'll do the telling now, and in the future. Because do you know what, Danny boy? I've just made a decision, a very important decision. I'm going to take my father up on his offer. I'm going to pack in the guards and take over the business. And do you know what that means? That means that you will have a new boss, a new man in the back of the Merc. A new man to take to the golfing dinners, to the girls in the massage parlours. A new man to live out your life for, waiting on his every whim and every move for as long as you can stomach it. But somehow, Danny boy, I don't think it will be for very long, because, somehow, I think you're suddenly going to be made redundant.'

He turned towards Rachel again. He lifted the bottle of whiskey from the table and took a mouthful.

'And as for you, you bitch, you're redundant from right now. So why don't you put that gun down and piss off out of here, and make sure that you and that brat of yours never come back?' He made as if to walk past her. She tried to block his way.

'No,' she said, 'I love you, Martin. It was nothing between Dan and me, it was just something that happened. It didn't mean anything. Please, you've got to believe me. Please, Dan. Please, you tell him.'

And suddenly Martin had turned on Dan, was reaching for his throat, and there was something in his hand, a knife, a kitchen knife. And she screamed out loud, shouted out to warn him, and then there was a noise so loud that her ears rang with pain. And a smell, the smell of a shotgun fired at close range. And Martin was on the floor. He was shocked, he was bleeding, his thigh was ripped open but he was still alive. He called out, 'Help me, Rachel. Help me.' And then there was a second shot, point blank, up close. And this time he was silent, not a sound from his open mouth. His eyes closed, then he whimpered once. And then there was silence, just for a moment, and then she heard her own voice screaming out, 'What did you do that for, why did you that, what have you done?'

And Daniel looked at her, and looked down at the gun in his hand and said nothing.

And she noticed her nightdress, that it was covered in small drops of blood, and she said, 'What are we going to do? We'll have to call the police. We'll have to tell someone. How will we explain to everyone about how it happened? What will everyone think? Dan, what will we do?'

And he explained to her, slowly, calmly. He would fix it all. He pulled her nightdress over her head. He got her a change of clothes from the bedroom. He dressed her. Then he got Martin's handcuffs from his car, and he tied her to the radiator. He said he would take her car and he would dump it. He would dump the gun and everything else somewhere they wouldn't be found. He would do it all. She wasn't to worry. She was to trust him. Sooner or later someone would come for her. And then she was to tell them the story. She was to tell them what he had said. And it would be all right. They would believe her.

But they didn't. She had trusted him and she had paid for it all. Become an old woman, with a shrivelled body and a dead heart. No one to love her. No one for her to love.

Not even the girl who walked with her friends from the bus stop at the corner of Stephen's Green. Black hair cut close to her head, dark eyebrows that outlined the curve of her eye socket, sallow skin with a faint flush of pink on her cheekbones. Laughing and joking, breaking into song. Until she saw Rachel waiting for her and then her expression changed. She walked more quickly, leaving the others behind, brushed past Rachel, ignoring her outstretched hand. Walked up the steps to the school door. Paused. Looked at her. Said just loud enough for only Rachel to hear. 'I told you before. I don't want to see you. Go away and leave me alone. I mean it. I really mean it.'

And then she was gone. The other girls passed by. One of them pulled a fifty-pence piece from her pocket. She pressed it into Rachel's palm, then turned to her friends and sniggered. 'Good deed for the day, isn't that it?'

It was such a cold day, that day in March when

Martin died. She sometimes felt that she had never warmed up again. She turned away and walked towards the canal. She opened her fingers and let the coin drop to the footpath. It spun on the stone by her foot and tumbled into the gutter. Like me, she thought. That's where I belong. And the sun disappeared behind a cloud, and the day went dark.

CHAPTER SIX

BLUE AS FAR as the eye could see. Pale blue of sky
meeting the darker blue line of the water, twelve miles
out on the edge of the horizon. And below him the
dense dark green of the pine trees on the clifftop, the
bright gold of the gorse in flower, and between them
and below them the bronze and brown of the bracken.

Daniel Beckett leaned over the parapet and looked
down. Children's toys were scattered across the smooth
front lawn. A bicycle dropped on its side, wheels still
spinning. A pram parked neatly, the large pink and
white doll propped carefully up against the lace-edged
pillows. A long rope with a wooden seat slotted into it
swung gently from the lower branch of a huge macro-
carpa tree. Backwards and forwards, forwards and backwards as if animated by a giant unseen hand. And from
somewhere in the distance he heard the sound of his
son and daughter – playing, shouting, laughing, crying
out – and the voice of his wife, calling to them, telling
them it was time for bed, time to come in, time to say
goodnight.

He leaned further over, pushing his body across the
stone ledge, craning his neck to see where she might

be. But she was out of sight. In the vegetable garden, he thought. And he imagined the way she would look, her long fair hair pulled into a plait, her shirt tucked into the waistband of her jeans, the bones of her spinal column showing clearly through the tight material as she bent and stood – digging, pulling, cutting, coaxing and nourishing, creating order where once had been chaos.

And he thought of the way his life had been. Before he met her. And felt again that familiar sense of panic and dread as he straightened up and moved away from the ledge, back towards the room in the bell tower, high above the garden. His special room. He put out his hand to open the French windows and saw himself reflected in the glass pane. A shadowy figure. Dark hair that fell back from his broad forehead to his shoulders. A dark beard, now with just a few streaks of grey, like the colour of his eyes, pale in contrast to his sallow skin. He stood and looked at himself. He noticed the bulk of his body, spread and softened by years of comfort and ease. Happiness, he supposed he could call it, now that he was in control of the company that his father had started, that he had wanted once to hand over to his younger son. But then after that son had died he had turned back to Daniel, the oldest, for help and succour.

Daniel moved towards the filing cabinet in the corner. He took out his bunch of keys and unlocked it. He pulled out a large box file. He placed it on the desk and opened it. He flicked through the collection of newspaper cuttings and saw for the first time in years the face of the woman he had thought to put behind him, safely locked away, out of sight and out of mind, until today.

'You'll remember her, won't you, Dan?' It was one of the guys who did some part-time work for him who said it. He was a guard in the local station, getting married next year, looking to earn the deposit on a new house. 'I'd say you'd remember her. Seems like a lot of people do.'

He remembered her all right, remembered everything about her. The colour of her hair and eyes. The feeling of her hand in his hand. The sound of her voice as she called out to him. How much he had wanted her. How he had snatched her from under Martin's nose. Got such pleasure from her and the thought of how his brother would suffer if he knew. And he had waited until that night, when she had rung him and asked him for help. And he had given it to her. He had helped her all right. Taken the gun when she had handed it to him. But she had not been grateful and she had suffered for her ingratitude.

And now she was back. He looked up from the pile of cuttings, out again towards the sea. He moved to the open door and heard his wife calling out. Calling his name.

'Daniel,' she was shouting. He listened to her voice with its American slur and drawl. 'Daniel, where are you? Come outside. It's lovely out here. Daniel. Daniel.' A sudden wind spiralled up the cliff face, snatching the words from her mouth and flinging them away as the door to the balcony banged shut. And all now was silence.

CHAPTER SEVEN

'SO, TELL ME, why did you do it?'

'Do what?'

Andrew Bowen sighed and swung back in his chair. He took off his glasses and placed them on the desk in front of him. He gently rubbed the bones beneath his eyebrows, then picked up his glasses again and swung them from side to side.

'Rachel,' he said slowly, 'don't play silly buggers with me.'

The complaint had come through yesterday afternoon, just as he was about to leave the office. It was from Amy Beckett's social worker. It seemed that Amy had arrived home at lunchtime, distraught. Her mother had turned up outside her school that morning, harassing her, embarrassing her in front of her friends, so she said. Her social worker wasn't having it.

'She's always been absolutely clear about it, completely upfront. Told us all, including her mother, as soon as it looked as if the woman was coming out on temporary release. There was no way she wanted to have any contact with her.'

Andrew had listened, made notes. He knew the

social worker well. Her name was Alison White.
They'd done their training together in Trinity College
years ago.

'I'll grant you, it's not what we would have wanted,
you know that, Andrew. We've always tried to encour-
age the relationship between the two of them, difficult
and all as it was. Amy's a very bright girl, knows her
own mind. She doesn't want her mother around. And
at her age, about to do the Leaving Cert., she's old
enough to make her own decisions. Anyway, Andrew,
you know how the system works. If Rachel Beckett
was that keen on seeing her daughter she knows what
to do. She should have asked you to arrange it or
contacted me. Not just turned up on the bloody
doorstep like that. It's just not on. Am I making
myself plain?'

She was. But then she had always been like that.
Blunt to the point of rudeness. A lot of people didn't
like Alison White. She didn't care. She used to laugh
about it, say it was because she was a Northern
Protestant. Andrew remembered getting drunk with
her and the others from their class. Well, they were all
getting drunk. Alison never did. And there was always
a point when Alison would say loudly, 'God, you
Catholics are a hoot. Mad keen to have a united Ireland
but have you ever thought what it would be like filled
with a million stroppy Prods like me, making your
lives a misery? Wanting to change everything? Getting
rid of your bloody Angelus bell on the radio, for a
start? Introducing a bit of plain-speaking into your
devious Jesuitical little world.'

There would be silence for a moment, then, before the backlash, Andrew would order the last round and start making tracks for home. Before Alison said too much, burned too many bridges.

'So you'll have to do something about it, Andrew. Make sure it doesn't happen again, because if it does I'll have to do something about it, and Rachel might not like that. OK?'

It was quiet in Andrew's first-floor office. The computer on the desk hummed softly, and from outside came the sound of voices, loud for a few moments as a door opened, then gone again. He looked across the desk at Rachel. A couple of weeks ago he wouldn't have recognized her if he had passed her casually in the street. But now, watching her, he could see that the changes in her were only on the surface. In the colour of her hair and the pallor of her face. When she looked straight at him, managed to maintain eye contact for a few moments, she was the same woman he remembered from all those years ago. Now she was looking down at her hands. They moved constantly, her long thin fingers smoothing out the wrinkles in her skin, sliding up and over the bones in her wrists, clasping and reclasping her forearms, then slipping back down again. She fiddled with the narrow gold ring on the third finger of her left hand, twisting it round and round, then sliding it up and over her knuckle, almost to the tip of her finger, then pushing it back again to safety. As he watched her she shifted on the hard wooden chair and he noticed the way her breasts moved beneath her white shirt. She crossed and uncrossed her legs, twisting one calf around the other, and he saw that her hips bones protruded through the denim of her cheap faded jeans. Then she lifted her head and looked at him.

'I went to see my daughter, because that is what she is. My daughter. Nothing can change that, nothing can make that anything other than it is.'

'But she doesn't want to see you, Rachel. She has told you. And you have agreed. It is, unless I am mistaken, one of the conditions of your temporary release. And you must abide by them. Otherwise this could turn into a hell of a messy situation. Do you understand?'

She stared down at her hands again. He watched the way she touched herself. Gestures of comfort, he thought. And he thought of the nights that he lay alone, his hands between his thighs, drifting in and out of sleep, waiting for the sound of Clare, crying out in fear or pain, asking for help and succour. Once they had slept together, their bodies curled fern-like, one around the other. But long before she had become ill he had moved out and into a room of his own. He had made all kinds of excuses. But how could he explain that he had woken up one morning and realized that he no longer loved her? That he had made a mistake? That she wasn't the woman with whom he wanted to spend the rest of his life? And then as he drifted in the free fall of indifference he met someone else, someone who was brave and beautiful, who challenged him, made him think, opened up new worlds, new possibilities. But Andrew was, as always, indecisive. Frightened of making the move, of committing himself again. And just as he was poised to go Clare told him that she was ill, that she would soon be helpless and dependent, that she could not live without him. And that was that. On reflection, he now realized that he had been relieved. He could take the coward's way out. Now he was Andrew the good, Andrew the saintly, Andrew whose opinions could never be challenged. Perhaps, if he had left Clare when her illness was barely perceptible, she might have found someone else, someone who would really love her and want her, not just someone like him who went through the motions.

Rachel raised her head and looked at him again for a moment, before dropping her eyes to her hands.

'Tell me, Rachel, why did you want to come and live here? Surely this place, this area must have so many memories for you? Surely it must make it all much more difficult?'

She stared at him, a look of puzzlement on her face. Then she spoke. 'Where else would I go? This is my home as much as anywhere, outside the prison, that is. And I have spent the last twelve years dreaming about the sea. I had to be by it again. You've no idea how wonderful it is to see it every day from my window, to walk beside it, to smell it, to feel saltwater on my skin again. You've no idea.'

He nodded. 'Fine. That's what you say. But I'm warning you. Any more messing around and you'll be back inside. It's extremely important, particularly for your first six months or so, that your behaviour is impeccable. Temporary release is just that, Rachel.

There is nothing fixed and immutable about it. You are still serving out, you must remember, a life sentence. We cannot afford for there to be any trouble or scandal associated with you. We've been lucky that the media haven't found out that you're not still in prison. But it's probably just a matter of time. Your case was such a huge story, there's bound to be some snotty-nosed journalist poking around where they're not wanted. And if there were to be any bad publicity we'd have no choice but to reconsider your position. And tell me,' his fingers drummed on her file on the desk, 'how *would* it feel to go back inside now?'

She stared at him again, and this time her eyes did not drop. Her cheeks reddened, then the blood drained away from them and she was white again. She stood up.

He watched her on the video monitor as she closed the street door behind her. She paused, hesitated, then turned towards the camera. She straightened her shoulders and smiled right up at him. Even the distortion of the wide-angle lens could not hide the transformation in her face. For an instant she was beautiful again. But then, as quickly as it had come, the smile faded and in its place was an expression of defeat and resignation. He watched her until she had gone beyond the camera's narrow range. He had wanted to ask her how she felt about her husband now. How she felt about his death. He wondered how she had grieved for him. He wanted to understand how grief and guilt would combine. He wanted to know what she had thought about all through those years. When she lay in her cell in the dark, what pictures of her husband did she see? And what lies did she have to tell herself in order to stay in control? He wanted to know because he wanted to know how he was going to feel. Afterwards. After he had taken the decision and acted upon it.

He got up from his desk and walked out on to the landing. He took a bunch of keys from his pocket and unlocked the door to the wooden cabinet screwed to the wall. He reached inside and pressed the stop/eject button on the video recorder. The machine clicked and whirred and a cassette slid smoothly out. He picked up a new one from the shelf above and fed it into the recorder's wide-open mouth. Then, with the old tape in his hand, he walked back to his office. He labelled it, dated it, then turned on his own machine. He watched the tape slide in, click into place, then he pressed play. He looked at her face, joyful in the sunshine, and wondered how long it had been before she could smile like that again. He watched her and wondered. Over and over and over.

CHAPTER EIGHT

IT WAS DISAPPOINTING really, Jack Donnelly thought as he wandered through the shopping centre, eating an apple and thinking about what he'd do for lunch. There had been, after all, no real mystery about the death, the murder, in fact, of poor little Karl O'Hara. He was just another junkie killed by just another dealer. It was shocking, tragic, depressing, all those sentiments. But it wasn't a mystery. Jack had gone to visit all the people whose names had popped out of the computer, including Karl's girlfriend. She had sobbed bitter tears all over the baby boy who bounced happily on her knee as she told how Karl had tried going on methadone, stuck to it for a while, then slipped back to the real thing. Then when she'd had the baby he'd told her he was going to give it all up, try to get himself together. And for a while it seemed fine. They'd been offered a flat by the Corporation, and there was some money coming in for a change. But then she realized that Karl was dealing as well as using. She'd tried to get him to stop. But he told her it was only until he got a few bob together. Then he'd give it all up, buy a van, get into the delivery business like his old man.

'So, what happened?' Jack leaned towards her and tickled the kid beneath his ample red chin. The baby looked at him with an expression of amazed surprise, then looked away, looked back, and burst into peals of excited laughter.

Karl was trying the oldest trick in the book, and the one least likely to succeed. He was using more of the gear than he was selling. Helping himself to samples of the product. Something had to give, and at the end of a very long day it was Karl's frail, under-nourished and wizened little body that succumbed.

The girlfriend's bags were packed for London. She was going to stay with her sister.

'I've had it with this dump,' she sobbed, while the baby pushed himself up on his sturdy little legs and pulled at her nose and hair. Jack reached over and took the child from her, taking care not to rest his wet and reeking bottom on his lap.

'And before you go,' he said, unpeeling the kid's sticky fingers from his tie, 'you'll tell me who was the bollocks who threw your Karl into the sea, won't you?'

She did. And she told him a lot more than he'd asked. All kinds of intelligence that would be very useful in the days to come. As he passed the baby back to her, surreptitiously wiping his hands on a piece of crumpled tissue from his trouser pocket, he pulled out a couple of twenty-pound notes.

'You might need these, for the little one.'

She turned away, her sobs even louder. He slid the money under a plastic bowl half filled with soggy cornflakes and stood up.

'Good luck,' he said, and meant it.

Poor kid, he thought as he turned into the supermarket and joined the queue at the sandwich counter.
Not a great start in life for either mother or child. He
thought of his own daughters. They were aged six and
ten – bright little things, cute and lovely. Well
behaved, got on fine at school, no trouble at all. They
even seemed to be coping with his split from their
mother. He couldn't quite believe that he'd actually
made the break. He'd been living on his own for three
whole months in a one-bedroomed flat in the new
development, just by the inner harbour, barely big
enough for the three of them when they came to stay,
every second weekend.

It was the younger of the two, Rosa, who asked all
the really difficult questions.

'Don't you love Mammy any more? Do you love us
still? Why did you leave us if you say you love us? Do
you love anyone else? Mammy says you have a girlfriend. She says you're going to get married again and
then maybe you'll have more children, and you won't
want us any more. Is that true, Daddy? Are you coming
home tonight? Why won't you come home tonight?
Mammy's cooking your favourite dinner, roast chicken
and lots of crunchy potatoes. Please, Daddy, just come
home for one night. Please, Daddy, we miss you.'

That was typical of Joan, leaving him to make all
the explanations.

'And, Daddy, we don't like her new friend. He
smokes. He makes a smell everywhere. He sleeps on
your side of the bed, and he always wants to watch

football when we don't. We want you to come home and tell him to go away.'

He didn't like being a cuckold. He could see that everyone at work knew. They were polite about it. But he'd caught the smirks, the whispered asides. He wondered if Joan had slept with any of his friends. He asked her, when eventually he got around to confronting her about the messages on the answering machine, the cigarette butts in the ashtray in the sitting room, the used disposable razor in the bin beneath the sink, when his electric model was there on the shelf.

'That's all you care about, isn't it, Jack?' she screamed at him. 'That I might have fouled your miserable little patch. Thinking about yourself for a change, is that right, Jack? You don't give a damn about me. You never have. Why did you marry me? Tell me why? Or maybe I should tell you, get it all out in the open for once.'

He'd cringed then, waiting for it.

'You liked fucking me, didn't you? I was easy. I was pretty then, and I was available. And do you remember when we got engaged, whenever we had a row or a disagreement over anything, what was your answer to it? You'd go out and you'd get plastered, and then you'd come to my flat and we'd fall into bed and that would be that. But it couldn't carry on like that, could it? Sooner or later you were going to have to start talking to me, getting to know me, letting me get to know you. But you didn't want that, did you? And even after I had the girls, I thought you'd want it then, but somehow you didn't. You were happier talking to them, getting to know them, than you ever were getting to know me. So don't you give me a hard time about what I've been doing. Just don't try it.'

She said a lot more that night too. About the way he lived his life. Or rather the way he didn't. She was right about a lot of it too, he had to admit. And he wondered for a moment if maybe this might be the catalyst that could make it all happen between them. He tried to kiss her, but she wasn't having any of it. She told him to go. And it was easier to do what she wanted, although he could see what the bitch was up to now. Rewriting history, coming the injured party with everyone they knew, so there was no sympathy heading his way.

And what had he done with the rest of his life? Catching petty thieves and locking them up. Catching mad bastards and locking them up too. It was all pretty pointless, he thought. Not so high on the list of services to humanity. But on the other hand who was he to be so dismissive of the whole business? There were plenty of other guys, he knew, who loved the way of life and got real satisfaction from it. Who relished every masculine moment. But not him. The trouble was that he didn't love anything else either. Aimless, that's what I am, he thought as he cast his eye across the list of sandwiches on offer, and picked, as always, Swiss cheese and tomato, aimless and truly pathetic.

He paid for his sandwich and walked out of the shopping centre. Bright sunlight pricked at his eyes, making them water. He fished around in his jacket pocket for his dark glasses. He sat down on a bench in the little paved area between the shops and the new cinema complex that had just been built. The metal back to the seat was comfortingly warm as he leant against it and took a bite of cheese and tomato. In spite of his gloom he was looking forward to picking up that bollocks of a dealer this afternoon. Now that was useful, that was worthwhile. He could see examples of the guy's handiwork everywhere around him. In the pale, sullen faces of the kids who lolled around him, shrieking abuse at each other and anyone else who came too close. Junkie voices, he thought. An unnatural tone that had nothing to do with accent and everything to do with unreality.

He finished his sandwich and leaned back. His eyes closed behind the tinted lenses, his head dropped on to his chest. He dozed. And woke suddenly, jerking upright as a car alarm nearby began to sound. He blinked, took off his glasses and rubbed his eyes, then put them back again, stretched and straightened, glancing at his watch to make sure that his lunch break wasn't yet over. He noticed for the first time the woman seated by herself in the corner diagonally across, squashed between a row of parked cars and a litter bin. She was taking items of food from a plastic container. An apple, an orange, a small sandwich, a bottle of water. She arranged them carefully beside her on the bench. She looked around as if she was checking to see if anyone was watching, then she began to eat. Quickly, neatly, breaking the sandwich up into small pieces, cutting slivers from the apple with a plastic knife, breaking the orange into segments. Her movements were precise and tidy. She reminded him of the sparrows that hopped on springy legs between the lunchtime strollers, picking up scraps of food invisible to the human eye. It was only as she was finishing and stood up, turning to face him as she pushed scraps of orange peel into the litter bin, that he recognized her. Andy Bowen was right. She wasn't gorgeous any longer.

He stayed very still, wondering if she would see him. But she was completely self-absorbed. She sat down again on the bench and began to pack away her lunch box. She drained the last of the water from the bottle and put it back in her bag, then she stood up and began to walk away.

To follow or not to follow? He thought of the way it had been that day in the house. Detective Superintendent Michael McLoughlin bending over the body. Blood everywhere. So much of it. The post-mortem report said that he was exsanguinated, that he'd bled out. He remembered McLoughlin talking about it afterwards, saying that it looked like someone had taken a hatchet to him, and commenting on how calm she was. They'd thought it was shock, because she'd been there in the same room with him for at least twelve, maybe even fourteen hours. She'd have watched him die. And then when they let her go, cut the handcuffs off her wrists, then she got upset, started to cry all right. But it was the daughter she was worried about. Made them phone the hospital immediately to see how she was after the accident. That was all she seemed to be worried about, that the kid was OK, that

she wasn't upset. McLoughlin always said they should
have suspected something wasn't right immediately.
But she was so clear about everything, about what had
happened that night in the house.

The house. That he had been invited to how many
times? He remembered the first time was for the baby's
christening. Martin had sent out a general invitation.
Everyone was welcome. It was a beautiful sunny day.
And one hell of a party. It went on all night. Martin
was the life and soul, until he got so drunk he keeled
over. Looking back on it now, with two children of his
own, he wondered how Rachel had coped with them
all. And there had been that moment, he had remembered it afterwards, when he had gone upstairs, looking
he supposed for the bathroom, opened a couple of doors
off the landing, and had seen her feeding the baby. It
was dark in the room and he had pulled back quickly,
embarrassed by the sight of her bare breast, so full and
white in the light from the stairwell. He noticed that
there was someone else with her, sitting cross-legged
on the floor beside her low chair, his hand on the
baby's head, and recognized that it was Dan. Well, he
was the baby's godfather after all. He'd been carrying
her around all afternoon, showing her off, giving
Rachel a hand with the food and the drink and
everything. While Martin had done what Martin
always did. Hung out with his buddies. The other
guys from Special Branch. The elite, they liked to
think. Always a group apart.

He remembered that he had felt – what was it? –
guilt, somehow, that he had intruded into the quiet,

calm world of the baby. And suddenly responsible for the racket that came up from downstairs, for the crowd of stragglers drinking their heads off in the kitchen and living room, and for the stench of alcohol and cigarettes that wafted into the small, quiet nursery. He wondered if he should leave. But Martin had grabbed him by the arm as he came down into the hall, shoving a pint glass and a plate of sausages into his hand, and that had been that.

It was a lovely house. Or it had been. He was one of the team who searched it, looking for secrets. There had been none. There had been nothing hidden. Just the lingering smell of gunpowder, strongest in the sitting room, beside the stained carpet. He remembered too that he had taken the nightdress they had found in the skip and compared it with the others in the chest of drawers and the clothes in the wardrobe. Same brand names, same size, same range of colours. And he had felt bad, guilty and awkward as he turned from the cupboard and looked at the bed. It was unmade. A cup of tea had been spilt across the bedside table. Underwear was lying on the floor, and a pair of shoes were thrown awkwardly in a corner. The air was stale and rank.

Had she been back there since then, he wondered as he waited and counted to ten. Then he stood up and moved out on to the footpath, turning right to walk up the main street. He could see her up ahead. Her grey hair stood out clearly among the crowds of lunch-time shoppers. And he remembered her father who had taught him when he was a student in Templemore.

Old Gerry Jennings. A good guy, one of the best. So proud of his daughter. The first one in the family to go to university. To become an architect of all things. Making things, building things. Making money, Gerry, someone had said, and they all laughed. And he laughed with them. Yeah, making money to keep me in my old age, when I'm shot of all you lot.

She had stopped at the traffic lights and was waiting for them to change. He hung back, turning away from her, watching her in the reflection of the newsagent's window. When the lights changed she hesitated, then rushed across the road, barely missing bumping into a young woman with a baby in a buggy and a child by the hand. He turned and crossed too, quickening his pace to catch up with her, just in time to see her disappear through the large bronze doors of the huge modern church which dominated the town centre.

Perhaps a fit of penitence, he thought as he paused, dipped the first two fingers of his right hand into the holy-water stoop and muttered, automatically, the words coming without thought, 'In the name of the Father, the Son and the Holy Ghost, Amen,' feeling as always his mother's warm hand on his, hearing his mother's low voice breathing in his ear. It was much darker inside, apart from the light that streamed through the floor-to-ceiling stained-glass windows at the northern end of the nave. St Michael, the archangel, vanquished evil in yellow, blue and red, with the Holy Ghost in the shape of a large white dove looking on from its vantage point in Heaven. Mass was being celebrated and he saw that Rachel had taken her seat midway between the altar and the last pew. She had slipped on to her knees, bowed her head and buried her face in her hands. Her grey hair was not out of place here, among this congregation of the elderly faithful. He sat down in the pew closest to the door and closed his eyes. She had looked very striking on the day of her husband's funeral. She had worn black, of course, but he remembered that she had carried a white rose. The photograph that had been on all the front pages the next morning was of the moment when she had thrown it into the open grave. A small white splash against the darkness that surrounded.

He remembered the drive from the morgue at St Vincent's Hospital to the huge Spanish-style church at the top of Kill Avenue. He had helped carry the coffin up the aisle. He shifted, suddenly uncomfortable, remembering its weight, and the way it had cut into his shoulder. He had tried not to think what was inside it. But in spite of himself he had begun to imagine Martin's body, the way it would look if the polished oak of the coffin fell away. The thought had made him stumble, almost slip on the shiny marble floor, and to straighten himself he had clutched at whoever was on the opposite side, feeling the warm roughness of the heavy dark blue uniform. A relief when they had reached the altar and their burden could be laid down on the waiting trestles.

Such a public occasion. So high profile. The playing of the last post, the removing of the flag, the careful folding and handing over of it. The Garda Commissioner coming to shake her hand and commiserate. Even the Minister for Justice and the President's aide-de-camp and a gaggle of politicians. TV cameras, newspapers. The works. And all she probably wanted was to be on her own, to grieve by herself, without the public scrutiny. But the public scrutiny of the funeral was as nothing compared to what had followed. A lot of lives had been ruined that night all those years ago.

Silvery bells rang and he opened his eyes. Around him the devout were preparing themselves for communion. On the altar the priest raised the silver salver and jug.

'Take this, all of you, and eat. For this is the body of my son which he has given up for thee. Take this, all of you, and drink. For this is the blood of my son which he has given up for thee.'

The bells rang again. On cue the men and women in the seats around him began to shuffle into the aisle. He watched the silent column form and waited to see if she would join in. But she didn't move. He stood up and took his place in the queue. As he passed by her seat he glanced down. She was staring ahead. Tears were streaming down her face and she was mouthing silently to herself. He stood before the priest. He held up his hands, one palm crossed over the other. He closed his eyes and heard the muttered intoning, 'the body of Christ, the body of Christ, the body of Christ'. He felt the wafer against his skin and raised his hands to his mouth. The saliva on his tongue received its dryness and it began to melt. He swallowed. A sense of peace flooded through him as he turned and walked back to his seat. The miracle had happened as it always did. He believed again. All doubts washed away. Now he knelt to pray, the words tumbling one over the other. 'Holy Father, help me now and forever. Holy Mother, protect me and my children from sin and darkness.' He leaned forward and pressed his forehead against his knuckles. 'Thank you, Lord, for this gift of eternal life. Thank you, Lord. Thank you.'

Rachel had noticed the man at the back of the queue for communion. He was much younger than everyone else and he wasn't usually here at this time, in this place. It had become her habit to sit in the darkness of the church and listen to the sound of the Mass. There was comfort in the familiar words and no one ever noticed her. All eyes were on the priest and the altar. And she liked that. But he had looked at her. She had felt rather than seen his glance in her direction as he walked past. She had watched him bow his head and hold up his hands to receive, and she had expected him to look again at her as he walked back to his seat. But his eyes were lowered, his expression turned inward.

She got to her feet and edged out of the pew. It was time, she was sure, to go back to work. Today, Mickey, the nice man who worked alongside her in the dry-cleaner's mending shoes and cutting keys, had asked her to have lunch with him. But she had refused, found an excuse. His feelings had been hurt, she could see that. He had looked down at his hands — callused, hardened, shoe polish ingrained around his fingernails and lodged in the lines of his palms, so they seemed, she thought, like an etching or a woodcut – and turned them over this way and that. Then he had looked at her face again and said, 'Some other time maybe,' as he put on his coat and lifted the countertop and walked away. She had nodded at his back, the bile rising into her mouth. How could she explain that it was nothing personal? That twelve years of eating on her own, in her cell, had made it impossible for her to imagine how it would be to eat in the company of another. Biting, chewing, swallowing, all such actions must be done privately. She could no more eat in public now than she could walk naked down the street. It just wasn't possible. That was why she always went back to her room at lunchtime, or to the corner outside the shopping centre, behind the parked cars, where no one else ever came. But she would have never been able to tell him or anyone else that. They wouldn't understand.

And then as she passed the man seated at the back by the door to the street he looked up at her, looked straight into her face. And she saw who he was, and knew him, and cringed away from him as she remembered. The searches and the interrogation. The parade of witnesses during the trial. The words that were spoken about her. Against her. She tried to think. Was there a name that went with that face? Did it matter? He was one of them. The people who had spoken lies about her. Who had turned her into this pathetic creature. Whose memories were so confused that sometimes she thought she would never be able to sort the chronology of her recollections into any kind of order. Before, after, then, now, it was all a muddled blur.

And the only way to make it clear again was to complete the task that she had planned for so many years. The time was nearly right to begin. Nearly, but not quite. Soon she would be ready, and then everything would be different.

CHAPTER NINE

ANOTHER FACE THAT might or might not be familiar. Plump cheeks, wide lipsticked mouth, long gold
earrings that caught the light and twinkled, and a
charm bracelet snagging on the wool and tweed of the
suits and coats that the woman piled on the counter in
front of Rachel.

'There's no rush for these, dear. Just getting all the
winter clothes sorted out. I do like to make sure that
everything's nice and tidy before the summer holidays.
You know that way.'

Rachel had never heard the woman's voice before.
In the days when she had sat in Court Number Four
and watched and listened as the case against her was
laid out for public scrutiny, she had heard the voices of
the barristers, prosecuting and defending, the judge,
the witnesses, but never the voices of the twelve
members of the jury. Apart from the man elected to be
their foreman, who would make known their decision.
Freedom and vindication or prison and disgrace.

Eight men and four women were selected from the
panel of jurors. She had watched the selection proceed.
Her solicitor explained, prosecution and defence could

object to four each. But the objection could be based on nothing more than appearance and instinct. They would try to get as many women as they could for her. Stands to reason, her solicitor said. Women would be more sympathetic to her situation. Precedent suggested that anyway. But they were unlucky.

Rachel had sat opposite them for the six days that the trial lasted, shifting uneasily on the hard wooden seat, trying not to slump or sag, straining to look alert and interested, to look like the kind of person they would believe. Behind her sat her father. Always. Every day. Her mother stayed at home. Rachel waited to see who would support her and believe in her. Once she had friends. Girls she had met at school and at university, who had stayed in touch through their years of work, marriage and motherhood. A few of them came, in twos, and stayed for an hour, sometimes less. Mouthing excuses across the crowded courtroom.

Sorry, got to go. Got to collect the kids from school, crèche, football practice. Got to get back to work, got a deadline. Sorry, talk to you soon. Keep in touch. Don't worry. It'll be fine.

While the jury sat and listened. All twelve of them. The eight men and the four women. Including the woman with the dangling earrings and the clinking charm bracelet, the powdered cheeks and the red mouth who now was pushing the piled clothes across the counter. Whose face had crumpled with anguish, her plump shoulders shaking, tears spilling down the ridges on either side of her nose as the foreman of the jury rose to pronounce the verdict.

She had cried silently then, and she had continued to cry while the judge pronounced sentence. And afterwards? Rachel did not know. Because afterwards there had been no time for anything or anybody except to say goodbye to Amy, to hold her for one last moment, breathing in the musky sweetness which rose up from beneath her bright blue sweater as Rachel kissed her and kissed her. On her cheeks and forehead, her mouth, her chin, the soft folds of skin around her neck, her hands and fingers, red with cold on that raw November day. Until the prison officer tapped her on the shoulder and told her that she had to go. That it was time. That the van was waiting.

'The van?' Rachel had looked up at her and back down to Amy, who had begun to whimper.

'The van, the prison van. Come on now, Rachel. Don't keep us waiting.' And she put her hand on her forearm and gestured to her to stand up. 'This way, now. There's a good girl. Don't make a fuss.'

Rachel stood in the Round Hall and looked from side to side. At her father, who had picked up the child and was cradling her in his arms, promising her sweeties and treats 'if you're a good girl for Grandad'. So that was the way it was to be. Mother and daughter, their obedience demanded. One by threats, the other by bribes.

Her solicitor and barristers were walking briskly towards the front door. The crowd who had milled around her since the trial began, the journalists, the guards, the vicarious onlookers, were leaving. Buttoning up their coats against the damp chill, picking up their bags and briefcases. Their conversations drifted past her.

'Tonight? I fancy a film. What about you?'

'Dinner would be nice, then a couple of pints.'

'I'm for a night in. A hot bath and a bottle of wine. I'm wrecked. And I've another big case starting tomorrow.'

She stood beside the prison officer and watched as the Round Hall emptied, like the tide going out, leaving her behind. And somehow or other she realized that it was all over.

The trial, the parade of witnesses, the chain of evidence, the testimonies, the legal arguments, the disputes about procedure. She had heard them all. She had listened as the days passed. And the story of her husband's death had been laid out in front of the court. The prosecution had produced their evidence. The shot-gun with her fingerprints on it. Her clothes stained with his blood. The forensic evidence that the spread of droplets was consistent with being in the position from where the shots had been fired. The medical evidence that the first wound to his upper-right thigh severed the femoral artery causing haemorrhage. That it was not, however, necessarily fatal. If he had received medical attention he would have survived. That it was the second shot that penetrated the pelvis that caused his death by damaging the left iliac artery, so he haemorrhaged into his abdomen. That the cataclysmic bleed caused him to exsanguinate, to bleed to death. That he went into a state of shock, that he lost consciousness immediately, that he died within half an hour. The evidence from her neighbours who said they had heard the sound of an argument. And yes, they had heard something else, a couple of loud bangs. They had thought it was a backfiring car. But no, they hadn't seen anyone else at the house. They'd seen no one come or go that night. Nothing except they'd heard a car drive away sometime late, after eleven or so.

'And did you see whose car this was? And who was driving it?' The prosecution barrister leaned forward as he asked the question.

The young woman from next door had hesitated. She couldn't be sure, she said. Oh, she was sure that it was Rachel Beckett's car, she knew that all right. And she thought it was Mrs Beckett in it, but she wasn't absolutely certain.

'Not certain, I see. In percentage terms what would we be talking about? Seventy-five, eighty, ninety per cent?'

Again the hesitation. Rachel stared at her, willing her to look back. But she ducked her head and paused, then said, 'It was pretty dark, but I'd say I'd be over ninety per cent sure that it was her.'

Rachel waited for the cross-examination from her defence. But it didn't come.

'Why didn't you go for her?' she had asked her barrister afterwards.

'Because,' he said, 'that way we still had a doubt. If I'd pushed her further who knows what she might have said?'

She had watched Daniel when he was called to give his evidence. She had never seen him so calm and confident. He told his story cogently. Mrs Beckett, Rachel, his sister-in-law had phoned him. Said that she was frightened, that she and Martin were having a row, that Martin was drunk.

'Did she ask for help?'

'Yes, she did.'

'And what did you say?'

'I said I would come and speak to Martin.'

'Did she tell you what the row was about?'

'She did.'

'And?'

'She said that Martin had found out that we had had a relationship a number of years ago. That he was furious. That he wanted to end the marriage.'

'So what did she want you to do?'

'She wanted me to come and tell Martin that it meant nothing. That it was casual. That it was all over.'

'And did you do that?'

'Well, I was going to, but when I got there Martin was asleep. He had passed out on the couch. So there didn't seem to be much point in hanging around. So I left.'

'So what do you say to the testimony of the defendant? That it was you who fired the second fatal shot and you who told her that you would get rid of the evidence – the gun, her clothes – that you would take her car and dump it, make it look as if it had been stolen. And it was you who concocted the story, the ridiculous story about who it was who had killed her husband.'

She watched him. She tried to catch his eye. She knew when he saw what was happening that he would do the right thing. And then she heard his words.

'That's completely untrue. Who would believe anything like that? My brother was alive when I left the house.'

'And where were you between the hours of ten p.m. and midnight on the night in question?'

'I was at my mother's house in Greystones. She hadn't been well. I had rung her when I was leaving work and she had asked me to come and sit with her, because my father was away. And I did, I stayed the night.'

She had watched Mrs Beckett give her testimony. She listened carefully to the words she used. She looked frail and old, her hands shaking, but her voice was strong.

'My son was with me. He put me to bed. He sat beside me till I went to sleep.'

'And what time was that?'

She hesitated. The court waited. Then she spoke. 'It was nine o'clock. I remember I heard the clock in the hall chime. I couldn't sleep. He brought me a video, one of my favourite old films, *High Society* with Grace Kelly and Bing Crosby. I love that film. I fell asleep. He was so good to me that night. He woke me up for the ending, because he knows I love it so much, and then he came into me every hour to make sure I was all right.'

And Rachel looked at her and listened as the barrister questioned her. Asked her over and over again.

Are you sure?

Are you positive?

Do you know?

And to each question she answered yes, yes, yes.

Until finally the judge intervened. Said he'd heard quite enough. That there was no further purpose to this line of questioning.

And now it was all over. And she was walking through the car park to the van, feeling the wind from the river tugging at her hair and her coat, the chain from the handcuffs tugging at her wrists as she looked up and around her, at the lighted windows of the court buildings, and the crowds outside the gates heading for home.

She did not cry then, not until sometime early the next morning as she lay in her prison clothes, underneath her prison blankets, and tried to understand what had happened. This cannot be, she said out loud. This is a mistake. I am not this person. I am not this woman. I am a good woman who loved her husband and loves her daughter. I made a mistake, that is all. I should not be punished for it like this. Tomorrow they'll let me out. As soon as it gets light I'll tell them it's all been a mistake. And she banged on the door and shouted.

But no one came to her. And she saw nothing except the sudden bright point of light as the spyhole was jerked open, every fifteen minutes throughout that night. And then the tears began to flow and saltwater stung her lips.

Now her hands touched the woman's hands as she

pulled the piled suits and coats towards her. The woman had long fingernails, painted crimson. They were hard and pointed, manicured and cared for. Rachel drew back and turned to the cash register, adding up the amount for each item. The machine spat out a pink ticket. Rachel tore it off and turned back.

'When would you like these?' she asked, and for the first time their eyes met. There was a pause.

'There's no rush. The end of the week would be fine.'

'And your name?' Rachel's pen hovered, waiting. This time the pause was longer.

'Lynch, Mrs Lynch.'

She pushed the top half of the pink slip across the counter. Long red nails fiddled with it, then fingers grasped it and slipped it into a black leather bag. Rachel picked up the other half and pinned it firmly to the rough stubbly tweed of a man's sports jacket. Around them was the bustle of trade and commerce, the echo of footsteps and loud music pouring from a speaker set in the ceiling tiles. She looked up again. The woman called Mrs Lynch was fiddling with the clasp of her purse, adjusting the floral scarf at her neck. Rachel dumped the pile of clothes in the waiting bin. She turned back to the counter.

'They let you out. Finally. They let you out.'

'That's right.'

'I'm so glad. It should never have been like that. I couldn't believe they would do that to you.'

Rachel smiled, just for a moment.

'I've thought about you so often, wondered how

you were. Please, if you need anything. I'll be back for the clothes on Friday. Tell me then, if there's anything I can do.'

Rachel watched the tears well up in her large blue eyes as the next customer stepped forward, holding out his ticket, waiting for service. The woman called Mrs Lynch turned away, then turned back again towards her.

'I'm so pleased, it's been such a long time.'

Rachel took the man's ticket. She moved to the racks of polythene-wrapped clothes that hung in rows, like so many sleeping beauties, she thought, waiting to be brought to life. She ran her finger along the hangers, matching up the numbers. She found a dark suit and, nestling against it, a dress. Cream silk, with tiny pleats that would fold and mould themselves around the body beneath, a halter-neck top, a low back and a long skirt. The plastic was cold and slippery beneath her hand as she pressed her palm up against it. She pulled the dress from the rack. She wanted to hold it next to her skin like the special dresses she had worn before. Once upon a time. Silk and linen, satin and lace. Her thighs crossing beneath her skirt, her stomach pressing against her waistband, her breasts pushing up and into her bodice as she watched Martin, how he was watching her.

'Hey.' She heard the loud voice behind her. 'What's keeping you? Is there a problem?'

She turned quickly, folding the dress and suit over her arm.

'Sorry, I'm sorry.' Her face reddened as the words

rushed out. 'No, nothing wrong, not at all. I was just,' she paused, 'just admiring this dress. It's lovely.'

Notes thrust at her as she folded the clothes and put them carefully into a plastic bag. Change snatched from her hand, and a curt nod of the head in acknowledgement as her apologies still poured out. She crept back and away from public view to stand, head bowed, among the silhouetted shapes of other people's lives.

The Matron had told her to come at two.

'You'll see him at his best then. We have music in the afternoon. He loves the music.'

She was late. There had been a mix-up over the cash in the till. It wasn't her fault. She was only supposed to work until one. But the boss had insisted on counting the money, and there was a tenner missing. She had made Rachel wait until everything had been accounted for. Until the money had been checked and rechecked. The sums done. And somehow the missing note had appeared again. Rachel had met Mickey's eyes above the pile of coins. He had winked and smiled apologetically.

She had to run to get the train out along the seashore to Bray. She had the name of the old people's home scribbled on a piece of paper, but she wasn't sure where it was. She had to stop to ask. Twice, three times, unable to concentrate on the directions she was being given. Running from street to street, peering at the names on the gates, until she found the right one. Sylvan View it was called. A long drive, a garden filled with evergreens. And, standing apart from its neighbours, a large red-brick house, with granite steps and a concrete wheelchair ramp curving up one side.

Her father was seated at a long table. A nurse was beside him. She lifted a double-handled cup to his mouth, coaxing him, urging him on, until he sipped tentatively, as if, Rachel thought, this was the newest experience in the world for him.

'Good boy, there's a good boy,' the nurse muttered, holding up a small square of toast, placing it against his lips. Again the pause, again the encouragement, the urging on, until eventually he opened his mouth and accepted the offering.

'It's the memory,' the nurse said, looking up at Rachel. 'They forget how to eat.' Forget how to eat and drink, how to dress and wash, how to read and listen. Forget how to be human in the world.

'But there's one thing they don't forget,' the nurse said as she led him into the large room which looked out on to the garden. Double doors opened on to a sunny lawn. Inside it was dark. A young man sat at an old upright piano. He was playing a tune that Rachel recognized. Her father and the others took their seats in a large semicircle around him. Their grey heads were bowed, their arms hanging passively by their sides. Rachel stood in the doorway, uncertain. The man at the piano smiled a big broad grin.

'Come on, lads and lassies. Take your partners for the waltz. Quick about it now.'

Rachel watched her father. He began to sway from side to side on the chair, his feet in their slippers moved backwards and forwards in a familiar pattern.

The nurse looked at Rachel. She gestured to the old man. Rachel took his hands and drew him up to standing. His hands felt so soft now, and small and withered, in hers. She remembered the way they had been in the years before. Large and strong, callused and capable. She thought of all the things he had taught her. To shoot and fish. To sail a boat. To grow vegetables and fruit. To drive. She could see his hands on the steering wheel. The veins stood up, blue ridges against the skin, brown, always brown, winter and summer. Now his hands were white and flecked with pale brown marks. Once he had always seemed to fill the space around him, now he seemed so small. Once he had been substantial, rock-solid in his uniform with his stiff peaked cap and his shoes that squeaked as he walked. Now his wrists were so thin she could have joined her finger and thumb around them, and his back was bent so his head was, for the first time ever, at the same level as hers.

They shuffled slowly around the room.

'Sing, everyone.' The man at the piano stood and waved encouragingly with one arm. The nurses clapped in time. Rachel opened her mouth and the familiar words poured out. Her father sang too. Around and around they turned together. His hands grew warm in her grasp and his voice grew louder. She listened to the words he was singing. He knew them all, verse after verse.

'Dada,' she said, 'it's me. It's Rachel. I'm here. It's been such a long time, but I'm here now.' He didn't answer. He just kept on singing.

Irene goodnight, Irene goodnight,
Goodnight Irene, goodnight Irene
I'll see you in my dreams.

Round and around they waltzed. Rachel watched
her father's face. His expression had begun to soften
and relax. He was losing that look of frozen immobil-
ity, the 'lion face' as she had heard it called. The man
at the piano increased the pace, and the dancers spun
more and more quickly. And then she saw her father
smile, that same open, joyous expression that she had
carried with her in her memory for so many years.
Unseen all the time that she was in prison, when he
had come to visit her, reluctantly, once a month. The
prison surroundings filling him with revulsion, so he
had drawn away, unable to engage in anything but the
smallest of small talk. Once, she remembered, she had
leaned across the table to touch him, but he had
flinched and looked in the direction of the watching
prison officer and quickly pulled back, out of her
reach. It was shame, she knew. Of her betrayal of her
husband, her infidelity, her public humiliation. And
she could barely bring herself to look at him and see
her shame reflected back at her from his watery-blue
eyes. And then he told her, six months or so after
she began her sentence, that they couldn't keep Amy
any longer. It was too much. They were too old.
And besides, she was difficult. Her behaviour was
disturbed.

'She has nightmares. She wets the bed. She's cheeky.
Your mother can't cope. We thought maybe the Beck-

etts might take her. But it's impossible. We can't bring ourselves to speak to them.'

And she said no, she didn't want her going there, and please, please could they not just hold on for a bit longer. She'd be out of here soon, she knew she would. But he said no. He had spoken to the social worker. They would find Amy a foster-family. It was common practice. It would be better in the long run.

But now the music had stopped and the man at the piano had closed the lid. There was a sudden silence, then a sob as one of the old ladies began to cry. She stood by herself in the middle of the floor, her hands reaching out, her feet still moving, taking delicate little steps from side to side. One of the nurses stepped forward and took her by the arm, leading her away, hushing her sobs, distracting her with offers of chocolate biscuits. The others followed without protest. Rachel's father dropped her hands. He turned away from her, his head bowed. His feet in their slippers shuffled forward.

'Dada.' Rachel tried to take his arm but he pulled himself away. 'Dada, please, won't you stay with me for a bit longer?'

He paused. He looked at her. His pale blue eyes met her own. For an instant there was recognition. She smiled and held out her arms to him. She stepped towards him again, but he moved away.

'No,' he said, 'not you, you're not my girl. You made me feel bad. Your shame brought me shame. My girl was good. You were bad. You did a bad thing.'

'No.' She took hold of his sleeve. 'No, I didn't. It

wasn't me. It wasn't my fault. Please, you must believe me.'

But already he had joined the line of bowed grey heads moving towards the double doors that led back to the bedrooms. She made as if to go with him, but the nurse turned to her and blocked her way.

'He's tired now. They're all tired. They'll want to rest for a while. Come back tomorrow if you like. Oh, and before I forget,' she paused and Rachel waited for the familiar expression of curiosity to spread across her face, 'Matron said would you drop into the office on your way out.'

It was late when she got back to her room and she was very hungry. She felt so weak that she wasn't sure she was going to make it up the last steep flight of stairs. Her hands shook as she fitted the key into the door, her stomach cramped, waves of pain and nausea that reminded her of childbirth. She kicked the door closed behind her and frantically jerked open the cupboard above the sink. She pulled out a small loaf of bread and began to tear at it, ripping off hunks and shoving them into her mouth, until at last her panic began to subside. Then she sat down on the floor beside the wide bay window, rested her head against a cushion, folded her arms tightly, slipping her hands underneath her armpits and closed her eyes.

It was almost dark when she opened them again. Below her on the busy road from Glenageary to Dun Laoghaire the street lights glowed, bright points of orange like candles on a birthday cake. She felt stiff and cold. She pushed herself up to sitting. Beside her on the floor was the small leather suitcase that she had brought with her from the old people's home. The one that the Matron had told her that her father had wanted her to have.

'He said to me when he came here first – after your mother died and he couldn't manage by himself any longer – he said to me over and over again, when he was still lucid. He said that one day you would come to see him, and when you did I was to give you this.' She turned back from the large locked cupboard in the corner of her office, with the brown case held out in front of her like a votive offering.

Rachel picked it up and rested it on her knees. The remains of a tattered label clung to the lid. She read aloud the words printed in faded blue-black ink. Kathleen Simpson, Belacorick House, Co. Mayo. Her mother's name, her mother's home. Long forgotten that she had come from that place by the river. Run away with Gerry Jennings, the young guard who came to the village. Changed her religion, brought her children up in the ways of their father. Punished for years by her own people. Denied her birthright.

Rachel put her thumbs to the metal locks and pushed hard. They clicked open. She lifted the lid. Inside was a large brown envelope and a piece of lined paper. The crabbed writing, recognizably her father's, said: *From your mother. She wanted you to have this. Something to help you get back on your feet.*

Rachel lifted out the envelope. It was heavy, bulky. She turned it upside down. Wads of money, five- and ten-pound notes dropped out and scattered on the floor. She sat up quickly and began to gather them up, smoothing out the stiff, waxy paper, placing them in piles, counting them. Five, ten, fifteen, twenty thousand pounds all together. More than enough to make a difference.

She stood up and rummaged beneath the sink. She found a supermarket plastic bag and bundled the money into it. Then she knelt down beside her bed and carefully, with the point of a knife, unpicked the stitching around one corner of the base. She pulled back the stained fabric and squeezed the plastic bag and its precious contents inside, pushing it down between the springs, then threaded a needle and quickly and neatly restitched it. She had never been the best at hiding precious belongings when she was in prison. There were others whose skills were legendary, spoken of with awe by both prisoners and screws. But this would do, for the time being, until she could find somewhere more secure, more permanent.

She lay down on the bed and wrapped a blanket around her. Beside her hung her map. She looked at the coloured shapes she had marked out on it and lifted up her hand to touch them. Soon, it would be time. She turned her head away and closed her eyes. She slept.

CHAPTER TEN

OUT NOW. OUT for a month. Every day it was easier. To walk by herself through the streets. To take longer and longer strides. To know that she could go further than a hundred yards without stopping to wait for a gate to be unlocked, for a door to be opened, for the commands that would tell her she could come or she could go.

Out now. Out for a month. Every day something new to learn and discover. The supermarket was her favourite place. She liked to wander with her basket. Watching the lights bounce off every shiny surface, making all the packets and tins and parcels glow and sparkle. She was getting better about food now. Every day she would try something different. Cheeses that dripped and smelt. Herbs that were new and unfamiliar, like coriander and basil. Feathery dill and bunches of peppery rocket. Black olives. New breads. Rolls with poppy seeds and sesame seeds. Hot spicy sauces and relishes that she ate with a spoon from the jar. And fish. Hake and brill, wild salmon and thick slices of tuna and swordfish. But not meat. She never wanted to eat meat again. Not since that night when she had seen Martin's body torn apart, bleeding. Now when she saw meat hung from butchers' hooks or swathed in plastic, the flesh so red, the fat so white, she could feel the bile rise in her mouth. It smelled, even in the air-conditioned coolness of the supermarket counter, of decay and rot and misery. It smelled of prison.

She had looked at herself in the mirror. Caught sight of herself in shop windows. Seen how she looked now. Strong and healthy, the prison demeanour gone from her. Her head lifted, smooth confidence in her step. She was nearly ready. Almost. And now she wanted to see, to test herself.

She had begun to go further away from her bedsit, the shopping centre, and the grid of streets in the town centre that she knew. Walking to the station, deciding. Which way today? South to Bray, along the coastline. Looking up from the window to the houses on the cliff above. Looking out for the one with the bell tower, the red-tiled roof just visible through the dark green of the pine trees. Thinking of the photographs she had seen of it on the society pages of the magazines that had found their way into the prison. The parties given, fund-raising for charities. Paper lanterns slung around the terrace. Gardens stretching off towards the sea. A marquee, a string quartet. The gracious, generous host with his beautiful wife and perfect children at his side. The pictures she had torn out and kept, pasted into her scrapbook. The details of their life that she had memorized.

Or north to the city and beyond to Howth. Watch-

ing, waiting, looking out for just the right person.
Like the man who was lying beside her now with one
arm flung over her waist. She lay quite still for a
moment, then she opened her eyes. She was lying on
her side facing a window. The light from the street
filtered through the slats of a wooden Venetian blind
which was lowered but not closed. Her head throbbed
and there was a foul taste in her mouth. Her neck felt
sore and stiff as if she had slept with it twisted. She
shifted carefully, moving her legs, trying not to disturb
him. She rolled on to her back. As she turned so did
he, away from her, gathering his arms and legs together
and lying on his other side with his hands tucked
neatly between his thighs. She pulled herself up and
leaned over him. In the half-light the fair stubble on
his face gleamed. His mouth was open and a bubble of
saliva rested on his full red lips. His skin was smooth,
unblemished, unmarked. Unlike her own body, which
seemed wrinkled and weathered, soiled and stained.
Not that he had said that as he watched her undress.
Or could she remember what he had said? Or who he
was or where she was now?

She turned away and reached over to the bedside
table, picking up a glass of water. She drank. The
water tasted stale, chlorinated. City water, like the
water in prison, she thought. She rested the cold glass
against her cheek and let her eyes drift around the
room. It was bare apart from the bed and an upright
chair by the window. There was a framed print on
the wall opposite, one of Gustav Klimt's bejewelled

Viennese ladies. She seemed to remember that he had said, last night, that it had been on the wall when he rented the apartment.

'They're all like that, you know, all these apartments on the Quays. They're all furnished exactly the same way. Same sofas and chairs, same wallpaper, probably the same people in each one.'

And he'd laughed. She didn't like his laugh. It was hooting, far too loud. Drew attention to him. Made people turn around and look. And she didn't like that. She'd been surprised by the laugh. It didn't go with the rest of him. The rest of him was smooth and pretty. She'd picked him out immediately. To follow. Just for fun. To see where he was going and what he was doing.

A game, that's what it was. The girls inside used to play it when they were let out. They'd tell her all about it.

'What you do,' they'd say, 'is you spot someone. In the street, or in a bar, or maybe even on a bus or a train. And you watch them. And then you go wherever they go. And after a while they notice you. But they don't notice that you've been following them, they just think you look familiar. And then it's dead easy, fucking ridiculously simple.'

'What is,' she asked, the first time they told her. 'What's simple?'

'To do what you want with them. Fuck them, rob them, have fun with them. It's the best game.'

And she had told them they were crazy. It was stupid. It would get you into trouble, big bad trouble.

'After all,' she said, 'they'll recognize you, they'll

know what you're like, they'll go to the police, and they'll be able to identify you. Won't they?'

And the girls had giggled and sniggered and nudged each other. And told her she didn't understand.

'For all your brains and fucking degrees and that kind of crap, you don't have a clue. About people, that is. They don't do anything about it, because they feel guilty, responsible, stupid. They've let you in, they've opened themselves up to you, they've judged that you're OK, and they can see how crazy they've been. And you know, Rachel, specially men. They've such huge fucking egos, they can't stand admitting that they've been wrong. So you're made.'

They were right. She wished she could tell them. They were right and she was wrong. It had worked just the way they said it would. And she had done it. She had spotted him on the train. He was young, good-looking. A tourist, perhaps, or a visiting businessman. He had a guidebook open on his lap, and he was tracing his route with one well-manicured fingertip. She moved her seat so she was sitting diagonally across from him. She stared out of her window, watching him in the reflection that played like a wide-screen movie in front of her eyes. He was wearing an open-necked shirt and a pair of light-coloured trousers. The sleeves of his shirt were rolled up, showing tanned forearms, covered with fine fair hair that gleamed as the sun fell upon it. She glanced over towards him, making sure not to catch his eye as he stood and stretched up to open the top part of the window. She watched the way the muscles in his back and buttocks tensed and moved as he struggled with the catch. She looked away and waited. Not for long.

'Excuse me, I can't seem to get the hang of this.' His accent was North American. His voice was low. She didn't respond immediately.

'Sorry. Miss?' He had that quaint, old-fashioned courtesy, like something from an old American TV series. 'Could you give me a hand?' He took a step towards her, moving awkwardly as the train gathered speed.

She had shown him how to open the window, answered a couple of questions about the passing scenery, then retreated to her own seat again. And when he got off the train at Pearse Station she had followed him. It was surprisingly easy. She had never followed anyone before, but maybe it was because she could tell that he had no purpose to his wanderings that she could easily keep him within her sights. He rambled along Nassau Street, then turned left up Kildare Street, heading towards the museum. She walked on the other side of the road, her heart leaping suddenly as she saw the uniformed guards on duty outside the Dáil. Felt the sight of their blue shirts, their silver buttons, their peaked caps take her breath away with anxiety. So she waited until her breath had slowed, her pulse had calmed, before she followed him through the ornate wrought-iron gate, and stepped into the cool dimness inside.

It wasn't hard to find him. He was looking at the exhibit of ancient gold. The light from the glass case shone up into his face, showing up the fine lines and wrinkles under his eyes and around his mouth. She moved closer and looked down at the gleaming yellow necklets, the metal twisted into fine spirals, the huge flat buttons and cloak-fasteners, the heavy ornate collars. She saw both their faces reflected in the glass and the way he was looking at her, recognizing her from the train. She smiled.

'It's beautiful, isn't it?'

She was proud of herself, the way she had managed to initiate the conversation. She had opened her mouth and wondered if the words would come. She knew about these things. She had studied archaeology in first year in college, part of her degree. The knowledge was all still there. Lodged in her memory. She explained. The kind of artefacts they were. The date they were made. She talked about the people who had worn them, the way they had lived. And he was charmed, she could see.

'Here.' She led him from room to room.

'You're better than a tour guide,' he said, his hand casually brushing against her back as they walked out into the sunshine again. And the hairs on her arms rose up as she felt her skin tighten.

'Can I buy you a drink?' he asked. 'As a thank-you for your time.'

And she nodded, unable for a moment to speak. She could see that he hadn't noticed. He was too busy telling her all about himself. He was thirty-two. He was divorced. He was from Ottawa. He worked for a software company, installing telephone and computer systems. He was in Dublin for two months, working

on a big job debugging some of the programmes here.
And he laughed his loud, ugly laugh.

'You wanna see the mess that some of your guys
have made of the system. And will they be told? You
wanna bet?'

He was lonely, he said as he moved closer, his thigh
rubbing against hers, one hand sliding up and under
her shirt, pressing against her vertebrae. She could
smell his sweat. She watched him drink. The way he
lifted up his chin as he raised the glass to his lips. The
way the skin stretched tightly over his throat, so she
could see clearly his Adam's apple and the tendons in
his neck. His hand clutched her thigh under the table,
his fingers digging into her crotch. She reached down
and slid open her zip and felt him touch her, then take
her own hand and press it hard against himself. So
long since she had done this. Years and years and years.
She felt his mouth against her ear, and his whispered
instructions.

'Come with me, come back to my place. We'll have
some fun.'

She followed him out of the bar, waiting while he
hailed a taxi, gave an address somewhere on the Quays,
then pushed her back against the seat, forcing open her
mouth, his hands reaching for her breasts. So long
since she had felt anything like this. And she remembered suddenly, so vividly that she wanted to cry out,
her first time with Martin. Outside in the open air.
Midwinter. The night they met. A retirement do for a
friend of her father's. She hadn't wanted to go but her
father had persuaded her. Bought her a new dress.

Halter-neck. Silk. Pleated. Beautiful. And she had met Martin, the son of her father's friend. And left with him, long before the speeches were over. Walked out of the hotel. Walked as far as the car park. Opened her coat. Felt the cold on her breasts and the warmth of his mouth. Leaned back against a tree and felt him inside her. Laughed out loud at their pleasure together. Afterwards they drove away in his car to sit by the little beach at Sandycove and watch the sun rise over the sea. And they touched each other as if each was precious and new and perfect.

There was a security gate at the apartment complex. He punched in his code. Five, eight, three, seven. She remembered it. She looked for cameras. There were none. He used a swipe card to open the door.

'Better than a hotel,' he said as he pulled her in behind him.

More private, she thought. He put on music. She knew it. The Cranberries. The girls inside had been mad about Dolores O'Riordan. She looks like one of us, they always said. He turned up the volume.

'Aren't you worried?' she asked him as he poured glasses of vodka and took a plastic sachet of what she was sure was cocaine from his briefcase. 'About the neighbours complaining?'

'Neighbours, complaining? It's live and let live here. I don't know them, nor could I give a fuck. And the feeling, I'm sure, is mutual.' He looked down at the two lines of coke he had laid out carefully across a small rectangular mirror. 'Now.' He handed her a rolled-up ten-pound note. 'Ladies first, I do believe.'

They'd have been proud of her, all her old friends from the prison. Not just the way she snorted the coke with practised ease but also in the way she sorted through his clothes before she left the next morning. Taking the cash from his wallet, his credit cards, the identity card for his job. She hesitated over his passport. It was worth money, lots of it, but on the other hand he'd have to report it stolen to get it replaced. No embassy official would believe that he had just lost it. And she didn't want to do anything that would force him to go to the police. Just in case, she wiped her prints from everything she had touched. Except his skin, she thought. He was still sleeping deeply when she had dressed and was ready to leave. Sleep suited him. He looked young and beautiful. It was a pity about the sex, by the time he was ready for bed he couldn't manage it at all. Too much drink, too many drugs. The girls had always said that the stories about coke and sex were a myth.

'It's just like any other drug,' they told her. 'Once they've got a taste for it they're fucking useless when it comes to bed. You always end up finishing it off by yourself.'

Such a pity, she thought, that they were right.

She stood by the river in the early morning sunshine and watched as a school of grey mullet made the journey from the sea towards O'Connell Bridge. They hung five-deep in the murky water, a lazy flick of their tails pushing them forward. What brings them up here, she wondered, away from the cleansing tide into the sluggish greasy sink of the river. Then she answered out loud her unspoken question. 'Food, of course, what else.'

She turned and walked away from the city towards where the river opened out into the bay. She raised her hand to her face. She could still smell him. His aftershave and his sweat. He had been so helpless, lying there beside her when she woke. She had sat and watched him. She had pulled back the sheets and looked at his body. She hadn't seen a naked man since Martin had died. As he rolled over towards her she saw the place where the shot from the gun had torn Martin apart. She remembered the colour of the blood as his heart pumped it from his body. Now she watched the pulse at the base of his neck, rising and falling. She reached out and touched it. It didn't take much to end someone's life. They had talked about it inside. The ways it can be done. The quickest, cleanest, neatest. They had told her and taught her, and she had listened and learned, stored up the knowledge for later, for when she would need it. She put her hand around his neck and felt his blood throb against her skin. He stirred and made as if to turn. She opened her fingers and pulled her hand away. She got up. She left.

Now the sun shone upon her face. She closed her eyes and tilted back her head. Then she pulled the credit cards and the money from her pocket. She had no need for them. She had all the money she could possibly want lying neatly in its hiding place in her room. She just wanted to know that she could do it. Break the commandment. Thou shalt not steal. Then get away with it. It was practice, that's what it was, for what was to come. She held her booty out in front of her, then flung the lot of it down into the river. She watched it settle on the surface, then waited until slowly and gradually the water dragged down the plastic and paper until all that was left was a tiny spreading ripple. Then she turned away.

CHAPTER ELEVEN

MORE ADVENTURES NOW. Every day something new to discover. Every morning there were exercises to do. Yoga poses she had learned in prison to drag her muscles out of their state of inertia. The cat, hollowing and arching her back, breathing in and out smoothly, rhythmically. The cobra, lifting her ribcage up out of her abdomen, the palms of her hands and her pubic bone flattened on the wooden floor. The dog, hips high, feet stretched, heels pushing down. The triangle, legs wide, feet turned first to one side, then to the other. And balancing poses, one leg raised, one foot anchored, one arm above her head, her gaze fixed to a dark spot on the wall, keeping her straight, keeping her upright, keeping her focused. Then down on the floor again, her knees bent, hands clasped behind her neck and she lifted and lowered her head, feeling the contraction in her stomach muscles. Twenty, thirty, forty times, sweat breaking out on her forehead. Hearing the voices of the women in the prison gym, shouting at her, urging her on, telling her to do it, to make it happen. She stood in the shower and scrubbed and scrubbed, and felt as if there was a new Rachel breaking through the skin of the old one.

The new Rachel who waited at the bus stop opposite the house just outside Dalkey village and looked at the cars parked on either side of the narrow road, haphazardly, some half up on the footpath, others carelessly blocking the gateway. It was twelve-thirty. Going-home time for the twenty or so small children who spent their weekday mornings at the Little Darlings crèche just outside Dalkey village. She had been here before. Every day this week. She would arrive just before twelve-fifteen and take up her position at the bus stop on the other side of the road. The bus, she knew, wouldn't come until well after twelve forty-five and no one would notice the woman who waited so patiently, leaning against the crooked metal pole.

It was the same routine every lunchtime here. The first of the mothers and the au pairs came at about twelve-twenty. The early birds would sit in their cars, listening to the radio or reading the paper. Then gradually all the others would arrive. Those on foot would walk past the parked cars and wait just inside the gate, leaning against the granite wall, chatting quietly. And the rest of the sleek, well-groomed women would arrive soon after, parking where they could find space, a steady rhythm of slamming doors announcing their presence as they too made their way into the drive. And then, sometime just after twelve-thirty, the children would appear, led by two teenage girls. They would always be carrying a present for their mothers. Paintings on large pieces of flimsy paper,

bright splashes and smears of colour to be fussed over
and cooed about, and interpreted endlessly over lunch.
Or lumps of clay, whose function was equally obscure,
but whose reception was guaranteed to be ecstatic.

Had it been like this for her, Rachel wondered as
she watched. Did she see herself and Amy among the
group? Was she the mother who crouched down beside
the little girl with the red curls, praising, encouraging,
urging her on with loving words and kisses? Or was
she the woman in a hurry, barely greeting the chubby
boy with glasses, before gathering up school bag and
painting, and hustling him out of the gate and into
the back seat of the car? There had been a time, she
remembered, when her kitchen walls were decorated
with Amy's paintings. Every day a new one to add to
the collection. Each one dedicated. To Mummy or
Daddy. To Grandad and Granny. To Uncle Dan. What
had happened to all of them, she wondered. Lost,
thrown away, dumped, she supposed. When the house
had been sold, after she had gone to prison, and Amy
to Rachel's father and mother, and then, when it had
all become too much for them, to the foster-family.
The house and its contents had belonged equally to her
and Martin. It was their family home. But Martin's
family had argued that the proceeds should go only to
Amy. That Rachel should not be allowed to profit in
any way from Martin's death. She could have fought it.
Her solicitor told her she had a case. But she had no
stomach for the fight. She agreed. Asked only that her
own belongings be parcelled up and sent to her father.
But what had happened to them when her mother died

and Alzheimer's disease took her father away from her? She had no idea. And now she no longer cared.

She was late today, the woman who Rachel had come to see. It was twenty-five to one. Most of the children had gone home. There was just the one still waiting, still being looked after by the teenage minders in their tight jeans and T-shirts. A girl, a sweet little thing with straight dark hair and a solemn expression. She stood by herself, the thumb of her left hand in her mouth, the other hand holding on to a large piece of cardboard on which were stuck some things that looked like seashells. The child was getting anxious. She was beginning to edge towards the gate, one step at a time, then stopping and looking back at the girls who were now deep in animated conversation. Rachel watched her. The child pulled her thumb out of her mouth, wiped it carefully on the skirt of her dress and moved to the edge of the footpath. She peered up and down, taking a step forward, then pulling back. She was talking to herself. Rachel couldn't hear what she was saying, but she could see the small mouth opening and closing, the plump cheeks dimpling. Soon, Rachel thought, there would be tears.

She looked beyond the child to the two girls to see if they had noticed what was happening, but they had turned their backs even more firmly on her, their heads together as they furtively lit their cigarettes. Time passed slowly. The little girl edged further and further away from the gate. Rachel looked up and down the road. It was quiet now, no passers-by, no pedestrians, just the occasional car taking a short cut to avoid the traffic congestion of the village. Driving fast, too fast down this narrow road. Rachel stepped forward. She crossed over to the child. She stopped in front of her. She bent down.

'Hallo,' she said, 'are you all right?'

The little girl looked up at her, squinting her grey eyes against the bright midday sun.

'I'm waiting for my mummy. I'm hungry. I want my lunch.'

'Do you now? Would you like this?' Rachel opened her plastic bag and brought out a peach. She held it to her nose and breathed in deeply.

'Yum,' she said, 'it's delicious.'

The child put out her hand for it, then pulled back.

'Are you a stranger?' Her voice was anxious. 'I'm not s'posed to talk to strangers.'

'Me?' Rachel drew away. 'Of course I'm not a stranger. I'm your friend. I have a lovely peach for you. I know little girls love peaches. I have a little girl just your age and they're her favourite fruit.'

'Where is she? Your little girl. Is she here?'

The child looked around, anxious again, then once more reached out for the yellow peach.

'No, she's not here, but would you like to meet her? She's your friend too.' She took hold of the child's hand. It was damp. She lifted it to her lips and kissed it gently. It smelt of crayons and stale milk. She turned it over and looked at the palm. It was grubby, playground dirt lodging in the clear-cut lines.

'You'll come with me, won't you?' she said, and the child looked up at her and nodded. Rachel bent down and rested her cheek against the child's downy skin. She breathed in the musky sweetness that rose up from beneath her bright blue summer dress.

'You're such a good girl, aren't you?' she said.

The child nodded. Rachel could see the saliva beginning to gather in the corners of her mouth as her hands grasped the peach's furry surface. And then she heard the sound of the car. The black Saab, the new model, very shiny, very perfect, just like the woman who sat behind the wheel, driving quickly, careless in her anxiety. Stopping suddenly, pushing the door, leaving it standing open as she hurried towards her daughter. Rachel put the peach back in her bag and without looking around began to walk away, heard behind her the mother's anxious apologies as she swept the child up into her arms, heard the sound of car doors slamming shut, then turned around and watched. Saw the older child, a boy, in the front passenger seat, and another in the back, a baby strapped in. Saw the woman look in the rear-view mirror, then expertly, smoothly, without a glance in Rachel's direction, pull away.

Just as the bus came into sight, slowed and stopped, the driver waiting impatiently until she had boarded, paid her fare and swayed up the aisle to a seat in the back. From where she could turn and watch as the Saab accelerated. Through the village, up along the coast, the cliff edge falling away below the road, then turning in through the high granite pillars, the wrought-iron gate, the gravel of the drive spitting out from beneath the car's wheels, stopping outside the two-storey house built of buttery yellow sandstone, with the high bell tower, the gardens stretching away to the sea. And the girl and boy, the perfect children, running across the lawn into the shrubbery, chasing each other through the walled kitchen garden, stopping at a swing that hung from the lower branches of the macrocarpa tree, while all around, from every direction, the blue of the sea threw up a bright reflected light.

It was Mrs Lynch who had found them for her. The woman and the children. The house in the photographs. She had insisted when she came back to collect her dry-cleaning that Rachel come to visit.

'I won't take no for an answer, dear. You must come for lunch. I'll collect you and bring you home.'

They lived, the Lynchs, in a red-brick house just off upper Glenageary Road. Deep carpets, a smell of furniture polish, a grandfather clock that tick-tocked like a slow, steady heartbeat. Mr Lynch barely spoke but he smiled at her, grasping her hand with his dry, birdlike claw, leaning over to pat her knee from time to time. Lunch was served at the mahogany dining table. Mrs Lynch talked. Rachel listened. Tales of children and grandchildren, holidays in Florida and Marbella. Rachel listened to the litany of proud achievement. She watched as Mrs Lynch sipped her soup from the edge of the spoon, tore her white roll in half and spread it with a smear of butter, dabbed at her lips with the linen napkin, punctuated her mouthfuls with conversation. Is this the way to do it? Rachel

tried to remember, and tried to copy, to replicate the
woman's neat movements.

'More, more, have more, dear. You look half
starved. What you need is someone to look after you.
Why don't you come and stay with us for a while?
Daddy wouldn't mind, would you, Daddy?'

Mr Lynch smiled indulgently, accepting without
complaint the nickname. He wouldn't mind, he said,
but he thought that Rachel probably wanted to get on
with her own life, instead of being stuck with two
fuddy-duddy old pensioners.

The hall and sitting room were hung with paintings
and black and white photographs. Graceful old yachts,
gaff-rigged, their huge white sails like seagulls' wings.
Rachel looked at them closely, admiring their lines.
She recognized a young Mr Lynch at the helm of the
most beautiful.

'I used to sail,' she said. 'Dinghies mostly. I had
my own Enterprise. It was a lovely boat.'

Mr Lynch nodded.

'Then I had a Dragon. Now that was a beauty. Like
one of yours.'

Mr Lynch nodded, his eyes wandering towards the
pictures on the wall.

'I crewed a lot for other people too, anyone who'd
have me. Cruisers, racers, you name it. I loved it, out
there in the bay.'

Mr Lynch spoke. 'There's nothing like it, the waters
of the bay and the Irish sea. The tides can be tricky.
There's a real tidal race. Four knots in either direction.
You'd be amazed how far they can carry you.' He

paused and sipped his coffee. 'You must have missed it,' he said.

After lunch Mrs Lynch insisted again. 'We'll go for a drive now. We'll go out as far as the Sugarloaf Mountain. That would be nice, wouldn't it? Such lovely views. Daddy will go in the back, and you, Rachel, in the front, no arguments.'

As they turned out on to the main road Rachel asked, 'Would it be all right, do you think? Could we go through Killiney, up the Vico Road? Could we go that way?'

And fifteen minutes later Rachel had found where they were. The red-tiled roof with the Italianate bell tower, just showing over the high granite wall. The wrought-iron gates, and the bonnet of a car nosing insistently out into their path, so Mrs Lynch had to stop suddenly, complaining.

'Honestly, these people who live in these big houses, they think they own the road.'

And Rachel had seen the woman and the children in the new black Saab and known what she had to do. It was easy, really so easy. The girls inside always said it was easy.

'You don't realize,' they had told her, 'how fucking soft most people are. They have no defences. They're not expecting trouble, so when trouble comes they don't know what's hit them.'

So easy. To hang around outside the house. To watch the car coming and going. To see the little girl wearing her special red sweatshirt. 'Little Darlings Crèche', it said on the front. And on the back the address and the phone number. They were right, the girls inside. It was dead easy.

To take the train to the station by the beach below the house. To walk across the shingle, up on to the rocks. To climb up the cliff path and over the few strands of rusty barbed wire on to the railway line. To scramble through the broken fence and into the garden. Careful at first in case she might be noticed. Then moving more openly, as her confidence increased, around the edge of the rocky promontory on which the house was built. Looking back up at it through the gaps in the trees towards the smooth green lawn where the swing hung from the lower branch of the macro-carpa tree. Seeing the children flit past, hearing their shouts and cries. Their mother's voice calling them in. Facing down the dog, the black Labrador who stood in front of her, barking and barking. His legs firmly planted, a line of hair rising on his back as she held out her hand to him. Feeding him scraps, biscuits and squares of chocolate. Watching the threads of saliva fall from his loose black lips as she held out her peace offerings. Then patting his big heavy head, looking into his dark brown eyes while he licked her hands.

Mrs Lynch was so kind. She took her shopping. She bought her new clothes. Trousers in linens of grainy black, sludgy green and purple the colour of day-old bruises. Crisp white shirts and blouses. And a jacket made of soft suede, the colour of a chestnut pony. Sandals with straps around her ankles, like the ones that Roman centurions wore, and new shoes that smelt of leather and held her feet gently and carefully. The first real shoes she'd worn for twelve years. And a new bag, leather too, big enough to carry a book and a newspaper, even a carton of milk and a loaf of bread, with a wide strap and little pockets inside. A purse with a zip for coins and a place for notes.

'And your hair, dear, we must do something about your hair. When did you last get it cut? You used to have such nice hair, I remember that it was a lovely colour, dark brown, nearly black but not quite, and it waved so prettily. You probably never needed to do anything to it then, but now . . .'

She collected her from the dry-cleaner's and took her to the salon in Glasthule, where Rachel sat for hours and listened to the chatter and gossip, while her head was massaged and rubbed, her hair was washed, cut and dried. She looked in the mirrors that lined the walls and watched the woman with the sleek grey curls, whose clothes perfectly complimented her slender body, as she moved about with grace and assurance, comfortable and at ease, suddenly at one with her brand-new skin.

'Thank you,' she said to Mrs Lynch as they walked out together. 'You are very kind. I really appreciate all your help.' And she leaned over and kissed the older woman on the cheek, smelling her face powder and the rose-scented perfume that drifted up from her body as they stood together in the warm sunshine. 'More than you can imagine.'

And Mrs Lynch took her hand and said, 'I always believed what you said. About that man, your husband's brother. I never believed him. I tried to convince the others. To get them to see it the way I saw it. But they said there was too much evidence against you. Your fingerprints were on the gun, and his weren't. I couldn't understand that either. But I knew there must be an explanation for it. I knew you'd never have killed your husband. Not when he was your daughter's father.' And she turned and walked away, stopping once to look back and wave.

The dog recognized her. And so did the little girl. Her name was Laura. Rachel had heard her mother call out to her and the child respond. She sat on the beach in her smart new clothes, with her jacket and bag lying beside her, and watched the shiny black Labrador running towards her, the two children, the boy and girl, struggling to catch up, and further away, a small figure in the distance, the tall blonde woman with the baby in a sling on her chest. She put out her hand to the dog and stood up. She picked up a piece of driftwood and threw it in a wide curving arc. He ran and leapt into the air, catching the stick in his slobbering jaws before it landed. And the two children laughed and jumped up and down and shouted, 'Do it again, do it again.' And when their mother caught up with them, Laura was already telling Rachel that this was her mummy and this was her brother and that was her baby brother. It was so easy then to smile at the tall blonde woman, make a casual remark about the beauty of the day and the sea, and the niceness of her dog and her children. So that within half an hour they were all eating ice creams that Rachel had bought from the shop on the beach. So easy, then, to walk with them to the gate that led from the sea up the side of the cliff to their house. To wave them goodbye. And say to the little girl with the straight dark hair and the solemn expression, 'Yes, of course, Laura, I'd love to come and see your pussy cat some day, of course I would.'

Smiling ruefully at her mother, who was shooing her on ahead. Sharing those 'aren't children funny?' kind of expressions, then waving goodbye and walking back along the beach, taking off her beautiful new sandals and rolling up her trousers, paddling in the waves which washed so gently up and down on the shingle and the shells which gleamed beneath the water. Feeling the sun on her back as she walked away from the tall blonde woman and her three lovely children, knowing that it was so easy, and that soon she would be seeing them again. She repeated the name the woman had given her. Ursula Beckett, Mrs Ursula Beckett, wife of Daniel Beckett, Martin's older brother, Rachel's former lover. And the man who had fired the shot that killed her husband. All those long years ago.

CHAPTER TWELVE

THIS TIME THE smell was even stronger. Even the young lads who prided themselves on having stomachs of burnished brass and an attitude to match were looking decidedly green as they clustered around the covered mound on the ground. Jack approached warily. He'd had a bad night. The girls had come to stay and Rosa had insisted on sleeping with him. He didn't mind, in fact he usually enjoyed her skinny little body curled up against his. But nightmares had jerked her, shrieking, out of her sleep, and then, when he thought he had finally calmed her down, she had suddenly and without warning wet the bed. And by the time he had changed her, himself and the sheets, it was dawn, and although she instantly drifted off, her thumb firmly planted between her lips, he had lain awake, watching the minutes click by on the digital clock until finally, and with a great sense of relief, it had been time to get up.

Now, four cups of coffee later, he felt dizzy and disorientated and not at all ready for what was lying here, down by the railway line, between Salthill and Seapoint, and stinking to high heaven.

How to describe the smell of rotting flesh? It didn't, he had once decided, smell like anything else. There were no possible comparisons to be made. You couldn't say that it reminded you of the scent of a particular flower or shrub. It wasn't similar to any food or drink. It was like nothing other than itself. Perhaps it was possible to discriminate between one kind of rot and another. Certainly rotting fish had a particularly potent stench. But, he wondered as the smell rose up and engulfed him, was there a qualitative difference between dead rat, cow or human?

'Jesus Christ,' he said out loud to no one in particular as he pushed his way through the tangled mixture of gorse, trailing briars, and buddleia gone wild. 'What on earth do we have here?'

He took a deep breath and lifted away the white plastic cover. What lay beneath was human, that much was obvious. But not much else. It was swaddled in a white sheet, wrapped tightly, criss-crossed like a large bandage, over and around its head, torso and legs. It lay on its back, its feet pointing towards the sky. It looked small and neat, a woman, he thought, or perhaps a prepubescent teenager, or an old person, shrunk with age and osteoporosis. Its arms appeared to have been folded over its chest, reminding him, for all the world, of a crusader and his wife he had once seen lying on a slab in an old English church somewhere in the north of England. York was it? He couldn't quite remember. He squatted down to have a closer look. Something with very sharp teeth had torn at the material, pulling it away, revealing the skin underneath. Bite marks gouged into the body's pale flesh on the thighs and stomach. But there were no signs of bloodstains anywhere, on the sheet itself or on the green rubberized tarpaulin on which the body lay.

Jack stood up and moved away. He tasted his breakfast, bitter, curdled. He turned towards the sea, which today at high tide lay smooth and flat, milky blue, just on the other side of the railway line, stretching across Dublin Bay as far as Howth Head. He breathed deeply, filling his lungs with cleansing salt air. Then he took a handkerchief from his pocket, covered his face and turned back to the body.

'Where did this come from?' He touched the groundsheet with the toe of his shoe, looking over at the group of uniformed guards, some of whom were busily organizing the crime scene cordon. 'Did one of you lot put this down?'

Of course they hadn't. Who did he think they were, fucking amateurs? They knew better than to interfere. They knew all about preserving the scene, all that stuff they'd had drummed into them time after time.

'So, tell all. Who found it, and when?'

It was, it seemed, a local authority surveyor. A young lad, newly qualified, sent down to the stretch of wasteland along by the railway line to begin the preliminary work on the new park the Corporation were planning. Jack could hear the raucous screech as he vomited, somewhere just out of sight behind a large sycamore tree.

'He stepped on it and fell over. Landed right on

top of it. It was wrapped in the groundsheet. All nicely parcelled up.' Tom Sweeney filled in the details.

'So why isn't it still nicely parcelled up, as you so delicately put it?'

'Because,' Sweeney's tone was resigned but caustic, 'because, as he was getting to his feet he couldn't help but hold on to the body and in doing so he pulled the plastic off it, and that was when he realized what it was.'

'It?' Jack knelt down, index finger and thumb clamped over his nostrils. 'It? Of course we don't think it's an "it", do we, Sweeney? What're the odds? Not great, I'd say. How about two to one that this here nice little parcel is a "she"?'

They waited in the sunshine for Johnny Harris, the pathologist, to arrive. In the old days, before they'd all become so scientific, so careful about procedure, they'd have pulled off the sheet themselves and had a good look. But not any longer. Now it all had to be done by the book. And the book said don't rush into anything. So they waited. Jack moved away and climbed the stairs to the old iron bridge that crossed the railway line. He rested his eyes on the sea, gazing across the bay to Howth in the distance. He dreaded what was lying back there under the briars and net-tles. He remembered the days when he had relished it all. The quest, the chase, the hunt, the tracking down. Now all he felt was the pain of the family, the fear of failure. He looked back down to where the body lay covered. He wasn't even sure how he was going to react when he looked at it. If he could even bring himself to look at it, at her, as she was now, lying there, rotting.

They were all silent as Johnny Harris carefully pulled the sheet away from her face. Her eyes were open. She stared up at them as if in wonder.

'Female,' he said, and someone laughed nervously.

Above their heads a blackbird burst into song, trilling loudly up and down the scale. A train passed by and, as a sudden breeze blew in from the sea, the trees and bushes around them shook their branches, the bright green summer foliage whispering and hissing.

Johnny Harris peeled some more of the sheet away.

'Age? Late teens, early twenties.' He moved her neck gently with his gloved hands.

'Probable cause of death? Strangulation.' He worked his way down her bare white body, revealing her arms, folded, one over the other. He touched the piece of cloth that was threaded through her small fingers.

'What do you reckon, Jack?' Jack moved closer and leaned over. 'Looks like a man's tie, doesn't it? Those diagonal stripes, the same colours repeated. Looks like a school tie, university, something like that.'

'How about the Garda Representative Association?' Tom Sweeney put in. And they all sniggered again.

Jack watched as Johnny Harris carefully peeled away the covering from her lower abdomen, her genital area and her upper thighs.

He tried to remember the words of the Act of Contrition. They hovered on his lips. He closed his eyes. *Oh my God, I am heartily sorry for having offended thee, and I confess my sins above every other evil.*

He lifted his hand and blessed himself. Johnny Harris pointed his finger at the bruises that mottled her skin. He differentiated between the marks that had been made by a fist before death and the teeth marks that had occurred more recently.

'Rodents,' he said, 'possibly even cats.'

There were small puckered scars on the wrinkled skin of her knees. Traces of childhood, he thought, falls from swings, and bicycles, grazes and scratches. Her feet were thin and white, with high insteps. Her nails had been painted scarlet. Like Rosa's toenails. She had shown them to him this morning as he was buckling her sandals. Look, Daddy, aren't they pretty? Mummy did it for me.

'Look.' Johnny Harris pointed again. 'See how they've grown. Even since she's been dead.' Jack looked at the thin line of white that showed above her cuticle. Then he stood back and watched as they carefully placed her inside the body bag. The metallic zing of the closing zip pushed all other sounds away. Johnny Harris peeled off his gloves. They dangled from his hands. Like an insect's discarded skin, Jack thought, and felt sick again.

'I'll give you a call when I've had a closer look,' he said, stepping out of his overalls.

Jack nodded. 'Fingerprint her, will you? Just in case.'

A name, that was what he needed. First and

foremost. And with the name would come its own particular list of suspects, motives and opportunities. And with a bit of old-fashioned luck everything else would fall into place.

It was early evening by the time he saw her again. He was tired. A thorough search of the wasteland by the railway had revealed nothing of interest. A heap of old beer cans and plastic cider bottles. A variety of shoes. Plenty of dog shit and some of the human variety. But no footprints, no handy dropped clues. None of the junk with which the average detective novel was littered. Unfortunately, he thought sourly, feeling a headache work its way up his neck and settle itself behind his eyes. They'd already started their house-to-house questioning. So far, so predictable. No one had seen anything unusual. Of course, there was always such a large amount of traffic turning off the sea road at Monkstown, heading down the hill to the car park next to the station. Even more since it had been extended recently, making room for extra commuters. One old biddy in a dingy flat on the top floor of the terrace of houses above told him there were always odd goings on there, night and day. Jack noticed the pair of binoculars on the window sill.

'Bird watching?' he asked, lifting them up and putting them to his eyes.

She grinned broadly. There was a great view from her front window. And of course the added bonus that the car park was well lit at night-time.

'Who'ye looking for?' she asked, pouring him weak tea from a tarnished silver pot.

'To be honest, we haven't a clue.' He sniffed the smoky-bacon flavour of the Earl Grey, turning down the offer of milk.

'Was she killed down there?' She picked up the binoculars and fiddled with the focus.

'You tell me. At this point in time you probably know more about it than I do.'

'Well, I'd say, if you want my opinion, she wasn't,' she said. 'You'd be surprised how quiet it is here at night-time. I don't sleep much any longer. Not now I've the sleep of eternity waiting for me just around the corner. I've often seen people going into those bushes. Often. But I've always seen them come out again.'

He asked Johnny Harris the same question. Was she killed down there, among the briars and the nettles?

He shook his head. 'I'd say not. I'd say from the distribution of blood in her tissues that she was lying there for three, maybe four or even five days. I'd say she was placed there, rather than dumped. The way she was lying was a bit too careful if you see what I mean. On her back, her arms folded, her legs together. I'd say she was put there before rigor mortis set in. Easier to handle her that way. That would make it within seven hours or so of death. And another thing.'

'Yes?'

'She was washed. It's normal in these situations for

the bowel and bladder to evacuate. But there's no sign of urine or faeces on her body. Also she was raped. Vaginally and anally. Considerable force was used. It looks to me like she was penetrated with something sharp. A small knife, perhaps, or a scissors. But again, all blood has been washed away. She's very clean, apart, that is, from the inevitable decomposition. And before you ask, no, there's no semen.'

'And how did she die? Did she die from the rape?'

'No. She was strangled. From the abrasions it looks to me like it was something like a clothes line. A synthetic material that burns the flesh easily.'

'So it wasn't the tie?'

He shook his head. 'I don't think so. The marks on her neck aren't consistent with that type of cloth. But it's interesting, unusual, the way that the tie has been twisted through her fingers. Like so.'

He pulled back the covering green sheet and lifted up her small hands. He separated her fingers to demonstrate. Jack felt his knees soften and weaken, the sweat break out on his forehead. He forced himself to look.

'She's very fair, isn't she? Is her hair naturally that colour?'

'Completely. Very unusual. She reminds me of a Swedish girlfriend I had once. Practically white her hair was.'

They stood in silence. The girl's hair was long and very thick. It was parted in the middle. It lay now on either side of her small heart-shaped face.

'What else can you tell me?'

Johnny Harris sighed. 'She was pregnant. About twelve weeks, I'd say. She also had some liver damage consistent with alcohol or drug abuse. And there are scars on her arms, here. See?' He pointed to the marks in the crook of her elbow.

'But she's clean. No heroin. No drugs at all. Not now anyway. And she's healthy apart from all that. And well looked after.'

'How do you mean?'

'Her teeth. Regular visits to the dentist. A few fillings, but not many. And some evidence that she'd had orthodontic treatment at some stage in her life. And see here, these teeth at the side.' He pulled open her mouth and pointed with the end of his biro. 'The X-rays show that she's had root-canal fillings and crowns. Very expensive. If you're asking my opinion, I'd say she was once a nice middle-class girl.'

Which wasn't what the fingerprints showed. The fingerprints told a different story. Within the last three years she had been arrested fifteen times. For possession of heroin, for possession with intent to supply, with soliciting, with assault, with larceny. Pearse Street had her records, her photograph and her name.

'Judith Hill? Jesus. We know her well.' The station sergeant looked at him in amazement. 'And you're telling me that Judith's dead? A year or so ago I wouldn't have been surprised. She was up to her neck in an awful load of shit. But she's been on the straight and narrow for the last while. Ever since she came out of prison. She's even going to college. Trinity, would you believe? Just across the road so she can drop in from time to time and say hallo. Not.' He paused and sniggered, then looked down at the file on the counter in front of him, turning it around so Jack could see the picture clearly. 'Christ, are you sure it's Judith? I only saw her recently. Last week or the week before. She was looking great. Oh, good God almighty, her father will go mad.'

Her father, Dr Mark Hill. His name, followed by a string of letters, on the brass plate screwed to the front railings of the tall red-brick house in the quiet square in Rathmines. It was late now. After ten. Jack slumped in the passenger seat of the car, while Tom Sweeney parked it carefully.

'I hate this,' he said. 'I fucking hate this.'

It was later still by the time he got home to the apartment overlooking the harbour. Such a relief to be on his own. No need to explain himself, make excuses, justify his sour mood. He walked into the bathroom, shedding his clothes, dropping them in small heaps on the floor. He turned on the taps. He walked back into the kitchen. He poured a double measure of gin into a tall glass, added ice and tonic, and a slice of lime. He drank half of it in one swallow and topped it up again. He got into the bath, lay back and closed his eyes. He didn't want to think about all that had happened tonight, but it wouldn't go away. The scene kept on replaying itself over and over against his closed eyelids. The father's denial, his refusal to accept that it might be his daughter who was dead. His insistence that she had changed. She wasn't involved in any of that 'business', as he called it, any longer.

'So have you seen her recently, have you spoken to her at all?'

Well, no, he hadn't. But she wasn't living at home at the moment. She'd moved into rooms in college to be close to her brother. He'd been helping her with her exams.

'But it isn't term time now, Dr Hill, is it?'

Well, no, he agreed. But she had said she wanted to do some extra work, preparation for next term. She's very dedicated, he said. She's studying history of art. She loves it. And she knows that she's wasted so much time with all that 'business'. She wants to make up for it.

'And boyfriends, other friends, anyone who was close to her?'

There was no one, he said, just her brother Stephen. They're very close.

And Jack especially didn't want to think about what had happened in the mortuary. When Dr Hill gazed down at his daughter's face. He had expected the usual. Shock, horror, tears. But not anger. Not rage. Not disgust. Not the words that poured from the man's mouth, in an unstoppable torrent. Words that made them all, Jack, Johnny Harris, Tom Sweeney, draw back and away.

'You little bitch. You little savage. How could you do this to me? After all I've gone through for you. You promised me. You said you'd never do this again. You said you'd be good. The way you used to be. You said you'd given all that up. You said you were going to live your life my way now. That I would be proud of you. That I would be able to hold my head up for you. And now look at you, you little bitch. I hate you so much. I can't bear it.'

And for one dreadful moment he reached out towards her, his hands grasping the sheet which covered her body. His fingers twisting the heavy fabric, pulling. Until Johnny Harris stepped forward, put his hand on his arm and said, 'That's enough, that's quite enough. At least leave her with some dignity.'

And then there were tears, and gasping sobs, and a sound of pain, a moan that came from deep inside him, as he sank to his knees on the cold tiled floor.

They drove him back to his front door. They offered to phone for help. Friends, family, anyone. But he got out of the car without answering. It was Sweeney who spoke first, who broke the silence as they stopped at the traffic lights.

'Did he do it?'

Jack shrugged. He let his breath out in a long sigh. 'Your guess is as good as mine. But we'll be back to him in the morning, ask him to give us a sample for DNA, sort out who the baby's father is. We'll have a go at the house. Quickly before he realizes what we're at. Talk to her mother. There's been no mention of her so far. And don't forget there's the brother. He probably knows a lot more about Judith than daddy-oh. Do you want to have a crack at him or will I?'

It was very quiet now. No sound from the car park outside. No sound of traffic from the street. He got out of the bath and wrapped a towel around his waist. He poured himself another large gin, then pushed open

the door to his small balcony. The sweet smell of
night-scented stock wafted into the room. A present
from Ruth, the older of his daughters. She had grown
them herself from seed. He stepped out on to the
balcony and sat down. So she'd been in prison a
number of times. Johnny Harris had called her a nice
middle-class girl. There weren't many of them inside.
What was it the prison governor always said about the
inmates? That they all came from Dublin's four inner-
city postal districts. Not from the nice suburb where
the Hills lived. Or for that matter from the area a
couple of miles from here where Rachel Beckett had
lived. A coincidence or what? He'd ring Andy Bowen
first thing. Someone else to be put on his list for
questioning.

He picked up his glass and swirled the ice cubes
around. The doors to the balcony next door opened,
and light and music came flooding out. And the sound
of voices, laughing, then silence, then other sounds, so
familiar. He listened. He wanted to hear. He wanted
to imagine what it was like. The ice cubes melted in
his drink, and a cold chill crept down his bare back.
But he didn't get up. He didn't go inside. He waited
until it was all over. And he had got what he needed.

CHAPTER THIRTEEN

THE TIE WAS the same. The same narrow diagonal stripes of red, grey and dark green against a dark brown background. Except that now there were two of them. One was crumpled and stained and in the plastic evidence bag which Jack had in his briefcase. The other was pressed and clean, slipped beneath the collar and flattened down over the buttons of the white shirt that Dr Mark Hill was wearing beneath his navy-blue blazer.

The tie was the first thing that Jack saw when Dr Hill answered his knock early the next morning. He waited until the pleasantries had been observed, and he was sitting with a cup of tea in the small dark kitchen at the back of the house, before he mentioned it.

'You don't mind if we stay in here, do you, Inspector, um, what did you say your name was?'

Jack told him for, he was sure, the fifth time.

'Ah yes, Donnelly, of course. You don't mind it in here, I hope? The housekeeper comes today and tidies up for me. I'm not very good at that sort of thing, so the rest of the house isn't really presentable.'

Jack nodded sympathetically.

'And your wife, Judith's mother? Is she here?'

Dr Hill gazed at the worn quarry tiles on the floor. When he spoke his voice was bitter. 'My wife, Judith's mother. Not my favourite topic of conversation. We've been separated for many years, since the children were quite young. She lives in England. We don't have any contact. I prefer not to think of her.' He sipped his tea, a look of distaste on his fleshy features.

He preferred, it seemed to Jack, not to think of many things. He preferred not to talk about Judith's drug addiction, her prostitution, assault and larceny charges. He preferred not to say where she had been for the last couple of weeks. Who her friends were. What kind of person she was. What sort of life she was leading. Her pregnancy. And above all, he preferred not to discuss her death. As the list of Jack's questions grew, the look of distaste on his face grew too.

Jack placed his cup and saucer on the kitchen table. He reached down and took the plastic bag from his briefcase. He rested it on his knees. He cleared his throat.

'I'm wondering, Dr Hill, about this.' He tapped the plastic with his fingertip. 'I had hoped that I might find some explanation for it in the answers to my questions. But I haven't. So I must ask you, can you identify it?' He held it out to him. He watched as the doctor took it tentatively in his large hands. He turned it over, then got up and went to the window, holding it out towards the light.

'Of course,' he said. 'It's a Trinity tie. Like this one, the one I'm wearing.'

'So it is.' Jack rocked gently on his stool. 'And do you know where it was found?'

If he had been expecting an emotional response, he'd come to the wrong place. Hill looked at it again, then handed it back to him.

'There are,' he said, the distaste now spreading into his voice, 'at a rough estimate, probably twenty thousand such ties in existence. What does it have to do with me?'

'You didn't notice?' Jack picked it up again and shook the tie around inside the bag. 'Here, see that, see that name tape. Recognize it? What does it say? Let me see.' He paused. 'Mark Patrick Hill. Now who could that possibly be?'

A look of consternation passed across the man's face, and his voice when he spoke was low and, for the first time, hesitant. 'Where,' he asked, 'where did you say you found it?'

'Did you get much out of the brother?' It was lunchtime and Jack was hungry. Last night's gin had taken its toll and his stomach felt empty and hollow. He took a large mouthful of roast beef and mashed potato, washed it down with a long swallow of cold milk and wiped his mouth with a paper napkin. It was ages since he'd eaten in town. He must remember, he thought, to congratulate the guys in Pearse Street for recommending this pub. The food was great. Straightforward, uncomplicated, just what a hangover needed.

Sweeney shrugged his shoulders. 'Not much. He's

very shocked by it all. Kept on bursting into tears. Couldn't think straight, so he said. I'll tell you one thing about him though, he's the image of his sister. Same colouring, same build, same look. They could be twins.'

'I assume it's their mother they take after. Not much of the father there.'

'He didn't say. I asked him about her. He was very circumspect. All he said was that the parents had split up when he and Judith were small. The mother had gone to England. And then there was a bit of a to-do about custody. Apparently the father got it, but she came back and snatched them. He says he doesn't really remember much about it. Except that after that they didn't see her at all.'

'And Judith, what did he tell you about her? Did he know she was pregnant?'

'He says not. He was very shocked when I told him. He became practically hysterical.'

'Any suggestions as to who might be the father?'

'Nah, nothing. He'd nothing to say about other friends, boyfriends, the drugs and all that carry-on. He wasn't involved at all, he said, not his scene. He said she'd left it all behind, that she was a dedicated student. He kept on saying, she promised me, she promised me.'

'Did you get to see her rooms?'

Sweeney nodded, his mouth full.

'And?' Jack shovelled the last of the meat into a heap on his fork.

Sweeney swallowed, then burped.

'Jesus, Tom, give us a break.' Jack flapped his hand at him in mock disgust.

'Sorry, boss, sorry.' He gulped some water. 'Well, apparently she'd been writing some kind of essay about this biblical character, Judith. Anyway, there are a number of well-known paintings, so the brother said, that show this Judith character in the process of killing someone. Very fucking bloodthirsty. All done in a good cause, of course, to save her tribe from annihilation. You know the kind of thing, invites him into her tent, gets him drunk, then offs him. Great big bloody sword. Chops off his head. She had prints of them stuck up all over the place. Put you off your lunch.'

Judith and Holofernes, that was it. The widow using her womanly wiles to save her people. Summoned to the chieftain's bed. Intent on murder. He knew the paintings. He'd seen them that morning reproduced in a book that was lying on the table in Dr Hill's kitchen. He'd opened it, idly flicking over the pages while he waited for Hill to come back from making a phone call. He'd noticed the inscription on the title page: *To Elizabeth, who knows how to love. Forever, Mark.*

He'd waited for Hill. He wanted to confirm with him that he'd come into the station. To be fingerprinted. To have a DNA test. To cooperate with their investigation. But Hill had insisted on phoning his solicitor.

'Fine,' Jack said. 'Go ahead. He can come with you, if you like. I'll just wait here until it's all sorted out.'

And while he waited he had turned over the pages, looking at the paintings.

'And,' Sweeney put his hand into his pocket, 'I've got something for you. I know your interest in this, so I thought I'd give you a bit of a treat. Here.' He handed him a photograph. 'It was stuck on to one of those pegboard things. In her room.'

Two women. One older, one younger. Their surroundings were drab, nondescript. They were looking, not at the camera, but at each other. They were smiling, happy. Their arms were around each other's waists. The older woman was taller and very thin. Her hair was thick and wavy, greying. The younger woman's hair was long and straight, white blonde, parted in the centre so it lay evenly on either shoulder.

'Well, what do you know? Nice middle-class girls together. Just as I thought.' Jack laughed out loud and turned the picture over. There was an inscription on the back: *Me and Rachel. Joyful Days!! August, 1997.*

'And what did the brother say about that? Anything interesting?' Jack had started on dessert. Apple tart and a lavish helping of cream.

'Nah.' Sweeney shook his head. 'Just said it was some woman who Judith had made friends with in prison. Didn't seem to know anything else.'

'And did you ask him if—'

'Of course I did, of course I asked him.' Sweeney snorted with indignation. 'I was just about to tell you. I asked him if she'd seen her recently. He said he didn't know. But then he sort of blushed. You know, he's got that kind of skin, very pale, the slightest thing makes him colour up. And then he said that he knew that Judith wasn't supposed to have anything to do with people she knew from prison. That it was a condition of her early release. That she was still on probation. So,' Sweeney reached over, took the spoon from Jack's hand and helped himself to a dollop of cream, 'what do you think?'

What did he think? He thought a lot of things. He thought that they needed to find out whose baby Judith was carrying. They needed to find out where she was killed. They needed a list of all her former contacts. They needed to know who would want her dead and why. And what was the nature of her relationship with her father. He wondered about the mother. Elizabeth, he presumed. Why had she left and why had she not been given custody of her children? His heart sank as he thought of the work that lay ahead and for a moment he began to panic. He hated these high-profile cases. He could see the headline on the early edition of the *Evening Herald* that the woman at the next table was reading. '**Sex Slaying Mystery**' it said in bold black capitals. Jesus Christ. He gestured to Sweeney, and nodded in the direction of the paper.

'Here we fucking go,' he said, getting to his feet, weary already before the day had half begun.

CHAPTER FOURTEEN

'SO YOU'VE HEARD about the death of the girl you knew in prison. What was her name? Julie, Judy, Jill?' It was nine-thirty in the morning. Her weekly visit to Andrew Bowen's office. She stared at the floor as she answered.

'Judith. It was Judith.'

'Jack Donnelly came to see you?'

'Yes. He came yesterday.'

'Good, good. And of course, you gave him whatever help you could? You told him anything you thought might be useful? Because it's very important. It's not great when someone who you knew in prison . . . Well, when there's any trouble or anything like that, it's very important that you come clean about it. That you're straight with the guards. You don't want any messing, do you, Rachel?'

It was a beautiful morning. She had gone to sleep the night before with the shutters open, watching the half-moon make its slow progress across the piece of sky visible through her window. And she had been woken early by shafts of sunlight falling across her face. When she turned over, shielding her eyes from the brightness, the pillow beneath her cheek was wet. Sodden. And then she remembered. Judith was dead. She had died more than a week ago and Rachel hadn't known. Hadn't even suspected. She had been so caught up in her own plans that she had barely given Judith a thought.

Jack Donnelly had arrived early and caught her unawares. She had recognized him immediately from the church a couple of weeks ago. And then, from the time before. He had shown her a photograph. She remembered it well. It was taken in the prison school, the day the Leaving Certificate results had come out. Judith had done brilliantly. A1s in English, History, French. Bs in Geography and honours Maths. The teachers had thrown a party. Fizzy drinks and biscuits and a chocolate cake. Paper hats and streamers to decorate the prefab where the classes were held. She had watched Judith celebrate and known what it meant. They would let her out now.

He wanted to know, he said, all about her. Who were her friends? Who was her dealer? Who was her pimp?

'I don't know anything about that,' she said, suddenly frightened. 'I didn't know her outside. I didn't know her when she was part of that world. And I'm telling you now. I haven't seen her since I came out. For just that reason. I've enough problems of my own. I don't need hers.'

He took his time before he told her Judith was dead. He led her on. To betrayal.

'OK, all right, she did give me some names. The guy she worked for. Not that it was much of a mystery. Half the girls inside had worked for him at some stage. And Judith swore she wasn't going to get back into all that when she got out.'

'And what about her father and her brother, what do you know about them?'

She shrugged, then said, 'Why are you asking me all this? What's going on here?'

'Nothing to concern you. I just want to know. Now tell me. Her father and her brother, what kind of a relationship did she have with them?'

But now she knew. She could tell. This wasn't right.

'Did?' she said. 'Why do you say did?'

She waited while he described how they had found Judith's body, how she had been killed, what had been done to her. And then she could say nothing more.

'You hadn't seen her, had you, since you got out?' Andrew Bowen's voice was soft so she had to sit forward in her seat to hear what he was saying.

'You know I wasn't allowed to.'

'That didn't stop you harassing your daughter, did it?'

Rachel looked at him. The clock behind his head said nine-forty. There were twenty more minutes of this to endure. Half an hour every week.

'You could have asked me for permission to see her, to see Judith. It would have been understandable, and it seemed from what I hear that she had been doing well since her release. She might have been able to give you some help with your own rehabilitation.'

Had she known this man all those years ago, in her life before? His face might have been familiar, but then again it might not. She could never tell these days.

'I would imagine that it must have been a bit of a relief for you when Judith fetched up in prison. Some-one you might have something in common with, someone educated, intelligent.'

'There was plenty of intelligence inside.' Rachel sat up in her chair and stared at him. 'There are a lot of very clever women in there.'

'But not educated, in the conventional sense. Not like you. University background, that sort of thing.'

She wondered. He could have been in college when she was there. It was such a small city, Dublin. So difficult to hide your background, your past. So hard to have secrets.

'But I'm sure it was definitely a relief for Judith Hill to find someone like you there already. A shoulder to cry on, a bit of help and understanding. She was an addict, wasn't she? Tough corner to be in, getting convicted in that state.'

'She wasn't the first. She won't be the last.'

'But you helped her, didn't you? I'm sure you did.'

'Judith didn't need much help. You forget, Mr Bowen, I was the one who had been in prison for nearly ten years when Judith was sent down. She had been out in the world. She knew her way around already. She had a reputation which followed her. The girls called her Snow White, you know, because of the way she looked. And because she was special.'

He'd got it wrong. Big time. It was Judith who helped her. Oh, Rachel had looked after her when she was coming down from the heroin. Cleaned up her vomit, hauled her on and off the toilet. Read aloud to her when she was too sick to get out of bed. And what did Judith give her in return? She gave her love.

'OK, I'm beginning to get the picture now. We have this "special" girl, who was in prison with you. And I think we all know the nature of your relationship with her. At least the prison staff certainly did, and your probation officer inside did too, and of course all this information has been passed on to me.' He paused.

She looked away. She could feel Judith's head on her shoulder, her slight body curled up against her side, see her long white fingers linked through her own.

'So this "special" girl suddenly winds up dead, very dead, not a mile and a half from where you're now living. And the guards can't quite figure out why she was found there. Why she wasn't found near her home, near her university. There doesn't seem to be much sense to it, does there? Apart from the inescapable fact of you. You can understand why Donnelly is so interested.'

She nodded. She felt sick. Donnelly had shown her the photograph taken in the mortuary. She had tried not to look, but he had waited until eventually her gaze had slid across the coloured print.

'This is what happens when you die from strangulation,' he had said to her, his voice neutral. 'This is what you look like. It's not pretty, is it?' He had pushed the picture closer to her as he continued. 'Let me see if I can remember what the forensic pathology textbooks say. Face and neck grossly congested, puffy, bloated. The conjunctival tissues of the eyes and ears haemorrhage. The facial blood vessels, the vessels of the eyelids and lips rupture. An awful sight, isn't it?'

She had struggled not to give way before him. Her fingernails dug into the palms of her hands. This was not Judith, this creature in the photograph.

'So, Rachel,' Andrew Bowen rocked back in his chair, 'I'm warning you now. I'm firing a shot across your bows. Metaphorically speaking. You told Donnelly you hadn't seen her, but I happen to know that you lied to him. Just as you have lied to me. There are witnesses who saw the two of you together. A number of people have told me where and when you and she met. So I hope you've got your story straight, got your alibi sorted out, because you of all people know the importance of an alibi, how it can make or break a case, don't you?'

She looked at him, then looked away out through the window, watching a flock of pigeons wheel and turn, their wings dark against the light blue sky.

'It's coffee time, you'll join me of course, won't you?' He stood up and walked to the glass coffee jug resting on its element on top of the filing cabinet. He filled two mugs, and then with his back still turned to her he opened the top drawer and took out a bottle. He unscrewed the cap and added whiskey to one of the mugs. She saw then how thin he was, how his hands shook as he passed the coffee to her. How his face was pale, his eyes bloodshot, his lips cracked at the corners. He sat down again and drank. There was silence in the room. Then he spoke again.

'I've been wanting to ask you something for a while, Rachel. I've been wondering. Do you remember me?'

She didn't answer.

'It's odd because I remember you. My wife was friends with some of the girls in your year in college. Maybe you remember her? Her name is Clare. Her maiden name was O'Brien.'

There was a face that came to mind. Heart-shaped, very pretty, lots of make-up. One of the Loreto girls who still hung around together in their sixth-form group. She nodded.

'Yes,' she said.

'That's good. I'm glad because I want you to do something for me. And I will be grateful for your help. So grateful that I will forget that I know anything about you and your "special" girl. I won't suggest to Jack Donnelly that he takes you in for questioning. I won't spread your story around and attract any kind of unwanted attention to you. I won't demand that you come to see me more often.'

And he told her about his wife. Her illness, his despair.

'You see, we've talked about you a lot recently. She remembers you well. She says that you all kept in touch for quite a few years after you graduated. She says that her friends were all in awe of you. You were so clever, so brilliant, indeed. First-class honours degree. Offers of scholarships in America, in France and Italy. They were all amazed when you got married. And to a guard, of all things. She says she remembers how dismissive you were of your father and all his friends. She says she remembers going to your house for some kind of class reunion. She said it was lovely. Full of colour and light. She remembers especially your garden, and your beautiful conservatory. It was so unusual then. Not like now when every Joe Soap has a bit of plastic and glass stuck up against his back door. And she says that she thought it was a terrible shame, a waste that you were designing kitchen extensions and attic conversions when you had such talent. Genius was what she actually said.'

She said nothing for a moment. Outside the pigeons still banked and wheeled against the pale morning sky.

Then she nodded. 'My conservatory, yes,' she said, 'it was lovely.'

She had designed it. She wanted to do it as a wedding present for Martin. At first he was interested. Then his interest waned. As it always did. Drifted away. Back from the world of family and women, back to the world of men. But Daniel understood. Said he'd build it for her. That summer, when Martin was away on duty, in Donegal, on the border.

Andrew cleared his throat.

'You see, Rachel, my wife needs to be looked after. Especially at night. I want someone to be with her at night. Not every night, but from time to time. Shall we say three, maybe four evenings a week? So I can go out, have some time to myself. Clare is very fussy about who she'll let close to her. She won't have a nurse. She won't have anyone who'll feel sorry for her. But she will have you. She says you're a wounded person, a broken person. Like her. You won't have to do anything very much. Just sit with her, perhaps read to her. Then make sure she takes her pills. I'll leave them for you. I'll take care of the dosage. You just make sure she takes them. That's all.'

He stood again, and again poured whiskey into his mug. This time he didn't offer her anything. He sat down. He drank. He looked at her over the rim of his mug. He put it down on a pile of papers on the desk.

'You'll accept my offer, of course, won't you?'

She looked at him. He turned away for a moment, and she wondered what he was thinking about. He turned back towards her.

'You will, won't you?'

She nodded.

He fiddled with his tie. 'I'll be in touch. I'll tell you when I want you. And you don't need to worry about that other business. It'll be our secret, won't it?'

Outside in the street the air was warm, but she buttoned up her denim jacket, folding her arms tightly over her breasts as she hurried home. It was so hard to keep secrets. She had said to Daniel, 'You won't tell Martin, will you? Promise me. I do care about you, you know that. You're very special to me. And we will always be friends, won't we? But please, please don't tell Martin.'

And he didn't. And after a while she had almost forgotten what had happened between them that summer. When he had come to stay, and the sun had shone every day for three weeks. Every morning when she got up Daniel was there cooking breakfast. She'd spread out the drawings on the table and they'd plan the day's work. She would bring him glasses of home-made lemonade and sandwiches, then cook him dinner, and they would sit in the garden until it got dark and talk. He told her then all about what had happened when he was a teenager. How he'd got into trouble. Fallen in with older kids. They'd stolen a car. Driven it at high speed. A woman and her child had been walking along the footpath when the car went out of control. Both had died. He'd been sent to borstal.

'Look,' he said, and showed her his tattoo. A rose on his left shoulder.

'I was a disgrace to the family,' he said. 'And Martin never lets me forget it.'

'No,' she protested, 'Martin doesn't think that. He loves you. It's just, you know the way he is, he has very high standards. He expects a lot from everyone, from me, and from you.'

'But I can never match him,' he said, 'he's so good at everything.'

And she had laughed and told him there was one thing Martin wasn't good at.

'Come with me,' she said, and drove him down to the harbour. And together they launched her dinghy down the slippery granite slipway. Daniel had never sailed before but he took to it immediately.

'Now,' she said, watching the way he used his balance, how quickly he learned to anticipate shifts in

wind. 'Now, Martin can't do that. He hates it. He gets
seasick. And do you know something, Dan? Don't tell
him I told you. He's scared of the sea.'

And it must have been that night that she heard
her bedroom door opening. Saw him standing in the
half-light waiting. Sat up and reached out to him.
Pulled him into bed beside her. Buried her face in his
neck. Felt his hand on her breast. Lay all night
hovering between sleep and wakefulness. Then opened
her eyes to a bright blue day. The smell of rashers
frying, and Daniel in his faded blue jeans and torn T-
shirt, singing along to an old Beatles song on the radio.
Toast popping, the table laid and a nasturtium flower,
streaks of red flushing through its pale orange, lying
on her plate.

But it was Martin she loved. Truly. Once she'd got
over the novelty of Daniel's gentleness, his sweet
eagerness to please. And she was relieved when Martin
phoned to say he was coming home.

'It will be our secret, won't it, Dan?' she had said.
And he had nodded and kissed her goodbye. On the
cheek. And kept his distance.

Rachel had wanted Judith to keep her distance. She
hadn't been pleased when she came out from behind
the racks of clothes in the dry-cleaner's and saw her
lolling against the counter.

'How did you find me?' she asked as they walked
through the shopping centre together.

Judith shrugged and smiled.

'The grapevine,' she said. 'That old prison thing.'
And then said, 'But why didn't *you* find me? I thought

I'd hear from you when you got out. I thought you'd want to see me. I thought you'd want my help.'

But how to explain. That she had no room for her any longer. That she had other priorities. No room now for sweetness or tenderness, gentleness or kindness. So she sent her away. And now she was dead. Donnelly had said they weren't sure when she died. But she had been lying beneath the briars and nettles by the railway line for at least five days. Barely a mile away. When she could have been loved and protected. Looked after. Judith had told her about the baby.

'I can't have it. I don't want it. Will you help me?' she had asked.

And Rachel had said no. That she couldn't. She had other things she had to do.

'Ask your mother,' she had said. 'She's in England. She'll sort it out for you. Or get the father to give you a few bob. He owes it to you, whoever he is.'

Judith had looked at her with disbelief, and left without saying goodbye.

And what did I do, Rachel thought. I was glad she'd gone. I was scared someone would see her with me. I couldn't wait for her to leave.

The guard had left the photograph behind. He had propped it up against the kettle. She picked it up and looked at it. Long and hard. And wept. And wept. Until there was nothing left inside but sour bitterness and anger. She remembered the book that Judith's brother had sent her for her birthday when she was in prison. Paintings by Caravaggio. There was a bookmark, a piece of scarlet cord, tucked inside so it opened of its own volition at one particular painting. It had made Rachel gasp and put the book down on the tarmacadam of the exercise yard for a few moments before she felt able to look at it again.

'You know what it is, don't you, Rachel?' She felt Judith's breath on her cheek.

'Of course I do. Of course. It's just . . . It's just such a strange, surprising image.'

The sword cut through the bearded man's thick neck. The girl stared intently, seriously at him. She pulled his head back and down, her fingers twisted through his hair. She remembered her own head pulled back and down, her own hair trapped between Martin's fingers.

'It's wonderful, isn't it? It's our favourite, Stephen's and mine. One day we're going to Rome, to the Galleria Nazionale d'Arte Antica, to see it. Together. Will you come with us?'

She had made a choice when she left prison. And the choice did not include Judith. She could not afford to be sorry. She could afford nothing now, nothing except her resolve. She closed her eyes. She would think just for now how it all might have been. But after that she would think no more about her.

CHAPTER FIFTEEN

IT HAD BEEN easy for Daniel Beckett to find Rachel. The guard who did nixers for him had got hold of her address. He had read the conditions of her release too. Said to him, 'She'll be no bother to you, boss. But if you're worried we can warn her off.'

But what was there to worry him? She was harmless, she was helpless. She was on her own.

He drove to the house in Clarinda Park. The one with the row of dustbins outside, in the area in front of the basement, with the discarded crisp packets and chocolate bar wrappers lying jammed up against the front railings. He had driven slowly past to see if he could see any sign of her behind the sagging net curtains that drooped across the big bay windows on the first and second floors. He had slowed to a stop, the engine idling, and looked out, then put the car in gear and moved slowly up the hill, and driven right around the top of the square to park on the other side. And wait.

He had found the daughter too. His daughter, he reminded himself as he sat in the café on the seafront at Howth and watched her move from table to table, taking orders, clearing away dirty crockery. A summer job, he supposed, between school and university. The name of her foster-family and their address had come from the same source as Rachel's. All in her file in the Garda station. And it had been easy to watch the girl's house and follow her down the hill to the town and the café.

'Yes?' She stood beside him, her notebook in her hand, her pencil poised. 'What can I get you?'

He ordered cappuccino and a ham sandwich. Then called her back to change his order to black coffee and a Danish pastry. Then called her again, said he wanted tea and a cheese roll.

'Brown or white?' she asked, in a tone of exaggerated patience.

He dithered, watching her expression of resignation turn to irritation.

'You decide. I'm useless, can't make a choice to save my life,' he said and smiled up at her. She rose to the bait and took it. Picked wholewheat for him.

'It's better for you, you know. Healthier.' And she smiled back. It had been years since he had seen her. He had heard when Rachel's parents had given her up to be fostered. And he had wondered whether he should intervene. But he thought it through. Rachel had never told anyone that he was the child's father. He had waited for it to come out as evidence in the trial. But she had said nothing. He had seen her face that day when he was giving evidence. Her shame at the way their relationship was talked about in open court. She didn't want her child to become part of that mess. He knew that was it. He had wondered about the kid, what she looked like as she grew up, what kind of a person she was becoming. And then he had met Ursula and she had changed everything for him. She had given him children of his own. So he didn't need that child of his imagination any longer. And he realized now, as he watched her, that he had all but forgotten her.

He left her a tip and waved goodbye at the door. He watched her for a moment through the plate-glass windows. She reminded him of someone. Not Rachel, he thought. He would never have known that she was Rachel's daughter. And then he saw who it was as a cloud crossed the sun and his own reflection formed in front of him. She turned towards him and waved again. She was very something. He couldn't decide. Not pretty exactly, with her cropped black hair and her strong, sturdy body. And then he realized what it was. She was very sexy.

Like her mother, he thought. Or the way her mother once had been. Long-limbed and graceful, with a sweet smile as she woke. So beautiful and capable. So much his brother's wife, and then, as if by some magic spell, his very own. For how long? Two weeks, maybe three. A perfect time. Turned over in his mind like a pocketful of loose change. Then pushed away with all the other memories. Until now, and the woman he saw walking up the hill from the town. She was nothing like she was then. She walked with a slight stoop, her back rounded. Her steps were short and hesitant. She stopped every few paces and paused, as if she was catching her breath. She looked around, as if she wasn't sure how far she could go, then walked on, as if, he realized, she was waiting for permission. She passed within feet of him. He averted his gaze, looked down at the newspaper on his knees. Felt his heart begin to leap in his chest. She was so close he could have put out his hand and twisted his fingers through her thick hair. Grey now, not dark and glossy the way it was before. But he didn't. He shrank back into his seat and watched her walk the rest of the way to the house. Watched her pause on the front step, stand staring at the door, then put her hand in her pocket and take out the keys. Watched her fumble and fiddle with them, before finally the door opened and she walked through. Waited to see if she would appear at any of the windows in the front of the house. And when she didn't he drove around the square and back out on to the road, finding himself behind the row of houses, counting them up from the end until he spotted the right one. Parking on the side of the road, looking up, until he saw a shadow against the pane, then, as the bottom half of the sash opened, her face as she leaned out, catching the breeze on her face. Lifting her head to the sky, closing her eyes so for a moment he recognized her for the woman she had been. He waited until she had disappeared back inside the room. He imagined himself there with her. Watching her, curious to know. Would her skin still feel the way it did? Would he still want to lie awake beside her, fearful of losing a moment of sensation? Would he still feel that moment of triumph when she turned and smiled at him and he knew she wanted him as much as he wanted her?

And then it was time to go. He turned the key in the ignition and moved slowly away up the hill. A curious symmetry to all this, he thought, watching mother and watching daughter. He liked knowing where they both lived and worked, he decided. He liked even better that they knew nothing about him. That was the way he wanted it. And that was the way it was going to stay.

CHAPTER SIXTEEN

ANOTHER HOT DAY. Another day to be enjoyed. Midsummer's day. Hours of brightness ahead. The sun on her face so she put on her dark glasses and lay back on her rug against a rock on the pebble beach at Killiney. A new experience to view the world through tinted lenses. She didn't wear them before. She had never liked the way the colours of the natural world were altered, made artificial by the glass. And she had never needed to hide before, to keep her emotions to herself, as she had yesterday. The day of Judith's funeral.

They had all been there. The guards, Jack Donnelly and a group of others she didn't know. And Judith's father and brother. They were both, she could see, in a state of shock. Rachel remembered how it felt to peform mechanically, to greet the congregation with fixed smiles and firm handshakes. She sat at the back and watched. And saw the tall, slender woman with the white-blonde hair cut in a ragged pageboy and her daughter's face, ruined now by age, who followed the coffin, from the brightness outside into the gloom within. Judith's mother, Rachel thought. Elizabeth, that was her name. She watched her take her seat behind her husband and son. There was no contact between them. No recognition on either side of their relationship. She remembered what Judith had told her. Her mother's infidelity with a family friend. How her mother had left home. How she had come back and there had been a court case for custody. How she had lost it and been granted limited access. How she had arrived after school one day and taken the children, driven to the ferry to England, driven all the way to Kent where she was living. And how the police had come three days later and taken them home.

Rachel watched her as she left the church after the service. Saw how she stood apart from the other mourners. On her own, running her thin fingers absent-mindedly through her hair. Jack Donnelly was the only person who spoke to her. He took her aside, his hand under her elbow. He looked as if he was asking her questions. She responded with nods and shakes of her head, her hands moving expressively. Rachel remembered the postcards that she had sent to Judith in prison. Regularly, once a week. Watercolours of flowers and birds. Detailed, beautiful. Her name was in small print at the bottom. She was an artist, Judith said. She worked in a nature reserve. It was like something out of a fairy story. A cottage in the woods.

'Or that's how it seemed to us at the time. Stephen and I were Hansel and Gretel in the gingerbread house.'

She had torn a piece off the edge of the card and twisted it into a tube to fit into the end of the joint she was rolling. She lit it and inhaled. The smoke came out of her mouth in a gasp of breath. Then there was silence.

'She wants me to go and visit her when I get out.'

Judith passed over the joint. Rachel took it from her.

'And will you?' she asked.

'Do I have anything to say to her, after so long?'

Rachel waited until Donnelly had moved away and Elizabeth Hill was once again on her own. She walked towards her and held out her hand. Elizabeth looked at her, recognition in her eyes.

'You're the woman in the photograph, aren't you?'

Rachel nodded.

'You were her friend, weren't you?'

Rachel nodded again, unable to speak.

'Thank you, thank you for all you did for her. She wrote to me about you. She told me all about you, and she told me how much she loved you.'

Elizabeth's grip was firm, her hand warm. She put her arm around Rachel's shoulder. She kissed her cheek.

'Be strong,' she whispered in her ear. 'Be strong for me and for Judith.'

Rachel looked at her watch. It was two o'clock. At this time yesterday Judith had been cremated. Her battered, beaten body transformed now into a pile of ash. Jack Donnelly had asked her who would have wanted to hurt Judith in that way. She didn't know what to say.

'It was deliberate,' he said, 'not an act of passion or anger. Her injuries were designed to be agonizing. So who hated her enough to want to do it? Or was it the case that someone wanted to make an example of her? Was that it?'

She couldn't answer him. She wouldn't answer him. Even when he threatened that he would make sure that she was back inside in a matter of days if she didn't tell him. But she just shook her head dumbly and tried to shut out the pain and keep the tears from spilling over and showing her weakness. They spilled over now and ran down her face behind her glasses. She closed her eyes, squeezing them tightly together.

'Rest in peace, my sweetest heart,' she said out loud, then stood up and walked to the water's edge.

Today was a special day. Today there would be more than ice creams. There would be a picnic and she had prepared it as carefully as she had prepared her story. Fresh brown bread. Smoked salmon sliced in fine slivers, with a lemon cut into quarters and wrapped in cling film. Smoked mackerel pâté and black olives from the deli in Glasthule. A piece of ripe goat's cheese, and Carr's Table Water Biscuits. A carton of strawberries and a tub of whipped cream. Some grapes, a bag of nectarines. And a bottle of white wine from New Zealand, suspended in a rock pool in a plastic bag. A book to read, and she was ready. To wait all afternoon if necessary. Until she saw the woman, the dog and the children walk down the steps cut into the rock to the beach.

And her story? It was as flawlessly constructed to attract as her food and drink.

Age? Forty-two.

Marital status? Separated, soon to be divorced.

Number, age and sex of children? Two sons at university. Both away for the summer.

Place of birth and current place of residence? Born in Dublin, brought up in Ranelagh, moved to London when she married her husband twenty years ago. Visiting Dublin for a month, house-sitting for a friend in Monkstown.

Occupation? School teacher. Didn't work while her children were young, but returned to work six months ago after her husband left her for a younger woman.

Husband's occupation? Something in the city. Something to do with the stock exchange.

Hobbies? Gardening, painting, printmaking, cooking.

State of mind? Distraught, lonely, isolated.

Needs? Friendship, someone to talk to.

It would have been almost too hot on the pebble beach, the sunlight splintering into sharp points of brightness on the tops of the waves that rolled in from the Irish sea, except for the gentle onshore breeze that flicked at the pages of her book, turning them over with a sound like the riffling of a pack of cards as she laid it down on the rug beside her and watched, behind her glasses, the group of children who were playing nearby with a long string of seaweed. Tugging and pulling at its fronds, whirling its whip-like tail over their heads. Flicking it out so it caught at the back of the legs of the little ones. Licking at their salty wet skin, then stinging, so they cried out and jumped away. Not sure whether this was a game to be continued or abandoned. Someone was going to get hurt, Rachel could see that. As she could see the two children who had appeared at the bottom of the steps cut into the cliff face, hurrying away from their mother, who was slowed down by the baby strapped to her chest, and the weight of the large canvas bag slung over her shoulder.

Rachel sat up straight and watched. The boy was ahead of his sister. She wondered, looking at his long skinny legs, how old he might be. She had lost that easy facility that she, like all young mothers, had once possessed. That ability to age and place every child. Before, all those years ago, she would have looked at him and thought instantly, oh yes, seven and a half, maybe going on eight, then begun to compare and contrast the unknown boy with her own child's abilities and progress. But now he was just small to her adult eyes. Ungainly, uncoordinated, his feet in runners with thick wedged soles, slipping and sliding over the wet, shifting pebbles. She looked from him to the woman with the baby. They were very alike. Despite the difference in age and sex their relationship shone out in their long limbs and high cheekbones, eyes that were narrowed against the sun, and hair that gleamed, clean and bright.

His name was Jonathan. She could hear the little girl, who straggled along behind him, burdened by a plastic bucket and spade, calling out.

'Jonathan, Jonathan, wait for me.'

It was a long name with too many syllables. Rachel

watched her, how she seemed to pause and gather breath before she used it. It must have been a struggle to master, she thought. Many attempts at getting it right. She watched the little girl pursue him, refusing to lag behind any further, desperately wanting to catch him up, beginning to run, her voice getting more and more frantic as she saw that her brother was nearly gone from her.

They didn't look alike, these two. She was round and dark, her hair cut so it framed her face. Her body was strong and solid, her calves already muscled, her feet in red leather sandals with straps and buckles, gripping the pebbles like the prehensile toes of a monkey. But her face was soft, her cheeks plump, a little roll of fat beneath her square chin and large dark eyes, which now were filling up.

'Wait for me, Jonathan. Please wait.'

But he had gone, disappearing into the group of other children, his fair head bobbing and dipping, lifting and falling as he too became part of the game. And she was left, standing by herself, tears dripping down her face and Rachel watching, waiting, wondering when she should intervene.

The tall, fair woman had sat down now on a flat rock. She was busying herself with the baby, manoeuvring it out of the sling, laying it down on the blanket she had taken from her bag, unfolded and smoothed out. She was preoccupied with her youngest. While the girl stood looking around her, the bucket and spade dropping from her hands, and bumping slowly over the tumbled pebbles towards where the waves broke in a surge of white foam on to the beach. And then, great sobs shaking her voice from her diaphragm, she took a step towards Rachel and said, 'I know you, don't I? You're not a stranger. You gave me a peach and a yummy ice cream. I like you. You're nice. But he's not nice. He won't wait for me. He never waits for me. He can run faster than me. All the time. I hate him.'

And then suddenly the gang of children had turned, were coming back towards them. The oldest and fastest whipped the younger ones into a mass of shouts and screams, pushing and falling as they struggled to keep together. And Jonathan, pulling his sister into the middle, reaching out to grab at her arms, then twirling the long piece of seaweed over his head, like a cowboy with a lasso, bringing it down on her back, so she cried out and lost her balance and fell, on to the hard wet stones, with the others prancing around her as if she were a sacrificial captive.

On her feet before she realized what she was doing, Rachel pushed her way through them, reaching down to pick up the child, turning on the others, shouting that they had no right to behave in this way, threatening them with their parents' wrath, lifting the girl up, smoothing down her hair, picking pieces of grit, small stones and crushed shells from her skin, taking her by the hand and leading her away from the rest. While her older brother, Jonathan, stood, unsure what to do next, turning first towards Rachel and his sister, then back to the rest of the children who were now drifting off, some looking anxiously towards their own mothers further up the beach, others still defiant, making angry gestures, kung-fu kicks and punches in the air. While Jonathan twisted and turned, like a dead leaf hanging from a branch. One minute defiant and angry, the next, frightened, sorry, repentant.

And then their mother was beside them too, calling out in alarm, the baby snatched up from its doze on the blanket, red-faced and yelling. And Rachel, calming, soothing, explaining, making everything all right again, sitting them down on her rug, offering food, pulling the loosened cork from the bottle of wine, handing the woman, Ursula Beckett, a glass, sipping one herself. Watching relief and comfort soften her body as she sat with the baby cradled on her lap, the girl melded to her side, even the older son relenting and sitting down beside them, accepting some strawberries and cream. So that ten minutes later all was quiet and peaceful as the sunlight splintered into sharp points of brightness on the tops of the waves that rolled in from the Irish sea.

'You're so good with them. They really like you. I've been so busy since I had the baby that I just don't seem to have had any real time to spend with them.'

It was getting late. They had eaten and drunk. They had played hide-and-seek, and catch, and skimmed pebbles across the tops of the waves. The baby had slept, and woken, been fed and changed, had slept again, and now he lay on Rachel's lap, looking up at her as she angled her neck and bent her face down to his. Smiling and frowning, watching how he twisted his mouth into a reflection of hers, contorting his upper body with delight, and waving his hands as he tried to reach out and grab hold of her hair. She stroked the top of his head with her forefinger, feeling the gentle indentation where the bones of the fontanel had still not completely closed over. She thought of the last time she had done this. A visit in the prison. A privilege granted. A meeting in one of the prefabs, in private. A boy baby too. Very big and strong. Already bursting out of his new towelling suit. Bottle-fed. His clothes smelling from the last time he had got sick, in the bus, stuck in traffic on the North Circular Road on the way to the prison.

'Jesus, Rachel, he stinks, doesn't he? I should have brought something to change him into.'

The air thick with tobacco smoke. Her old friend Tina, early release to have the baby, sticking to the conditions of her probation. In love, Rachel could see, with motherhood. Come back to visit, to show off her beautiful, healthy, six-month-old son.

'Isn't he lovely? I love him so much. I'd do anything for him, anything, Rachel.'

'Will you stay off it all, will you do that for him?'

'Anything, I'll do anything. He's so perfect and sweet. And he's mine.'

The baby, pushing himself up on her knees, reaching out to his mother, grabbing at her hair as she pulled him from Rachel and buried her face in the folds of his neck. Laughing at the smell of baby puke, taking delight in the daily routine.

'Jesus, Rachel, I never knew you could do so much

washing. All fucking day long, I'm washing and drying and changing. But you know what, I love it.'

Tina, the worst of them all. The scar on her face running from behind her left ear down to the corner of her mouth. Countless convictions for drug offences, robbery, assault. A surface as hard as the metal grid on the window, but inside as soft and sweet as could be. A lover of stories.

'Read it, again. Rachel, read the one about the princess and the frog. I love that one. Tell me another story, tell me about the children of Lir, the ones with the stepmother who didn't want them. Make me cry, Rachel, so I can let go. Let me feel love. Look after me, Rachel.'

'He'll be dark, like Laura,' she said, smoothing down the fine, soft fuzz which covered his scalp. 'And his eyes, what colour will they be?'

'They'll be grey.' His mother stretched and rolled over on her side, lying with her head propped up on her elbow. 'He's going to be just like his father. Laura's the image of him. It's funny that, isn't it?' And she sat up, taking a comb from her bag and running it through her hair, smoothing it down, and fastening it at the nape of her neck with a large tortoiseshell clip. 'The way children in a family can be so different. Jonathan, for instance, is so like my father. He has all his expressions and mannerisms. It's quite odd, because my father died five years ago. Jonathan barely knew him.'

It was beginning to get cool now. The beach was

nearly deserted. Only a couple of people walking with a dog far off, their figures silhouetted against the sweep of the bay and the dark hump of Bray Head off in the distance.

'Your sons. Tell me, what are they like? Do they take after you or your husband?'

She would describe the two boys.

'The older is very dark. He's not really academic but he works hard. He loves the outdoor life. He's a very good sailor. And a great swimmer. He had some problems when he was a child. Reading difficulties, but he got over it all with a bit of remedial teaching. He's very affectionate and he seems easy-going. Shy but not to be crossed. He's not at all like his younger brother. If you didn't know they were related you wouldn't think it.'

'And the younger one, what's he like?'

'Oh, he's quite a star. Very clever, always did very well at school. Good-looking too, I must say. Tall and slim, light brown hair that goes fair in the sun. Very blue eyes. But a bit cold. Self-centred. Ambitious. And very moody. Can go from sunshine to thunder in the blink of an eye. He can be frightening when that happens. But in a funny contradictory way it makes him very attractive. Already the girls are after him.'

'It must have been such a shock when your husband left you. How did they take it?'

'It's hard to know really. They don't say much. They keep their emotions to themselves.'

'And you, it must have been terrible. Were you very hurt? Did you know he was having an affair?'

Rachel was silent.

'I'm sorry.' Ursula reached over and took the baby from Rachel's lap. 'I didn't mean to pry. I'm just being nosy.'

'No, no. It's fine. It's good to be able to talk about it. Most people, our friends, were so embarrassed. And they didn't want to take sides. And no, I was your classic stupid wife. I didn't realize that he was involved with anyone else. And then he came home one night and said it to me straight out, and said she was pregnant and he wanted to marry her.'

'And your sons, were they much help to you?'

Rachel stood up and began to pack away the remains of the picnic. 'They have their own lives to live. I don't really want to drag them into it. You have to let them go, you know. It's one of the first things you learn as a mother, I think. The importance of letting them go. Doing without them.'

The girl and the boy were still down by the sea. They were playing an elaborate game. It involved building fortifications with some of the larger stones, constructing a waterway for the waves to wash through. Rachel stood and watched. It was quiet now. Behind her the woman was busy with the baby. She was changing his nappy, making him tidy for the journey home. Rachel turned and looked at her, then looked away. She moved quietly over the wet stones, down towards the children. The dark head and the fair head were together, concentrating on their task. They didn't hear her feet sliding towards them. They didn't look up. She could hear their voices, disputing, arguing. They looked very small there, before her. The sea rushed up, around their ankles and their calves. She could see the way it dragged back with it the smaller stones and pebbles. She saw how their bare feet dug into the soft clinging sand. She stopped and watched them. And wondered. Just for a moment. Thought of their mother and father and how they would feel. If something should happen to their children.

She stepped closer and closer. Still they did not see her. She looked around once again. The mother was bending over the baby. He was crying. He sounded tired, fractious. Off in the distance she could see the people with the dog. They were far away now. They would not hear, no one would hear the double splash as the two children hit the water, as they thrashed and struggled, their legs and arms making the sea white with foam. And she would be there too. Wading in, wet to her knees, her thighs, losing her balance so she could no longer stand, her feet no longer able to grip the shiny, slippery stones beneath. Beginning to swim, reaching out for the children. Taking a deep breath and diving, reaching out and pulling them down to her, holding them close to her, their bodies limp now as all the air was pushed from them by the steady flow of the sea.

No one would ever see, no one would ever know. I did everything I could, I tried, I tried, she would say. Watching the grief on their faces.

And then the girl, Laura, looked up, turned her face towards her and called out, 'Rachel, look at this. Isn't it great? And isn't my bit the best, much better than his? Aren't I the cleverest?'

A look on her round face that Rachel had seen before. So many times.

'Look, Mummy, look what I've done.'

'Look, Mummy, look at this.'

'Look, Mummy, am I good? Am I a good girl? Am I the best girl?'

She squatted down beside her, so the sea water pulled at her own ankles and legs, licking the hem of her trousers, and put her arms around the small solid body, feeling the smoothness of her skin against her cheek, as she whispered so only Laura could hear, 'You're wonderful, my sweetest heart, you're the best. Always. The best.'

CHAPTER SEVENTEEN

'I'VE ASKED YOU both to be here to witness this search.' It was early morning, eight-thirty. Bright outside, although already the sky was beginning to fill with threatening dark clouds. Jack stood in the sitting room in the Hills' house in Rathmines. Dr Hill and his son Stephen stood before him. Their expressions were sour and unhelpful.

'I've asked you to be here, as I said, to witness this search which I am about to undertake of the house, the gardens and the garage. I am informing you that I have the necessary documents to authorize this action. I have obtained a search warrant from the District Court for this purpose. You will be told of any objects that we wish to remove from these premises. I am sure that you will cooperate fully.' And even if you don't, he thought, looking at their faces, trying to read the mixture of emotions which paraded across them, even if you don't, you can do fuck all about it.

Dr Hill spoke first. 'I don't understand why this is necessary. I cannot believe that you seriously think that Judith was killed in this house. And by implication that I, or Stephen, had something to do with her death.

We have both told you what we know. We have both been as helpful as we can to you and your,' he paused as if to gather breath, 'your ridiculous investigation. It is as plain as the nose on your face that this terrible crime had absolutely nothing to do with any civilized person, and everything to do with the scum, the gutter rats, the prison fodder with whom she spent two years of her life.'

Would that it was that simple, Jack thought. He cleared his throat.

'You may think that, Dr Hill, and that is the way it may appear. And please accept that I understand your grief and how you must feel at having lost your daughter in this way. I too am a father. And I have seen many others suffer what you are suffering. But try to look at it from where I'm standing. If you consider the evidence so far, from our point of view, you may see it very differently. For example, we have established that Judith was strangled, and that she was strangled with a length of rope. The kind that is commonly used as a clothes line. We have already, with your permission, taken a sample from your clothes line, and we have noticed that a piece was cut off the excess of it, and it matches, I'm sorry to say, perfectly, the piece that was used to kill your daughter. We know, roughly speaking, the time frame in which Judith died. And we have witnesses, your neighbours, who will say that they saw her here, in the house, during those couple of days. One neighbour is very specific. She says that as it happens it was her birthday and Judith called in with a bunch of flowers for her.'

He paused and looked at them again. He was interested in the difference in their expressions. Stephen Hill now looked bored and disinterested. He yawned, openly, exposing his small white teeth in a way that reminded Jack uncomfortably of Judith's, the way she had looked in the morgue when Johnny Harris pulled back her lips to reveal her gums. Sweeney was right. Brother and sister were very alike. The doctor, on the other hand, was nervous. He tapped his foot impatiently and fiddled with his tie, his belt, his expandable watchstrap, and one hand slipped into his trouser pocket and jingled the coins.

'And then,' Jack took out his notebook, flicking through the pages, 'and then there is the question of the blood group of the foetus. The baby boy that Judith was carrying. The baby's blood group was O. The same group as Judith. And also the same group as both of you.'

'What on earth are you suggesting?' Dr Hill straightened up. His face was suddenly red. 'Do my ears deceive me? Can you be saying what I think you're saying? Can you really be suggesting that my daughter, Stephen's sister was carrying a child fathered by either of us? You're mad, that's what you are, Inspector Donnelly, stark, staring, raving mad.'

'Really? Is that what you think? And you, Stephen, what do you think?'

Stephen Hill looked at him for a moment, then smiled. 'I think, Inspector Donnelly, that these days there are tests which are a lot more refined, a lot more conclusive than the crude blunt instrument of forensic science that you are wielding. So I suggest, before you make any more accusations, that you use them.'

Touché, Jack thought, you little bollocks. And wondered just how long it would be before they got the results of the DNA analysis that they had requested. Join the queue, was the response from the forensic laboratory. Helpful as always.

'All right.' Jack moved towards the door. 'Why don't we just get on with it?'

There were five detectives in all making their way systematically through the house. They knew what to look for. Anything. Anything at all. But in particular they wanted a match with the sheet in which the girl had been wrapped. A knife or scissors, some sharp cutting object whose blades matched the cuts inside her vagina and anus. Any traces of blood, no matter how small. And anything else, useful or otherwise.

He walked through the hall towards the staircase which curved upwards. Dr Hill had made as if to come with him, but Jack had put him off. Said he'd prefer it if he stayed downstairs. Asked him to explain the layout of the house. Then left him drinking tea with Sweeney.

Downstairs there was a small study, two large interconnecting rooms – a sitting room and dining room – and a dark poky kitchen. All were furnished with heavy antiques. Mahogany table and sideboard, high-backed sofas and chairs covered with faded chintzes, and sombre portraits that gazed down on every side. The garden outside was neglected and overgrown. Two apple trees heavy with fruit stood in the middle of the lawn. And on either side were long herbaceous borders, the plants smothered with bind-weed and dock. Behind was the garage, a substantial brick building. Jack noticed that those of the neighbouring houses had all been converted into architect-designed mews.

Upstairs on the first floor there were four bedrooms and a large bathroom. Jack could see that very little had been done to change the basic structure and fabric of the house over the years. The walls were covered in faded flowery paper. The carpets were threadbare. There didn't appear to be central heating, and the bathroom was spartan in its fittings. A large free-standing bath, a heavy enamel hand basin, and next door a separate lavatory, with a cistern fitted high on the wall. Above again, up a smaller staircase, there were three more rooms.

'There's nothing up there,' Hill had told him. 'Just a couple of rooms that were servants' quarters. In the days when you could get servants, that is. And there's a storeroom too. Lots of old junk and rubbish. I keep on meaning to get around to clearing it all out, but somehow or other I never have the time.'

'And Judith's room, which was hers?'

'When she came out of prison first I made her sleep in the room next to mine. I wanted to be able to keep an eye on her. So I suppose that's what you could call hers. She's been living in college for the last few months and she's taken a lot of her books, clothes, personal things there with her. You won't find much of anything there.'

He was right about that. It was a small narrow room and it was virtually empty. A high old-fashioned bed, neatly made, faced the door, flanked by a chest of drawers on one side and a small table on the other. The room was painted a dull cream. A faded rug covered the black-painted floorboards. The walls were bare. No posters, pictures, decoration of any kind. A tall dark wardrobe was pushed behind the door. He opened it and stepped back in surprise as he saw his own reflection swing suddenly into view in the full-length mirror inside. He smiled at himself and straightened his tie. He didn't look so bad these days, he thought. Given what he'd been through recently. Especially given that he didn't have a clue who had killed Judith Hill.

And there were no clues here. A couple of pairs of faded jeans hung on wire coat-hangers. There was a coat of some kind of tweed and beside it a green wool blazer with a school crest on the top pocket. That was all. He stepped back and let the door fall shut again. There wasn't much of use in this spartan, cell-like place. No books, no letters, no diaries or notebooks. Hardly even any clothes. And they hadn't found too much either in her room in college. A lot of library books, lecture notes, and a box containing computer disks. Sweeney had scanned through them. All the files were related to her studies. Jack was surprised there was no diary of any kind. She seemed, he thought, for no particular reason, like the kind of kid who would have kept one. But they found nothing of that nature. And no letters either. No references to her mother, father or brother, at all. And none to Rachel or anyone else connected with her time inside.

He had tried again to get Dr Hill to talk about his wife. But he had drawn a complete blank.

'I have nothing to say on that subject. As far as I am concerned the woman no longer exists.'

Stephen Hill was equally reticent. 'My mother,' he said, pursing his lips. 'Now to whom exactly would you be referring?'

'But she was there, at Judith's funeral.'

'Was she? I didn't notice.'

'And your father, does he feel the same way as you?'

Stephen smiled, a narrow rictus of the face and lips. 'My father,' he said, 'is a passionate man. He is capable of great love and of equally great hate.'

And a possessive man too? Jack pondered the question as he stood in the doorway of the room at the top of the house. It must have once been an attic. The beams and timbers of the roof were exposed, and a large dormer window had been let into them. North-facing, he reckoned, so the light that came through the panes was pure and clear, untainted by the gold of direct sunshine. It fell now upon a large easel that stood in the middle of the floor. And lit up the canvas which rested against its uprights. Jack stepped forward and looked at it closely. It was a painting of two children. It was unfinished, he could see that, but it was still very beautiful. The children gazed into the eyes of the viewer, and as he moved away from them their gaze moved with him. He could feel their eyes on his back as he walked slowly around the room. Looking at the shelves, the stacks of canvases, some framed, others rolled and standing in bundles, the boxes of paints and brushes, the piles of paper of differing weights and gauges. In one corner was some kind of a press, ink-stained, and beside it a large rectangular sink. He leaned over it and smelt immediately the pungent stench of acid. There was a row of black and white photographs framed on one wall. He could see immediately who they were. Judith and Stephen as babies and small children. And Mark Hill too as a young man, handsome and strong in swimming trunks and tennis whites. And sitting on a canvas stool outside a small tent, tending a Primus stove, waving a wooden spoon in one hand, and laughing. In one corner of the room was what looked like a large cupboard, surrounded with black curtains. When he pushed them aside he found a photographic enlarger, a workbench, and a sink with running water. Everywhere there was paint. Spattered and dripped all over the floor, the work surfaces, even on the walls up to waist level. And such colours. Blues, greens, bright yellows and purples. And above all reds. Scarlets, vermilions, crimsons, and a red the colour of ox blood, deep and dark. What a strange man, Jack thought as he stared around him. He hates his wife so much that he won't even mention her name, and yet he has kept all this untouched for years and years and years. Possession by proxy, would that be it?

He leant over and looked down at the dark red drops that formed a haphazard pattern over the bare floorboards. They were slightly raised, slightly bubbled. He scratched at them with his fingertips and saw that they had coloured the edge of his nails. He lifted his fingers to his nose and sniffed. There was no characteristic smell of paint. Just another smell like an old-fashioned butcher's shop. He stood up and took a clean handkerchief from his pocket. He wiped his fingers carefully on it, looking at the smears of red across the white cotton. He walked over to the workbench. There was a row of tools lying neatly in place. A couple of sharp knives, and a number of gouges of different sizes with wooden handles. The kind that were used for making lino cuts, he thought, remembering art classes at school. He picked them up carefully, one by one, using his handkerchief to handle them. He thought of the way the lino would peel up from the tile in a thick coil of brown. He walked to the centre of the room, underneath the skylight. He held each of them up and noticed that the largest had a fine line of red trapped between the edge of the metal and the wood into which it was set. He laid it down again, carefully, on the bench. Below was a row of long drawers. He pulled each open in turn. The top two contained drawings, nature studies of plants and animals. Very beautiful, very detailed. The next had paintings, sketches in watercolours, faded now, muted and delicate. He bent down to pull open the one at the bottom. It was filled with sheets and sheets of paper, all blank as far as he could see. He reached down and flicked through them, and felt beneath his fingers something else. Shiny, hard to grasp. He squatted and took hold of the drawer, pulling it from its runners. He turned it upside down, spilling its contents all over the floor, and felt his heart jump and his breath catch in his throat. Polaroid pictures of Judith lay scattered around him. He picked them up and looked at them in turn. In all she was naked, her body arranged in poses that made nausea suddenly rise up from his stomach. In some she was alive, and in some she was dead. She looked terrified, hurt and vulnerable. Her living eyes and her dead eyes stared directly into his. Asking him for help. Begging him to save her. But it was too late. Far too late for Judith now.

Chapter Eighteen

Tom Sweeney would do the interrogation. Tom Sweeney was good at it. Jack would sit in the corner and watch. Make notes, monitor what was being said, intervene if he thought that Tom had let anything slip by. Except that Tom never did.

'OK, before we start let's summarize what we have.' It was six in the morning. They were going to pick up Dr Hill in half an hour. They would hold him for six hours, then they would renew the order. Twelve hours to get a confession. An admission of guilt.

'Crucial question number one. When did Judith Hill die?'

Today was the 23rd June. It was a week since her body had been found. Johnny Harris reckoned she'd been dead for about six days. So she was killed, they thought, somewhere around the 10th of the month.

'How was she killed?'

That was easy. They knew she had been strangled. Again Harris considered, from the damage that had been done to her neck, the kind of force that had been used, that her killer was most likely to be a man. And a large one at that.

'What other injuries did she have?'

Laceration of the vagina and anus. Severe bruising on the thighs and external genitalia. Also heavy bruising on the ribs and stomach, which had caused rupture of the uterus. Bleeding from the vagina. Bruising to eyes, cheekbones and nose. Probable cause: blows to the face and head before death. Bleeding from the nose and mouth.

'What physical evidence do we have?'

Bloodstains found in the upstairs room. Bloodstains on the lino-cutting tools. Dr Hill's fingerprints everywhere. Photographs of Judith taken both before and after death. Evidence that the rope used to strangle her had come from the house. The doctor's tie that had been threaded through her fingers. Hairs from Judith's body found in the doctor's car. The linen sheet in which she had been wrapped was identical in every way to other sheets found in the house. And Dr Hill himself had identified the rubber groundsheet as one that he had bought many years ago.

'What do you reckon, Jack? What's your considered assessment?' Sweeney's grin was getting bigger and bigger.

'I'd say it's a hole in one, most definitely. A birdie, an eagle, a fucking albatross, or whatever you call it. And I'd say we should get going.'

He sat in the corner and listened. Sweeney was taking Dr Hill through that weekend, the last weekend that he had seen Judith.

She had come to stay on the Monday before. It was

the housekeeper's annual holiday. He needed someone to cook for him, clean up after him, generally take care of him.

'Judith always did it, you know, before she got into trouble. From when she was quite young, ten perhaps, twelve, before she was a teenager. She was very good around the house. A very good girl. She always wanted to please me, make me happy. She used to come home from school and before she'd even started on her home-work she'd have prepared the vegetables for dinner.'

'So you must have enjoyed spending time with her, it must have seemed like old times.'

'Well, you know the way it is. I was in and out. I have surgery here twice a day. And then I do house calls as well. And I'd be visiting patients in hospital, keeping an eye on their progress. But we ate together every evening.'

'So explain to us, Dr Hill, if you would be so kind, explain to us how it was that you say you didn't realize that she had gone missing. I don't quite understand that.'

'Well, you see, I went away, that weekend. For the Saturday night. I was invited by friends who live in Wicklow, Laragh to be precise. They invited me for dinner and, because of the ridiculous laws about con-sumption of alcohol and driving, they suggested I stay the night. And when I got back home on Sunday, there was no sign of her. But everything was left perfectly clean and tidy, and there was even a stew in the oven, waiting to be heated up.'

'No note, no message, no nothing?'

'No, there wasn't, but that didn't surprise me. She had done what I asked of her. The housekeeper was due back on the Monday, so I just assumed that she had left, gone back to college, whatever. You know, I gave up trying to keep track of her movements a long time ago.'

They had checked, of course, with the friends in Wicklow. They corroborated his story, up to a point. They had asked him to come for pre-dinner drinks around seven o'clock. He hadn't arrived until eight-thirty. He hadn't given any explanation for his lateness. They had thought his manner strange, distracted. He hadn't spoken much. He had in fact behaved quite rudely. He had got very drunk that night. Not like him, they said, he was usually a temperate man. And then in his drunkenness he had talked a lot about Judith. How disappointed he was by her. He could never forgive the shame she had brought on the family. How after all this time she reminded him too much of his wife. And the shame that she had brought on them too. And they said he had left, quite abruptly, sometime after midnight. They had remonstrated with him, warned him of the dangers of drinking and driving. But he had just got up and gone. Just like that.

Sweeney was going through his polite phase. Jack watched him. He could hear the contempt in Dr Hill's voice. Sweeney was patient, persistent, thorough in his questioning. Dr Hill could barely bring himself to respond.

'So where did you stay that night? Your friends tell us that you most definitely didn't stay with them.'

'No, they're right, I didn't. I stopped the car at Kilmacanogue and I slept there until dawn. Then I went home.'

'Home to kill your daughter, was that it?'

Dr Hill didn't reply. He looked into the middle distance and sighed.

'Your friends, your old friends, they were very concerned about you that night. They said your behaviour was uncharacteristic, unusual. They were quite shocked by you. Can you explain what was on your mind?'

'Explain to you? Why should I? What business is it of yours whether I'm drunk, sober, polite, rude. Whatever I am?'

Jack listened to Sweeney explaining why it was in his own interest to be more forthcoming. There was silence. Sweeney sighed. He put his hand in his pocket. He pulled out a large yellow envelope. He held it upside down. The photographs dropped on to the table. Sweeney fanned them out. Jack waited for the response. But there was none. Dr Hill looked away.

'What do you expect me to say?' he said. 'What do you want me to do? Cry, beat my breast, is that it? Well, I won't.'

'Why not?'

'She disgusted me when she was alive. She disgusts me now she's dead. I didn't take those photographs. I don't know who did. But I'm not surprised by them. Not that long ago Judith did that sort of thing to pay

for her drug habit. She was used to it. I asked her once
how she could bear it. She just shrugged her shoulders
and said, 'Needs must.' Can you credit it? I saw her,
you know. I went looking for her one night. I drove
into town. I drove around Fitzwilliam Square, then
down by the canal. There was a row of women, all
waiting. I drove slowly so I could see her. She didn't
realize it was me. She turned around and she pulled
open her blouse. I saw her breasts. My own daughter. I
remembered how I used to bathe her when she was
small, after her mother went. It was a nightly ritual.
The two, my beloved son and daughter, in the bath
together. They had such perfect beautiful little bodies.
And afterwards I would dress them in their pyjamas
and put them to bed and read to them until they fell
asleep. Then I would sit and watch them in case they
might have bad dreams, nightmares, and they might
want me. And this was the payment I got for all that
love and devotion. My own daughter waving her tits
at me on a cold, wet, bloody awful night.' He stopped
and buried his head in his hands, then he looked up.
'You asked me why I behaved so uncharacteristically,
as you so delicately put it, that night. Well, my
daughter had just told me that she was pregnant. She
asked me to help her get rid of the baby. She asked me
in my capacity as a doctor. Not as a father. And that,
my friends, is the last thing that I will say to you. I
will now exercise my right to silence.'

They kept him there until the last possible
moment. And then they let him go. The statement
went out to the media. A man had been arrested and

questioned for the murder of Judith Hill. He had been released. A file was being prepared and would be sent to the Director of Public Prosecutions. And in the meantime, Jack thought, they would watch him and they would wait.

Rachel heard the announcement on the nine o'clock news that night. She was sitting beside Clare Bowen's bed. The light was turned off in the small room. A strong smell of new-mown grass drifted in on a gentle breeze. She got up and made as if to shut the open door. Clare put out her hand and plucked at her sleeve.

'Leave it. I like it like that.'

Rachel liked it too. The grass on the lawn at the back of the house had been ankle-deep when she arrived in the early evening. It was strewn with daisies and buttercups, and crowned with the waving heads of plantains. She had dragged the lawnmower from the shed and tugged hard at the cord until, with a couple of splutters and groans and a gush of grey smoke, it had burst into a raucous screech. She had raked the clippings into soft piles, then taken off her shoes and walked barefoot up and down, feeling her toes sink into the soft springiness of the grass. Then she had lain down on it for half an hour and dozed until Clare had called her in.

Now they watched the television pictures. An old photograph of Judith, taken, Rachel was sure, when she was sixteen or so. Shots of the outside of the house and the place where her body had been found. The Garda team at work. An interview with Jack Donnelly about progress so far, and then the shot of a man being bundled from the station into a waiting car. A coat was held over his head, but Rachel recognized him immediately. A big man. A strong man. Judith had dreaded his visits.

'Why does he come?' she had said. 'He hates it here. He hates me. We have nothing to say to each other.'

'And was it always like that?' Rachel had pulled her head on to her shoulder to comfort her.

'Oh, I don't know,' she had replied. 'Maybe when I was small we got on OK. I was always so good. I was polite and thoughtful. I always put him first, but then as I got older. I don't know. It was different.'

'You knew her, didn't you?' Clare tried to lift her head from the pillow, but the effort was too much for her.

Rachel nodded.

'What was she like?'

'She was lovely. She was clever. She was very funny. A great mimic.'

'And that man there. Do you know him?'

Rachel shook her head. 'No, but I know who he is. He's her father.'

There was silence then. Rachel got up and went into the kitchen. She opened the cupboard and took out the container of pills. Antibiotics and painkillers. Opiates, DF 118s and sleeping pills. Halcyon was the name printed on the label. Rachel smiled at the notion. Andrew Bowen had counted them out and left them.

'Give them to her with some juice,' he said. 'There's

orange and passion fruit in a carton in the fridge. It's her favourite.'

Rachel put ice cubes in a tall glass and filled it to the top. She sat down beside the bed again and lifted Clare's head.

'Here,' she said, 'it's time for your pills.'

'Not the sleeping pills, not yet. I want to stay awake for a bit longer.' She opened her mouth for the others and swallowed them down with a gulp from the glass. Juice ran down her chin and on to her nightdress. Rachel bent and wiped it away.

'You're kind.' Clare's voice was barely audible. 'Very kind.' She lay back on the pillow. 'He's paying you, I hope, for this?'

Rachel nodded.

'He needs his time by himself. He has a woman he goes to. I know all about it. It's not love. It's never love with Andrew.'

Rachel lifted the sheet away from Clare's body, then smoothed it down, tucking her in firmly all around.

'It wasn't love with me either. In the beginning maybe, but not for long.'

'And you, what was it for you?' Rachel fluffed up the quilt and tidied the books into a neat pile beside the bed.

'It was love for me. No one could understand what I saw in him. He was gawky and clumsy. But he was clever, so bright and funny. I laughed all the time when I was with him.'

'Here.' Rachel held out the sleeping pills. 'You should take them now. It's late. You need your rest.'

The woman in the bed smiled. 'It's not sleep I need. It's something a bit more permanent. We've talked about it, a lot. In the beginning we talked about when would be the best time. And then I got better and for a while I thought it had all been a mistake, a misdiagnosis. And then the symptoms came back and this time there was no mistaking them.'

Rachel watched her eyes flick uncontrollably from side to side.

'And so we've decided. It'll be sooner rather than later. The problem is how to do it. These pills, these things I have to take, you can't overdose on them. They're benzodiazepines, unfortunately, not barbiturates. They bring forgetfulness, a respite, but it's only temporary.'

'Shh.' Rachel knelt down beside her again.

'The thing is, I'm worried about what it'll be like for him. Afterwards. How will he feel? I want this, I don't want to go on like this, but I don't want him to suffer. I'm scared he'll feel guilty. That's why I wanted to ask you.' She paused, her breathing laboured.

'You wanted to ask me what?' Rachel looked down into her face.

'Oh, nothing, it's nothing.'

'No, go on, tell me.'

Clare closed her eyes, then opened them looking directly in Rachel's.

'I want to know how you felt, after you killed your husband. Did you feel any guilt? What was it like for you all those years in prison? Could you bring yourself to remember him, the way it had been before?'

Rachel stood up and moved away.

'I didn't kill him,' she said. Her voice was measured, controlled. 'How many time do I have to say it. I did not kill my husband. Yes, I admit I shot him, but I didn't kill him. It was an accident. It was my brother-in-law who did it. No one would believe me. In some ways I don't blame them. I should have told the truth right from the start. But I didn't. I lied. And my lies were found out.'

She sat down on the side of the bed.

'And yes,' she said, 'I did feel guilt. I felt dreadful guilt. I still feel dreadful guilt. But I feel other things too.' She handed Clare the glass of juice and the pills. She waited until she had swallowed them, then she sat back and listened to her breathing. Until it was slow and shallow.

'If he is human he will feel guilt.' Her words were soft, her voice gentle. 'But he will get over it, like I did.'

She stood up and turned off the television. She turned back towards the bed. She bent down and stared into Clare's face, watching her closed eyelids flicker. Then she smoothed her thin hair back from her forehead and stepped through the door into the garden.

Outside it was still warm. It had been hot earlier in the day. The kind of heat that brings a garden to life, she thought. And she thought of how she had spent that afternoon.

'It's as if you can see all the plants actually growing, the energy flowing through them,' she had said to

Ursula Beckett as they walked together through the garden centre. They stopped beside a bed filled with irises. Their flowers were tightly furled, like small neat umbrellas, but as they stood beside them, she noticed that one of the petals, white, tinged with pale blue, had begun to edge its way free.

Today they were on their own.

'Would you like to come with me?' Ursula had asked her as they said goodbye at the beach that day. 'If you're interested, that is. There's a garden I'm designing, out past Bray. I need to organize my stock for it. There's this wonderful nursery I go to. The same family have owned it for years. You'd enjoy it.'

They had driven off the dual carriageway and taken a turn that led them up a winding wooded road to an old stone farmhouse. Ursula had told her how kind these people had been to her when she started her business. They had helped and encouraged her, shared their knowledge with her, and they had introduced her to her husband.

'My lovely Daniel,' she said. 'You'll have to meet him. He's such a sweetheart. I know you'd like him. He seems a bit gruff when you meet him first, but that's because of his job. He runs a security company. He's under a lot of pressure, there's always a lot of money involved. But when you get to know him, underneath all that macho stuff, he's a dote.'

She was beautiful, this woman whom Daniel had married. He had chosen well. Rachel watched her as she walked ahead of her through the rows of plants. She was graceful and confident, sure of her place in the world. Rachel compared them, one to the other, and felt awkward and clumsy.

'So, tell me,' she said as they stopped to sit on an oak bench, beside an arbour covered with climbing roses, 'tell me how you met.'

Ursula explained. A number of years ago, there had been a terrible spate of robberies out here. It was far enough from the city so the roads were clogged with snow in the winters, but close enough so the glow from the lights just over the horizon seeped into the night sky. Men had come in a van in the early hours of the morning. They carried shotguns and iron bars. Black balaclavas covered their faces. They knew what they wanted. Money, jewellery, silver, paintings, furniture. It happened more than once. After the third time, when the family had been tied up in the cellar and threatened, they got sense. They called in a security company.

'As luck would have it, I was here the day Daniel came to see them. We kind of started chatting, and then you know the way it is, one thing led to another, he took my phone number, and then he called me and we went out together. And somehow we ended up getting married. It was very unexpected. I was planning on going back to the States where my family live.'

'What brought you to Ireland in the first place?' Rachel kept her face turned from Ursula's gaze.

'Oh, the usual Irish-American thing. I was mad about the music and the culture, and I came over to trace the ancestors. I had relations who were living out here. They had a big farm down the road. Sold now, houses built all over it. But back then my aunt was a keen gardener. She got me going, got me interested. I never thought of staying here permanently. I was always about to go home. I even had a boyfriend waiting for me. But there you go. That's life. Here I am. Married with children.'

'And how long ago was that?'

'Oh, let me see. Laura is four. Jonathan is seven. So I guess it must be eight years or so. Yeah, that's right. It's our anniversary the week after next. We'll be having a party. You must come.'

Eight years ago, when she had been in prison for four years. The worst four years of her life. She thought of it now as she sat on the wooden bench, stroking the smooth grain with her fingertips, feeling the sun on her face, listening to the sound of a woodpigeon in the branches of an ash tree nearby. Further away a cow bellowed, one long drawn-out note. A warning sound. And the noise of prison sounded in her ears. The shouts, the threats, the screams. The clanging of metal on metal. And the solitary loneliness within it all.

'So, you must miss your family. Whereabouts in America are they?'

'They're in Boston. They come over quite often to visit. And I go back to see them every year. I take the kids with me. Daniel won't come. He doesn't like to fly. He says if he could sail across the Atlantic he'd have no problem. He likes boats. God knows why.'

'You don't?'

She smiled and grimaced. 'Can't stand them. I get seasick real easily. Daniel has a yacht. He's in love with it, I'm convinced. "She", as he insists on calling it, "she's" moored, or whatever you call it, in the harbour in Dun Laoghaire. It's the only thing we disagree about. He wants to go sailing on the weekends, and I want to stay in my garden.'

'And what about Daniel's family? Oh, sorry,' she paused, 'now I'm the one being nosy.'

'No, not at all, it's fine.' Ursula patted her on the knee, her touch warm and generous. Inclusive. Confiding. 'Daniel has a kind of a tragic story in his background. He had a brother, a younger brother. He was murdered, years ago. His wife killed him. It was terrible. And what was worse, if anything could be worse, she tried to implicate Daniel in the whole thing. She said that they'd been having an affair and her husband had found out, and there'd been a dreadful row and that Daniel had shot him. Of course, it was nonsense and no one believed her. But it was terrible for the family at the time. Daniel's mother never got over it. She died not long afterwards, from alcohol. And his father, too, suffers that way.'

His wife killed him. How strange to hear it said like that, so bluntly, so matter-of-fact. His wife killed him. She wanted to say the words out loud, try them out for size.

'You're very quiet.' Ursula leaned towards her, looking into her face. 'Have I shocked you?'

'No.' She smiled. 'Of course not. I was just wondering, what happened to the wife? Did she go to prison?'

'She most certainly did. She got a life sentence. Daniel says they'll never let her out. She's bad through and through. You know, I'm an American, and we have a different approach to questions of justice. I think that someone like that, who commits murder, then tries to blame another person, deserves the death penalty.' She paused and looked again at Rachel. 'Now you're shocked, aren't you? That's not a popular senti-ment here, I know. My friends always tell me to shut up when I get going on the subject, but I'm afraid that's the way I feel.'

Rachel said nothing in reply. She had thought about death often. She had wanted to die more than once. She turned her wrist over so the scar shone whitely in the sunshine. She fingered it gently. The skin still felt different even after all this time. She had tried to open her radial artery one day, using a sharp piece of plastic she had broken from a biro. Blood had flowed all over her clothes, all over her bedding. She had felt sick and light-headed. She had held her arm away from her body and watched the blood drip on to the floor until the screws found her. And that was the end of that.

'Come on.' Ursula stood up. 'I've got work to do. And you're going to help me. You know something about plants, don't you? I can tell. I have a feeling that you're quite a gardener, that your garden at home is something special, am I right?'

What could she say? How could she answer? That it was something special, that it had been something special. That it had been beautiful and precious. She smiled up at her and stood.

'Once,' she said, 'once I had a lovely garden. But then we moved away, and I've never been able to get it right since. But now, perhaps, I will.'

She stood in the doorway and listened for the sound of Clare Bowen's breathing, then heard the phone in the corridor outside, ringing. It was Andrew. He was drunk.

'You can go now,' he said. 'I'll be home in ten minutes.'

'I'll wait, I don't mind.'

'No.' His voice was loud and insistent. 'No, I don't want you to stay. I want you to go. Do you understand me? Do I make myself clear?'

She listened again for the gentle sound of Clare's breath. Then she left the room, and left the house. It wasn't far from the quiet road where the Bowens lived to the sea road. She walked quickly, then broke into a run. Her stride was smooth and fluid. She had been running regularly along the west pier every day. Her breath flowed evenly in and out of her nostrils. She ran faster, the thick soles of her trainers cushioning her ankles and knees on the hard concrete of the footpath. All around her was dark and still. There was hardly any traffic. She ran on, smelling the sea before she saw it. The tide was out. She could taste the salt on her lips and feel the thick black mud that lay just beneath the sandy surface, the way it would ooze through her toes. Soon she saw the shape of the trees beside the DART station. She ran down the hill to the car park and pushed her way through the bushes. It was very quiet here. Ahead she could see something white, fluttering, the tattered remnants of the crime scene tape. She bent down and ducked beneath it. She saw the dark shape where the guards had cleared the undergrowth away from the place where Judith had lain. She sat down on the ground, then lay back, flat, staring up at the sky. There was no moon tonight, but the stars were bright and clear. She rolled over and rubbed her face in the earth.

She thought of the offer that Ursula Beckett had made her. To come and stay for a couple of days, while her husband was away.

'He's going sailing with some of his friends from the yacht club. I don't like being on my own with the kids. The au pair is useless. She's just another kid too. I'll give her the weekend off. Come and stay, it'll be fun. I'd like it.'

'What should I do, Judith?' she whispered. 'Should I do it? Will it be worth it? Will it help?'

She turned on her right side and pressed her ear to the ground. She listened. Then she lay back and looked up again at the stars. She smiled and spoke again. 'Goodbye, Judith, and thank you. For your love and kindness. For your generosity. For helping me choose how I would live my life in the future. Rest now, rest in peace.'

The tears ran from her eyes. She pulled her legs up to her chest and wrapped her arms around them. Deep sobs shuddered from her body as she rocked herself from side to side, listening to the murmur of the sea as slowly the tide crept in across the ridges of sand.

She had planned what she would do when she left prison. Worked it all out. Every step, every move. And now it was working. She was on her way. Soon she would have what she wanted. Soon it would come. She rocked herself some more. She closed her eyes. And saw her future so clearly now in the darkness.

CHAPTER NINETEEN

IT WAS ONLY an hour and a half by train from the centre of London, but it was a landscape unlike anything that Jack had ever seen before. Huge square fields, ten acres at least, densely covered by a grid of wire which was supported at each corner by tall wooden poles and draped with row after dense green row of long vine-like plants. Small brick cottages with tiled roofs the colour of dried blood stood neatly by the railway line, their gardens packed with summer flowers. And every now and then the sea of green was interrupted by what he realized must be oast houses, their conical snouts pointing skywards. So these were hop fields, these strange unnatural structures like giant vineyards. Or was it hop gardens, wasn't that what they were called, he vaguely remembered, thinking of stories of happy cockneys picking hops in their summer holidays or some such thing. He sat back into his seat and clutched a cardboard cup of lukewarm coffee, staring out as field after field whipped past.

It had been a very early start this morning. The six o'clock flight from Dublin to Heathrow, the train to Paddington, the tube to London Bridge, and then another train out through all those commuter towns with quaint English names like Chislehurst, Petts Wood, Orpington and finally to Tunbridge Wells in Kent. He wasn't convinced that it would be worth the effort. But he was intrigued by the phone call he had received yesterday morning. It was from Elizabeth Hill.

'I am phoning you,' she said, 'because I have just read in today's *Irish Times* of the arrest and questioning of a man who, from the description in the paper, I recognize as my ex-husband. And I am absolutely stunned that you would think that he would have had anything to do with my daughter's death. It is inconceivable that he would have harmed her. I cannot understand what you think you are doing.'

He had explained that they had sufficient evidence to arrest him. And they anticipated that they would have a sufficiently strong case with which to charge him. He's definitely, Jack told her, in the frame.

There was silence for a moment.

'You're wrong about this, Mr Donnelly. I don't know what you think you're doing, what kind of logic you're using. I don't even care what evidence you think you have against him. You are absolutely and utterly wrong.'

A sudden pang of anxiety had made his stomach twist, his mouth go dry. She was wrong, of course she was wrong, but why would she rush to defend the man who so obviously hated her? This was the question he pondered as a taxi drove him from the station at Tunbridge Wells, through the narrow lanes, the hop fields towering above them as they passed by, and into the forest where Elizabeth Hill now lived. It was, he thought, like something from one of his daughters' story books. All darkness and mystery, with the sun pushed out of sight by the trees that crowded in on either side of the road. Jack imagined what it must be like at night-time. Pitch black and silent, except for the occasional hoot of an owl. And he smiled at the thought. The kids would love the idea of it.

The taxi slowed and stopped at a five-barred gate.

'I might as well leave you here. It's not much further, just around that bend in the road.' The driver jerked his head in the direction. Jack fumbled in his pocket and pulled out a handful of pound coins. He counted them out and dropped them into the man's upturned palm.

'You a friend of hers from Ireland?' The driver twisted his thick neck around to get a better look at him.

'Yeah, that's right. Do you know her?'

He shrugged, then pulled out his receipt book and began to fill it in. 'Not really, but everyone hereabouts knows who she is. She's the official artist for the nature reserve. She does all kinds of stuff. Calendars, cards, posters. Birds and animals, all very pretty. Not my taste though. I prefer the other kind of birds, if you know what I mean.'

God, Jack thought, bloody taxi drivers.

'So, she lives by herself here, does she? Must be pretty lonely.'

'By herself. You obviously don't know her very well. She's always got a lodger or some such staying.'

And the man sniggered, his jowls shaking. 'She's a bit of a one really. But then you know what artists are like.'

Jack waited until the car had driven off before he began to walk along the lane. His feet made no sound as they scuffed through the fallen pine needles. The air smelt fresh and sharp with the scent of resin. He suddenly felt a long, long way from home. He thought of the drive from the station. How neat and tidy all the hedgerows had been. No tattered plastic bags hanging from the branches of the hazel and wild roses. All the signs on the road were freshly painted, perfectly legible. And there was no litter, no abandoned cars or dumped black plastic sacks oozing with someone else's rubbish. The villages they had passed through had village greens and he had even seen a pond with ducks, and a cricket pitch, with a quaint little wooden pavilion. It was very English, very afternoon tea and cucumber sandwiches. Very different.

Elizabeth Hill's cottage was different too. It was built of old brick, a variety of colours, muted reds, pinks, creamy yellows, and it was half-timbered. The roof was steeply pitched, with tall ornate chimney pots. The windows were small, the panes diamond-shaped, shining in the sunlight, and the top half of the front door was open, fastened back against the wall. He stood and looked inside. It gave directly into what he supposed was her sitting room. It was dark, shadowy, except for the bright spotlight mounted on the ceiling, which shone down on to a drawing board, a sheet of paper, and a woman's fair head bent over her work. He stood outside and watched. She didn't look up. He waited, his hand on the latch.

'Come in,' she said. 'You're late. I was expecting you an hour ago.'

He stood in the middle of the room and looked around him, at the murals that decorated every square inch of wall. Trees grew from the skirting boards upwards, their crowns stretched out across the ceiling. Birds flew from branch to branch and from behind the mass of leaves small faces peeped. Children with large eyes and blonde hair, their hands outstretched. Even the floorboards were decorated, painted with detailed strokes, dense green grass so he could almost feel the softness beneath his feet as he walked towards her.

She was seated on a high stool at the drawing board. She was wearing baggy white cotton trousers and a loose yellow shirt. The sleeves were rolled up to reveal long slender arms covered in small freckles, and as she moved silver bracelets slipped up and down from wrist to elbow, a constant tinkling that sounded like a musical soundtrack accompanying her every gesture. Her small feet were bare. They were also freckled and brown, with high arches and long straight toes. He remembered. He had seen those feet before. She looked like a child, this woman with her ragged fair pageboy and her lithe compact body, but in the brightness of the spotlight he could see the cross-hatch of lines around her eyes, her mouth and across her forehead.

She offered him coffee and homemade scones with rich dark honey.

'It's good,' he said, leaning back into the cushions of the low sofa.

'It's local,' she replied. 'My neighbours on the next farm keep bees.'

There was silence as he munched. He licked his fingers then said, 'You've lived here how long?'

'I left Dublin fourteen years or so ago. I was lucky. I got this job very quickly. I like it here. It's almost my home.'

'Almost?'

'Almost. As much a home as anywhere can be, apart from the place of one's birth.'

'So you think that, do you? That it's not possible to replace one home with another?'

'It's the emigrant's dilemma, isn't it? The yearning for something that's changing all the time. Never being able to be happy with what you have.'

'So do you go back to Dublin often?'

'Don't be so disingenuous, Mr Donnelly. You must know that I don't. You probably also know that when I went back for Judith's funeral, it was my first time since I left.'

'So you didn't return when she got into trouble? When she went to prison.'

'You know that. You know that I didn't. In fact, I wasn't even aware of it at first. Judith didn't choose to tell me. And my husband doesn't keep me up to date on the goings-on with my children. Not since all that nastiness, all those years ago. He's never forgiven me, I'm afraid, for the way I betrayed him. Having an affair was bad enough, but having an affair with a woman was completely beyond the pale.'

'Hold on a minute.' He sat up straight and looked at her. 'Having an affair with who?'

She laughed out loud at the look of surprise on his face.

'You're shocked,' she said. 'You who's seen every-thing. Did no one tell you? I'd have thought they'd all be dying to reveal the true extent of my disgrace.'

And then it was his turn to laugh when he thought about it. How everyone had just said a relationship with a family friend, and he and the others had all made the automatic assumption.

'You see, I'm not only an adulteress, but I'm a lesbian too. Doubly shocking. And my husband had to bear the knowledge that he had been cuckolded by a woman, and, worse still, by someone he knew and liked. Sweet Jenny Bradley. She was married. She and her husband were neighbours of ours. We ran away together. We both left our families, our men and our children. But she went back. She couldn't bear it. She realized she loved them all more than she loved me. But that wasn't the way it was as far as I was concerned. And Mark never, ever forgave me for the disgrace, the public humiliation. That was why our custody battle was so bitter and protracted. That was why I did what I know was a shameful thing and took the children and brought them here.'

'A shameful thing? Was it? It was, I would think, a rather foolish thing. You must have known

that the British police would find them and take them
back.'

She nodded. 'I suppose I did. I don't quite remember what I thought or knew then. But I did know after
that dreadful day when they were, how shall I put it,
"removed from my custody", that I had to let go of
them. That there was no future in this. And in spite
of everything I knew that Mark was a good father. A
better father than I was a mother. He truly loved them.
And their home was with him. So I made a decision
that I would stay away from them. I knew that if I
tried to have access it would be bounded by conditions,
rules, regulations and I couldn't bear all that shit. So I
rationalized it, I decided that when they were older
they could choose. To see me or not to see me.'

'But weren't you worried that your husband's opinion of you, his view of what happened, his influence
would prevail? Surely he would make sure that they
wouldn't want you?'

'That was a risk I was prepared to take. But I know
him. I know him very well. I'd known him since I was
a small girl. We were part of the same world. Both from
Church of Ireland families. We lived in the same part of
Dublin. Our families were friends. We were practically
like brother and sister. I should never have married him.
I knew from the word go it was a mistake. And I also
know this.' She stood up and took a cigarette from a
carved wooden box on the mantelpiece. She lit it, then
sat down once again on her high stool, the light shining
on her face. 'I know he would never, ever do something
like that to Judith. You're so wrong about him.'

'So who would? Tell me that, because we have plenty of evidence, you know.' And he told her then, about the studio, the blood, the tools, the photographs, and watched the colour drain from her face. She stood up and went to the tall cupboard in the corner. She opened it and took out a bottle and two small glasses. She poured. She drank. He hesitated.

'Go on,' she said. 'It's good stuff.'

He sipped warily. It was apple-based, he could smell it in the spirit. She poured herself another glass. He shook his head.

'It's local too,' she said. 'Another neighbour who grows apples for cider makes it. You could call it own-brand Calvados. It's very good for emergencies.'

She turned away, her head bowed. The room was quiet. Somewhere outside he heard the revving of a tractor's engine. Full throttle then dying down to a low rumble. He waited. He looked around him again. There was a desk against the far wall. A computer squatted on it. Ugly and plastic. Unlike anything else in the rest of the room. Above it were a number of photographs, framed. He stood up, glass in hand and walked over to look at them. He recognized them. Judith and Stephen as children. The same pictures that were on the wall in her studio in the house in Rathmines. And other pictures too. A woman with dark hair in a thick fringe. She looked familiar. He looked down at the desk. There was a pile of pages in a plastic-covered folder. And beside it a small print, a painting that he recognized immediately.

'This Caravaggio here. It seems to be a bit of an

obsession with all of you. This is the third time I've come across it since Judith died.'

She lifted her head and wiped her hand across her eyes.

'It's grotesque isn't it? I should get rid of it. I used to admire the way it was painted. That strange mixture of explicit realism with a kind of heightened dream-like quality. But it's the kind of picture you can only enjoy if violence has never touched you. But now, to me, it's pornographic. It glorifies and glories in the act of murder. It celebrates it.' She walked over to the desk. She pointed to the folder. 'Judith's essay. She sent it to me to read. I was impressed. It's an excellent piece of work. But I can't look at that painting any longer. It makes me feel sick.' She picked up the print and tore it into pieces, flinging them into the grate of the fire. She poured herself another measure and drank half of it in one go. She stood beside him, looking at the photographs. 'That's her,' she said, touching the face of the young, dark woman. 'That's my Jenny. She was so beautiful then.'

'And now?'

She smiled. 'Now she's a middle-aged woman with a good haircut and a bad figure. I saw her when I was over. She came to the funeral. She barely acknowledged me. And afterwards, after the service, she had invited everyone back to her house. But it was very obvious that "everyone" didn't include me.'

Of course, now he could place her. The neighbour whose birthday it had been that weekend when Judith was killed. The neighbour to whom Judith had given the flowers.

'Is there anything else you want to know, Mr Donnelly? If not, I'm afraid I'm behind with my work.' She switched on the computer and pulled an upright chair to the desk.

'I'm surprised,' he said, picking up his briefcase and pointing at the screen. 'I thought you were a pencil-and-paper kind of person.'

'Needs must,' she replied, her right hand fiddling with the mouse. 'I use it all the time now. The graphics package is quick and simple. And in spite of myself I have become a fan of the Internet. I can read the Irish papers every day and keep up with what's happening at home. So, Mr Donnelly, I'll be watching what you do, have no fear.'

She walked with him as far as the gate and waited until the taxi came. He thought of the way she had looked when he arrived that morning, almost like a child in her simple clothes and bare feet. Now she looked like an old woman. Her skin was grey and sagging. Her eyes dull. Her movements slow and awkward.

'Please remember what I have said to you about Mark.' She put her hand on his arm. 'I'm asking you to take it seriously. I do not believe that he killed Judith. Please do not carry on with this line of investigation. Nothing good will come of it. He has suffered enough through the years. Please don't add to his suffering.'

*

He was exhausted by the time he got to the airport. He just wanted to get back to Dublin, find himself a quiet corner in a quiet pub, and get stuck into a couple of pints. But the plane was delayed. First of all for half an hour and then for a further forty minutes. He sat at the bar and nursed a drink. All around him he could hear Irish voices. Comforting, familiar sounds. You're a dreadful wimp, he said to himself. A day away from home and you're a mess. No sense of adventure at all. And then he heard his name being called. He turned around and recognized the small blonde woman behind him.

She had been in London for two days for a conference on fostering, she said. It was very dull, no fun at all.

'Here,' he patted the stool beside him, 'take a pew. What're you drinking?'

They had met a number of times before, he thought. Always with Andy Bowen. In fact he seemed to remember that once he had thought there might be something happening between them. But Andy had said no and laughed at the thought. Not Alison, he had said. She's far too bloody upright and principled to have anything to do with a married man. And added, sourly, 'More's the pity.'

He waited for the inevitable questions about the murder, about the arrest, about the investigation. But they didn't come. Instead she talked about her garden.

'It's ridiculous,' she said. 'I've been away for three days and all I can think about is the greenfly on the roses and whether or not the loganberries will have ripened enough to eat. And I planted a couple of silver birches last week, and I hope the next-door neighbour's kid will have watered them for me like I paid him to do.' She laughed, her round face dimpling. 'Since I moved into this house in Sandymount last year I've become a complete gardening bore. I'm like someone who's just had a baby. I've only one topic of conversation.'

'That's what I need,' he said, offering her peanuts. 'A hobby. Something to take my mind off work.'

'Yeah,' she said, between crunches. 'Yeah, I used to be obsessed with my job. Couldn't stop thinking about it, talking about it too. All the kids, the ones whose fostering I supervise, they were like my kids. I was always on call for them. They used to ring me up night and day. Bothering me, badgering me. And then the parents. Christ, they were worse. And there was me, muggins, stuck right in the middle.'

'And was Amy Beckett like that? She's one of yours isn't she?'

'Ah, Andy's been talking, I see.' She shook another handful from the bag. 'Actually, I've never had any bother from her or with her. She was dead lucky with her foster-family. They're a very nice bunch and they all hit it off right from the start. Which was a good thing, because I can tell you, you wouldn't want to get on the wrong side of that kid. She's tough. Single-minded. Focused. All that and more.'

'Like her father, that's what she sounds like.'

'Yeah.' Alison, looked at him. 'Of course, you knew him, I suppose. I never had the pleasure.'

Jack reached over and took the bag of peanuts from her, tipping it up and gesturing in mock horror that it was empty.

'Sorry.' She smiled. 'Here, let's have some more. I'm starving.'

'And let's do ourselves a favour,' he said as he waved to the barman for another round. 'Let's not talk about anything remotely connected with work. I'm sick of it and I'm sorry for raising it. Give me some nuts and tell me again about your garden.'

She kept him entertained until they were called for take-off. He was surprised by her. She didn't seem to square somehow with the way Andy had described her. He watched her fair head during the flight and fell into step beside her as they moved through the arrivals area at Dublin airport.

'No luggage,' she said, pointing to her neat little bag on wheels. And when they emerged into the twilight outside it made sense for him to offer her a lift. And even more sense for her to ask him in for something to eat, and maybe something nice to drink.

'You put me to shame,' he said as he wandered around her large, beautiful sitting room. 'How do you manage to make it all look so perfect?'

'It's love,' she said. 'I fell in love with the house two years ago. It was a mess, practically derelict. It's taken me this long to get it even half right.'

The rooms on the ground floor were painted with bright jewel-like colours. Mossy greens and deep blues. The kitchen was vivid yellow. He thought of his flat.

White walls. No decoration. And of the house in which he had lived with Joan for all those years. She had nagged and pleaded, cursed and threatened. And he had never given in. He would do nothing to it. Now he sat and watched Alison as she prepared a meal. Making a tomato sauce for pasta. Slicing red peppers and breaking up pieces of feta cheese to go with a crisp lettuce for the salad. Her movements were neat and precise.

'Here.' She turned towards him, a bottle and a corkscrew in her hands. 'Man's work.'

He sniffed the cork. 'Mmm, that smells good.'

She took the bottle from him and poured.

'Not half as good as it tastes,' she said, and lifted her glass. He looked at her neck as she swallowed. It was long and white. He suddenly wanted to catch hold of her skin with his teeth. He could feel himself blushing as he thought about it. He lifted his own glass and drank. The wine was rich and fruity, with a slightly acid aftertaste. She watched him.

'Nice,' he said. 'What is it?'

'Guelbenzu. One of those Spanish vineyards that have suddenly got really good.'

'Oh, you know about wine, do you?'

She smiled and refilled their glasses. 'Only so I get to drink the good ones. That's all. Like this.'

'You like good things, don't you? Good food, good wine.'

She took a step towards him. She put her hand on his shoulder. He could see the shape of her breasts through her white shirt.

'Yes, I do. I like to be satisfied. I like to enjoy myself.'

He put his hand on her shoulder, then ran the tips of his fingers along her collarbone and rested them in the hollow at the base of her neck. She swallowed and he felt his fingers rise and fall with the movement. When she spoke he could feel the vibration from her larynx.

'I've often wondered about you, Jack. Andy would never say much. He's too discreet. But I did hear that you're separated now. Is that right?'

'That's right,' he said. He took another swallow of wine. He leaned forward and kissed her on the cheek. She moved her face so her mouth was on his. He kissed her again and felt her lips open.

She pulled away from him and reached out to turn off the gas burner. 'We'll eat later,' she said.

CHAPTER TWENTY

HAD SHE EVER seen such a sunset before? She couldn't remember that she had. She sat on the terrace outside the house and looked out to sea. The dark blue of the horizon lay before her, twelve miles out, and above it the pale blue of the sky streaked with clouds that were coloured improbable shades of pink and orange and gold. She sat and watched until the view before her was refracted and distorted by the tears that filled her eyes. So this was how it had been during all those years when she was locked away from the world. Evening after evening Daniel Beckett and his wife had sat here, on this bench, at this table, and looked out on the beauty that lay before her now. And she had not known.

She lifted her drink and smelt it. The sweetness of the gin, the astringency of the tonic and the tart bitterness of the wedge of lemon. She swirled it around, watching bubbles rise in long beaded strings to the surface, hearing the musical tinkling of the ice, and then she drank. She was getting better about alcohol. Those first few weeks after she came out of prison she had found it terrifying. The way her body ceased to be her own. The way her voice thickened and slurred. The surge of emotion, elation, well-being, excitement that rushed over her, carrying her along like a wave pounding up the beach, then dumping her in a miserable heap at the tideline.

But now she was more measured in her attitude. She drank and felt the coldness slither down her throat and a flush rise in her cheeks. Today had been near perfect. And tonight was going to be even better.

She stood up and walked to the doors that led into the long bright living room. She paused and listened. There was music playing, Frank Sinatra singing. And from the kitchen next door another voice singing along with him. She called out.

'Ursula, do you need help? Is there anything I can do?'

Ursula appeared at the door. She pushed a couple of strands of hair back from her face and wiped her hands on her striped apron.

'No.' She smiled. 'You've done plenty. Getting the kids into bed is quite enough for any adult to do in one night. Here,' she held out the bottle of gin, 'have a refill.'

She had played with the children, hide-and-seek in the garden. They had shown her all their special secret places. The garden shed with the lock that was broken. The plastic polytunnel in which they sheltered on rainy days. The three huge compost bins. One full with a dark crumbly mixture, one stuffed with garden and kitchen waste, and the third empty, big enough to scramble into, with a lid that was easy to open and close down again. There was a platform built into the sturdy branches of an oak tree, and a rope ladder to climb up into it. Just enough room for an adult, a small adult. And a great view in through the bedroom windows of the house. And all the little pathways and tunnels through the dense bracken, the gorse and the pines on the clifftop.

'We're not really supposed to play outside the garden fence,' Jonathan confided. 'They're worried that we might fall down on to the railway line or on to the rocks. They think we're stupid.'

'Yes.' Laura nodded her head up and down, stretching out her chin as far as it would go, then touching it to the buttons of her blouse. 'Stoopid, they think we're stoopid. But we're not, are we?'

'No.' Rachel kissed her. 'No, you're not stupid, either of you. You're clever. Now. Show me some more. Show me some really amazing hiding places, where no one would ever think of looking for you.'

They had taken her around the side of the house, sneaked, fingers to lips, past the glass door that opened into the kitchen, and slid back the door into the garage.

'Look.' The boy pointed with his toe to the boards that lay neatly fitted together in a slight indentation in the floor. 'That's a good one.'

'But we're not allowed to get into it. Daddy says it's dangerous.' Laura looked anxious.

'What is it?' Rachel bent down to have a better look.

'It's for, you know . . .' Jonathan put his hands on

his hips and assumed a look of manly importance. 'It's for fixing things. When there's something underneath the car that's broken. Daddy does it sometimes. He likes fixing it himself.'

Rachel reached down and prised one of the boards apart from its neighbour. An inspection pit, of course. Daniel had always been good with mechanical things. Good at taking engines, clocks, sewing machines, transistor radios apart, and carefully putting them back together again.

She put her hands on each of the children's shoulders and said, 'I don't think you should hide there. I think your daddy's right on this one. It's probably very oily and smelly down there too.'

'And very dark.' Laura's face was crumpling.

'But dark is nice,' Rachel said, bending down and looking into her face. 'Dark isn't scary, dark keeps you safe.'

She sat beside her bed and watched her. Watched the way her jaws gripped her thumb, her small cheeks quivering as she sucked and sucked, and then as she drifted deeper and deeper into sleep, relaxed and let go, so her thumb dropped from her mouth, wet and glistening, a smear of saliva leaving a silvery snail's trail across her chin. Rachel lifted a corner of the sheet and wiped it away. She stroked the child's soft dark hair and kissed her once more, resting her lips against her cheek. Then she stood up and walked away.

Ursula had decided they would eat outside. Make the most of the fine evening. Enjoy it while they could.

'Here.' She handed Rachel a corkscrew. 'You do the honours.'

It was one of those wooden ones, with a long curling spike, and a top and a bottom section which were supposed to twist against each other and pull the cork effortlessly from the neck of the bottle. Rachel tried to make it work. She could feel Ursula watching her. She was getting anxious, impatient. The food was waiting, the large bowls of chowder beginning to cool.

'I'm sorry.' Rachel looked over to her. 'I can't get the hang of this. I've never come across one like this before. You do it. I'll get the rest of the food from the kitchen.'

There were rolls, warm from the oven to go with the soup, and homemade hamburgers. She had watched Ursula knead with her hands the mince meat with onion and parsley, and bind it together with the large orange yolk of an egg, and felt sick. But cooked, seared black on the outside they didn't seem so bad. She had made chips, French fries she called them, thin sticks of potato, crisp and salty. And there was a salad, lettuce, tomato, chives. 'All from the garden here,' she said with pride in her voice. And a bowl of mayonnaise and jars of mustard and pickles of every variety.

They ate in silence. It was good. It was delicious. She watched Ursula. She was greedy. Cramming her mouth with food. Opening it wide so Rachel could see its contents, then lifting her glass and swilling wine into it. Rachel felt her stomach heave. She pushed away her plate.

'That was a truly a feast. Thank you.'

'You're not finished? There's homemade apple pie, and ice cream. And cream too, if you'd like. Come on, Rachel, I don't often do this. I'd never fit into my clothes if I ate like this too often. But I thought we'd have a treat tonight. You look like you could do with one. Here, give me the corkscrew. I'll open another bottle.'

Rachel watched her hands, the way she tore the foil from around the cork. It was sharp. She had cut herself. A small line of red appeared on her fingertip. But she didn't seem to notice. She stood up to pour, and swayed, slopping wine on to the tablecloth, drops spattering her white trousers.

'Shit.' She began to laugh. 'I knew I'd do that. I'll just go and get a cloth.' The phone inside began to ring. 'You get it, Rachel, will you? If it's Dan tell him I'm busy. Tell him I'm fine. Tell him I love him.'

There were phones everywhere. She had noticed that already. Every room seemed to have at least one. She passed by the red handset in the sitting room. She walked out to the hall. She closed the door. She lifted the receiver. She listened. She spoke. She put the receiver down, then lifted it again, listened and laid it beside the phone. She backed away and out, hearing the sound of water running in the kitchen.

'Who was it?' Ursula's voice was loud, too loud.

'It was nothing. It was a wrong number.'

It was getting late. It was getting dark.

'You get the dessert, Rachel. It's all in the fridge.

And there's a bottle of Baileys on the sideboard. Let's have some of that too. I love it.'

She poured the liqueur carefully into two glasses. She looked over her shoulder out on to the terrace. Ursula had lit candles and an outside lamp, which hung from a bracket on the wall. The light flickered over her as she leaned back in her chair, her eyes drooping. This would be easy, Rachel thought. She put her hand in her pocket and pulled out a plastic pill bottle. She opened it. She took two of the red capsules from within. She carefully pulled apart their plastic shells and poured the fine white powder into one of the glasses. She looked over her shoulder again. Ursula had got up and had walked to the edge of the terrace. She was swaying gently from side to side. Rachel picked up a teaspoon and stirred until the powder had dissolved. She bent her head to the glass and breathed in deeply. All she could smell was cream and coffee and alcohol. She walked outside and handed Ursula a glass. She watched her bend her head over it.

'Wow,' she said, 'that smells good.'

She was asleep before she had finished it. Her head slumped forward on to the table. Rachel sat and watched her. She didn't look so perfect now, with her stained trousers, her slack face, her mouth open, snores pouring loudly from it. She thought of Daniel's voice, how it had sounded on the phone. She hadn't heard it since that day in court. When he had denied her and turned away from her. When he had betrayed her.

'Hi, babe,' he said, then when there was no response

he spoke again. 'Is that you, Ursula, how are you, love?' And then when she didn't reply he spoke again. 'How's things, how're the kids, how are you getting on with your lame duck lady? Having fun?'

'Who's that?' She spoke in a voice that didn't belong to her. 'You've a wrong number.' Then she hung up.

He would have tried again, but he would have got an engaged signal. And then he'd have stopped trying. He'd ring again in the morning. But in the morning his wife would remember nothing of this night.

Rachel got to her feet. She walked around the table and hauled Ursula to standing. 'Come on,' she said. 'It's bedtime.'

Ursula's eyes flopped open, then closed again as her body sagged. Rachel half carried, half dragged her into the sitting room. She laid her down on the long sofa. She undressed her. She went to the cupboard in the hall and found a blanket. She wrapped her in it. She stood and looked down at her. Sleeping like a baby. Sleeping like her children upstairs. And now, thought Rachel, the house is mine. She picked up her glass. She turned to the long mirror that covered one wall. She saluted herself. She drank.

It was morning when she woke. It was the cry of a baby that woke her, insistent, getting louder and more demanding all the time, and a tug on the bedclothes, and the girl's voice in her ear, calling to her.

'Wake up, peaches lady, please wake up. The baby's

hungry and he's soaking wet and I don't know where Mummy is.'

She lay on her side, the sunshine turning the bright yellow of the curtains to cream. She lifted her head. Laura was standing, balancing her small brother on her knee. His face was scarlet, a mixture of tears and phlegm running down his fat cheeks. He sobbed and gasped, frantic with hunger. He smelt of ammonia. She pushed back the bedclothes and stood up.

'Here.' She reached over and took hold of him. 'Mummy's asleep downstairs. Don't disturb her. Show me where his nappies are kept.'

It was all so simple and natural. So familiar. She laid him down on the bathroom floor on a towel, stripping off his soaking Babygro. She washed him, powdered him, fastened on his clean nappy. She found him a terry-cloth suit. She wiped his face and kissed him.

'And now,' she said to Laura and Jonathan who had joined them, 'who'd like breakfast?'

The kitchen downstairs was spotless. She had washed up, cleaned up, left everything ready for the morning. She put the baby in his highchair and heated him a bottle. She poured cereal into bowls and put slices of bread into the toaster. She handed the older children glasses of orange juice and made a pot of coffee. Soon all was peace and harmony. And then they heard a noise coming from the sitting room.

'What's that?' she asked.

'That's Mummy,' the boy replied. 'She slept on the sofa last night. I think she's being sick.'

She left the children eating and walked through. Ursula was sitting up. Her face was ashen. The sour smell of vomit filled the room. Rachel stood and looked at her. Ursula covered her face with her hands.

'What happened?' she asked.

'You don't remember?'

There was silence.

'I think,' said Rachel, slowly, 'that you had a mite too much to drink. You passed out here, so I thought it best to leave you.'

'And this, how did I get like this?' She looked down at herself, clutching the blanket tightly.

'Ah, you don't remember that, no?'

A shake of the head.

'You wanted to dance. And then you wanted to strip. There was no stopping you.'

Tears began to drip down Ursula's wretched face. For a moment Rachel almost felt sorry for her.

'And don't worry,' Rachel said. 'What you said to me last night. That's between us. All right?'

Ursula's face reddened. She looked away, then back up at Rachel.

'The children?' she said.

'They're fine. I've changed the baby and fed him and the other two are having breakfast. Don't worry about them. Look.' She sat down beside her and took her hand. 'Look, it was just a bit of fun. I didn't mind. I'll tell you what. You go upstairs, have a bath, then go to bed. I'll stay and mind the kids for the day until you're feeling better. How does that sound?'

She brought her a tray upstairs to her bedroom. A cup of tea and some toast.

'Ugh.' Ursula made a face as she drank. 'I don't take sugar.'

'Drink it,' Rachel said. 'Sweet tea is just what you need for a hangover. My father used to swear by it.'

Tea with sugar and two more sleeping pills. That would keep her quiet for the day. She watched her sink back against the pillows.

'I'll take them for a walk, shall I?'

Ursula smiled sleepily. 'Take the car if you like. You're so kind, so thoughtful. I really appreciate this. And I am sorry.'

Rachel stood in the doorway of the bedroom and watched as her eyes closed. It was a beautiful room, this room where she had slept last night, with long windows that looked out across the garden to the clifftop and the sea beyond. It was a room full of secrets. The safe under the carpet in the corner. The jewellery box in the top of the wardrobe. The diary in the top drawer of the little ornamental desk. They always said it, the girls inside. You'd be amazed the way people write things down. The PIN number for their bank cards. The code for their alarms. The combination lock for their safe. She knew them all now. As she knew the house, inside out. She had gone up to the room in the bell tower last night. Daniel's room. She had switched on the lamp and sat at his desk and looked at the row of photographs on the shelf. She had looked for traces of her own life and found them. The picture of Martin in a silver frame. Taken by Daniel, using her camera, one summer's day before they got married, in the back garden of his parents' house. She turned the frame over and pushed away the little clips that held it in place. She laid the glass and cardboard backing down on the desk and pulled out the photograph. Half of it had been folded over, hidden from view. It was the half that showed her. Martin was sitting in a deckchair. He had taken off his shirt. His skin was pale. She was sitting on the grass, looking up at him. She looked so young and pretty. She looked up now and saw her reflection in the dark of the window. She looked down again and pondered, weighing it up, wondering what she should do. And then with a sigh, she folded it back again, and again reassembled the frame and replaced it on the shelf, exactly where it had been before.

She had found the attic room too. The children had shown her the little staircase and the small door at the top.

'It's locked,' Jonathan said. 'We're not allowed up there. It's where Santa keeps our Christmas presents.'

But she had taken the bunch of keys that Ursula had left on the kitchen table and found the right one. Opened the door and stepped inside, bending down her head. Felt for the light switch. Seen that the room was empty, apart from a camp bed in the corner, a sleeping bag, a pile of boxes. Closed the door and locked it.

And now she was driving Ursula's car. Trying to remember. What should she do with her feet and her hands? How to coordinate them, move them in tandem. Remember to use the rear-view mirror, remember to indicate, snatching at the wheel as she rounded a bend so the car slewed out over the white line. And the boy in the passenger seat beside her lifted his head from his Game Boy, sighed and said, 'We do have power steering, you know. This is a top-of-the-range Saab. Latest model. It was very expensive.'

She smiled at him as she said, 'Thanks, Jonathan, I'm not very good with cars.'

They effortlessly climbed the hill to the village, and she thought of the times she had panted up the same stretch, always the only person on foot, everyone who passed her by driving cars just like this one.

They stopped at the top. She parked carefully, conscious of the boy's knowing glance as her foot slipped from the clutch as she reversed, so the car shuddered to a stop. But there were ice creams to be bought, then eaten, a distraction for a while as she drove down the other side of the hill to the nearest shopping centre. This time she managed to ease the car into a parking space without mishap. She took the keys from the ignition and said to Jonathan in the front, Laura and the baby in the back, 'Now you stay here. I won't be a minute and when I come back where would you like to go? To the beach, to the amusements? You decide.'

She walked quickly along the row of shops until she found what she wanted. The key cutters in the little kiosk at the end. She handed over the whole bunch. House keys, car keys, keys to the garage, keys to the safe. She waited. She took the copies and put them carefully in her pocket. She walked back to the car. Caught sight of herself in the wing mirror. Pushed her hair back from her face. Smiled. Saw the children's faces light up as she opened the door and took control once again.

It was mid-afternoon when she drove them back. They were tired. They had worn themselves out on the dodgems, the carousel, the pin-ball machines and computer games. She drove slowly and carefully. They didn't seem to notice where they were going. She turned into the quiet cul-de-sac and drove around the green, looking for the house she wanted. She stopped the car.

'Now,' she said, 'Laura, I want you to come with me, just for a little while. Jonathan, you stay here and mind the baby. OK?' She had expected complaint but he just nodded his head and reached out to fiddle with the radio. She took Laura's hand and they walked to the front door. Her heart thumped beneath her ribs. She pressed the bell. She heard footsteps and saw the shape of a woman through the frosted-glass panel.

'Can I help you?' She was barefoot, wearing a loose flowered dress. She must have been in the garden, Rachel thought, looking at the woman's hands in their heavy rubber gloves.

'I'm sorry to bother you, but I was wondering. I used to live in this house a number of years ago. I've been away for a long time and I was just curious. Would you mind if I had a quick look around?'

She was kind, she was polite. She stood back and let them in. Rachel looked down the hall towards the kitchen.

'Go ahead,' the woman said. 'It's a bit of a mess. Sunday, you know?'

Rachel walked with Laura into the sitting room. She could feel the sweat breaking out on her fore-head, on her back. She looked towards the garden, towards the conservatory. She put her hand up to her mouth.

'It's gone,' she said. 'It's all different.'

'Yes.' The woman bent down and picked up a pair of runners and a baseball cap from the shiny parquet floor. 'Yes, I think it's changed a lot over the years. It had a bit of a history, this house. Did you know about it? Was it before your time?'

'A history?'

'Someone was murdered here. Oh, ages and ages ago. But a lot of work was done to the house after-wards. Not by us, but by the people who bought it next. We got it cheap, in fact, because of that. We used to get a lot of people coming just to have a gawk. Because of what had happened.'

Rachel walked to the door to the garden. It was all gone. Her careful planting, her pond, her border. Now there was just a lawn with a gang of boys playing football on it. She felt Laura's hand clutching her jacket and heard her begin to whimper. She bent down and picked her up.

'She's tired,' she said. 'She's had a long day.'

'She's lovely. I've always wanted a daughter, but it's

boys all the way with me.' She patted her round stomach. 'This one too, another little David Beckham.'

Rachel smiled and stroked Laura's silky hair.

'Her older sister was a baby here. Her room was upstairs. Can I show her?'

'Of course, why not? Just don't mind the mess.'

She took her time, walking from room to room, explaining it all to the child, who rested now sleepily on her shoulder. The woman was waiting for her at the bottom of the stairs.

'Thank you,' Rachel said, 'you've been very kind. I appreciate this. It means a lot to me.'

'Does it? I'm surprised.' The woman's expression was curious. 'I wouldn't have thought you would want to come back. After what you did.'

Rachel looked at her. She tried to speak, but no words would come.

'You're her, aren't you? I thought it was you as soon as I saw you. Revisiting the scene of the crime, is that it? I'm amazed. I thought they only did that in the movies.'

Rachel put her hand on the latch.

'It's OK. I don't mind. I'm just surprised, that's all. I thought you were in prison.'

'Please.' Rachel put out her hand. 'Please, don't say anything else.'

The woman smiled. 'You'd better go. My husband wouldn't be so keen on you being here. But me, well,' she shrugged her shoulders, 'it was a long time ago. Live and let live, that's what I say. But the child, she's hardly yours, is she?'

It wasn't far from the quiet cul-de-sac to the house on the cliff. Three or four miles, that was all. She drove quickly down the hill from the village. The tyres squeaked on the hot surface of the road. The baby had fallen asleep, and he rocked from side to side in his chair. Laura was drowsing beside him. Jonathan's eyes were closed. There was a bend in the road. Beyond it she could see the bracken and gorse of the cliff and the sea beyond. She put her foot on the accelerator. The car shot forward. Jonathan's eyes opened. He sat up.

'Fast,' he said. 'It's too fast. Slow down.'

The house was silent as she carefully carried the sleeping baby to his cot and laid him down. She paused at Ursula's bedroom door and looked in. She too was fast asleep. She heard the television go on downstairs and then the phone ring. She could hear Jonathan's voice as she walked past the sitting-room door.

'Yes, Daddy, we've all been out with the lady. Mummy's sick. She's got a bad headache. She's in bed. Are you coming home soon? Good. Bye.'

'What did he say?' She felt her heart begin to beat faster.

'He's on his way. He'll be here in an hour.'

She put the keys back on the ring by the kitchen door. She looked around once more. Everything was as it had been. She made the children sandwiches and brought them glasses of milk.

'I'm going now. I'll see you again.'

They lifted their heads and looked at her. Laura stood up. She walked over to her and put her arms up. Rachel bent down and kissed her.

'Bye-bye, my little girl. See you soon.'

She walked quickly across the lawn towards the clifftop. It would be easier to leave this way. She didn't want to risk meeting his car on the road. She felt the keys jingle in her pocket as she moved. And she thought of all she had left behind. Fingerprints on every imaginable surface. Hairs on the pillows and the mattress of the bed where Daniel and Ursula slept and a pair of bead earrings hidden in the dust beneath it. Fibres from her clothes left on the furniture and a button from her jacket underneath the cushions on the sofa. Everything was in place. Everything was ready. And soon she would be too.

CHAPTER TWENTY-ONE

NOW THERE WAS another map pinned up beside the first one above her bed. Rachel had drawn it herself, when she got back from the house on the cliff. The house named Spindrift. The spray that blows along the surface of the sea. Whipped up by the wind, twisting and turning, a layer of white that obscures the tops of the waves, making it impossible to see their height. But now she could see everything in her mind's eye. She had sat down with a large sheet of paper, a pencil and a ruler, and she had drawn it all out. The plan of the house, floor by floor. Put in all the rooms, the windows, the doors. Marked out the boundary to the garden and coloured it with different pens. The vegetable patch, the herbaceous border, the lawn, the trees. Then put in the family. Drew the figures, stick-like, but recognizable. Daniel with his dark hair and beard. Ursula with her long fair plait. And the children. Finished it off and sat back to admire it. Then stuck it up beside the other one. It was good. It was done.

And now there was something else she must do. She must meet her daughter once more. This time she had gone through the proper channels. She had asked

Andrew Bowen to arrange it. He had spoken to Amy's social worker. They had agreed between themselves. Rachel and Amy would meet in what they called a neutral venue, as they had so many times in the past, when she was still in prison. She would have liked it if, just once, they could have met in the open air. Perhaps at the end of the west pier, where the huge blocks of granite, which kept the sea at bay, were warmed by the sun. Or even in the one of the city's parks. St Stephen's Green where Rachel used to take her when she was small to feed the clamouring mallards. Or Merrion Square to sit on the grass between the formal beds, bright with fleshy begonias. Or best of all in the Iveagh Gardens, hidden behind the long grey buildings of the Concert Hall and the National University, overgrown and wild, its statuary half broken, fallen down among the shrubbery. A place she used to visit, when she was a student, to lie in the sun and dream.

But it was not to be. Andrew Bowen had told her. She was to go to the headquarters of the Probation and Welfare Service.

'They're in Smithfield, where the old cattle market used to be. But you wouldn't recognize the place now, it has so many fancy new buildings. Do you remember how to get there? Would you like me to come with you, or would you prefer to go on your own?'

She had chosen to go by herself. To walk up the Quays, passing with sudden dread the Four Courts, feeling the heavy bulk of the pillared building, with its green copper dome, leaning over towards her, threatening to topple into her path. She remembered those two weeks, twelve years ago, walking in from the street every morning, pushing through the crowds of reporters and photographers, who squawked at her. 'Look here, Rachel. Give us a smile, Rachel. How's it going, Rachel? What do you have to say, Rachel?'

With her father by her side, his face tightening, despair cutting deep grooves in the flesh of his forehead, in the space between his eyebrows and on either side of his mouth. And making his eyes hooded and blank. And on the last day, Amy in her arms as she tried to find a way to bring her into the Round Hall, looking for the entrance at the side of the building, through the swing doors where the barristers passed, hearing the sudden shout as one of the photographers saw her and called out to his friends: 'Here, look, she's here, with the kid.'

And then when the jury had delivered their verdict, she had been so sorry that she had brought her. It had been selfish and foolish. Not the sort of thing that a decent, proper mother does, to expose her child in that manner. How could she have done it? The desire to see her child before she was sent away, that was understandable, wasn't it? Any mother would have felt like that, wouldn't she?

She had begun to doubt herself immediately. And now she had no sense of her own rightness. Had she ever had any real maternal instinct? Was there such a thing, she wondered as she turned away from the river, towards the large cobbled square, and stopped to look at the row of modern office buildings where once had been an uneven, irregular skyline of houses, shops and pubs. And why was she choosing now of all times to test it? Why had she asked to see Amy, when Amy had made it so plain that she did not want her back in her life? She walked across the open space and leaned against the railings. She closed her eyes and turned her face up towards the sun, calming for a moment the sense of panic that was beginning to take hold of her body. All she wanted, she thought, was to be in the same room with her. No, she corrected herself, that wasn't strictly true. She wanted more. She wanted to stand close, put her arms around her, fold her young supple body into her own. Lean her cheek against the soft skin of her daughter's cheek. Breathe in her warm scent. Soap and newly washed hair and that indescribable smell of child. Feel the weight of her daughter's head as she let it droop on to her shoulder. Whisper in her ear that she, Rachel, was in spite of everything still her mother. That she, Amy, was after all that had happened, still her daughter. That they were bound together by the nine months that Amy had spent inside her mother's body. By the five years of nurturing and loving that they had spent together. And as she stood with her face to the sun, her eyes closed, she could feel her lips part in a sudden involuntary smile.

She opened her eyes and looked around, blinking rapidly, dazzled for a moment by the brightness that flooded in and saw the car that had stopped outside the largest of the buildings. The one with the long plate-glass windows at street level and the lettering across its glass doors. Department of Justice. Probation and

Welfare Service. She stood up. A man and woman were seated in the front. The girl was in the back. She watched as the woman got out of the passenger seat and held open the door behind her. She saw her daughter, close-cropped black hair, row of earrings in her right lobe, tight jeans, short top which revealed a tanned stomach, runners with thick wedge soles and a cigarette dangling between the fingers of one hand. She watched as the woman put an arm around her shoulders for a moment, squeezed her tightly and kissed her quickly on her cheek. Saw the expression on her daughter's face. The resentment that twisted her features so she looked sulky, angry, unattractive. She flung the cigarette down on the footpath and ground it with her toe, before dragging open the heavy glass doors and slamming them behind her. The woman turned back to the car, shrugging her shoulders, an expression of hurt resignation on her face. She saw Rachel, stared at her for a moment, a grimace of distaste tightening her mouth into a narrow line, then opened the car door and got inside. As they moved slowly away, the tyres reverberating over the cobbles, their two faces peered out at her. And then they were gone.

It was a bright room, the one into which she was shown. Its large windows faced west, and the rays of the afternoon sun lit up the specks of dust that floated above the long polished table. Rachel stood by herself just inside the door and waited. Amy was seated in a chair in the corner. A small blonde woman was standing beside her. Her hand was on Amy's shoulder. She smiled at Rachel and began to speak. She introduced herself. Her name, she said, was Alison White. She was Amy's social worker. Perhaps Rachel remembered her? They had met once or twice before, some years ago.

Rachel nodded, then said softly, 'It was twice, we met twice.'

The woman smiled and looked down at the note-book in her hand. Then she continued. This was, she said, a difficult occasion. As they all knew, Amy had been very reluctant to meet with her mother since she was released from prison. And of course Rachel hadn't made things any better by attempting to see Amy in what could best be described as an ad-hoc manner. Amy had been very upset by this and had felt threat-ened by Rachel's behaviour, which was, the woman said, unacceptable. However, Rachel had obviously learned from her mistake, and this time she had put her request through the proper channels.

Rachel looked towards where Amy was sitting. As Amy felt her gaze fall upon her, she shifted in her seat, twisting her upper body so her head was turned completely away. An awkward position, uncomfortable for any length of time, hard to maintain. Rachel could see the bones, the knobs of the vertebrae at the back of her neck, stand out in the space between her hair-line and the stretchy material of her lipstick-pink blouse.

'It is my opinion,' the woman said, 'that it would be a good thing if Amy was to re-establish some kind of contact with her natural mother. Although Amy is extremely fond of and close to her foster-mother, and the rest of her foster-family who have made huge efforts to care for her in every possible way, still the natural bond between birth mother and child cannot be ignored, and in my experience there always comes a time when it reasserts itself.'

She paused.

'And it is my experience that it is better if this can be handled properly, that guidance can be given to both mother and child to see them through this difficult period of adjustment. And now, before I leave you two alone, shall I pour the tea?'

She pointed to the tray with a metal teapot, milk jug, sugar bowl, two cups and saucers and a plate of chocolate biscuits, which was sitting in the middle of the table.

It tasted the way all institutional tea tasted. Stale and stewed, bitter and brackish. Rachel drank, forcing the liquid into her stomach. She put down her cup. She looked across the table at Amy. The girl had disdained the drink that Alison White had offered. Instead she had pulled out a packet of cigarettes and lit up, despite the no-smoking signs stuck on the back of the door. But then she obviously wasn't the first to smoke here in this room, Rachel thought, looking at the large round ashtray that Amy had dragged from its place on the table to a position from where she could comfortably flick her ash.

'Well, I'll go now. I'll be next door if you want me.' Alison White looked at her watch. 'You have an hour or so before this room is needed. But if you want longer there are other rooms down the corridor.' She smiled, a look of apprehension flickering across her pretty face, just for a moment, then she backed away.

The door clicked loudly behind her. Rachel sat down. She leaned across and picked up the teapot. It was heavy. She could feel her wrist bending, as if at any moment it would give way. The brown liquid gushed from the metal spout, splashing into both cup and saucer and casting drops in an arc on the table. She put the pot back on the tray and felt in her jeans pocket for a tissue, hastily wiping up the spilt tea. She scrunched the soggy paper up into a ball and leaned over towards the ashtray.

'Do you mind?' she said, and dropped it in.

Amy shrugged and drew heavily on her cigarette. Rachel watched the yellow-tinged smoke as the girl funnelled it out of her mouth, her lips forming a tight 'o' as she blew neat little smoke rings, which floated slowly up towards the ceiling tiles.

'Not bad,' Rachel said. 'Not bad at all. Some of the women I was in prison with could blow the most amazing shapes. Circles within circles within circles. They were absolute experts at it.'

'So?'

'So, nothing, nothing in particular. I could never do it, that's all. Even when I was a heavy smoker, before I got pregnant with you, of course, when I was a student. When smoking seemed to be the coolest thing in the world.'

There was silence. Rachel leaned across the table and picked up the plate of biscuits. She held them out.

'Would you like one? They're chocolate digestives. You used to love them when you were little. You couldn't get enough of them. I used to have to pretend they were all gone, otherwise you'd have driven me mad trying to get at them.'

All gone, all gone, Amy.

All gone, all gone, Mumma. Bikkys all gone.

Amy stared at her blankly, then took another cigarette from her packet and lit it from the butt of the first.

'Lying to me even then, were you? Not telling me the truth, the whole truth and nothing but the truth, so help you God.'

'Sorry?' Rachel started back, feeling suddenly cold here in this warm sunny room.

'Sorry. Are you?' For the first time Amy looked at her. Directly. Meeting her eye, holding her gaze.

'I am sorry, of course I'm sorry. I'm so sorry about everything that has happened between us. To you and to me. To us. And I want an opportunity to try to put things right.'

'Put things right. I see. And how do you propose to do that?' Amy leaned back in her chair, crossing one leg over the other and resting the tips of her runners on the tabletop. She began to push herself backwards and forwards.

Rachel cleared her throat. She thought of the words that she had practised, rehearsed. All the things she had wanted to say. The explanations, the reasons, the justifications. It had seemed so simple and straight-forward, all those nights when she had lain in her bed in her room in Clarinda Park, looking at the map on the wall beside her. Remembering. And Amy's reaction had been so wonderful. She had heard her return the words of love and sorrow. Of regret. Of sympathy. And her resolution that now they would be able to go forward together into a new life.

'I'm waiting.' The speed of the rocking had increased. The chair creaked. The rubber of the soles of Amy's shoes squeaked as they peeled off and on the wood of the table.

Squeak, squeak, squeak.

The rubber wheels of the pram, backwards and forwards on the shiny wooden floor.

Hush little baby, don't say a word,
Poppa's gonna buy you a mocking bird,
And if that mocking bird don't sing,
Poppa's gonna buy you a diamond ring.

Tiny baby shrieks, little legs that kick and flail, little arms that wave above the swaddling blankets. Go to sleep, Amy, love. Mummy's here.

'Having problems, are you? Not quite the happy reunion you thought it was going to be? Thought we'd weep and moan and fall on each other's necks, is that it? Thought it would be like one of those made-for-TV movies that you get cheap at the video shop. Well, Rachel, Mrs Beckett, whatever I should call you, you can forget it. If you haven't already realized it, get it through your head now. I didn't want this meeting. I have nothing to say to you. I have no feelings for you.

And as soon as I possibly can I'm out of here. For good. Do I make myself plain?'

The girl's voice bounced around the room. Rachel felt as if at any moment the windows would begin to shake and rattle, the cups and saucers would crash to the floor, the ash in the ashtray would rise in a fine grey cloud above their heads. She waited until there was silence. Then she cleared her throat, lowered her gaze and began to speak.

'I don't expect forgiveness, understanding, or love. I don't want anything from you, Amy. Except that I want you to acknowledge that I am your mother, and that you are my daughter. That is all I want. That is why I have asked to see you. That is all I need. Nothing more. That would be enough for me to take away from here. And if I felt that I had that, I would not need to trouble you any further.'

She paused and looked up. Amy was blowing smoke rings again. Her face was contorted. Her eyes were cold. Rachel bowed her head and continued.

'I completely accept your relationship with the Williams family. I have never doubted their integrity or their desire to protect and love you. We have both been very lucky with the Williamses. When I went to prison and my role and responsibility as a mother had been taken from me, I needed a family like them to step in. You needed a family too. And I am very grateful to them. I hope they realize that. I know that I have missed out on the most important twelve years of your life and nothing will ever make up for it. But now that you're almost an adult, that you're entering a new phase in your life, I just want to know whether there might be some role in it for me in the future. If there is,' she paused and looked up again, 'if there is, well, I would be so grateful and happy. If there isn't . . .' She shrugged her shoulders, staring down at the table's grainy surface. 'If there isn't, well, I would have to accept that too. But I want you to know, that no matter when or how or under what circumstances you might want me or need me, then I would be there for you.'

There was a crash as Amy jerked her chair back down on to the floor.

'You mean the way you were there for me that night you murdered my father, is that what you're talking about? The day you were there for me when you dragged me into the Four Courts to have my picture all over the papers, so I can never be free of it. So every time anything ever comes up about the case, or whenever they're doing one of those stupid chronicles of the decade, or whatever, there I am, on the fucking telly. All of five years old, crying my eyes out, snot dripping down my face. My teddy bear hanging out of my hand. Do you think I like seeing that? Do you? Do you think I like having to remember back to that time? Are you surprised that I've changed my name? That I'm Amy Williams now. That as far as I'm concerned the only Beckett I'll admit to knowing anything about is Samuel Beckett.'

'You like him, do you?' Somehow Rachel found herself speaking, saying something, anything to interrupt the flow of Amy's voice.

'Like him? I don't give a fuck about him. All those stupid words. Lies, that's what most words are. Like your words. Why didn't you just admit that you killed him? Why didn't you just admit it and plead guilty to it? Then we'd all have been spared the trial and every-thing that went with it. And then maybe, maybe . . .'

She stopped. Tears teetered on her bottom lids making her eyes shine and glitter. Then tears and words spilled from her. 'And then you wouldn't have been in prison for so long. They would have let you out sooner. And I would have had a date or a time in the future to look forward to. I could have had a calendar on my wall and I could have crossed off the days with a red felt pen. That's what I could have done. I could have known when you would come home, that's what the difference would have been. But I never knew anything. All I knew was that you were a bad woman.'

Rachel looked at her, at the sudden anguish on her face, an expression she hadn't seen for years. And when she spoke her voice was pleading. 'How can you say that? Didn't I always tell you that I hadn't killed your father, that it wasn't me, that I wasn't responsible for what happened? Didn't I always say that to you? Every time they brought you in for visits, I always said to you that I was telling you the truth. And I couldn't lie about it, go along with what everyone else wanted. I told you so many times. And I told everyone else so many times. I didn't kill him. It wasn't me. But no one would believe me. I thought perhaps that you might. But I don't blame you or feel anything other than responsibility for it. Not now. I thought I'd been able to let you know. When I held you and cuddled you and kissed you and played with you, all the time I said to you, Amy, you're my daughter, my baby, and above all else I love you.'

'But that was the lie, wasn't it, Mother?' The sound of the word on her lips made Rachel's stomach heave and her knees weaken. 'And I don't believe your denials. And I don't believe that you loved me above all else, because if you had you wouldn't have killed my father. So stop now, no more denying it.' Amy was on her feet. Suddenly very adult, very composed. 'Whatever you say, it doesn't make any difference. What's done is done. You left me, effectively, an orphan, without even any memories to carry with me.'

'But that's not true.' Rachel put her hand in her bag and pulled out a small plastic wallet. 'Don't you remember? I gave you one just like this. With all these photographs in it. Look.' And she opened it, flicking over the plastic leaves, pulling out pictures, dealing them like a pack of cards on to the table. 'Don't you remember?'

'Remember, of course I remember, Mother.' Again the use of the word, again the intonation of disgust and contempt. 'But the memories that I had were polluted by you. I used to keep my pictures under my pillow. I used to kiss them goodnight before I went to sleep. These strange and beautiful people. This lovely woman, this handsome man, this pretty baby. But then it got to the point where I couldn't even look at them, because all I felt was the pain that you had caused. So do you know what I did with them, Mother?'

Rachel watched her, mesmerized. She wanted to look away, but she couldn't. She had to keep her eyes on this girl who was turning into a woman in front of her.

'Shall I continue, shall I go on? Shall I tell you what I did, Mother?'

Rachel nodded, her throat constricted.

'One day I go down to the kitchen, I suppose I must have been about ten or so, and I climb up on a stool and I open the cupboard where Mummy, Mummy Williams, keeps the matches. She keeps them there so that none of her children will get hold of them and light them and hurt themselves. But I find them and I take them back up to my room and I strike them one after the other and I burn my photographs. Of course, I'm old enough to know all about fire and things like that. But when the pictures begin to burn, suddenly they set fire to the bedclothes and, when I try to put the fire out, my pyjamas go on fire too. And I get burned. See.' And she pulled up the tight sleeve of her blouse to show the striated red and white skin of her forearm. 'They didn't tell you that was what happened, did they? What did they say? I spilled a kettle of boiling water over me, I got too close to the fire, something like that? Something that would lay the blame on the Williamses. They didn't want to have to hurt you any more, you see. But it wasn't their fault. They were far too good at being parents to let something so careless happen. And do you want to know something else? I wanted to fade away, and blacken, and disappear too. Just like the people in the photographs. And afterwards I was sorry that I hadn't.'

Now tears poured unchecked down Rachel's face. She wept silently, making no attempt to wipe them away. The drops fell on her hands and rolled off on to her thighs, darkening the blue of her jeans. She heard the sound of the door behind her open. She felt the movement of air past her as Amy left the room. She heard the door close and still she wept. She got to her feet and walked to the window. She looked down into the square below and saw the car that had just driven up. The man who got out and put his arm around Amy's bowed shoulders as he opened the back door and ushered her in and out of sight. Rachel drew back into the room. She opened her mouth but there was no sound. She hunched herself down, her arms wrapped around her chest, her hands clutching at her shoulders and waited until the spasm had passed. Then she stood up, pulled her shirt from her waistband and used it to wipe her face. Picked up her bag. Glanced down at the pictures still spread out on the table. She walked to the door, opened it, and moved towards the lift. Pressed the button with the arrow pointing downwards. Heard its mechanical whine as it came closer and closer. Stepped into it. Looked at the face of the woman reflected in its polished walls. Stepped out into the lobby. Walked to the glass doors. Moved into the brightness of the afternoon. Breathed in the warm air. Then turned and walked away.

CHAPTER TWENTY-TWO

THE PEACHES LADY, that was what Daniel's daughter called her. His wife called her something else. She had said her name was Barbara Keane, the first time he asked her who was this woman the kids were always talking about. Now she looked up at him from his desk, the file of newspaper cuttings spread out in front of her, and said, 'I didn't realize you'd kept all this stuff. You never told me.'

He leaned over her, gathering the pieces of paper into a heap.

'In fact,' she continued, 'I seem to remember that when I asked you about her you told me you had thrown everything to do with her and your brother and the trial away. So what the fuck is going on? Suddenly this bitch is in my house. And I only found out by chance, when I was looking through the filing cabinet for the kids' birth certificates. So I could get them their American passports.'

He soothed her and calmed her, gathered up the file, and told her he would go to the police about her.

'She's sick,' he said. 'She's always been crazy. She's probably even worse after all her years in prison.'

'But you told me she'd never get out of prison.' Her voice was high pitched, on the edge of hysteria. 'They'd never let her out. So what does she want now? What does she want with me and my children?'

He had tried to find out what happened that weekend that the woman they called the peaches lady came to stay. But Ursula wasn't telling.

'Nothing, nothing much. We just had too much to drink. I felt dreadful the next morning, and she took the kids out for a drive so I could sleep.'

He asked the children.

'We had fun,' Jonathan said. 'We went to the amusements. She took us on the bumper cars. We ate popcorn.'

'And candyfloss,' interrupted Laura, 'and lots of coke. It was great.'

Now he checked the house to see if there was anything missing. But everything looked as normal. Nothing was out of place. It was as if she had never been there.

'Don't worry. It's all right. I'll take care of it.' He watched the sudden uncertainty, anxiety on Ursula's face. And wondered how Rachel had done it so successfully. Had breached their security, their sense of rightness in the world.

He'd take care of her if need be. He watched her window, parked up on the footpath at the back of the house at night, and looked up at that bright rectangle of light. Watched her go to work and come home. Watched the way her back had straightened, her stride had lengthened, her face and body had rounded and filled out. Saw the smile on her face as she greeted neighbours, stopped to stroke the cat which lay on the steps of the house next door, bent to pull a stalk of lavender and hold it to her nose as she felt in her bag for her keys.

He thought about the police. How he had never been charged with the murder of his brother. How they had believed his story and the alibi that his mother had given him. Believed her when she said she had heard the grandfather clock on the landing outside her bedroom door chiming the hour. Didn't know that he had opened its glass front and moved the hands back, then clicked it shut again. Sat with her and played her videos until she fell asleep, then moved the hands of the clock forward again. So easy. So simple. The last thing he wanted was some nosy young copper taking out the case, examining it, looking through the evidence, spotting holes where there had been none before. The last thing he wanted.

So he'd watch her and he'd wait. And in the meantime he'd go on visiting the café by the harbour where the girl worked. He was getting on well with her. She liked him. She'd told him her name.

'Amy Williams,' she said, with a shrug and a grimace of distaste.

'Amy, that's a nice name.' He leant back in his chair and looked up at her.

'Yeah, too nice, too sweet, too pretty.' She lifted up his cup and saucer to wipe away the crumbs from his pastry.

'No,' he said. 'It's subtle and different. It's like

you.' And watched the flush on her cheek, and the smile that followed it. Now he could see her mother in her. In the way she looked down as she spoke, her gaze flicking back to his for an instant, then away again.

Patience, that's what was needed, a bit of biding his time. Martin had been good at that. He could do no better than follow his little brother's example. Martin had told him often enough: 'Don't rush into situations, don't make snap decisions, bide your time. It'll be worth it in the end. It always is.'

Martin was right about most things, he thought. Except for that last time. But now he'd do what he counselled. He'd wait. He'd bide his time. He'd stick it out.

CHAPTER TWENTY-THREE

THE PHONE CALL woke Jack out of a deep dreamless sleep. The best sleep he'd had in months, if not years. What was it that the kids in school used to say? Two kinds of deep sleep. The sleep of the just, and the sleep of the just after. This was definitely the latter. He rolled over, moving Alison's head from his shoulder, and felt for his phone, hearing the warbling ringing tone. *Eine Kleine Nacht Musik* played at double time. It was Ruth who did it. She was always fiddling around with it, changing the settings. Like most ten-year-old kids she knew more about mobile phones than anyone else in the universe.

He was sure he had thought to leave it somewhere findable. Unlike the rest of his belongings, which were scattered inelegantly across the bedroom floor. His fourth night in a row at Alison's. The weekend spent juggling kids and fatherly duties, but still managing to find himself winding up in Alison's squeaky brass bed.

His fingers closed on its plastic case. He looked at the LED display. It was five past nine. It was Sweeney's number. Shit, he thought, I'm bloody late. And then he thought, no, it's not that. I'm taking today off, my first free day in weeks. So what is this? It must be trouble.

The body was still hanging where it had been found, dangling from the banisters, down into the hall, twisting gently in a slow and stately pirouette as the rope around its neck wound and unwound. The housekeeper had discovered it. She had let herself in as usual, just after eight-thirty. She had been looking down at the rug in the hall, thinking, she said, that it was getting very threadbare around the edges. That really she should speak to Dr Hill about it. It would be dangerous soon, easy to trip on, and really that wouldn't do with so many people traipsing in and out of the house every day. So she didn't notice it immediately. It was only when she was right underneath that she saw him. That she saw his feet hanging just above her head. His poor feet, she kept on saying. She'd never seen his feet bare before. He was always so meticulous about everything, always kept himself really well. He has beautiful hands she said, real healer's hands. But his feet, what a mess. The toenails need cutting, calluses all over his heels, and a corn on his middle toe. Jack met Sweeney's eyes above her head. He winked and instantly felt dreadful. Sweeney was trying not to laugh.

'So, love, what else did you see?'

'Nothing else,' she said. 'I got such a fright I just stood there looking up at the poor man and then I phoned for an ambulance, and when I told them what he had done they said they'd send the guards. Straightaway.'

The doctor had hanged himself from the banisters on the first floor. Jack looked at the rope. It was clothes line. Faded, orange, exactly like the rope used to strangle his daughter. He had left a note. It was stuck in the pocket of his shirt. A single page, torn from what looked like a prescription pad. His name, address, phone number and surgery times printed on the top. And underneath, in small, barely legible handwriting, the date and the message.

I did not kill my daughter, Judith, or hurt her in any way. I do not know who did it. But I cannot bear the thought of further shame and humiliation. I know that I will be charged with her murder, that I will be tried and found guilty. I could not go to prison. It's better for everyone this way.

It was not signed. Jack watched as Johnny Harris supervised the removal of the body from its suspended position. He leaned against the panelled wall of the hall. In spite of everything, he was feeling wonderful. He could barely keep the grin off his face. He looked at his watch. It was ten-thirty. Alison was doing home visits all day. He had said he would phone her. They might be able to meet for lunch. But anyway she was coming to his flat for dinner and the rest. He closed his eyes. He could still feel her breasts pressing against his chest, her legs wrapped around his hips. Still smell her skin and taste her mouth.

'Hey, boss, wake up.' Sweeney prodded him in the ribs. 'There's someone at the door who wants to see "whoever's in charge". I suppose that would have to be you, wouldn't it?'

This time he recognized her immediately. The middle-aged woman with the good haircut and the bad figure. She was waiting outside on the front path.

'I was wondering what's happened. What all this is for.' She gestured to the ambulance and the three Garda cars parked underneath the plane trees. 'Is there something wrong? I'm not just being nosy. Mark Hill is a very good friend.'

He thought she was going to faint when he told her. Her face flushed, then the colour faded from it. She staggered and he put out his arm to support her.

'Here, I'll take you home.'

Jennifer Bradley, that was her name. He remembered the house. Next door up on the left. And the flowers that Judith had given her for her birthday.

'Shall I come in with you, will you be all right?'

She nodded, struggling to control her voice. 'Thank you, but my husband's here. He'll be as shocked as I am by all this. We've known the Hills for years and years. We both moved into these houses at the same time.'

'You were friendly with Elizabeth Hill, weren't you?' He tried to keep his tone as neutral as possible.

She looked at him and smiled coldly. 'I was. I'm sure you know all the details.'

He nodded. 'Not all,' he said. 'Just the important ones. I'm just curious, if you don't mind. You and your husband worked it all out. You stayed with him. And you and Dr Hill were also on good terms, is that right?'

'Yes.' Her voice was even colder. 'I made a mistake. I realized that. I allowed a certain,' she paused, 'a certain emotion to take over my life. But I could see that it had no future. My future was here with my family.'

'But Elizabeth didn't feel like that?'

'Elizabeth Hill was always a rebel. That was one of the things that made her very attractive. But I wasn't. And Mark knew the difference between us. And he didn't hold it against me. I tried to help him with the children as much as I could. Judith and Stephen were always in and out of my house. They used to come to me and my husband when Mark was busy. And Judith used to babysit for my younger children. She was almost like their older sister. We all loved her very much. We are all so diminished by her loss. And now this. It's so unfair.' She began to cry, her face crumpling. She took out her keys and opened the front door.

'I'm sorry.' Jack held out his hand to her. 'I didn't mean to add to your pain, but sometimes these questions have to be asked.'

Someone would have to tell Elizabeth. He supposed it would have to be him. His sense of well-being vanished. Better get it over with. He walked slowly back towards the Hills' house. He would do it out here in the street where it was quiet. He took out his phone and his notebook. He found her number. He began to punch it in. And then he felt a blow on his back, followed by another and another. He turned around. Stephen Hill was behind him, an expression of fury on his small white face.

'You bastard, you fucking bastard. Look what you've done to my family. You've destroyed it. You've destroyed my father.' He began to flail at him again, his fists jabbing into his stomach, his solar plexus, his lower abdomen. Nervous laughter burst out of Jack's mouth as he put up his own fists to defend himself. And felt excruciating pain as Stephen lifted one foot and kicked him hard and accurately in the testicles. He bent double, gasping for breath, agony flooding though his body, vomit rushing up into his mouth. He heard rather than saw Sweeney dragging Stephen Hill off him, hustling him back into the house, as he slumped against the railings waiting for the pain to subside.

It was much later when he finally got around to making the phone call. He waited until Johnny Harris had been in touch. He confirmed that Dr Hill's death was suicide.

'I'm surprised,' he said, 'about one thing. Hill had access to all kinds of drugs. Just a quick look at his surgery and I could see he had plenty of morphine there. Enough to die painlessly. Yet he chose to die by strangulation. And there's no doubt about it, it hurts. But then that's the pattern. Women take pills, men choose a more active, aggressive form of death.'

'I know why you're ringing.' Elizabeth's voice sounded subdued, distant. 'Stephen has already phoned me. He's distraught. I'm coming over this evening. I'll take care of the funeral. He told me how he went for you. He's sorry now. He knows it wasn't your fault.'

But was it? He sat on the balcony with Alison beside him, watching the sky darken over the harbour.

There were boats tied up along the harbour wall, visitors from England, Germany, France. They could see their lamps and navigation lights glowing, and hear their chatter and music from their radios. Alison took his hand and kissed it.

'It isn't your fault, Jack,' she said. 'All you've done is your job. Who knows why he killed himself. A lot of suicides are not spontaneous. A lot of them have been planned in some way, conscious or unconscious, for years. He hadn't done his grieving for his daughter particularly well, had he?'

'How could he, if he had killed her? How could he have grieved for her at all?'

'But that's the dilemma, isn't it?' She poured more wine into both their glasses. 'Just imagine the combination of grief and guilt that man was carrying. I saw it in Rachel Beckett yesterday when she came to meet Amy. You can see the toll it's taken on her. It hurts looking at her. It doesn't bear thinking about.'

But he couldn't stop thinking about it. And that night, as he lay with Alison's head on his chest, every time he closed his eyes he saw Mark Hill's face. His tongue protruding from his mouth, his purple swollen cheeks and his bare feet, white and soft, traces of talcum powder still clinging between his toes.

Grief and guilt. He felt them both himself. And there was no way of leaving either of them behind. Not now. Not ever.

Chapter Twenty-Four

RACHEL HAD BEEN watching the next-door neighbour's cat all afternoon. Her attention had been attracted first by the sudden darts of movement across the paved terrace, towards the little oval pool, then the rush and leap up into the solitary old apple tree, which even now at the height of summer was still without all its leaves.

She had watched the way the cat's black tail thrashed from side to side as it crouched by the rockery, something small and dark between its front paws. She had noticed the way it pulled back just for a moment, as if its attention had been distracted, and then as the small dark something tried to move away, it moved too, once again alert, aware, its shiny black ears pricked upright.

She had opened her window as high as it would go and leaned out as far as possible, trying to see what it was that was keeping the cat so amused. She could hear, above the noise of the traffic, the yowls and low cries that came from its mouth as it circled its prey. And then when she could bear the suspense no longer she had gone down the three flights of stairs to the door which led out into the yard, crammed with piles of wood and discarded broken pieces of furniture. Junk that her landlord had abandoned, but which provided a useful ladder so she could pull herself up on to the top of the wall and look down into the ordered beauty of her neighbour's small garden. The square of concrete paving, the pool with its water lilies and fish, the patch of lawn surrounded on three sides by a narrow bed crammed with summer flowers and vegetables. And on its own, the apple tree, its trunk splitting into a fork, like two fingers held upright. Where the cat now sat, opening and closing its yellow eyes against the brightness of the sunshine. While at the foot of the tree, spreadeagled on the close-cropped grass, lay a frog.

She watched it. It appeared as if it were dead. She pulled herself on to the top of the wall, then dropped the few feet on to the ground. The cat turned its face towards her and crouched down into the black ruff of fur around its thick neck. She looked towards the house, but there was no sign of activity behind its gleaming windows. She moved quietly across the grass to the foot of the apple tree. She crouched down and examined the frog. It was about four inches long. Its legs, mottled with green and brown markings, were splayed out behind. They looked almost human, she thought. Elegant. The princeling wearing the cross-gartered stockings. She picked up a piece of twig and gently touched its back. It made no move. She pushed at it, but its body did not seem to register the pressure. Above her head she heard a rustle and the sound of claws on bark as the cat began to slither down the trunk towards her. She put one hand in the pocket of her jeans and pulled out a bundle of paper tissues. Carefully she picked up the frog, holding it gingerly, and half ran to the pond. As she bent down over the water suddenly the frog squirmed and pulled away, leaping out, its legs already making swimming movements as it disappeared with a small, musical splash. Down, down, beneath the lily pads, into the darkness. She looked up at the cat, who had followed behind. He stared fixedly into the murk, then crouched again on his haunches, his tail thrashing from side to side, and a sound of disappointment coming from his throat.

'Go away,' she hissed at him, nudging his ribs with her bare foot. He moved quickly to the other side of the terrace. But already as she dragged herself back across the wall she could see that he was inching slowly and deliberately towards the pool. And by the time she had reached her room at the top of the house she could see that once again he had something between his front paws as he crouched by the side of the rockery.

She had to admire his persistence, that big black cat that lived on the other side of the wall. Or was it persistence? She supposed not, in an animal. It must be an instinct, she thought, something from which he cannot escape. And then she thought of other cats she had known. Who had been more than happy to lie in a warm spot for most of the day, purring and preening and rolling over to have their soft stomachs rubbed and patted. Beautiful creatures, they were, she remembered. Secure in their bodies and sure of their place in the world.

Like the people whom she saw now at Ursula and Daniel Beckett's anniversary party as she stood beneath the pine trees at the edge of the garden, watching the groups of twos and threes, glasses in their hands, who moved behind the picture windows. She could hear through the open door the hum and burble of their voices rising above the music, which came from the group of musicians seated on a small raised platform on the lawn. She watched Ursula move among her guests. She knew the kinds of words she would be using. Welcoming, supporting, confiding, flattering. She watched the children, dressed in their best, running in and out of the house, fetching and carrying. She drew back for a moment into the trees and turned to look out to sea. It was still very bright. The water below the cliffs gleamed in the evening sunshine. Dark green close to the shore, dark blue further out, and a line of light along the horizon. And the beginnings of the sunset touching the clouds with a fine feathering of pale pink and grey. She took a powder compact from her bag and opened it. She looked at herself, critically moving the small mirror from feature to feature. She smoothed down her eyebrows with her fingertip and pulled out her comb to settle her hair. Then she turned back to the house. She took a deep breath. She lifted her head and gazed towards the lighted windows. Now was the time. Now she was ready.

It was easy to slide in through the wide open door. No one noticed her. No one was watching. Except the white-coated waiter, who immediately spotted a guest without a glass and held out his tray in her direction.

'Drink, madam? Wine, mineral water or perhaps some champagne?'

She hesitated, her hand hovering, looking down at the colours. The dark red, light yellow, pale lemon fizziness. She picked up a glass of white wine. She held it to her nose and breathed in its essence before she drank as her eyes scanned the room, looking for the man with the thick dark hair and the equally dark beard, whose face she remembered from the time before. Whose photograph she had seen in the articles he had cut from the pages of the glossy magazines. She moved forward, carefully easing herself through the throng, picking up snatches of conversations as she passed.

She could see Ursula's blonde head and hear her voice, her accent rising above the hum of the room. Rachel walked slowly towards the doors to the garden. She sat down at a table on the terrace and looked out to the sea, watching the line of clouds along the horizon.

She finished her glass of wine and signalled to the waiter for another. She drank some more. The alcohol was changing her demeanour. She felt bright and alive, confident, capable of anything. She stood up and moved away from the house again, towards the marquee that had been put up on the lawn. It was empty still. A group of musicians were setting up in the corner. She could smell damp canvas and crushed grass. It reminded her of holidays when she was a kid. Camping in Wexford. Rain on the roof of the tent and the smell of the Primus stove. She walked into the centre of the wooden floor and leaned against the pole. The band had begun to tune their instruments. Guitars, a mandolin, a violin, and a huge concertina. She watched them, then leaned back against the wooden support and closed her eyes. They began to play. Their music sounded like gypsy tunes. Rhythmic, romantic, nostalgic. She swayed from side to side, humming along with the familiar sounds, then felt something tugging at her skirt. She opened her eyes and looked down. Laura stood beside her. Rachel bent and kissed her cheek, resting her lips against the child's face.

'Would you like to dance with me, sweetheart?' she asked. The child nodded and held out her hands. Rachel took hold of them and together they swayed around the wooden dance floor. The band began to play more quickly. Around and around they twirled. Laura was laughing. She was pulling back against Rachel's grasp. Rachel could feel dizziness beginning to push her off balance. She slowed down and lifted the child up, holding her on her hip as she moved in waltz time, her feet sliding across the wooden floor of the huge tent. Laura was laughing out loud, leaning out to counterbalance Rachel's movements as they spun around and around and around.

And then stopped as Ursula suddenly was beside them, pulling the child from Rachel's arms, shouting at her, demanding to know what she thought she was doing, why was she here, how dare she invade their privacy in this way.

Rachel pushed her hair back off her face. She was breathless. She gulped in air, then she picked up her glass of wine and drank some more.

'But you invited me,' she said. 'That day when we were out in the nursery, you told me to come. And you told me again that night when I stayed here with you. You gave me an invitation. Don't you remember?'

She watched the expression on Ursula's face change. Doubt replaced anger.

Rachel moved towards her. 'Yes, you said to me how much you'd enjoy having me here, inviting me to meet all your friends, how much you wanted me to meet your husband too. You do remember that, don't you?'

The band had stopped playing. People had begun to drift into the marquee to see what was happening. They stood in a curious semicircle around the two women.

'Yes,' Rachel continued, 'you told me there would be music and we could dance together, the way we danced that night, Ursula. Don't you remember? You had such a great time of it that night, you said we'd do it again. Why don't we, why don't we now? I'm sure everyone here would like to see it, the way we danced that night.'

She reached out and took her hand. And then she saw him, standing slightly apart from the rest of the guests. Those bright, shiny people, with their extravagant gestures and their confident movements. Their jewellery, their make-up, their glittery surfaces. Who faded away to nothing now as she saw Daniel watching her. And she looked at him. Saw the streaks of grey in his dark hair, the extra flesh on his body and face. Remembered how she had created him, called him up from the depths of her memory as she lay in her cell, night after night. Thinking of the way he had looked and felt. As her legs weakened beneath her and her mouth dried up so she did not know if she would be able to speak. For a moment there was silence. Then Laura ran forward, towards him. She clung to his knees, then stretched her arms up his thighs, pulling at his belt.

'Daddy, Daddy, pick me up, give me a cuddle.'

He leant down and put his hands under her armpits. He swung her high, up on to his shoulder. The child laughed and shouted out, 'Look, peaches lady, look. I'm the king of the castle.'

Daniel moved slowly towards her. He held out his right hand.

'Rachel, I do believe it's you. After so many years.'

She heard the voices then, the comments, the hum of recognition.

'How nice to see you. How interesting. I'm glad you've been enjoying yourself here. Enjoying our hospitality.'

He lifted Laura from his shoulders and put her down carefully on the terrace. He stepped forward and took hold of Rachel's wrist. His grip was tight, uncomfortable.

'But now,' he said, 'it's time you were leaving.'

He tugged at her arm and she stumbled forward. The remnants of her glass splashed down her dress, staining it darkly. He tugged her again, and again she stumbled. The crowd moved aside. She could see out through the open flap of the tent. Two men were standing, waiting. They were wearing dark blue uniforms, shirts with a logo written in white on front and back. Daniel nodded towards them, and they moved forward quickly. He let her go. The men stood, one on either side of her. Together, in step, they walked out of the tent, across the lawn, around the side of the house, up the drive to the gate. Their footsteps sounded loudly on the gravel. And then as they reached the road Rachel heard the sound of the band starting up again. A dance tune, another waltz. She heard the guitars, the mandolin, the violin, the concertina all playing together. She began to hum. The security guards opened the gate. They stood aside.

'Off you go, darling.' The younger of the two spoke. He gave her a shove in the small of her back. She fell forward, putting out her arms to save herself. The heels of her hands and her knees made contact with the hard surface of the road. She felt the sting of small stones pricking into her skin. Tears started into her eyes. She heard the sound of their shoes as both men turned and walked away. Then the heavy clank of the iron latch closing. She waited for a couple of moments until it was quiet, then she pushed herself up to standing. She turned away and began to walk up the hill to the village. The darkness pressed in on her, wrapping her in its comfort and safety. She stopped for a moment and tilted her head to look up at the sky. The half-moon hung above her the way it had hung above the prison. But now when she moved it moved with her, following her path, stopping when she stopped, drifting through the night as she began to walk again.

It was such a big house, the house in which Daniel and his family lived. Full of nooks and crannies. She had it all there in her mind's eye. She thought about the alarm system, the number she had written down in her notebook, the locks on the doors and the windows. She thought of the bunch of keys she had put carefully away in her cupboard. He would be going around checking them all before he went to sleep tonight, she was sure of that. And would he sleep tonight? Probably not, or if he did his dreams would waken him. But she would sleep well, better than she had slept for a long time. For years really, when she came to think of it. She would sleep like a baby. A baby that at last has been fed and nourished and cosseted. She was so looking forward to it. She couldn't wait.

Chapter Twenty-Five

It was the banging that woke her the next morning. Persistent, loud, eating into the warp and weft of her dreams, even though she turned on to her stomach and pulled the pillow over her head, flattening the palms of her hands against her ears. But it was no good. She was awake. She lay for a moment on her back, looking at the sunlight creeping across the ceiling, trying to remember where she was. She sat up, a sudden fright making her sweat, wondering, thinking was she back inside again? Was that where the noise was coming from? The screws working their way down the landing towards her cell? Keys in hand, the jangle, the rattle, the thunk of the lock, then the bang, the shout, the wakey wakey, rise and shine. Breakfast time, ladies. But the voice that was shouting her name now was a man's voice. A voice she knew from before, before prison even.

She would have wanted to have the time to brush her hair, wash her face, but now the noise was so loud that her neighbours from downstairs had joined in the racket. Banging on their ceiling so her floorboards shook. Driving her up and out of her bed to hasten to the door and unlock it. To stand back and let him in. To face his rage. To answer his questions.

'What do you want?'

'What on earth do you think you're doing?'

'Who do you think you are?'

'Conning my wife and children with that crazy story. The deserted wife, the two sons, all that crap. So tell me now. Why are you here? Now, after all these years. Why now?'

'I could ask you the same question, couldn't I? Why are you here, now, after all these years?' She wrapped her arms across her breasts, feeling suddenly cold. 'You should be thanking me that I didn't tell your wife all about you and me. When I realized who she was. That I didn't just spit it all out. The whole rotten story. That I kept it to myself. That I was cute enough to make up something else that she wouldn't suspect.'

'So you're telling me that it was just a coincidence that you met her, is that what you're saying? Well, I don't believe you, not for one moment. I know you, remember, Rachel. I know you very well.' His voice rose in a shriek of anger as he moved towards her, his hands in fists. As the door behind him opened and she saw the boy from downstairs standing there, his blonde hair in a crest like a small child, his eyes puffy with sleep.

'What the fuck is going on here?' He took a step further into the room, looking at them both. Then said, his voice concerned, anxious, 'Are you all right, Rachel? Is everything OK?'

She looked towards Daniel. 'No, it isn't. Get the

bollocks out of here. Now.' Her voice was harsh, her accent and tone suddenly not her own as she moved towards him and pushed him hard in the chest so he lost his balance and stumbled back, as the boy from downstairs became changed too, threatening, his slight body inside the sweatshirt and jogging pants, hard and tense. She slammed the door behind Daniel and they listened to the sound of his footsteps on the stairs and the hollow thump as the heavy front door swung back into place.

He was waiting for her when she finished work later that evening. His van was parked outside the shopping centre and he was leaning against it, flicking through a newspaper. She saw him a moment before he saw her. She was about to turn away, but he was beside her, his hand on her arm.

'Don't go,' he said. 'I want to talk.'

'You do? What on earth can we have to talk about?'

'Look, I'm sorry about what happened this morning. I didn't mean to frighten you. Please, let me buy you a drink. You look as if you could do with one.'

He smiled at her. She saw Amy in his face.

'Not here, not around here. Somewhere else.'

He took her to a big new pub out on the road to Bray. It was crowded, noisy. A wide-screen TV was showing a football match at one end. At the other a jukebox pumped out the latest hits. She had to sit close to him to hear what he was saying. She could smell him. Sunshine, fresh air, newly dug earth. A tang of sweat from his skin.

He looked well. He looked better than she had remembered him. He seemed to have grown. Taller, broader, fitter, stronger.

'How did you find me?' she asked.

He shrugged his shoulders. 'I could ask the same thing of you. How did you find me?'

'I used my head, Daniel. I used my prison head.'

'And now, what do you want now? Money, a job, a place to live? Go on, surprise me, give me a hint.'

She was drinking gin. It tasted good. She looked up at him and smiled.

'She's lovely, your Ursula. And so are your children. You're very lucky. You've done well, haven't you, since your brother died and you stepped into your father's shoes? If Martin had still been alive, he would have been the one to take over. And then where would you have been? His errand boy, his runner, his scapegoat. But when Martin died, all that changed. You know what, Dan? I think you owe me.'

They drank more. The light outside faded. The lights inside gleamed. A band had replaced the juke-box. Playing old favourites, songs they both remembered. Couples were dancing, lurching and bumping together on the small wooden floor.

'Come on.' Daniel held out his hand to her. She rested her head on his shoulder and closed her eyes. She remembered the tattoo. The rose, the line of red just beneath the skin. His hand pressed against the small of her back. She remembered then what it was to lie beside a man's body. How different from all those years inside.

When closing time came he drove her home. They didn't speak. She watched his face in the light from the road. As he stopped the car outside the house he turned to her.

'You do want me, don't you? You do want me to come in?'

Afterwards, when he had gone, she slept. This time so deeply that when she woke hours later she could barely remember what had happened. But there were traces of him everywhere. Dark hairs left on her pillow and in the folds and wrinkles of the sheets. A damp stain that she felt beneath her thighs as she turned over. And when she stood in front of the mirror and looked at her body she could read him in the signs. The dark red of the blood he had sucked to the surface at the base of her throat and on the white skin around her nipples. Bruises on the inside of her thighs, and on her wrists and upper arms. And when she sank into the bath she felt the sting in the long scratches down her back, and inside her, where the water gently lapped.

'Don't mark me,' he had shouted at her, pinning her hands together behind her head. And she had closed her eyes as she opened herself up to him. Twice. Dozing fitfully after the first time, then reaching out for him again, and finding him once more.

He had said nothing as he dressed and prepared to leave.

'I'll tell you what I want,' she said, lifting her head from the pillow, her voice low, so he had to lean towards her to hear what she was saying. 'I want to go out in your boat. I've seen her in the harbour. You remember, don't you, what it was like when we sailed together before? So, grant me one wish, Dan. Take me out on your boat, and I will never bother you or your family again. I promise.'

She turned her back on him, pulling her knees up to her chest, wrapping her arms around them, as she felt sleep dragging her under.

'OK,' he said, 'it's done.'

She smiled as she pulled the quilt over her head. It was warm and dark now, here. Dark is good, she had said to the child. Dark saves you. The child hadn't believed her. But she was right all along, she knew she was.

'Tell me, Rachel, what is it like outside now? Is it as warm and wonderful as it seems to me?'

It was night-time. Rachel sat on the floor, leaning back against Clare Bowen's bed. She had been reading to her. Tonight it was *Pride and Prejudice*.

'I want the chapter where Mr Darcy asks Elizabeth to marry him and she rejects him. I love that moment, don't you?'

Outside it was dark and silent. Inside the lamp on the bedside table cast a buttery glow over the two of them. Rachel turned towards her, holding the book up. She began to read. Clare settled back against her pillows. She sighed. She closed her eyes. When Rachel finished, Clare stirred restlessly.

'You're not comfortable, are you?' Rachel put out her hand and touched her forehead. It was warm and sticky.

'Would you like me to bathe you, make you feel fresher before you go to sleep?'

Clare opened her eyes and nodded.

Rachel filled a basin with lukewarm water. She pulled back the bedclothes and eased Clare's nightdress over her head. She rolled up her sleeves and dipped her sponge in the water. She lathered soap in one hand and gently wiped away the sweat that lay stickily between and underneath Clare's small, flattened breasts. Clare watched her, then reached out and touched Rachel's arm. She pulled it closer to the light.

'Where did you get those bruises?'

Rachel looked at them. They were deep purple against the paleness of her skin.

'If I tell you, do you promise me you won't tell your husband?'

Clare lifted her hand and pushed back the collar of Rachel's shirt. Her fingers rested on the marks on her neck. She listened in silence.

'Be careful,' she whispered. 'Be very careful.'

Afterwards, Rachel waited until Clare slept. She had given her her pills, holding her head up as she swallowed them. Then soothed and comforted her, knowing that Clare would fight the sleep that was coming. That she would be scared that this was the night from which she would not waken. Rachel heard Andrew's key in the front door, and his footsteps in the hall. She heard him stagger against the wall, the sound of water from the tap in the kitchen rushing into the sink, the clatter and crash of something breaking. She stood up and walked towards the front door. Andrew was on his hands and knees, picking up shards of broken glass from the tiles. He looked up at her, his face red, his eyes bloodshot.

'Thank you,' he said. She nodded, and turned away.

Outside it was still warm. She began to run, gaining speed as she neared home. There was no need for him to thank her. He and his wife were doing her a favour. It was just they didn't know it. Not yet anyway. But soon they would. Soon it would be clear to them and to everyone.

CHAPTER TWENTY-SIX

SO WHAT TO do about the Judith Hill case? Technically it was still unsolved. No one had yet been charged with her murder, that much was sure and certain. But with the prime suspect dead and buried, where to go now? Jack sat at his desk and looked around him. Most of the detectives who had worked on the case had been reassigned. Even Sweeney. And he was off on a fortnight's holiday.

'It's a really decent thing you're doing,' Alison had said when he told her. 'It'll be great for Joan to get away with her bloke for a change. You can hardly begrudge her. And you're always saying you don't spend enough time with your little ones. It'll be fun. You'll have them all to yourself for two whole weeks.'

Ruth had looked askance at him when he suggested that Alison might come and stay too. Just for the odd night.

'Where on earth, Daddy, will she sleep?' Her tone was one of moral outrage. 'Rosa sleeps with you, I sleep on the sofa bed. There's no more room, is there?' She glared at him and he felt his resolve crumble. But Alison was understanding.

'We'll manage,' she said in her calm no-nonsense way, kissed him and pulled him back down into her bed and held him tightly.

And it was fun, being with the girls all the time. Cooking for them, getting to know them all over again. Becoming smitten by Ruth's hard-headed intelligence and Rosa's wistful playfulness. So that Judith Hill and her father, her brother and her mother became hardly more than characters he might have read about in a book or seen in a TV series. This was real life. This waking each morning with his daughters, getting them their breakfast, sitting on the narrow balcony and watching the small boats come and go through the inner harbour. Watching all the kids who took part in the courses organized by the sailing school at the end of the west pier, splashing around in their wetsuits, falling in and out of canoes, capsizing their tiny sailing dinghies. So when Alison came to visit, he almost resented her presence, the intrusion into his domestic world. Until he got used once again to the feel of her warm soft body against his as he sneaked up behind her in the kitchen or beckoned to her to come into the bedroom for a couple of minutes.

And when it was over, and life went back to normal, he thought what a lovely time it had been. Those two weeks in the middle of the summer, that special year.

Rachel had seen Jack Donnelly and the two girls sitting on their balcony in the morning sun as she went for her daily run. They were all very alike. All very dark, with glossy, shiny heads of hair. She had seen them walking together on the pier, taking their time, stopping to look at the turnstones, the wagtails and all the gulls. Looking for the seals that swam out among the boats. Crying out with delight as they watched them surface and turn over on their backs, lazily extending a flipper, before diving deep and disappearing again. She had seen him at night-time too, recognized the blonde woman with him. The social worker, Alison White. Tried not to think of the last time they had met. The pain of being with Amy, and of watching her leave.

Daniel had told her how he had found Amy too. Boasted about it. Told her how he had gone to the café where she worked. Chatted to her, teased her, made her laugh. She's cute, he said.

'Did you tell her who you were?' she asked.

He hadn't, he said. He didn't want to upset her. He just wanted to know what she was like.

'And what is she like?'

'She's like me. And sometimes she's like you. And sometimes she's like none of us.'

They had seen each other a number of times since that night. He had phoned her, come to meet her after she left the dry-cleaner's. He had taken her around the city in his van. They had gone to different places. An apartment in a building that his company controlled. His office when no one was there. He had shown her round. Explained to her how after Martin's death old man Beckett had taken a back seat and Daniel had gradually assumed control.

'Not bad, eh? For the black sheep of the family. Do you remember, Rachel, how you made me feel better about, more confident about what you called my "intellectual capabilities"? You were good that way, weren't you? And with Martin gone, well, the old man didn't have anyone else he could trust the way he could trust me. After all, Rachel, I am one of the family, aren't I?'

Like I'm one of the family, she thought. Part of all that. Indelibly marked.

'Does Ursula know you've seen me again?' she asked. 'Aren't you worried she'll find out?'

'Worried? No. Ursula has the arrogance of her class and her background. She cannot believe that I would betray her. No one has ever betrayed her before. Everything in the world has gone right for her, ever since the day that she was born into a wealthy family who planned how her life would be lived. She knows no disappointment, she knows no fear. In fact,' he smiled at her, 'the only time I have ever seen fear on her face was that night at the party. She was scared then. Terrified.'

'So what does she think has happened to me now?'

'She thinks that I have gone to the police about you. She thinks that you have been warned off. She thinks that you are harmless. A broken, bitter woman with no future.'

'And what do you think?'

'I think I want to know what you want from me. I think you want me to help you, but I'm not sure how.'

'Kiss me, Dan, for a start. That will do. It's been

such a long time since I've been kissed. Then tell me why you killed my husband.'

He took her face in his hands. His fingers slipped down on to her neck. He pushed her head back. She could feel his thumbs pressing against her windpipe, her breath beginning to catch in her throat. He relaxed his fingers and held her close.

'You know why I killed him. He was going to ruin my life.'

'And instead you ruined mine.'

'No, I didn't. You ruined it for yourself. You lied to him. You cheated on him. And you paid the price. But now you can start all over again. You're young enough, you're still beautiful. You're bright and clever. I'll help you, Rachel. You know I will.'

He was nervous, she knew that. He wasn't sure. He wanted to keep her close. He asked her to the house to stay for a night or two. Ursula had gone away for a couple of weeks. Taken the kids to the States for a holiday.

'What about my trip in the boat, Daniel? You promised, remember?'

They agreed to meet, down at the harbour. Sunday afternoon. Three o'clock.

'I'll bring food, something to drink. How about that?'

'Sounds like a great idea.'

'And where will we go, which direction, north or south?'

'We'll wait and see. We'll go with the wind.'

She met him at the slipway. She had everything she

needed for the trip. A change of clothes in case she got wet. A heavy sweater in case it got cold. Food for the journey. He had all the rest. Wet gear, leggings and life jackets, stored in a canvas bag in the back of his van. It smelt musty as she pulled the bag open.

'I always keep this stuff here,' he said, 'just in case I get the chance for a sail. It's handy.'

There were oars too, to be fitted to the dinghy, leaning up against the sea wall.

'Here, give us a hand,' he called, and together they lifted it down the granite slip. She watched him load up, carefully distributing the weight fore and aft.

'That's a heavy one,' he said, hefting her bag. 'What have you got in it, all your worldly goods?'

She smiled. 'Just a few things for the trip. You know how it is, be prepared.'

He guided her into the bow of the small boat and took his seat opposite. He lifted the oars. His movements were quick and precise. She trailed one hand through the cold, clear water. It was deep and dark green, almost opaque like blocks of agate or greenstone. She leaned over and saw her face look back at her. She smiled. And watched the smile come back to her. She looked over towards him.

'Thank you,' she said, 'you've no idea what this means to me.'

His boat was wooden, thirty feet long, with a two-berth cabin.

'What's it to be, Rachel? Sail or steam?'

'What do you think? What would you do with this lovely wind?'

It was force four, so the weather forecast said. Visibility was good. Pressure was high. Together they hoisted the sails, the jib and the main. She stood with her feet wide apart, balancing as the boat began to buck beneath her.

'Are you ready?' Daniel shouted. She turned to him and nodded. She squatted down and lifted the mooring rope free. The boat swung around crazily, then straightened as Daniel took the tiller and hauled on the main sheet, turning its nose at an angle to the wind. She picked her way carefully back to the cockpit and took her place beside him. She took hold of the jib sheet, pulling it as tight as she could, feeling the rope cut into the soft skin on the palms of her hands.

'Tie it up,' he shouted to her, and she wound it quickly in a figure of eight around the brass cleat. She leaned back and looked up, shading her eyes against the sun. The huge white sail was stretched into a tight swelling curve, filled now with wind. Beneath the hull she could hear the rush and swirl of water as they gathered speed. She laughed out loud as pleasure filled her. She turned towards him, and reached out to touch his cheek.

'Thank you,' she said again. 'Thank you for this.'

They were heading north across the bay. The boat heeled steeply beneath them and water sluiced down the deck from the bow, pouring into the cockpit, soaking their legs and feet. She watched Daniel, the way he grasped the tiller confidently, checking the sail, its angle to the wind, making small, precise adjustments to his course. He knew what he was doing. She

could see that. He must have sailed a lot since that
summer when she first taught him. Sailed out here,
wind in his hair, salt spray on his lips, while she lay
with her face turned to the wall of her cell. She looked
away then, at the points of sunlight which sparked
from the shining surface of the sea. She looked back
behind her and watched the grey granite harbour walls
of Dun Laoghaire getting smaller and smaller. Up
ahead was the hill of Howth and the Bailey lighthouse.
And all around the gentle blue and green of the
mountains, the smear of darkness where the city spread
out and pressed up against their rolling foothills. She
wanted to cry out with pleasure, sing with delight. She
stared towards the mouth of the river that led up into
the heart of the city. The river that flowed past the
Four Courts, where her life had ended. The waters of
the canal flowed into it too. The canal that lay, sludge
green and putrid, outside the walls of the prison where
she had spent all those years. All those years of wasted
life.

'Will we stop?' Daniel shouted to her as they
rounded the Bailey and saw the little harbour of Howth
snuggled in behind it. But she shook her head and
shouted, no, she didn't want to land, she just wanted
to keep going, for as far as the eye could see. He
laughed and slipped his hand up under her shirt, and
cupped her breast and kissed her on the shoulder as the
wind blew and the boat heeled and the mast creaked
and the rigging rattled and banged. Brass and wire on
wood.

'Hey, Rachel, you promised me food, didn't you?

And something to drink. Come on, you have to take care of your skipper. Isn't that the first rule of the sea?'

She stood up, feeling the boat shift as she changed her weight. And then she was below deck, down in the small tidy cabin, two berths, a little galley with a table and a sink, a two-burner stove and a small fridge. She had brought bread and cold meat. Lettuce and tomatoes, cheese, slices of dark fruitcake. She opened cans of beer and passed one up to him, then laid the food out on the table.

'Dan, do you have a knife? I forgot to bring one.' She put her head out through the hatch, watching as he lifted the beer to his mouth and drank. Saw the dribbles of foam slip down his chin. Heard him say as he wiped his face with the back of his hand, 'The tool box, on the floor. You'd better wash it first.'

She pushed back the metal clasps, opened it, found the knife in the tray with the screwdrivers. She pulled it out. Its long blade was folded back, buried in its wooden handle. She eased it free. Pumped water into the sink, holding it underneath the intermittent flow, cleaning it carefully. Then rummaged around again in the tool box, looking for the whetstone. Taking a handkerchief from her pocket, wrapping it around the handle of the knife. Holding the blade at an angle to the stone, sliding it backwards and forwards, over and over again. Hearing the metallic rasp of metal on stone, making the hairs stand up on the back of her neck and her nipples tighten against her blouse. Then reaching into her bag, her fingers finding the smoothness of a small bottle. Taking it out. Unscrewing the top.

Taking a long swallow of brandy. Looking up again towards the hatch. Seeing Daniel there, his thick dark hair blowing back from his face. Hearing his voice. He was singing, muttering the words of a song. She dropped back out of sight. Took hold of the bottle and drank again, then picked up the knife with the handkerchief again. Held it in her right hand. Spread the fingers of her left hand, looked at them, then brought it down hard so it sliced between her thumb and her first finger. Sliced through the skin, the flesh, the muscle, the blood vessels. Sliced hard and deep into them all. So the pain shot through her fingers, up her arm, rushed into her heart. So she cried out, screamed, in agony, in fear.

'Daniel, Daniel, help me. I'm hurt!'

Saw the blood gush from her hand. Held it out in front of her, watched the way it dripped everywhere. On to the floor, on to the pretty flowered covers of the bunks, on to her trousers, her shirt, and then, as Dan was there in front of her, on to his shirt, dripping all over his clothes as he tried to take hold of it, tried to help her, while she screamed and screamed, seeing large black shapes dance in front of her eyes, as the pain poured through every nerve in her body.

'The knife, the knife, I didn't realize it was so sharp. Where is it? Pick it up, don't cut yourself on it. Put it somewhere safe.'

Afterwards she wasn't sure how he managed to bandage her. How eventually he managed to stop the flow of blood. Bring it under control so it no longer stained the gauze bandages he had found in the first-aid kit. Then calmed her down and held her, filled the little kettle with water, boiled it, made her tea, wrapped her in a blanket. Told her not to worry about the blood, which had stained everything. Said she was to rest, that he would clear it up. Said it didn't matter. It was an accident. Anyone can have an accident. Held her tightly to him and soothed her. Until she said, 'What's happening up there, Dan? What's that noise?' They heard the sound of the wind, tearing at the sails, tearing at the rigging as the boat lurched violently and began to tilt over and over and over. He clambered out on to the deck, screaming back at her.

'Get up here quick, put a plastic bag over your hand. I don't know what's happening, but we're in trouble.'

What was it the weather forecast said? Force four, increasing to force six or seven by early evening. Visibility good, but deteriorating. Pressure dropping. Gale-force warning in evidence from nineteen hundred hours. They were right. They were always right. She began to shout instructions at him, remembering what to do, how to do it.

'Get those sails down. Put in two reefs. Here, Dan.' She flung him a life jacket and a safety line. 'Clip yourself on.'

She began to laugh. It was perfect. It was just what she wanted. It was raining. She pulled on her waterproof jacket, zipping it up tightly. So tightly that the blood which was all over her clothes would not be touched by the water. She zipped him into his too. And thought of the knife, where she had put it, slipped

down between the little cooker and the fridge, left
there, safe and sound. She smiled at Dan as the rain
ran down their faces, as gradually he took control of
the boat once again. Turned her back towards home.
Sailed her though the storm, until the wind began to
drop as they saw the harbour lights ahead of them.

It was late by the time they had moored the boat
and Dan had rowed them back to the shore. They were
both exhausted.

'Quite a trip,' she said. Her legs trembled as she
tried to find her balance on solid ground again.

'Not really what you had in mind, I'm sure, was it,
Rachel? Not really your special day.' He smiled ruefully as he put all his gear in the large canvas bag
again, stowing it carefully in the van.

'I don't know, I think it was pretty near perfect,'
she replied, nursing her hand. 'Just the way it always
should be. Plenty of excitement and adventure, and
then a happy ending.'

'Here.' He reached out and tried to take hold of her
hand. She flinched away. 'You need stitches in that.
Let me take you to the hospital, get it seen to.'

She shook her head. 'No, really, you've done
enough. It's fine. I can manage.'

He frowned. 'Aren't you coming back with me? I
thought you were going to stay.' He reached out to
take hold of her arm, but she pulled away.

'No, I'm fine. I'll take care of it. You go. It's late.'

She waited until he started the engine. She could
see the doubt, the anxiety on his face.

'I'll call you tomorrow. Really, I'm fine. Just go.'

She watched the rear lights of his van getting smaller and smaller, then she picked up her bag. It was heavy. It had everything she needed. She walked through the boatyard and along the harbour road. She looked up at the apartments. The lights were off in Jack Donnelly's sitting room. But she could see that his door was open. She could see that he was there. She looked away. She kept on walking.

CHAPTER TWENTY-SEVEN

IT HAD BEGUN to rain every day now. The fine dry spell was over. The kids had gone back to their mother. He missed them. It wasn't the same without them. He felt lonely and depressed. Useless, somehow. Even though he was spending most of his time with Alison in her beautiful house, with its glowing pine floors and bright jewel-like colours on the walls.

'Move in with me, why don't you?' Alison had said.

He had wondered and dithered, and thought about the disinterested peace of his white-walled flat over-looking the harbour. An inability to commit, that was his problem. He couldn't even decide to paint the sitting room, let alone make any other decisions. Bloody pathetic, that's what he was.

He was depressed about the Judith Hill case too. He had rung her mother a couple of times, spoken to her, asked her how she was, how Stephen was coping. The news was not good.

'I'm terribly worried about him. He's acutely depressed. I'm trying to get him to come and stay with me but he's very hostile to the idea. You know, I had gone some part of the way with Judith. We were beginning to get to know each other. But I don't have anything much with Stephen, apart from the fact that I am his mother.'

'Where is he living? He's not at home, is he?'

She sighed. 'No. He isn't. He's been staying with the Bradleys. Which is another reason why it's very awkward.'

Jack could imagine. 'Look,' he said, 'would you like me to go and see him?'

There was silence. 'Actually, Mr Donnelly, it's kind of you to offer, but I don't think that would be a good idea. Best leave him alone, let him get on with it. I'm going to come over myself, I'm not sure exactly when, but sometime in the next week or so. I'll give you a ring then, maybe we might meet. But leave it for the time being.'

He supposed he should do that. After all, it wasn't as if he didn't have enough new cases to keep him busy. There had been another spate of drug-related killings. More broken bodies like poor little Karl O'Hara. More distraught mothers and girlfriends, fatherless kids. There were two deaths in particular that he was sure were connected. He wanted to talk to Andy Bowen about them. He picked up the phone and punched in his number. He hadn't seen him for a while. It was time for a pint and sandwich.

Andy didn't look good. He looked thin and very pale.

'I'm glad you phoned, Jack,' he said. 'Actually, I was just about to call you myself.'

'Missing me, eh? Missing all the scintillating conversation, the little nuggets of wisdom that drop from
my lips, is that it?'

'Piss off.' Andy smiled and lifted his glass to salute
him. He drank. No whiskey today, Jack noticed. Or
maybe he'd already had it before he arrived.

'No, it's something else. I'm not sure, it may be
nothing. But I'm worried about Rachel Beckett. She
hasn't shown up for a couple of her appointments. And
I got a phone call this morning from the woman who
runs the dry-cleaner's. She's missed work. And her
landlord's been on to me, too, to say she hasn't paid
her rent.'

'How long has it been since you've seen her?'

'It must be ten days or so. You see,' he paused and
drank again, 'I suppose I should tell you. I have this
arrangement with her. It's a bit unorthodox.'

'Oh, yeah.' Jack looked at him. 'You sneaky bugger.
Who'd have thought it? The black widow of all
people.' He smirked.

'No, it's nothing like that. Are you mad? No, I
thought it would be good for her.' And he told him
about Clare.

Jack looked at him and raised his eyebrows. 'That's
a bit odd, isn't it? Kind of a crazy thing to do, I would
have thought. To put a convicted murderer in a
position of trust with your own wife. Kind of mixing
the professional with the personal, isn't it? Not strictly
according to the rule book, I would have thought.'

Andy's face reddened. He sat up straight.

'And do you, any of you, always operate strictly according to the rule book? Come on, who are you kidding?'

'That's as may be, Andy, but I've never involved my family in anything I've done. That's different. That's dangerous.'

'Oh, for Christ's sake, Jack, get off your high horse. Rachel Beckett isn't violent or dangerous. You know that. What happened with her was a one-off. There was never any suggestion that she would reoffend. Not really. She shouldn't have served that sentence, you know that as well as I do. In fact, if the truth be told, a conviction of manslaughter would have been more appropriate. She was extremely unlucky. These days she might not even have gone to prison. And if she had she'd probably have been out in a couple of years. Anyway,' he took a long swallow from his glass and wiped his mouth with the back of his hand, 'anyway, it's worked out really well with Clare. They like each other. Rachel is very good to her. And it's made things so much easier for me.'

Easier for you to go out and get plastered all the time, Jack thought. And immediately felt sorry for him. He sighed. 'OK, well, whatever.' He pointed his finger in Andy's direction. 'I still think it's dodgy. And I don't think your superiors are going to be too impressed.' Andy made as if to interrupt.

Jack held up his hands, palms out. 'Yeah, yeah, I get the picture. You want me to make a few discreet enquiries, see if she's just taken off on a bit of a notion or something, fallen in love or whatever, discovered

God, gone on a retreat. Don't worry, I'll do it. And I'll keep my mouth shut. For the time being.'

But there was more that Andy wanted him to know. What his wife had told him. 'She said to me, when Rachel didn't show up for the second time, that she was really worried about her. She said that Rachel had told her something, made her promise that she wouldn't tell me. But now she wasn't so sure. Apparently Daniel Beckett had found out that Rachel had left prison. He'd tracked her down, found out where she was staying. And he'd been to see her. Clare says that Rachel was in a bad state afterwards. She was terrified. She said that he had raped her. She had bruises all over. Bad ones.'

'Why didn't she tell you about it?'

'Clare said she was terrified that this would upset her temporary release. That she would be sent back to prison. She said that she had told Dan that when she was more able to manage on her own she would move away. That she didn't want to cause him any problems. But according to what Clare said, she was badly frightened.'

'And do you believe her? What kind of mental state is Clare in these days?'

'Ah, come on, Jack, she's ill, very ill, but she's not that bad. She's not hallucinating or imagining things. Look, why don't you come and talk to her yourself? Make up your own mind. I just think it's odd, that's all. But I don't want to do anything about it officially until I'm sure what's going on. I feel I owe it to her to give her a bit of a chance.'

To say nothing of your own chance, Jack thought as he finished his drink. 'OK, I'll go and have a look around her flat. Talk to the neighbours. See what the story is.'

He remembered the way her room had looked that day he had come to ask her about Judith. Everything so neat and tidy and clean. The huge sash window was pushed right up, so a strong easterly breeze blew in off the sea, lifting the curtains and making the paper lampshade whirl around on its central flex. She had told him she liked it like that, even though it was cold.

There's no wind in prison, she had said. There's nothing like that inside. Even outside in the yard, you're still inside.

Today it was just the same, neat and tidy, everything in its place. Except the window was tightly closed. The room smelled stuffy, airless. He stood in the middle of the floor and looked around him. There was a bunch of flowers, wilted, in a glass vase in the middle of the small kitchen table, and a smell of decay that came from the cupboard beneath the sink. He pulled it open and lifted out a plastic rubbish bag. Tea leaves and vegetable peelings that had all gone mouldy. He poked gingerly around. Scraps of bread, some apple cores. Nothing much. He opened the fridge. There was a small carton of milk, sour, solid, and a couple of cartons of natural yoghurt and some cheese. He dumped them all in the plastic bag and opened each of the small cupboards. A pile of plates and bowls, a couple of mugs. And in the drawer next to the sink some cheap cutlery. He walked across the room and opened the wardrobe. Not much here either. A couple of dresses and skirts, two pairs of trousers and a suede jacket, which looked new and expensive, all hanging from wire hangers. On the row of shelves there were piles of underwear, T-shirts, some blouses and sweaters, all folded neatly. Nothing looked new, apart from the jacket and a pair of sandals, still in their cardboard box, in the bottom of the cupboard. He reached up to the shelf at the top. His fingers felt something hard. He pulled it out. It was a small brown leather suitcase. The remains of a tattered label were glued to its scratched lid. He sat down on the bed and opened it. Inside was a pile of old photographs. He flicked through them. A small child, an older couple. He recognized them all. Daughter and parents. There were a number of official-looking letters all on Department of Justice headed notepaper. And beneath them lay a large brown envelope. He lifted it up. It was heavy. He turned it upside down and tipped the contents out beside him. It was money. Wads and wads of notes, in different denominations, fastened together with thick elastic bands. He did a quick count. There must be a few thousand here. Five thousand at least. And crumpled in the bottom of the envelope a note, in faded handwriting:

From your mother. She wanted you to have this. Something to help you get back on your feet.

He stood up then and stripped the bed, pulling away the mattress. There was nothing to find. He lifted the rug from the floor, sliding it away, but again nothing but dust. He opened the door to the small bathroom. It smelt of damp. He tugged at the mirrored front of the cupboard above the sink. Inside was a packet of Anadin, a new tube of toothpaste, a couple of bars of soap. Some jars of face cleanser and moisturizer. A toothbrush lay on the sink, and a face cloth was folded over the edge of the bath. That was all. In the corner next to the bath was a wicker basket. He lifted the lid. A towel, a sheet, a pair of jeans, a pair of trousers made from something like linen, a blouse, a bra and a couple of pairs of pants lay crumpled in a heap. He pulled them out and threw them on the floor, and saw immediately, on the sheet, a smear of something that looked like dried blood. He picked it up and walked back into the bedroom, into the light. There was blood, that was sure, and something else. An opaque stain, sticking in a small ridge to the material. He stood by the window and looked around him. What of value had she brought to this room? What of value was still here? He looked down at the photographs, scattered now on the floor. The child with the straight brown hair looked back at him. He sat down on the bed again and noticed the large map on the wall. It was a map of the city, different areas outlined in different colours. He remembered he had commented on it that day.

It's my memory map, she had said. I needed it when I was in prison, when I began to forget what was outside. I'm keeping it for old times' sake.

He piled the money into a heap and began to count. Carefully, taking his time. All together there was six thousand, seven hundred and fifty-five pounds there. A lot of money for someone like Rachel Beckett.

He thought about the conversation that he had had that morning with the woman called Sheila Lynch. Someone else who Clare Bowen had told her husband about.

'Yes,' Mrs Lynch said to him, 'I know Rachel and I'm worried about her. I can't understand where she could have got to. I drop in on her from time to time. But the last time I called to the shopping centre to see her, they told me they didn't know where she was. I've bought her a few things, you know, given her a few presents. She has nothing, the poor girl. Absolutely nothing. And it's so difficult for her. She's not like the rest of those people who go to prison, you know. She comes from a good family. She was well brought up. It was so hard for her, for all those years. And now she's trying to make it right again, and she was so upset that her daughter wouldn't see her. I counselled patience. I told her how volatile teenagers can be. But I am worried. I can't imagine where she's got to.'

'What do you reckon?' he asked Alison that night as they lay together in her bed. 'You've met her. What do you think of her?'

'She's extremely vulnerable. You should have seen her that day she came to meet Amy. She was so nervous she could barely stand. And afterwards, after Amy blew her out, I actually felt like going after her, to see if she was all right. I wouldn't have been surprised if we'd had to fish her out of the river, she looked so shattered.'

'So do you think this disappearance could be suicide?'

Alison shook her head. She turned and kissed him on the shoulder, resting her lips against his skin for a moment. 'No, not really. Rachel must by now be what we call a hope addict. Hope has sustained her through her years in prison. Hope is all she has left.'

'Is that hope or fantasy?'

'Does it make any difference at this stage? I doubt it,' she replied, and lay back on the pillow, curling her body around his. He turned towards her. She looked very pretty, her eyes closed, her hair falling forward over her face. He kissed her gently on the forehead and pulled her closer. He reached out and switched off the lamp. He closed his eyes. He slept.

CHAPTER TWENTY-EIGHT

IT WAS A trap. Daniel Beckett could see that clearly now. She had set it, baited it, sat back and waited. And he had sprung it. Without even knowing what he was doing. Without a struggle, an ounce of resistance. He had accepted all the lures and temptations. And now he was paying for it. Hand over fist.

The police had been very polite when they had come to the door early that morning. He had heard the bell ringing somewhere far off, deep in the dream that was carrying him towards wakefulness. But he didn't want to open his eyes. There was something wrong. He knew it. There had been something wrong for the last couple of weeks. Ever since the Saturday that he had taken Rachel out on his boat, when Ursula and the kids had gone to the States for a couple of weeks to see her family, and he had stayed behind in the house by himself. Well, not quite by himself, because Rachel had been there with him.

They had been very polite when they saw him standing on the doorstep, clutching his dressing gown, his feet bare, his eyes filled with sleep, his mouth dry and arid. The politeness had lasted while they drove him up the hill to Killiney village, then down the winding road to the town below. It even lasted until they had put him first of all into a cell, then, after half an hour or so, brought him into what they called an interview room. Then the politeness had ended.

He had met them all before, the men who came and went throughout the day, asking him the same questions over and over again. The inspector, Jack Donnelly, was the one who was in charge. It was he who had turned up at the house and had spoken to Ursula the day after she came back, when she was still jet-lagged. Half asleep. Shown her Rachel's photograph. Asked her if she knew her. When she had last seen her. Then come back again, sometime later, when it all began to get much more complicated and difficult, and said casually, 'It must have been hard for you when you realized who she was and what her relationship had been with your husband.' Feigned innocence of the consequences of his question.

It was Donnelly too who had come to see him in the office that first time. Led him gently along. Allowed him to say that, yes, of course he remembered her. And, no, of course he hadn't seen her for years.

'Oh,' Donnelly had said, 'that's strange because your wife has told us that this woman, who she recognized from a photograph although she said she knew her by a different name, was at your house. At a party for your wedding anniversary, in fact. And that you definitely met her that night. Isn't that so?'

So he had to agree, said that it was an awkward situation. Of course he had been surprised to see her,

---

shocked if the truth be told. And he had asked her to leave, thrown her out in fact.

'And your wife really didn't know who she was? Who she really was?'

'Well.' He had paused and thought how best to answer this. 'To be honest, no, she didn't. Rachel had given her some story about how her husband had dumped her for a younger woman. The kind of thing that drives women mad, you know?' He had tried to laugh. 'And Ursula had felt sorry for her, and befriended her. There's no reason to upset her, surely, is there? You say that Rachel hasn't been seen for a few days. She's missed work. She didn't show up for her meeting with her probation officer. Well, I don't know much about these things, but it seems to me that that's a violation of the terms of her probation. I can't see that it has anything to do with me.'

But somehow he could see that this was a problem that wasn't going to go away that easily. He watched Donnelly and the man with him, a sergeant he supposed, called Sweeney, settle themselves down on the leather sofa in his office, the one Ursula had convinced him to buy. They looked comfortable there, he thought. Too bloody comfortable. They didn't look as if they were in a hurry to leave. And Donnelly even had the nerve to ask him if he would hold all his calls for a while. Just until they'd finished with their business.

'It's easier,' Donnelly said, after the third interruption. 'It's much easier and quicker for us all if you wouldn't mind just concentrating on the issue at hand.'

'And,' he had asked, 'what exactly is that?'

Donnelly had said they were worried about Rachel Beckett's safety. They were concerned about her state of mind. Apparently, she had had a very difficult meeting with her daughter some weeks ago, and there was some fear that she may have wanted to hurt herself. Do herself some kind of damage. So they were trying to find out as much as they could about her behaviour recently. Hence their visit to him.

'But surely this isn't a matter for the guards, is it?' He had tried to make his voice as neutral as possible.

'Well,' Donnelly rubbed the palm of his hand over the soft black leather of the couch, 'strictly speaking it isn't, but our colleagues in the probation service are very concerned, and of course if she has done a runner or something like that then it's a matter for us. So we're trying to narrow down the possibilities. Any-way . . .' Again the hand gently caressing, the fingers pressing into the fine-grained skin. 'Anyway, according to the other tenants in the house in Clarinda Park, a man answering your description visited her in her flat there on a number of occasions. And on one occasion, apparently . . .' And here he consulted his notebook. 'Yes, that's right. The kid from the flat below said that he heard what he described as one hell of a row, so noisy that he actually went upstairs to intervene. Would he be right about that?'

He felt suddenly nervous, the skin in his armpits began to prickle with apprehension. He cleared his throat. 'Well, that's a bit of an exaggeration, I'd say. I was kind of upset about her being at the party, and I was very upset that she'd lied to my wife about who she was. I just thought it would have been better if she'd been straight with Ursula. I didn't like the feeling that she'd made a fool of her. After all, Ursula was just trying to be kind.'

'So you had words?'

He shrugged and took a sip of water from the glass on his desk. 'I suppose I was a bit louder than I needed to be. That was all.'

'I see.' Again the palm slid over the smooth black leather. 'And then there was at least one occasion after that when one of the other tenants, who's on the same floor as Rachel and has the bedsit at the front, looking out over the square, said that she heard sounds that were distinctly those of what could be called "love-making". What do you say to that?'

Daniel shrugged again and again sipped from the glass.

'What's it got to do with me? Who's to know what Rachel's been getting up to since she left prison?'

'So.' A pause, and the hand again, pale against the dark leather. 'So the fact that the tenant in the bedsit at the front of the house says she saw a van parked outside, with the words Beckett Securities painted on the side, that wouldn't be significant. No?'

Daniel shifted in his seat, crossing one leg over the other, resting his right ankle on his left knee. His brown leather shoes were dusty. They needed polishing. They were too good to wear to work, he thought. All the mucky places he had to visit every day. The building sites, the factory premises, the industrial estates on the outskirts of the city. Ursula was right. She was always telling him he should stick to runners, that he'd ruin his good shoes like this. But he liked to wear leather on his feet. There was something about the look of rubber and canvas that made him feel stupid, inadequate, helpless, that reminded him of his teenage years, when he was always in trouble and at a loss, always out of control.

'Look, this is all a bit "so what" really, isn't it? So I gave her a bit of affection, a bit of comfort. She wanted it. She asked me. And I could hardly refuse her. I could see how lonely she was.'

Donnelly stood up. 'Right, Mr Beckett, I see. She's the woman who had been convicted of murdering your brother. You have just discovered that she has told lies to your wife about her identity, and yet you felt like doing her a favour, being nice to her. I have to say it seems a bit odd to me. But then,' he put his notebook away in his jacket pocket and gestured to the younger man, Sweeney, who was still lolling back into the cushions on the sofa, 'as I always say, there's nowt as odd as you know what.'

Sweeney stood up, a wide grin on his face, and together they walked towards the door. Donnelly paused and turned back towards him. 'It was terrible that whole business, wasn't it? I remember your brother well. He was a great guy. You were questioned too, about the murder, I seem to remember. She tried to lay the blame on you, didn't she? You must have been very angry about that, very, very angry. Anyway, not to worry, I'm sure she'll show up somewhere. We'll let you know what happens. We'll keep in touch.'

He had brought Rachel here too. She had lain on the sofa where the two guards had been sitting, while he finished off some work at his desk. They had drunk cold beers that she had fetched from the small fridge in his secretary's office. She had fallen asleep and he had watched her, remembering as he read through the invoices and signed the pile of letters that his secretary had left how she had helped him that summer all those years ago to make sense of everything that until then had been senseless. How she talked to him about books, ideas. Asked him questions, made him think. Argued with him, challenged him. Told him he should go back to school and pick up where he had left off when he got into trouble. Told him he was as clever as everyone else. That he could make something of his life, that he didn't have to spend it any longer in his brother's shadow. If I had you all to myself I could, he had thought then. And when she had thrown him away, gone back to Martin, he had felt that new world she had shown him fade and die. Until that night when Martin had lain bleeding on the floor and he had felt the gun in his hands.

He watched her as she slept, lifting his head from the paperwork and files spread over the desktop. Checking the computer screen, analysing flow charts and spreadsheets. Still fascinated that it was he, the stupid one of the family, who was running the show, calling the shots, the boss. She was beautiful, he thought, more so when her eyes were closed, when he didn't have to look at her expression, always guarded, watchful, ill at ease. And when he had put the last letter in its envelope and dropped it into the out-tray, he went over and lay down beside her, cradling her in his arms, waiting until she woke.

The politeness. He remembered it from the time before. When he had been asked to come into the station, 'Just to make a statement, you understand?' And his father had come with him. On first-name terms with every single guard he met, from the newest recruit to the chief superintendent, who came out of his office to exchange pleasantries, to compare golf scores. Then the politeness had stayed. They had believed him and the alibi that his mother had given him.

'It's a messy business,' the chief super had said to his father. 'I'm sure you understand we have to check this out. She's made accusations, allegations about the lad. We have to follow them up.' And his father had allowed himself to be reassured, then offered to meet for a pint, later on that day, or perhaps a game of golf at the weekend.

That time, he seemed to remember, he had been taken into a room which was close to the front desk. With windows and posters about neighbourhood watch and crime prevention on the walls. This time the room where they brought him was at the far end of the building. It stank. It had no windows or posters. And there was no politeness there either.

'I don't understand,' he said, 'what this is all about.

What you've been doing to me over the last few weeks. First of all you start harassing my wife, needlessly upsetting her by telling her things about my past which are my business and only my business. Then you start watching me, following me, going around all my sites, questioning my staff. Then you show up at my house again, asking me the same old questions over and over although I've already told you everything I know.'

'And not told us everything you know, isn't that the point, Dan? I've asked you repeatedly about where you might have gone with Rachel Beckett and you didn't tell us about the trip you made with her on your boat. A lot of people saw you that day. They saw the two of you down at the pier. They saw you get into the dinghy and head off with her. But no one saw you come back. So why don't you just get it all off your chest? Tell us what happened.'

He looked around the small stuffy room. There was Donnelly and Sweeney and an unnamed, uniformed guard standing in the corner. Every now and then there would be a knock at the door and someone else would come in to whisper in Donnelly's ear or pass him a note. Donnelly would smile or frown, consult with Sweeney in another whisper. It was all play-acting, Daniel knew. He'd heard his father talk about interrogations often enough in the past to know what was smoke and what was fire. But he wasn't taking any chances.

'Look,' he said, 'I've had enough. I want my solicitor. I know what my rights are. I told you to phone him. I told you to get him here and I'm not saying another word until you do. Do you understand?'

'Fine, no problem.' Donnelly nodded to Sweeney. 'Go and see what's holding the guy up, will you, and while you're at it bring in all the evidence. We might as well get started on that.'

They had served a number of search warrants on him. For his house, his office, his boat. Ursula had barely spoken to him for days now. The atmosphere in the house was poisonous. In vain, he had tried to tell her there was nothing to find, there could be nothing to find. Rachel Beckett was alive. He knew that.

'But what I can't understand,' she kept on saying to him, 'is what you were doing with her. Why did you see her again after that night at the party? I just don't understand it. I don't understand what was going on between the two of you.'

He had been present when they made their searches. He had seen the objects they had removed. Slipped in underneath the low double bed where he and Rachel had slept, where he and Ursula slept every night, they had found a pair of homemade earrings. Coloured beads on wire. They had found a button underneath the cushions on the sofa that matched, they said, one from a jacket of Rachel's. They had taken fingerprints from door handles and tabletops. And they had found in the remains of a bonfire of leaves and garden rubbish, down by the path to the cliff, a charred leather handbag with a matching wallet and a small pocket diary, with a number of entries in Rachel's handwriting. From his car they had picked hairs and fibres and found more fingerprints. And in the boot, in the canvas duffel bag in which he kept his sailing gear, they had found his jacket, dark brown smears all down the front. But it was what they had found in the boat that most worried him.

'Explain that to us now, Dan. Your solicitor is here, present. He will, I'm sure, make certain that you don't say anything that you wouldn't want to. But you do have to give us an explanation for this.'

Donnelly held up a clear plastic bag. Inside was a knife.

'So, Dan, tell us again what happened that Sunday when you and Rachel Beckett went out on your boat.'

The trap was being sprung. He thought of the rats he had seen his men and their dogs chasing on building sites for a bit of sport. He had watched the rats slither through impossibly tiny holes, flattening themselves to slide underneath stones, behind brick walls, jumping heights that might be eight, nine, ten times their own size. And then the moment of triumph when one of the dogs would seize the struggling rodent in its teeth. The sound of its frenzied screams made him cringe. He listened to the shrieks that were almost human in their pitch and intensity. And finally he would hear the dull sound as spade or shovel would flatten the animal against the ground. He thought of Rachel that day on the boat. She was wearing sunglasses, he remembered. They suited her, hid the tiredness of her eyes, made her look younger. He commented to her that they were expensive.

Where did you get them? he asked.

She smiled, her mouth opening, so her teeth peeped through her lips. *A secret admirer*, she said, then stretched herself out on the long seat on one side of the cockpit.

It was perfect sailing weather when they left the harbour. A south-easterly force four carrying them on a broad reach across Dublin Bay, past Howth, and onwards. He had forgotten what a good sailor Rachel was. She had an intuitive understanding of wind and wave. She moved with the boat, her balance perfect. As nimble as she had been years ago, although not as strong, he noticed, her hands soft and tender. But there were winches on this boat, so strength wasn't such an issue. It was a good solid wooden sloop. Bermudan rig. Thirty feet in length over all, with one cabin below, a tiny galley and a toilet aft.

How far are we going? she had asked him.

And in reply he had said, *How far would you like to go?*

And she had laughed and held one hand over her eyes, in an exaggerated ship's captain pose and replied, *As far as the eye can see.*

Time was a different commodity at sea. He had always noticed that. It was only his hunger that made him think of how long they had been out there, *Hey, Rachel, you promised me food. I'm starving. What'll it be?*

He could hear her singing to herself down below. Her voice was tuneless. He looked around him. There weren't so many other boats out today, despite the holiday and the weather. It was very quiet here. Very beautiful. Very lonely. He rested the tiller against his thigh, feeling the boat driving forward under the pressure of the wind. He closed his eyes and for a moment he drifted off.

He heard her voice. Saw her face looking up at him through the hatch. *Dan, do you have a knife? I forgot to bring one.*

Tool box, watch out, it's very sharp. Turned his face up to the sun. Contentment, practically happiness. Then heard a cry. Sudden fear in her voice.

What is it? he shouted.

She didn't answer.

Rachel, he called again, *what's the matter?*

Screaming, no words, just sound.

Help me, help me. I've cut myself. I was using your knife to slice tomatoes and it slipped. I'm bleeding like mad. There's blood all over everything. I'm so sorry. I'm making a real mess down here.

Then he heard her again. *Dan, can you help me? I feel weak. I think I'm going to be sick.*

He lashed the tiller in place and swung himself down into the cabin. She was sitting on the bunk, holding her left hand. Blood was running down her wrist, down her arm, dripping off her elbow. Blood on the flowered covers of the cushions, blood on the floor, blood all over her clothes.

Christ, he said as she reached out towards him, her face milky white, her eyes glazed, and fell against his chest. Blood on his shirt, blood on his jacket, blood all over the handkerchief he took from his pocket to bind the cut, the slice through the skin between thumb and first finger and down the pad of flesh beneath.

What did you do to yourself? How on earth did you do it?

It was your knife. I didn't realize how sharp it was. I dropped it somewhere.

She stood up.

There. Look.

The knife was on the floor by her feet. He bent down and picked it up, putting it carefully out of the way on the shelf where he kept his charts, his compass, his sextant. He felt in the locker beneath the fold-out table for the first-aid kit. Then held her hand over the small sink in the galley, ignoring her protests as he pumped water from the tap on to the cut, watching the water turn pink as the blood ran down into the drain below. Then fumbled with a pad of cotton wool, a bandage, sticking plaster, anything to stop the blood that continued to seep through. Finally, holding her hand, squeezing it tightly, ignoring the blood that stained his clothes, until eventually its flow ceased. Then bound her hand with a clean bandage and laid her back on the cushions to rest, while he found some brandy and gave her a glass then boiled the kettle for tea.

'I see.' Donnelly picked up the plastic bag again and looked at it. He turned it this way and that, then handed it to Sweeney. 'I see. She cut herself with your knife. Your knife which only has your fingerprints on it. Your fingerprints in the blood which has been identified as her blood. She cut herself so badly that she bled all over the cabin of the boat, despite someone's attempts to clean it up. She bled all over your shirt and trousers, your jacket, your handkerchief. And then, after she'd finished bleeding, she managed to slip the knife down behind the little cooker, in a place where it wouldn't be found unless you actually pulled the whole thing to pieces, which is what, unfortunately, we had to do.'

Pick it up, Dan, before you step on it and get hurt. He could still hear her voice. The concern, the anxiety.

I'm all right, she said. *I'm fine, really. I just need to rest for a little bit. But I think you'd better go back up on deck. It doesn't sound too good out there.*

'So.' Donnelly put the plastic bag back in the box again. 'A number of people saw you leave the harbour with the woman on the boat. No one saw you come back. Now why would that have been?'

She was right. It wasn't too good out there now. The wind had freshened. He reckoned it was force five, heading for six. It was cold suddenly and dark, clouds hanging low overhead, and streaks of rain, like wisps of dirty cobweb, visible on the horizon and getting closer. The swell had deepened and as he swung the boat around into the wind, struggling to gain control again, waves began to break over the bow and foredeck, sending streams of water rushing back into the cockpit. The weather forecast. Had it said this? He had asked Rachel to phone the recorded message. What had she said? Force three strengthening to four in the late afternoon. Visibility good. Possibility of light rain. Nothing like the storm that was gathering around him.

Can you manage? He saw her pale face looking up at him, still holding tightly on to the bandage, then reaching down into the cabin and handing him out his rain gear. *Here, put this on. You'll get soaked.*

He had struggled with the main sail, to reef it, to make it smaller, fighting to keep his balance on the slippery deck, feeling the tide still carrying them back down the coast. It was she, wasn't it, he was sure, who had said, the engine, use the engine, take the sails down. But when he checked the diesel he could see that the tank was virtually empty and the spare container was empty too.

Getting dark now, the lights from the houses along the coast glowing, wondering should he call for help. Then she was beside him, her hand wrapped in a plastic bag, wearing his old yellows, too big, so she looked like a clown. A smile on her face as she said, *It's all right. We can manage. Here.* Taking the tiller. Somehow finding a course. Beating out on a long tack that took them, it seemed, almost out of sight of land, then going about, the bow of the boat rearing up, seeming almost to fall back on top of them, then settling down, cutting a furrow through the waves. Going below to hand him up squares of chocolate, slices of thick rich fruitcake, singing to him in her funny tuneless voice. Sea shanties and pop songs from their youth. Making him laugh, forget his fear. And all the time, keeping the boat on course, so eventually he saw the Dun Laoghaire lights, the encircling walls of the harbour, and felt peace and calm fall over him as they moored the boat. Got into the dinghy and reached the shore.

'That's why it was so late. That's why no one saw us. Because of the storm. That's why.'

'And that's how you were able to cover her killing,

isn't it? Where did you dump her body, Dan? How far out did you go with her? And you were careful, weren't you? You took off her clothes, anything that might identify her further. And you dumped them too. But you know what, Dan? You should have given a bit more thought to the tidal drift in the Irish sea. Did you know that although there's a hell of a rush up and down the coast, once you get out a bit further it's like a bloody swimming pool. Nothing moves much. And that's how we managed to get this.'

Another clear plastic bag, and inside it the remains of a black sack and some clothes.

'Pulled out in some fishing nets. A trawler from Howth. The skipper was telling me. He said you'd be amazed what they find out there. You see, he said, the Irish Sea is like a tube. Once you get beyond the Kish lighthouse everything just goes round and round and round. You know what they are, don't you? It's what Rachel was wearing, wasn't it? A pair of trousers and a shirt. Her new clothes. The ones that her nice friend Mrs Lynch bought her. She recognized them immediately. And do you know what's in the shirt? Tears, rips, made with a very sharp knife. Just like the one we found in the boat. And do you know what else we found? Bloodstains. It's incredible, isn't it, the way even sea water can't get rid of them all.'

'But tell us, you took off her clothes, why was that? So she wouldn't be identified by them? Was that it? Or had you already taken off her clothes before you killed her? And why didn't you dump her bag out at sea too? Did she leave it in the car? Was that it? Or did she leave it in the house that day, and you found it when you came back that night?'

It was a trap, that's what it was. He could see it all so plainly now. He had assumed she was going to come back with him for a last night. He looked at her clothes, bloodstained, crumpled. He said, he remembered, *We'll stop off at your place. You can pick up something to wear. Then we'll go back to Killiney. A hot bath, a good bottle of wine. There are steaks in the freezer. I'll cook us a meal. I don't know about you, but I could eat a horse. Or maybe, here, let me look at your hand, will I take you to the hospital?*

But she had shook her head. Said, no, she was too tired. She was stiff from the boat. She wanted to walk for a bit. Stretch her legs.

Don't worry about me. I'm fine. If my hand is still bad in the morning I'll go to the doctor myself.

Then she had kissed him gently on the cheek and given him a little push. Said, *Go on, off you go. Thanks for everything you've done for me today. You'll never know how great you've been.*

'So.' Donnelly sat back, crossing his legs, folding his arms. 'So, where is she now, Dan? You say you didn't kill her, so where is she?'

He had thought they would charge him that night. But they didn't. They let him go. They were sending the file to the Director of Public Prosecutions. They would be in touch. Sooner rather than later.

'What do you make of it?' he asked his solicitor as they walked to the car.

The tall thin man with a pronounced stoop didn't

answer immediately. Then he sighed. 'I think we need some expert opinion on this. They've no body, but that doesn't mean they've no case. It's happened a couple of times before. There was one particular trial, I remember. A girl in Liverpool went missing. Never seen again. A barman in the local pub was questioned, charged with her murder on the basis of a piece of rope they found in the boot of his car. It had the girl's blood on it. He was convicted, sentenced to life. Even though they never found the girl's body.'

He got a taxi as far as the top of the hill. He felt like walking. His thigh muscles ached from the tension of the day. He felt dirty, contaminated. He could smell the staleness of his own sweat. He walked down the road towards his house. The black of the night pressed in around him. She had told him what prison was like. It's never dark like night-time, she said. And it's never bright like daytime either. It's always in between.

Fuck the bitch, he thought, anger breaking through his despair. I beat her once before and I'll beat her again. One way or another, she's not going to get away with this.

Ahead of him lay the house. It was in darkness. He put his key in the lock and opened the door, forgetting that he was alone. Calling out for Ursula, for the children, for someone, anyone. But the house was empty. He sat down on the stairs, his head in his hands. He had to hand it to her. What a trap. What a scheme. What a nightmare.

Chapter Twenty-Nine

THE HOUSE WAS very quiet now with Ursula and the children away. He had given the cleaning woman a month's pay and told her to go. The gardener could still be seen pushing the mower backwards and forwards across the striped lawn and bent double over the rows of vegetables in the walled garden. He supposed he would keep him on for the time being. Ursula would not thank him if the gorse and bracken of the hillside, the bindweed, buttercup, and scutch grass was to swallow up all her hard work.

He did not know when she would come back. She had taken the children and gone back to Boston. She had been adamant. They would not return until this mess, as she described it, had been sorted out.

'I will not put up with it!' she had screamed at him. 'I won't go through all that shit, with the newspapers and television, and everyone looking at us, and spying on us, and making judgements. I won't have it.'

He had watched her pack, noting the methodical, careful way she ticked off the items on her long list. Sending the children scurrying into their bedrooms to select their favourite toys. Laura had clung to his thigh, looking up at him with her round grey eyes, her shiny dark hair silky beneath his hand as he bent down to push her away. How old was she now, he wondered? That other dark little girl, who he had cradled in his arms when she was born, who he had watched as she grew, and grew more like him. Had he noticed it? Not really, not at the time. He had thought she had taken after her mother, rather than her father. And it was only that night when Rachel had phoned him and told him what had happened that he had seen her for what she was. His own daughter, his own flesh and blood. The only time he had ever had anyone who he could say was truly related to him.

'She's mine?' he had said to Rachel. 'You mean she's actually my child? Is that what you're saying?'

And he had felt joy, warm and golden, spreading through him, like the smile that he saw spreading across his face as he looked in the mirror hanging on the wall beside the phone. My child, my baby, my own. He listened to her sobs, heard her fear, soothed and reassured her, and said, 'Don't worry. I'm on my way. I'll sort it out. Don't you worry.'

He had thought as he drove to the cul-de-sac where Rachel and the child lived with his brother, that now, surely, she would leave him. Now that she knew that the child was his, when she didn't even have that tie to bind her to Martin any longer, now, surely, she would decide that he was not the man she wanted. And she would come to live with him, and he would build her a whole house, not just a conservatory. Maybe he would even build her a boat. Perhaps they would sail away together, to the sun, and start a new life, and maybe even have more children. A boy who would take after him even more than the little girl.

'Daddy.' Laura pulled at his fingers. 'Daddy, why aren't you coming with us to America? I want you to come. Please. Mummy, tell Daddy he's to come with us.'

But Ursula's face was set hard and frozen. She didn't reply. She just shooed Laura away, sent her off with a list of errands, and when he came up behind her and put his arms around her, cupping her breasts in his hands in the way she always liked, she pulled away from him and spat back over her shoulder, 'You should have thought about what you might lose before you started messing around with that bitch.' Then faced him again, screaming, 'How could you do it when you could see how she had deceived me? What were you thinking of?'

And when he didn't answer her immediately she pushed him hard, so he fell back out of the room, putting his hands over his ears as he heard the door slam behind him.

And now all was silence in the house. He wandered from room to room, looking around him as if in a stranger's home. Where had all this furniture come from? Who had picked the paintings on the walls? Bought the rugs which lay like pools of brightness across the dark wooden floors? Chosen the flowered Victorian tiles that decorated the bathrooms? He remembered the pleasure that Rachel had got from the work he did for her that summer as he had laid the simple terracotta floor, brushing the grout into place. And how they had sat and celebrated together and watched the moon rise above the garden, and she had named the constellations that under her guidance formed themselves into shapes he could recognize. The Bull, the Plough, the Archer, the Hunter and the Hunter's Belt. The same shapes that they had watched together here, sitting out on the terrace, while the light from the full moon fell upon the sea like handfuls of silver, and the breeze in the branches of the pine trees sounded like the exhaled breath of a large sleeping beast.

But now he took no pleasure from that same view. He felt as if a blind of some dense, opaque material had been lowered in front of it. So he could see it dimly, but as if in the far distance. And when he wandered out through the French windows on to the terrace, where he had met Rachel for the first time just a few weeks ago, and walked across the grass to the top of the cliff, all he could think about was the remains of the bonfire, sifted and analysed by the guards in their white overalls. The ash carried away in plastic bags to see what else they could find, apart from her bag and her diary and her make-up and her money.

'Why?' he had said to them. 'Why, if I was going to burn them, would I not have made sure that they burned completely? Why would I have left them partially intact? Why, if I wanted to hide something, why would I leave any evidence around?'

But Donnelly had just shrugged and said, 'You tell us, Dan. You tell us what happened.'

He thought back over those two days and nights when she had stayed there with him. He had had to go out for a while. Finish off some business. Would she come with him, he asked? But she had said no, that it was so beautiful here in this garden on the clifftop that she would like to stay behind. If he didn't mind, of course. She would cook him dinner. See if she could remember how to do it after so long. And when he had returned the kitchen was full of the scent of olive oil and basil. She had made pesto, picked handfuls of the fresh herbs from the raised beds by the terrace and crushed it in a pestle and mortar to make the sauce. That was all he could smell, even when they went to sit on the terrace after dinner, although he wondered if that was wood smoke he could see hanging in the air and was anxious for a moment, in case there might be a fire down among the dry bracken near the cliff edge. But she carried out a tray with a jug of coffee and a bottle of Calvados and a cigar in a metal tube.

'I remember,' she said, 'how you liked them. So I bought this one specially for you. It's from Havana.'

And he had felt almost disloyal, thinking how Ursula hated the smell and wouldn't have them in the house. And then felt ridiculous that he was feeling guilty about that when he didn't feel guilty about anything else. Then he thought that had Rachel done what he wanted that night, it might then have been the most natural thing in the world for the two of them to be here together on this beautiful summer's evening. And they could have been talking about their daughter, and what she was or wasn't doing. They could have been planning her future. They could have seen their own future stretching out before them, secure and comfortable. Full of love and commitment and small triumphs. But of course, he thought as he poured Calvados into two small Waterford crystal glasses and lifted the porcelain coffee cup to his lips, if Martin had lived all this would have been his. And where would he have been then? He lit the cigar and drew heavily on it, drawing the smoke deep into his lungs, so for a moment his chest felt as if it would burst open, and the blood rushed through his veins, roaring in his ears, drowning out every other sound as he thought of what might have been. A minion's job, a minion's life. Slave and lackey to his clever brother. Never able to cut his losses and go, for fear that he might miss out on some treat or other. And it might not have mattered if she had said that she would be with him. But she hadn't said that, that night, when he had stood at the door and seen through the frosted-glass panel the shadows of Martin and Rachel as they waited for him.

Daniel had said to her, as he pushed her into the hall and watched Martin walk away down towards the kitchen, 'Come with me, now. I want you. He doesn't.'

And she had said, 'Are you mad, are you crazy? I don't want you. I don't love you. Not the way I love him.'

'So, what am I doing here? Why did you ask me to come?'

'Because I'm scared. And you're the only person I can tell. I can't tell anyone else, because I'm so ashamed. Ashamed of what I've done. Ashamed of how I've betrayed him, betrayed the vow I made to him when I married him.'

So she was ashamed, that was it. But not ashamed that she was now betraying me, Daniel had thought, not ashamed that she has been prepared to deny my child her birthright. None of that bothers her. She was holding the gun all the time that they were arguing. He had watched its barrel, the way it swung around as she moved. And he had wondered. Which of them should I shoot? And then it happened, so suddenly even he was taken by surprise. Martin's insults had shocked him with their ferocity, Martin's temper had been frightening to behold. But so was hers. She had turned the gun towards them both, then moved it quickly downwards. The noise had been terrifying, and the smell and the colour of Martin's blood pumping out of his leg. And then she had turned to him, her face stricken, and said, 'What have I done?'

As Martin screamed out in pain, clutching at his shattered thigh. And it all clicked into place. All those years of insults and hurt and pain and rejection. And then she handed him the gun. He remembered the feel of the wooden stock in his hands. His hands in their gloves, the gloves he had worn that night because it was so cold. And he took aim himself and fired. And said to her as the sound of the shot died away, 'Now, now you won't have to be ashamed any more.'

It was getting cold now. There was a wind coming in from the sea, an easterly with just the faintest touch of winter. It rattled the long sash windows and sent a shiver rippling through the heavy curtains. He walked from room to room switching on all the lights. He sat down at the desk in his study and stared at the row of photographs, picking each up in turn. The one of Martin had gone. Ursula had ripped it from its frame and torn it to pieces, pausing only long enough to comment on the way Rachel had looked then.

He stood and walked to the front door. He put his hand in his pocket and pulled out his car keys. He closed the front door behind him and got into the car. He drove slowly up the drive and out on to the road. He looked in the rear-view mirror. Behind him was the usual pair of headlights, keeping the same distance away from him, as always. He drove slowly up the hill to the village, then down towards Dun Laoghaire. It was Saturday night. The main street was busy. He stopped at the newsagent's and pushed his way in through the late-night shoppers. He picked up a pile of the Sunday papers. He scanned the headlines.

'Missing Woman's Daughter's Disappearance.'

'First Mother, Now Daughter, Gone.'

And in huge black type: '**Who is This Man?**' And a photograph of him taken at the gate. And a whole page about his house, his wife and children, his involvement with Rachel.

He paid for the papers and walked out into the street again. He looked to the left and to the right and saw the unmarked car parked just behind his own. He walked towards it, bending down and knocking on the closed window. He waited as the glass pane slid open.

'Listen, lads,' he said. 'Just to let you know. I'm going for a pint. In Walter's. OK? I'll be about an hour, I'd say. But maybe,' he paused, 'maybe I'll be longer than that. I could do with a few tonight. But don't worry. I won't drive if I go over the limit. I'll get a lift home from you two. How about that?' And he sniggered as he walked away, turning back once to wave at the two guards slumped down in their seats.

He pushed open the swing doors into the bar and found himself somewhere to sit. He ordered a drink. He read. He ordered another drink. He read some more. The newspapers had given the story the full treatment. Rehashed all the details of the murder, dredged up their old photographs of Rachel, showed the outside of the house where Amy lived with her foster-family. Even got hold of pictures of Amy as a child. He scanned through them all quickly to see if his name was mentioned. There were references to a man who had been arrested and questioned in connection with the disappearance of Rachel Beckett, but nothing else. He put down the paper and finished his drink, then pushed his way up to the bar and ordered another. It was busy in here tonight. And noisy. Loud music pumping from the speakers, the crash and clatter of bottles and glasses on the cold shiny marble of the bar, the banging of chairs and feet on the hard wooden floors. Everything was glossy and shiny. New. And everyone was young.

He paid for his pint and pushed back to his seat. He looked at the girls all around him. Amy looked like one of them. Brash and confident, with her pierced ears and her bare stomach. He had gone as usual to the café, ordered his coffee and pastry, joked and laughed with her. Smiled up at her, waited for her to smile back. Then when he was leaving he said he'd like to meet her, take her out for a drink. And she had agreed instantly, pushing her small breasts out towards him and resting her hands on her hips. It was early evening when she finished work. He got out of his van and walked towards her. She had put on more make-up, and he could smell her perfume. He handed her into the front seat and drove off towards town. She was nervous, excited. She lit a cigarette. They stopped at a pub. She ordered vodka and coke. She fiddled with her earrings and waited for him to make a move. And then he told her who he really was. That he was her father. Watched her face. Waited for the shock to die away. Waited for the questions.

'How?'

'Why?'

'What happened?'

'I loved my brother,' he said. 'I loved him very much.'

'And did you love her?' The pronoun spat out with vengeance.

What should he say? Which did she want hear?

'I did at the time. At the time when you were

conceived, I loved her very much. But she wanted to stay married to Martin. If I had known that you were mine I would have made her tell him. But I didn't know until that night when he found out.'

'She said you killed him? Did you?' A hard stare, a look that he could not escape. He stared back at her.

'No, I didn't. She killed him. She was frightened and she was ashamed.'

'So she tried to blame you for it? Is that what happened?'

'Yes, she tried to blame me. And now she's trying to punish me. She's done this, this disappearing act. It's a game, that's all. The police think I killed her. They have all this evidence that she planted. But she set me up. Amy, I promise you. I didn't hurt her at all. I wouldn't hurt her. I'm not like that.'

'So why are you telling me all this now? Why have you been coming to the café for the past few weeks? What's going on?'

He took her hand. He turned it over and stroked the lines that criss-crossed the palm.

'I suppose,' he said, 'that I tried to forget all about you. I put all thoughts of you away in a drawer and I turned the key on them. I came to see you when you were living with your grandparents. But they didn't want me around. They didn't know what to make of me. They couldn't decide whether to believe me or their daughter. And then when they couldn't look after you any longer, and you went to the foster-family, I decided that it was better if I stayed away. Let you get on with growing up without any of that stuff, that bad and painful stuff from your past getting in the way. And then when I heard that Rachel had been released from prison, I thought of you again. And I knew I wanted to see you. So I found you. I didn't want to tell you all about it. I didn't want to upset you or drag you into a relationship that you might not have wanted. But for me, I wanted to see you, to see what you were like.'

She looked around her, then looked towards the mirror behind the bar. He followed her gaze.

'We're very alike, aren't we? I can see that immediately. We're much more alike to look at than she and I have ever been.'

'Yes,' he said, 'there's no doubt about it. You're my daughter. My firstborn. And now, Amy, I have to ask you something. I have to ask you to do something for me.'

He was drinking too quickly but he didn't care. He ordered another pint, waited until he had paid for it, then got up and walked around the bar towards the sign for the toilets. He walked down the stairs and along the corridor. He passed the door with the sign for the ladies. He walked into the men's toilet. He was alone. He stood at the urinal. He unzipped his fly. He watched his urine spurt out in a golden arc. He rinsed his hands and walked out into the corridor again. It was empty. He turned towards the back of the building and went through the door at the far end. Ahead was the emergency exit to the lane that ran behind the pub and beside it a payphone. He looked around once more.

Then picked up the phone, feeling for change in his pocket, and punching in a number. He spoke.

'Yeah, it's me. Are you all right? Have you eaten? Is the TV working OK? Can you get all the channels? Good, good. Don't worry. It won't be for long. You're all over the Sunday papers. She'll come running, don't you worry, and before you know you'll be back home again. And you know, Amy, how much I appreciate this, don't you? You do, you do know? I really, really am grateful to you for helping me. And afterwards, when it's all over, and I've the cops off my back, then we can start sorting ourselves out again. I'll never let you go now, you know that. You're my daughter and I love you.' He paused and listened, looking back over his shoulder. 'OK, have a good sleep. I'll talk to you tomorrow. No, I don't know what time it'll be. I have to be careful. I can't phone from home or use my mobile. You know that. OK, kid. I'll say goodnight now. Goodnight.'

It was late when he left the bar. Heading for two. The cops were still there, still parked by his car. He barely glanced at them as he started walking towards Glasthule. His step was unsteady. He swayed as he moved. He hailed a taxi just outside Sandycove. He gave the guy a big fat tip when he let him off at the gate to the house.

'Goodnight, mate,' he said, extra loud, and waited to see the cops arrive before heading for the front door. He dropped the newspapers in a heap beside his bed. He'd read them all again in the morning and listen to the latest in the news bulletins. And wait. But not for long. He knew that. It was the only way to make Rachel show herself. She wouldn't be able to stay away if Amy was in trouble. And Amy knew that too. That was why she had agreed to help him. He explained what he wanted to do. He would hide her in an apartment in the city. She would have everything she needed. It would only be for a few days, until Rachel came forward. And then she would be free. And he would be free. And Rachel would be back where she belonged. Behind bars again.

'You will help me, Amy, won't you? I'll make it up to you, all those years together we missed. You know I wanted you, I wanted us to be a family, but she didn't. She was prepared to deny you that, and me too. But once this is over we can never be separated again. Do you agree?'

And what would he have done if she had said she wouldn't go along with it? He had thought about that too. He was desperate. It had to be done one way or the other. One way was the easy way. The compliant way. The best way. The other was the bottle of chloroform and the pad of cotton wool, the handcuffs and the gag. He had wondered, when he asked her, which way it would go. But she just looked at him with his grey eyes, her straight black eyebrows furrowed together across the bridge of her nose the way his did, and said, 'Of course I'll do it. She can't be allowed to get away with this.'

And told him how she would go out with her friends, and meet him in town, and not go home.

'You won't be able to tell anyone, you know that,

don't you? Your foster-parents will be worried. You do realize, don't you?'

She nodded.

'That's OK,' she said. 'They'll understand, afterwards, when I explain it to them. They'll get over it.'

'I'll never be able to thank you for this, Amy,' he said, and he kissed her gently on her cheek.

And now he waited. Wherever Rachel was she would want to see the newspapers. She was waiting to see when he was going to be charged with her murder. And when she read about Amy she would know it was him. And she would come. And when she did, he'd be waiting.

CHAPTER THIRTY

ANDREW HAD STOPPED going into work. He had gone to the doctor, Clare's doctor, and told him that he couldn't cope any longer. He had asked for medication, antidepressants, tranquillizers, whatever they were called. The doctor had examined him, taken his blood pressure, noted his bad colour, his thinness. Told him he wasn't eating properly, that he was drinking too much, that he should watch it. He was no use to his wife in this condition.

'Perhaps the time has come, Andy, to get her some residential care. Give you a bit of a break.'

But he wouldn't hear of it. What would he have without her? His life was so bounded by her needs. He couldn't imagine how he would fill his time if he didn't have Clare to look after.

He went home, his pills in his pocket, and poured himself a large vodka. They sat together that night. The door to the garden was open. There was a smell of new-mown grass. The boy from next door had cut it. Piled it into little round hillocks all over the lawn.

She asked him to put on some music.

'You choose,' she said.

He picked Elgar. The song 'Where Corals Lie', sung by Janet Baker. He set the CD player to repeat. Over and over again. They sat in the dark and listened to the words. Clare asked him about Rachel Beckett, what was the latest news?

'I miss her,' she said. 'I liked her. Do you think she's dead?'

She began to cough. Her chest was congested. It was pneumonia again, he was sure of it. He listened to the words of the song.

> The deeps have music soft and low,
> When winds awake the airy spry,
> It lures me, lures me on to go,
> And see the land where corals lie.

'What did she have to live for?' he asked.

'Her daughter, her future. She wanted redemption. I know she did.'

He said nothing.

'We talked about, you know . . . We talked about how it might be for you after I've gone. I told her what we wanted to do. I asked her how you would feel. I asked her how she felt.'

'And.'

Clare didn't reply. He looked at her. She lay quietly curled on her side. Her eyes were closed. She had stopped taking her antibiotics. She told him she had had enough.

'It's time, Andy. Now it's time.'

He listened to the music.

'Andy, please, I'm so cold.'

He got up and walked over to the bed. He lay down beside her and pulled her head on to his chest. She coughed and coughed. He sat up and pulled her up beside him.

'Hush,' he said, 'hush. Go to sleep. It'll be better in the morning.'

He picked up her glass. He put her pills into her mouth. He gently poured the juice between her lips. She swallowed, choked, swallowed again. She closed her eyes. He listened again to the words of the song.

> *Thy lips are like a sunset glow,*
> *Thy smile is like a morning sky,*
> *Yet leave me, leave me, let me go*
> *And see the land where corals lie.*

He remembered one night he had come home and seen Rachel here with his wife. He had walked across the garden and watched them through the window. He had seen the way that Rachel held her, warmed her, wasn't afraid to be close to her. Wasn't frightened of her dependency, her pain. He listened now to Clare's breathing. It was quiet and slow. He laid her back down on the bed. He picked up the pillow. He pressed down hard against her face. He waited. One of her hands moved, stirred, lifted, dropped back down on the bed.

'No,' the word burst from him. He snatched away the pillow. He laid his head on her chest. Felt the tremor of breath. He held her face between his hands and kissed her gently on either cheek, and then finally on her mouth. She stirred in her sleep. He lay down beside her and pulled her close. He closed his eyes. He slept.

CHAPTER THIRTY-ONE

IT WAS A girl's voice. An adolescent girl's voice. Not yet the voice of an adult. But deeper, more resonant than the voice of a child. Jack had never heard it before. But he knew immediately who it was, this sobbing creature who cried out for help.

Mummy, Mummy, please. Mummy, help me. Are you listening, Mummy? Do you hear me? Please come and find me. I know you're out there somewhere. I know you want to help me. I need you now more than I've ever needed you before. So please, come back from wherever you are. Please.

And then the cry, a long howl of anguish and fear. Then silence. The tape ended abruptly. Nothing more but the hiss of the machine.

The package had arrived in the first post of the day. It had been lying on his desk with all the rest of the junk. He had picked it up, weighed the padded envelope in his hand, looked at the postmark, looked at the label with his name and address printed on it, then gone to the coffee machine. He was tired. Alison had stayed with him last night, and he didn't think either of them had got much more than a couple of hours of rest. When he sat down at his desk the longing for sleep had begun to wash over him. And for a moment he had contemplated going sick, sneaking home to crash out on the bed, burying his face in the pillows that smelt of Alison. But he had pushed the thought from him as he picked up the tape again, hunted in his top drawer for his Walkman, slotted it in, pressed play and listened, and felt the bile rise up into his mouth, and the sensation of a stream of iced water slide down his backbone. He pressed the rewind button, then pressed play, and listened again.

The mid-morning traffic along the sea road and over the toll bridge was nearly as densely packed as the rush-hour crush three hours earlier. He had brought the tape with him, and he played it again and again as the car crept forward. Outside it was raining. A steady leaden downpour that sluiced over the windscreen like the stream from a hosepipe. He sat and listened, the windscreen wipers turned to slow, and waited.

Her foster-parents had been sent the tape too. And the local guards who were dealing with the girl's disappearance. The parents were frantic. Phil Brady, the inspector from Clontarf, was at a loss. 'You'd better come over here, Jack. Give us a bit of a dig-out. Maybe you can make some sense from all of this. Because I can't.'

Christ Almighty, frantic parents. He felt he couldn't cope with them any longer. Or maybe it was just that he'd been better at the personal stuff when he was newer to the job. Or maybe it had just seemed easier, and maybe back then they hadn't set so much store by it. You weren't expected to have a post-graduate degree in meaningful dialoguing, or basic bullshit about bereavement as he privately termed it.

Not that, so far, bereavement was on the agenda. The girl was missing, not dead. Not so far. Although the parents, the foster-parents as he had to keep on reminding himself, didn't see it that way. They were doing a good job of preparing themselves for the worst. It was spelt out in the rigor of their stiff white faces, and the way they had already begun to speak of Amy in the past tense.

He sat with them in their small tidy front room, drinking tea, refusing biscuits. There was nothing in their demeanour to suggest that Amy Beckett, or Williams as she called herself, was not their own child. There were photographs of her everywhere. Along with the pictures of their other four children. But it was easy to spot the odd one out. The Williams brood were fair to mousy, with round faces and snub noses. Cute when toddlers but undistinguished as teenagers and young adults. The kind of people you'd pass in the street. The kind of faces that were never picked out in identity parades. Unlike Amy. He walked around the Williamses' sitting room, looking at the framed photographs hanging on the wall. Mostly school pictures. First communions and confirmations. Amy's steady gaze followed him as he moved. He could feel her eyes on his back as he turned away. He was reminded of the painting of the Sacred Heart that hung on their landing when he was a kid. The crucified Christ would catch his eye as he walked slowly up towards him, and he would still be watching as he turned quickly at the top of the stairs. That same steady mournful look.

He asked Mrs Williams if he could see the girl's room. She opened the door without a word and showed him the way. No Sacred Hearts to be seen on their landing, he noticed, just a series of watercolours. Flower paintings. Detailed, precise, like plates from a botanical reference book. He stopped and looked more closely.

'Yours?' he asked.

'No, my husband's.'

'A nice hobby to have.'

'Oh,' she looked back at him, 'not quite a hobby. More of an obsession. And one that Amy used to share when she was younger. They used to go off on collecting trips. She was quite expert, very sharp-eyed, great attention to detail. She would find the plants and Dave would paint them.'

'Would, was, not any longer?'

'Well,' Mrs Williams pushed open the bedroom door, 'as you can see, adolescence took over.'

So this was what he had ahead of him, he thought as he looked around at the posters that covered all four walls and the ceiling too.

'Quite a job, isn't it?' Mrs Williams craned her head to look up at them. 'That's our Amy. When she decides to do something she goes all the way.'

'Your Amy?' Jack sat down on the stool by the small wooden desk. 'You do think of her as yours, do you?'

'Well, whose else is she? She came to us when she was barely five. I think you could say we've taught her everything she knows. Our children taught her how to be a sister. My husband and I taught her how to be a daughter. My mother and father taught her how to be a granddaughter.'

'And her own mother, what did she teach her?'

There was silence in the small stuffy room.

'Well, I suppose to be fair she didn't have much of a chance. And she did give a her good start, I'll say that for her, especially with her intellectual development. Amy was always very bright. She already knew her alphabet when she came to us. She could count, she had her favourite books and stories. Look,' she stood in front of him, the skin of her face sagging with anxiety, 'don't get me wrong. I know she isn't ours, not ours by adoption. And as foster-parents we've always been very conscious that she might only be with us for a short time. We know all about that. We've fostered before. And if Amy had left us we would have fostered again. But there was always something special about her. Something very special. She's a very special person. Even that first day we met her, there was a quality about her that shone through. Even when she was like this.'

She picked up a framed photograph from the desk and held it out to him. He looked at the little girl in the bright blue dress, standing holding hands with a smiling man and woman.

'We took it that first day. We always did that with all the children. We thought it would make them feel wanted. And when they left us we gave it to them as a memento. So many of them, you see, don't have things like this.' Her voice broke and tears began to trickle from the corners of her eyes. She pulled a tissue from the cuff of her white blouse and wiped her nose. 'I'm sorry, I've been trying to keep calm, for everyone's sake, but I'm so worried about her.'

Afterwards, as he was driving back into the city centre, he could still smell the perfume that she was wearing. Blue Grass, that's what it was. He remembered one of his aunt's loved it. She had boxes of soap and talcum powder all with the same delicate scent stashed in the top of her wardrobe. It had always puzzled him, the possibility of grass being anything other than bright green. He puzzled now over the girl and what had happened to her. Mrs Williams had said that everything had been as normal. Amy was waiting for her Leaving Certificate results to come out. She had a job in a local café. She seemed perfectly fine.

'But how did she react when her mother went missing, and all that stuff in the papers and on TV, all the rehashing of the case? And then the suggestion that something bad might have happened to her. Didn't that upset her?'

Mrs Williams sighed deeply. 'She didn't say much about it. We hoped that it was a false alarm, nothing really serious. So I suppose we tried to play it down. Not deny it, of course, but just stress that no one was sure what was going on. She had been a bit quiet recently, but she goes through these silent phases anyway, from time to time, every now and then. She kind of withdraws. Spends a lot of time here in her room, listening to music, drawing, reading. We've got used to leaving her be. She comes out of it eventually, when she's ready.'

'And did she mention recently that she had met anyone new, that anyone had made any approaches to her?'

But of course she hadn't. She wasn't one who would tell everything. She would want to have her secrets. Still he thought he might as well show Mrs Williams the photograph of Dan Beckett. Just for the record. Just so he could say he'd done it. He watched her face as she gazed at the picture. She took her time, studying it slowly, then she shook her head.

'He looks familiar for some reason. But it strikes me that he's far too old to have been friends with Amy. No, I've never seen him. Never seen him at all.'

He asked her if she minded leaving him alone, here, just for a few minutes. She shrugged and said she supposed not, running her hand protectively over the flowered duvet and plumping up the pillows before she left. He sat back and looked around him. There was a cosy nest-like quality about the room, he thought. The small single bed looked inviting, and he had a sudden desire to lie down, although he could imagine how his legs would hang out over the end. 'Whose been sleeping in my bed,' he chanted quietly out loud. And smiled. This was a room a kid could be happy in, he decided, and then remembered Judith Hill's room and how it had looked that day when had gone to see her father for the first time. Cold, clean, empty. Nothing to say for itself. Not giving away a single clue or an ounce of information. And now all its secrets were buried in the family plot in Deans Grange cemetery. The one grave, the headstone with the two names on it. He had been surprised by that, but Elizabeth and Stephen had decided between them. Whatever else, Judith and Mark were still father and daughter, still the same flesh and blood.

How much did that matter, flesh and blood, the biological link, he wondered as he said goodbye to Pat Williams.

'You will let us know as soon as you hear anything, won't you? You will do everything you can to find her for us, please?'

She followed him out on to the footpath. Her hands fluttered like falling leaves. She couldn't keep them still. He wanted to take them and fold them together, wrap her arms around her body, keep her safe. Instead he just nodded and said that of course he would. He'd phone them later. They weren't to worry. He was sure that Amy would be home soon.

His phone rang just as he was bumping across the railway line at Merrion Gates. It was Sweeney's number on the display. His heart sank. It could be nothing but bad news.

'There's someone trying to get hold of you, Jack. She's insisting. She needs to see you. Here, you know the address.'

Again that dreadful smell of rotting flesh. It hit him as soon as he walked into the hall of the tall red-brick house in Rathmines. The front door had been on the latch, and when he pushed it gently, it swung open. He stood and looked around him. He remembered the sight of Mark Hill's body hanging from its noose. He called out.

'Mrs Hill, Elizabeth, are you there?'

There was no reply. He took a couple of steps forward and peered into the sitting room on the right. It was empty but in here the smell was even stronger. And then he heard voices coming from the dining room behind. He called out again, and this time she answered.

He opened the door and walked in. And gagged, vomit in his mouth. He pulled out his handkerchief and spat into it, unable to speak. He looked around him. There was blood everywhere and pieces of flesh. Shapes that were both recognizable and unknown. Elizabeth Hill was standing at the door that opened out into the garden. A tall heavy man was standing beside her.

'You remember George Bradley, don't you?' she said.

Jack nodded and looked around him. He tried to find words to ask, to question, but there was nothing there.

'Stephen did it.' Elizabeth spoke in a low monotone. 'This is all his handiwork.'

Flies buzzed over the remains.

'For some reason,' she said, 'he was trying to copy the picture.'

She pointed to the large print of Judith and Holofernes that had been pinned to the wall. Now it hung sagging, torn at the edges. Jack bent down, covering his nose to look more closely at the animal heads which were everywhere. Chickens, birds, the remains of a sheep, something that looked like a cat, even, he was disgusted to see, a couple of rats' heads. He felt his gorge rise again and backed away.

'Here.' Elizabeth stepped aside. 'You'd better go out and get some fresh air.'

She explained what had happened over a cup of tea in the Bradleys' bright clean kitchen. She had been coming to see Stephen anyway, she said. But when she arrived they told her that he was no longer staying with them, that he had decided to go home. They were worried about him. They had tried phoning, they had knocked on the front door a number of times, but there was no response.

'Of course, we knew he was in there,' George Bradley said, 'from our mews, which is where I have my office. You remember, I'm sure, Mr Donnelly. You visited me there after Judith died. And of course we can see clearly into the house from the windows. And I could see lights on, so I knew he was in there all right.'

Jack remembered. The bright modern office space. The converted garage. George Bradley had some kind of software company. Very high-tech. Although he had thought at the time that he didn't look the type. He looked more like a teacher in a posh school, with his grey hair and half-glasses, baggy cord trousers and sleeveless sweater.

'Anyway, to cut a long a story short, we finally

decided to go in and look for him. Jenny has a key,
you know. She'd been reluctant to intrude. But anyway, there he was, in the dining room, covered in
blood, with all those dreadful things around him. He
was completely incoherent.'

Elizabeth had begun to cry, quietly.

'I'm sorry,' she said. 'It's just so terrible.'

'Where is he now?' Jack looked at George Bradley.

'We got the doctor. He's taken him into hospital.
They've sedated him, and they're going to do a full
assessment.' Bradley stood up and opened a cupboard.
He brought out a bottle of brandy. 'Here, Elizabeth,
have a drop of this. It goes surprisingly well with
tea.'

Jack looked around him. The kitchen was filled
with sunshine. A tabby cat lay sleeping in a basket on
the countertop. It snuffled and snored gently, its
whiskers twitching. Above it was a pegboard covered
with notices, letters, photographs, cards all pinned
haphazardly together. He needed something like that,
he thought, for when the girls came to stay. He could
never keep track of their swimming lessons, their ballet
lessons, their term times, days off, holidays.

'Is there anything I can do?' he asked, finishing his
tea and refusing another cup.

She shook her head. 'I don't think so, but thanks
for coming anyway. I wanted you to know about this.
Oh, don't get me wrong.' She reached out and touched
his hand. 'I'm not blaming you. Stephen's mental
condition doesn't, I think, only have to do with what's
happened over the last couple of months. I bear a lot

of responsibility for it too, I'm afraid. Wouldn't you agree, George?'

George Bradley looked at her and for a moment his stare was hard and unforgiving. Then he smiled, a mechanical grimace.

'Not at all, dear. That was a long time ago. Water under the bridge and all that.'

He thought about forgiveness as he drove home. He had forgiven Joan her sins, he supposed. He hadn't enjoyed being deceived, being lied to, being made a fool of. But then he didn't really love her, so he wasn't hurt in that way. He thought about George Bradley and Mark Hill. One had forgiven, the other had not. One was alive, the other was dead. One had a family that was still intact. Children who were growing up with futures to anticipate. He thought about the terrible scene in that room. The stench, the sight of the sticky dried blood all over the floor, the fly-blown animal remains. What must have been going through that poor kid's mind? How had he got to the stage where he could do all that?

The rain had lifted by the time he got home. He parked the car and walked back towards the harbour. He sat down on a granite bollard. The slipway was crammed with people and boats. It was a happy, colourful scene. It would have been like this the day that Rachel went out with Beckett, he thought. They had taken statements from a number of people who had seen them. How did she look? he had asked. They all said the same thing. How does anyone look who's about to go off sailing on a nice afternoon? She looked normal, that was what they said. He went through the checklist of where they had searched for her. The ports, the airports, the train and bus stations. They'd found nothing. They'd put her photo and description out on the TV news. It had been plastered all over the newspapers. No one had seen a thing. She had got into the boat with Beckett and as far as they could tell she hadn't come back. And something had happened out there. Something that wasn't good. He rehearsed the evidence so far. Blood that matched Rachel's all over the cabin. The knife with her blood and Beckett's fingerprints. Blood too all over his sailing gear. And then there was the evidence they had collected at his house. Hairs and fibres taken from the bed, the sofa. Her bag on the bonfire. The clothes picked up by the fishermen from the Irish sea. The evidence of at least one violent encounter between the two of them. The statements from the other tenants and from Clare Bowen. She had bruises, all over, Clare had told him. She was frightened. So why did she go out in the boat with him? What hold did he have over her?

Did they have enough to charge him? Jack would have thought so. Beckett had the three essentials. Means, motive and opportunity. But the DPP hadn't made a decision. So they'd watch him. Drive him crazy. And sooner or later something would give. Jack was sure of it.

Poor Rachel Beckett, he thought. Andy Bowen was probably right about her. She should never have had to serve that sentence. He felt suddenly guilty. But what was it to him? He was barely involved. He was the new kid on the case. Older, wiser heads had made the decision to go for the murder conviction. Had refused to countenance a plea of manslaughter. Had insisted that she should pay the price for her crime. He put his hand in his pocket and pulled out his phone. He needed Alison now. A bit of comfort would go a long way on a night like tonight.

CHAPTER THIRTY-TWO

IT HAD BEEN easier than Daniel had thought to move the girl from the apartment just off the North Quays out to the house in Killiney. He had to hand it to her. She was pretty cool when it came to pressure. She knew how to look after herself. Not bad for a kid barely eighteen. Still, he supposed she hadn't licked it up off the street. Her mother had the same kind of calm. He remembered her that day out in the boat. The blood dripping down her wrist, the way she had reached out for him, asked him to pick up the knife. Scattered all those bits and pieces of evidence all around the boat, and his house and car. Left her markings to be sniffed out.

He could have left Amy longer in the apartment in town. It was safe enough in some ways. He'd been able to drop in and see her a couple of times a day. Leaving the van in one of the underground car parks where his company had the security contract, then slipping out through the crowds and taking a circuitous route through the city to the service entrance of the apartment block. She had seemed fine to him. They had talked. He had cooked meals for her. Spaghetti

Bolognese, his speciality, and garlic bread. Brought her bottles of wine. Chianti in raffia bottles. She had questioned him about what had happened then, all those years ago. She wanted to know everything, everything he could tell her about his relationship with Rachel.

'Why didn't she tell me herself?' she kept on asking him. 'Why did she go on telling me lies?'

He couldn't answer her.

'I suppose,' he said, 'she didn't want to make things seem any worse than they already were. She didn't want to drag you into the shame of it all. I suppose she was trying to protect you.'

'Protect me,' the girl had scoffed. 'It wasn't that. She was just a coward. She couldn't face me with the truth. But . . .' She leaned across the table and took his hand. Her cheeks were pink. The wine, he thought. 'But wasn't it very cruel of her to deprive you of me? After all, you had no one of your own. No one of your own flesh and blood, I mean. You would have wanted me, wouldn't you? You would have wanted us to be together, isn't that so?'

He supposed he could have left her in the apartment in town, but he could see that she was getting restless. She didn't like being locked in on her own. He kept on telling her that it wouldn't be for much longer, but after three days had passed she was beginning to get anxious. And he was worried. The apartment was registered in Ursula's name. But he wasn't sure how long it would be before some clever little prick of a detective would do a search of the Land

Registry and find it. So it would be better to bring her out to the house in Killiney. They'd already been over it with a fine-tooth comb and found nothing. And they wouldn't get another search warrant without further evidence. And it would be so much easier to have Amy close at hand.

So he'd worked it all out. And he'd waited. He knew the surveillance routine. They didn't hang around all night. Once they thought he was safe in bed, they disappeared. Watching the overtime claims, he was sure. So he waited and listened, then when all was quiet he slipped out of the house, down the cliff path, along the beach to the car park by the DART station, and found the van he'd arranged to have parked there. The one that belonged to the business, but without any logo to identify it. He drove into town. She was lying fast asleep on the sofa, turned on her side, with her arms wrapped around a cushion. A blanket was slung over her legs, and when he touched her on the shoulder, whispering her name, she shot up out of her sleep grabbing hold of it and pulling it up to her face, frightened for a moment. Confusion, surprise all over her small pale face, then quickly realization as she pushed aside the blanket, her legs bare underneath it, and stood and pulled on her jeans, shoving her feet into her runners, quickly bending down to tie the laces. Then picking up her leather backpack, running a hand through her short hair, following him out into the cold. Didn't ask him anything, just stood shivering, her lips trembling as he opened up the back of the van and gestured for her to get in. Showed her the sleeping bag rolled up on the mattress in the back, waited until she had pulled it up and over her body. Locked her in. Then unlocked the door when they had arrived back at the car park by the DART station. Told her to follow, then took her hand to pull her quickly through the soft sand, down on to the shore, showed her the way across the rocks, heard her breath coming in short gasps as she struggled to keep up with him. They scrambled up the path, through the pine trees and into the house, just as a faint streak of pale grey appeared along the horizon.

'For your safety,' he said to her as he unlocked the attic, switched on the light, showed her the camp bed against the wall, the pot in the corner, the bottles of water and the bread, cheese and fruit. The small transistor radio on the floor. 'It's better this way. You'll be safe here. You'd never know what's going on outside. Stay here for the day, sleep as much as you can, and this evening when I come home you can come downstairs and we can talk.'

He didn't pay any heed at the time to the expression on her face. Afterwards he realized it had been a mistake not to notice. That she was hurt that he was making her a prisoner in his attic, that he wasn't welcoming her into his home as his firstborn, his oldest daughter. He heard her calling out to him as he ran downstairs, and he paused and listened for a moment, and called back up to her, that she should sleep, and not to worry. He thought about her from time to time as he went about his business throughout the day but he wasn't anxious. The attic was secure.

There was only one tiny skylight, and it didn't open. The bolt on the door was solid. And anyway, this situation wasn't going to last for too much longer. He knew the impact the tape would have. Rachel would come running, scuttling out of her hiding place. He knew she would. And it would all be over.

It was late when he got home, after dark. The same set of headlights had followed him all the way out from the city and parked within sight of the tall gates. He had paused and flashed his hazard lights at them as he turned into the drive. When this was all over he was going to sue them for wrongful arrest. For harassment. For compensation. For fucking up his life. He was going to make that arsehole Jack Donnelly pay for all this. He parked the car outside the front door and let himself in. The house was silent. She'd be hungry, he was sure of that. Probably bored, fed up. He would let her out, run her a bath. Cook her a good meal, give her something to drink. Open a nice bottle of wine. Show her around the house. Show her how well he'd done. Who knows, he thought as he walked up the attic stairs, when this is all over maybe she'll come and stay with us. Ursula would like her, he knew she would.

Or perhaps, or perhaps that wouldn't be such a good idea. He paused on the small landing and listened. He could hear nothing from inside. He sat down on the top step and rested his head against the wall. So far only three people knew about his relationship with Amy. And that was the way to keep it. The last thing he wanted was anyone asking any questions, thinking back to Martin's death and wondering. Perhaps it might not be such a good idea if Amy went home after all this was over.

He stood up and listened again. There was still no sound from the attic room. He shot back the bolts and unlocked the door. He bent his head to step inside. It was dark. The light was turned off. She must be sleeping, he thought. He walked slowly towards the bed and called out her name, quietly, so he wouldn't startle her.

'Amy, Amy, wake up. I'm back. Have you been all right here all day by yourself?'

The room smelt foetid, stale, with a tang of urine. He couldn't actually see her anywhere. He could see the shape of the bed, the tumbled blankets.

'Amy, it's me. It's Dan. Wake up now. I'm going to cook you the best steak you've ever eaten.'

And then he felt rather than a heard a disturbance of air, just behind him, and turned, just in time, and just in time saw her standing holding something in her right hand. What was it? It was lighter in colour than anything else in the room. And as she moved her arm, began to bring it up over her head, he saw that it was a piece of metal, and realized that the camp bed was partially dismantled. That she was holding one of the struts, and as she stepped towards him, her arm up above her head, he moved away, just out of reach, so when her arm came down the metal bar struck him not on the back of his head, as she had intended, but on his shoulder. Pushing him backwards, making him lose his balance, so he crashed down on to the floor and saw that she was about to turn and rush through the door. Until, that is, he reached out and grabbed her around the ankle, feeling thumb and index finger joining around the bone. Tugging at her so she too crashed down beside him with a scream and a groan, while he pulled himself hand over hand, up along her leg, up over her knee, up her thigh, his fingers digging into her flesh, until he could grab her by the waist, pressing her to the ground with the whole of his weight, twisting her short hair in his fingers so she cried out in pain. Felt her small breasts flatten beneath him, smelt her sweat, her fear. He shouted at her, 'Going to do the dirty on me, were you? I thought we had a bargain. I thought we were agreed. I thought you supported me in this. That you agreed that your mother was an evil woman. That I had to get her to come back. I thought we agreed.'

He pulled her head back and knocked it down hard on the wooden floor, so she cried out again and again, tears starting into her eyes. He jerked her up to sitting and then to standing, twisting her hands behind her back, anger rising up through him so he wanted to hurt her, pay her back for the betrayal. He hit her hard across the face, so blood began to spurt from her nose, then crashed his fist into her stomach. And as she began to scream out in pain he flung her as hard as he could towards the camp bed in the corner and heard her begin to beg for forgiveness.

'I'm sorry, I'm sorry. I was frightened. I thought you weren't going to come back, that you were going to leave me here. I tried the door, but you had locked it. I couldn't cope with the feeling of being trapped. And I heard that tape being played on the radio today. I feel so bad. I heard my foster-parents being interviewed. And they're so worried about me. They were crying. It was terrible. And I realized I want to go home. I shouldn't be doing this. I must have been crazy. I don't even know you. Why should I believe you anyway? How do I know you are who you say you are? How do I know you're not lying to me?'

She pulled back and away from him, putting her hands up in front of her face to shield herself, and then it was that other night all those years ago and Martin lying there on the floor, holding his hands up in front of his shocked white face, hands that were already covered with the blood from the wound in his thigh, and an expression of bewilderment turning to realization as he saw how Daniel was lifting the gun to his shoulder.

As he now lifted his right hand, index finger extended, thumb cocked towards the ceiling, his other fingers curled in against his palm, and pointed it at her.

'Bang, bang,' he said. 'I haven't finished with you. I'll be back, and then you'll be sorry.' He backed away, standing for a moment silhouetted in the doorway, before slamming it shut, locking it, bolting it top and bottom. Hearing her crying out to him not to leave her. Begging to be let out. Breathing quickly as he took the stairs two at a time, not stopping till he reached the hall below, and the kitchen and the warmth and the light.

The light inside, the heavy brocade curtains slipping over the long dark windows on their smooth, noiseless runners. The bottle of whiskey on the table. Lifting it up, feeling the smooth hardness of the glass against his teeth as the liquid burned its way down his throat. Then pouring it into a large heavy tumbler, its crystal base leaving deep indentations in the flesh of his hand as he squeezed it tightly, gulping down the warmth and comfort. The adrenalin seeped from his body and his head began to droop, jerked upwards for a moment, his eyes struggling to focus, then sagged back down on his chin as the glass dropped from his hand on to the wooden floor, rolled over and around and around in a circle, and came to rest against the edge of the rug.

Until something jerked him back up out of his doze, so he found himself half out of the chair, his heart pounding, the breath coming out of his chest in short sharp gasps. And heard the sound of the dog, barking. The dog, of course, he had forgotten all about the dog, tied up in the garage now Ursula and the kids weren't here to take care of the stupid mutt. Making such a racket. Short, sharp yowls of anger and despair. So he pulled himself upright and walked into the kitchen, dangling the bottle by its neck, pouring himself another large shot as he hunted in the cupboard for the dog food, the tin opener, hearing his own footsteps on the tiled floor, loud in the empty house. He turned towards the glass door that opened on to the garden and stopped. And saw standing outside, staring in at him, a small, slim figure. Dark clothes, cropped dark hair, small white face. Smiling. Lifting a hand and placing it pressed flat against the glass. A hand with a long red scar bisecting the palm between thumb and index finger. And above it that face, familiar and unfamiliar at one and the same time. She had cut her hair and dyed it black. So she looked for an instant like the girl upstairs. And as he stood and watched she put her other hand in her pocket and pulled out a cloth, and then as she lifted her palm from the glass she used the cloth to wipe away the marks, palm print, prints from the pads of flesh on her fingertips, that she had left there. All the time smiling at him as the cloth moved up and down, up and down, side to side, side to side, until all was clean and shiny again. As she moved back and away and into the darkness, lifting her scarred hand in salute, and was gone.

And he was left, reaching for the key that hung on a ring by the door. But now there was no key. And the door was locked, and although he flung his weight against the panes of shatter-proof glass it would not budge. So with a cry of rage he turned on his heel and rushed for the front door and out on to the gravel of the drive, howling now louder than the dog tied up in the garage.

'Come back, you bitch, come back. I know you're here. I know you can't get away. Come here so I can see you.'

He began to run, around by the side of the house towards the vegetable garden, his feet slipping and sliding on the grass covered now with a heavy dew. Pulling out the spade that stood where the gardener had left it, imbedded in the heavy fertile soil, hefting it in his hand, feeling its weight, running his hand quickly across the metal blade polished by use. Then stopping, standing completely still and listening, listening. Hearing the dog's howls, a car changing gear as it ground its way up the hill from the beach. His breath slowing as he calmed himself. Further away he heard the sea on the rocks, the wind in the pine trees, and saw a bobbing light over in the corner where the old polytunnel was, where the kids played hide-and-seek.

Come, Daddy, come and play with us. Count to twenty backwards, then find us, find us.

He watched the light as it moved around the garden, then began to follow it, swinging the spade, feeling its heaviness drag his arm down. And then the light was gone and he heard the bang of the shed door as he ran towards it, crashing through the row of blackcurrant bushes, smashing them out of his way with the spade, reaching the shed, calling out her name as he blundered inside it. Tripping over a pile of plastic plant pots. Turning back to the garden, seeing the light again, this time up in the oak tree by the gate, where he had built the tree house for Jonathan for his seventh birthday. The light swung to and fro, high in the branches. But as he rushed towards it he saw the slight figure jump down just yards away from him. And the light go off. And darkness again.

He felt like screaming out with anger and frustration. He thought he knew his garden, every bush and tree, every secret place, but somehow she was

making it all seem so unfamiliar, so difficult to find
his way through. He turned back towards the house.
The dog had stopped barking. But there was another
noise now, coming from the garage. The clanging of
metal on metal. This time he moved more cautiously.
Slow steps forward. Then stopping to listen. It sounded
like a lump hammer, hitting the metal vice. When he
reached the open door he stopped. It was dark and
silent now. He put his hand on the light switch. He
clicked it on. Nothing happened. He clicked it up and
down. Still nothing. He stepped forward cautiously.
The dog was no longer in its place by its basket in the
corner. But there was something else moving on the
other side, near the bench where he kept his tools. He
heard his voice being called, softly, 'Daniel, Daniel.'

He walked forward. His feet felt hard concrete
underneath them. And then he was falling, down into
the inspection pit. Landing awkwardly, one ankle
collapsing beneath him. Pain shooting up his leg.
Toppling over into the mess of spilt oil. Screaming
again, 'You fucking bitch, when I get you I'll kill you!'

Dragging himself out, struggling to the door again,
leaning on the spade, his leg weak beneath him. Out
on to the gravel in front of the house, and suddenly
there was a blare of music. And he turned and saw the
curtains drawn back, the French windows open, and
the same slight figure standing, looking out towards
him. He began to run as fast as his damaged ankle
would allow, swinging the spade, remembering the
dull thump as the rats' bodies were flattened against
the earth. He lurched up and on to the terrace and into

the house, through the living room into the hall, the front door standing wide open. Heard her voice again, calling out to him.

'Daniel, Daniel, I'm going upstairs. Can you catch me? Can you find me?'

And remembered suddenly the Garda car parked as always just outside the tall wrought-iron gates. And the dark shapes of the two men inside, and a glow from a cigarette as he rushed towards them, shouting, 'She's here, she's here. I told you, didn't I? I told you she wasn't dead. She's here. Come on, come in and find her!'

Dragging open the door, half pulling the driver from behind the wheel, rushing before them as they walked towards the house. Shouting, 'I told you I was telling the truth all along. She is here. I've just seen her!'

Screaming at them, 'Search for her. Find her. She's here. She's upstairs. Go on, go up. I saw her there!'

Watching the two men go into the hall, up the stairs, as he waited for a moment outside, breathing great gulps of air with relief, smelling the coconut sweetness of the gorse on the hillsides around them rising up into the night air. As he turned towards the lighted doorway and saw again the small figure stand-ing there and the policemen on either side, holding each of her arms. Shouted out with joy and relief. Now they would believe him. Now he would be freed from this nightmare. Now he could have back the life he had lost. As he stumbled towards them. Then stopped, a look of amazement, then horror spreading across his face. As the guard stepped towards him and put his hand on his arm, and said, 'Can you explain this to us, Mr Beckett? Can you explain why this young woman was locked up in your attic? Can you explain her injuries to us?'

As she turned towards him and he saw, the cropped dark hair, the pale face, the bruised cheekbones and eye socket, the arm that she cradled protectively against her body, the torn and dirty black jeans. The smell of urine and vomit. The sound of her sobs as she cried out to them, 'He wouldn't let me go. He made me go with him. I was so scared. I thought he was going to kill me!'

The sound then of the spade as it clattered to the floor. He looked down at it, saw the remnants of the soil from the garden falling off on to the pale rug. Ursula would never forgive him for making such a mess. He bent down to pick it up. And for a moment, as he felt its weight in his hand, he thought of what he could do with it. The way it could come crashing down on the girl's skull, cutting off in mid-sentence her accusations, her complaints. And then he could use it on the guard, wiping that look of satisfaction from his smug, round face. Make him scream out with pain and terror. Leave him lying bleeding on the floor, humiliated, hurt. Damaged beyond all repair. And he weighed it all up as he swung the spade up and down, down and up, feeling it heavy in his hand, feeling the tick-tock of its pendulum arc. Until, suddenly, his arms were grabbed from behind, the spade was pulled from his grasp, and he could feel the sharp bite of the handcuffs as his wrists were locked together. And he was being half dragged, half pushed out of the door, up the drive and into the car.

A face appeared at the window beside him, and Jack Donnelly bent down and smiled.

'Gotcha,' he said, then banged the roof with his fist, a sharp angry sound, and stepped back as they began to make their stately progress up the hill. Away from the house, away from the sea, away from his freedom.

THE END

IT WAS A year later. It was Court Number Four again. The same court where Rachel Beckett had been convicted of the murder of her husband. And again it was packed to capacity. Spectators, journalists, guards, solicitors and barristers, and of course the jury, the witnesses and the accused. Daniel James Beckett, charged with the murder of Rachel Beckett and the false imprisonment and attempted murder of Amy Beckett. He had pleaded not guilty to all the charges. The State's case in the lesser counts of false imprisonment and attempted murder was strong, watertight it could be said. But there were still some doubts about the viability of the charge of murder. Rachel Beckett's body had never been found. Speculation had been endless. Precedents were raked over. There was the case of Michal Onufrejczyk, a Pole, who was convicted in Glamorganshire Assizes back in 1955 of the murder of a Mr Sykut, despite the fact that neither the body nor any trace of the body had been found and the prisoner had made no confession of any participation in the crime. He was sentenced to death. More recently there was the case of the British army undercover officer,

Captain Robert Nairac, who went missing in the 1970s in South Armagh. His body had also never been found, but eventually in 1977 one Liam Townson was convicted of his murder. And ten years or so ago the tragic case of Helen McCourt in Liverpool. Again, no body but bloodstained clothing and a piece of rope, also bloodstained, found in the boot of the accused barman's car were enough to convict him of her killing.

Jack sat and watched the proceedings. He stood in the witness box, took the oath, gave his evidence. He listened to Beckett's denials. His protestations of innocence, his account of the appearance of Rachel Beckett that night at his house, an account which had never been corroborated. The guards who had gone into the house had seen no one except the girl, Amy. They heard her screams and cries for help. They broke down the locked door and found her in a dreadful state on the floor. Head injuries, internal injuries, shocked, hysterical, slipping in and out of consciousness. And in no doubt that Beckett would be back. To finish what he had begun.

Jack watched the shock and anger around the courtroom when the girl Amy told what had happened to her. Said how he had convinced her that her mother was still alive. That the only thing that would bring her back was if she thought that Amy was at risk. Now he had forced her to stay with him in the house in Killiney. Refused to let her go. Then threatened her, said he would finish her off. He didn't want me, she said. He just wanted to use me, and then when that didn't work he wanted to get rid of me. After he had told me I was his daughter. Jack looked around him at the stunned faces in the courtroom. The silence was absolute as the girl told her story.

He listened carefully to the prosecution's summing-up. That Beckett had wanted to get rid of anything from his past that might embarrass him, that might upset or endanger his new life. That if he was ruthless enough to kidnap and attack his own daughter, then he was certainly ruthless enough to commit murder. He heard the forensic evidence detailed again. Blood-stains in the boat, a bloody knife with Beckett's fingerprints on it. Blood on his clothes. Rachel's clothes, stained and slashed, found in the plastic bag dumped in the sea. Testimony given of the angry encounter between Rachel and Beckett, and of her fear of him. He sat in the Round Hall and waited for the jury to decide. They took their time. The day passed. He spoke to Alison on the phone and to the girls.

'We saw you on the telly,' Rosa said, 'on the news. Everyone at school saw you too. You're famous, Daddy.'

The jury were sequestered over night. He couldn't decide whether it was a good sign or not. They had a lot to think about, so much evidence to sort through. He'd have loved to have been a fly on the wall in the jury room. And what if they failed to agree? He remembered it had nearly happened with Rachel's trial. The jury had asked the judge for guidance. He had said he would accept a majority verdict and that was what he got. And what if this group of men and women failed to reach even that? The judge might declare a mistrial. And then they'd have to start all over again. Christ, he couldn't bear the thought of it. And then word came. They were back. They had a verdict. Beckett was going down. For life.

Afterwards he realized how tense and anxious he had been. His legs ached, his neck and shoulders were like planks of wood. It took all Alison's skill and persuasion to untie the knots.

'Let's celebrate,' he said to her.

But the girls wanted to celebrate his new-found fame too.

'Take us out, Daddy,' Ruth demanded. 'We want to go to a proper restaurant, not McDonald's or Burger King, somewhere with waiters and candles. We've got something to show you.'

The something was a Polaroid camera. Joan's boy-friend had given it to them.

'It's so we'll like him,' Rosa said. 'It's a brime.'

'Not a brime, you thicko.' Ruth was quick to butt in. 'A bribe. It's a bribe.'

He took them all to the Brasserie na Mara in Dun Laoghaire. It had waiters, candles, tablecloths, good food and plenty of wine. Ruth appointed herself chief photographer. Soon the table was covered with snaps.

He woke in the middle of the night, his head pounding, his mouth dry. Alison had gone home. The girls still hadn't accepted her staying with him over night. Soon, he promised, soon I'll make them. Rosa was curled against his side. Ruth was snuggled into the sofa bed. She had left her photographs in a pile on the kitchen table. He drank glass after glass of water as he flicked through them. There was one in particular that he liked. Alison had taken it. Me and my girls, he thought as fondly as his hangover would allow. He picked it up and pinned it to the cork noticeboard above the fridge, beside the girls' school timetable. He refilled his glass and looked at it. It reminded him. What was it? Suddenly he saw Judith Hill's body, twisted in death and remembered the photographs that he had found that day in her mother's studio. The room at the top of the house in the quiet, leafy suburb. He was still not completely sure who had killed her. Her mother had been so adamant that it wasn't the girl's father. After his death, and after the brother, Stephen, had gone crazy, he had wondered if it might have been him. But eventually when they got the DNA test back from Judith's dead baby, it had matched neither father nor brother. He wished now that he was able to tell Elizabeth Hill that he knew what had happened to her daughter. He liked her. He felt for her. He knew how he would feel in her situation.

He finished his glass of water, rinsed it and left it to drain, then turned back to the board again, and this time it was something else that he saw. A similar collection of school notices, timetables for swimming lessons, letters from the council about bin collections. And photographs. Polaroids. Another family group. A middle-aged woman with a good haircut and a bad figure. A man of similar age, with longish grey hair and a lined face. A son and a daughter, late teens, early twenties, and two small girls holding on to the parents' knees. What was it Jenny Bradley had said? Judith had babysat for their younger kids. Next-door neighbours brought even closer together by the upset that had befallen them all. He wondered as he walked through the sitting room, bent down to kiss Ruth's flushed cheek, tucked the quilt tightly around Rosa's skinny little body. He wondered.

He wondered again next morning if he was completely wasting his time. But he might as well do it anyway. He put in a search request.

Surname: Bradley.

First name: George.

Address: 15 Plane Tree Parade, Rathmines.

Then he went off viewing houses with Alison. She had finally got him to commit.

'Come on, Jack. You put it off until the Beckett case was settled. Now it's time. We need a place of our own. Don't you agree?' There was a moment's silence. She spoke again. Her tone was blunt. 'Well, if you don't agree, I don't, to be honest, see much future for us. I'm not going on like this.' And for a moment he saw the Alison that Andy Bowen always talked about.

It was afterwards, when they'd gone to a have a drink to discuss the relative merits of the three properties they had seen, that his phone rang. It was Sweeney.

'You know that guy Bradley you were interested in? Well, here's a bit of a surprise. He was part of an investigation into allegations of abuse, sixteen years or so ago, at a school where he taught maths and physics. Some of the girls complained about him and another bloke. It didn't go far. In those days no one was interested. But Bradley left not long afterwards. That was when he got into computers. Set up his own business.'

Jack went back to the office and got out the file. Read over all the statements. Jenny Bradley had been very clear about that weekend when Judith died. It was her birthday. Judith had brought her flowers. She had arrived just after lunch on that Saturday. She stayed for a couple of hours. They sat in the garden. They gossiped. Mrs Bradley said how lovely it was to have the old Judith back again, the way she had been before she got involved with those dreadful drugs.

'Were you alone?' he had asked. He looked to see what she had said.

'Yes, we were. The children were all off doing other things and my husband was in his office. You know, at the end of the garden. We could see him in the window. Judith was waving to him. I remember she leaned over and whispered in my ear. Let's pretend, she said, that we're talking about him. And she cupped her hand around my ear and we both had a good laugh.

'And afterwards, what happened afterwards?'

'Nothing of any consequence as far as I can remember. Judith went back home. She said she had some tidying up to do. I asked her if she'd like to have dinner with us, we were having a bit of a special one. For my birthday, you know. But she said no, she was going back to college that night. And that was the last I saw of her.'

He looked at George Bradley's statement. Bradley

didn't mention anything about seeing them in the garden. In fact he said he hadn't seen Judith at all that day. He said he had been working all afternoon. A rush job.

'Even though it was a Saturday and your wife's birthday?'

Bradley had made some kind of disparaging remark, how at Jenny's age birthdays weren't something you wanted to celebrate. And then said that his wife knew what it was that paid the bills, kept her world ticking over.

Might as well go and see him. Nothing much else on the books at the moment. Might as well make the effort.

He arrived first thing next morning. He hadn't phoned ahead. He stood in the lane that ran behind all the houses and pressed the intercom on the modern steel door. The old stone of the original mews had been rendered and painted white and blocks of frosted glass had replaced the original windows. It all looked very sophisticated, trendy, up to the minute. There was building work going on next door where the Hill family had once kept their car, their bicycles, their gardening tools. He supposed the house had been sold. It was unlikely that Stephen would ever leave the secure hospital where he now lived.

If George Bradley was surprised to see him he didn't show it. His office was filled with light. Large abstract paintings hung on three of the walls. The fourth was a huge window that looked out over his house and garden, and Jack saw immediately the house and garden next door.

'Great view,' Jack said as he took the proffered seat.

Bradley grunted. 'It's for the light, not the scenery.' Then added, 'You'd better get to the point. I'm busy.'

They went back over the statement. Jack couldn't understand how he had missed it all before. The guy had no alibi. No one had seen him, been with him, from the time that Judith and Jenny Bradley had watched him from the garden until he had come home for dinner, sometime between eight-thirty and nine that night.

'You were here by yourself? There was no one else working with you?' Jack asked him for the third time. And for the third time Bradley stated that he was.

'This job you were doing, who was it for?'

Jack wrote down the details, and all the time his gaze kept on sliding across to the windows of the Hills' house. Downstairs, the dining room and kitchen, bedrooms on the first and second floor, and upstairs in the attic, the large dormer window set into the slated roof. North light, that was it, north light for the artist.

'Tell me about Judith,' he said. 'You'd known her for a long time, hadn't you?'

Bradley nodded.

'So?'

He swung around and looked out the window. 'So, she was a nice little girl. She was clever, but shy.'

'Pretty?'

Bradley looked at him and smiled. 'Yes, she was

pretty. In that way that girls are. But they go off, you know. They lose that bloom.'

'She doesn't seem to have been very happy though, wasn't that so?'

'It was hard for her and her brother. What happened with their mother.'

'And hard for you too, and your children?'

'We sorted it all out. We got over it. It was a stupid mistake on Jenny's part. She was overly influenced by Elizabeth Hill. But it's all in the past now. We've forgotten all about it.'

'So you forgave your wife?'

'Haven't I just said that? Of course I forgave her. She made a mistake. She admitted it. She atoned for it. And now if you don't mind, as I said, I'm very busy. I can't imagine why you're dredging all this up now. And I can't imagine what you think I have to do with it.'

He'd have to ask him. It had to be done.

'You know, don't you, Mr Bradley, that Judith was pregnant when she died. Of course we've tried to find out who the baby's father was. We've eliminated Mark and Stephen Hill. We've also eliminated a number of men with whom Judith had sexual relationships over the last few years. I'd like to be able to eliminate you. You'll agree to a DNA test, won't you?'

Bradley stood up and walked to the window. He leaned his head against the glass. His face was very red. He turned back into the room. His voice was loud and angry.

'You seriously think that I would have had sex with that girl after everything she'd done? What kind of a man do you think I am, that I would risk my own health and the health of my wife by having anything to do with her?'

'Your health, is that all that concerns you? Not the fact that she was young enough to be your daughter? That she was the child of your next-door neighbour. That she was a friend of your own children. That she was little more than a child herself.'

Jack couldn't keep the indignation out of his voice. He thought of his own daughters, and the thought made him feel ill.

'Don't give me that holier than thou bullshit, Inspector Donnelly. Judith Hill was a woman, and you know what women are like, don't you?'

Bradley had been questioned about the allegations that the two school girls made about him and one of the other teachers. He had denied everything. Categorically. He had said that the girls had a crush on him. That they were always trying to attract his attention, find ways of being alone with him. He had said that he had rejected their advances and this was their way of getting their own back. He had been believed. The girls had backed down when they were challenged. Their parents had been embarrassed. It wouldn't have gone away so easily now, Jack thought. After all the revelations about abuse in schools, orphanages, county homes. After the way in which men and women in positions of authority had been shown to use their power to wreak havoc on young lives. Now the girls would have been listened to more sympathetically. At least he hoped they would.

'So, you'll take the test, Mr Bradley? We can expect you at the station this afternoon. What time would suit you, three, three-thirty?'

He phoned Elizabeth Hill. Just to bring her up to date and to see what she would say. He was disappointed that her answering machine was switched on. He left a message asking her to call. Then he went off to look at some more houses. Alison was determined. They were going to buy, no matter what.

It was after lunch the next day when the desk sergeant called him. 'You've a visitor, Jack. A lady here to see you.'

That was quick off the mark, he thought. Elizabeth Hill must have been so excited at his news that she couldn't wait. But it wasn't Elizabeth. It was Jenny Bradley.

He took her across the road to the pub. The sun shining in the window showed up the deep lines across her forehead, the black circles beneath her eyes. Her voice was unsteady as she began to speak.

'I should have come before. I knew eventually you'd find out.'

'Find out what exactly?'

'Find out about George and those girls. You see, I knew he was lying about them. I knew he was like that. And I knew he was like that with Judith too.'

'With Judith?'

She nodded. 'It started when she was about thirteen

or so. She was very friendly for a while with our daughter Sally, who was the same age. She was always in and out of the house. She used to stay regularly and she'd often spend whole weekends with us. George was very fond of hill walking. He used to take the kids with him. In the summer they'd camp. Then Sally got sick of it. But Judith still went with him. I knew it wasn't right.'

'But you didn't do anything about it?'

She shook her head and stared down at her hands, twisting her wedding ring around on her plump fingers.

'I didn't for one very good reason. I thought that if he didn't have Judith he would try it with Sally. I rationalized it that way. I also made myself think that Judith wanted it, that at least this way she was getting some affection, some physical attention. Because I knew that her own father was extremely cold and distant. Somehow or another I made it all right. And then—'

'And then?' Jack felt suddenly sick.

'Then she got into all that trouble and instead of seeing it for what it was, a response to something that I had allowed to happen, I justified George's actions. I allowed her behaviour to legitimize what he had done.'

There was silence for a moment.

'I'd like a drink,' she said. 'Brandy, please.'

He ordered two. She picked up the balloon-shaped glass and drank. 'This test that you've done. You know, of course, what it will show, don't you? You know that the baby was his.'

'Are you sure about that?'

She nodded. 'As sure as I am that he killed Judith that evening. While I was next door icing my birthday cake, he was upstairs in Elizabeth's old studio.'

Jack looked at her. 'You know this for a fact, or you just think it?'

'Well, he didn't tell me, if that's what you mean. He didn't come bursting into the kitchen and announce it. But I know he did it. He was very loud that evening, full of bombast. And at one stage one of the kids asked him where the camera was. She wanted the usual family photos. He went and got it, but there was no film. And I knew there had been a film in it. But it was all used up.'

'Why are you telling me this now?' Jack picked up his glass and sipped.

'You're going to find out anyway. I always knew you would, that it was just a matter of time. I've given up trying to keep it a secret. I'm prepared now for the scandal in a way that I wasn't before. I'm also sick with disgust at my own behaviour. And I feel it's time I made amends.'

'So you'll make a statement, you'll stand over what you've said?'

She nodded. 'I'll do more than that. I'll show you the one photograph that he didn't leave in Elizabeth's studio the day when he'd finished what he was doing. I found it one day when I was cleaning his office.'

They sat in silence while they finished their drinks. Then Jack spoke again.

'Why did he kill her?' he asked. 'Do you know?'

She shook her head. 'Not for sure. But I presume she was going to spill the beans. She was quite a different girl when she came out of prison, you know. She was strong and self-confident. She had a whole new life ahead of her. I'm surprised that she had continued to have sex with him. But I suppose he still had some hold on her. Anyway, I could see that Judith had made some decisions about her life. I think it all had to do with that woman, the one who was in prison with her. Judith spoke to me about her. She said how much she had helped her. She said what an amazing person she was.'

It was late by the time Jenny Bradley had finished making her statement. Sweeney had gone to pick up her husband. He refused to speak. He asked for his solicitor and then remained silent. But they had the photograph and it said it all. The dead girl and the man with her body. There'd be no bail for him. Jack went back to his desk to tidy up. He looked at his watch. It was after midnight. He picked up the phone and dialled Elizabeth Hill's number. He knew it was late, but he knew she'd want to know what had happened. He listened to the phone's ringing tone. He could picture her room with the painted walls and ceiling.

'Hallo.' He heard her voice and behind it music.

'Hallo, Elizabeth, it's Jack Donnelly here.'

There was a silence for a moment, just the sound of a woman's voice singing.

'Jack, how are you? You've news for me?'

'Yes, that's right. I thought you'd like to know.'

He told her the story. He spared her no details. She

listened and said nothing. Then she spoke. 'Thank you,' she said. 'Thank you for not forgetting all about us.'

'Are you all right?'

There was a pause. She sighed. 'Yes, I'm fine. I'm just glad to know what happened. And that someone has taken responsibility for Judith's death.'

He was just about to say goodbye and hang up, when he heard her voice, a sudden urgency.

'Wait, just a minute. Tell me about that other case that you've been involved in. I've been reading about it on the Internet. The case involving Rachel Beckett.'

'Oh yes, of course. You knew her, didn't you?'

'Not well, but she was very close to Judith. I know that. And I know that she helped Judith hugely when they were in prison together. I was so sorry to hear what happened. I thought this would be a new beginning for her, a chance to put all that stuff behind her. But at least you got a conviction.'

'Yes, I wasn't sure how it would go, but the jury made the right decision. I'm sure of it.'

'He got life, didn't he?'

'That's right. And George Bradley was refused bail. So both of them will be enjoying themselves tonight, accommodation courtesy of the state.'

'George will appreciate that,' she said, 'he always fancied the spartan ideal. But tell me, before you go, the girl that your man kidnapped . . . Amy, isn't that her name? Is she all right? How did she cope with the trial and all that sort of thing?'

'Surprisingly well,' he replied. 'She's actually a

terrific kid. Very independent, very in control. And she's lucky. She has a great relationship with her foster-parents. They've helped her a lot.'

There was silence again, still the sound of the singing in the background. He yawned.

'Sorry,' she said, 'I'm keeping you up. You should be at home in your bed. Off you go now. And listen, thanks again, for everything.'

He left the station and walked outside. There was no moon tonight and pools of darkness lay between the orange streetlights. He walked down Marine Road and along by the harbour. He'd seen a house today with Alison. One they both liked. It was in a cul-de-sac just off the main road. Five minutes to the shops and the harbour. He was going to enrol the girls in a sailing course next summer. They'd love it. There was a beautiful if neglected garden with the house. Alison was delighted. Another challenge for her green fingers.

He stopped by the slipway and looked out at the sea. It slopped lazily against the harbour walls. He thought of the cottage in the forest where Elizabeth lived. It would be lonely at night, especially in the winter. He recognized the song she had been playing and the singer. It was Billie Holiday. One of Alison's favourites. He wondered if Elizabeth was alone. He hoped she wasn't. She was a nice woman, he thought. She deserved a bit of love in her life. He turned back and looked at the houses and blocks of apartments along by the harbour. All those people defenceless in their sleep.

A breeze blew in from the east, ruffling his hair, making him suddenly shiver. He closed his eyes and opened his mouth, gulping cleansing lungfuls of salty air. It was lovely out here tonight. So fresh and quiet. He thought of what it would be like to be locked into a prison cell. When he was still in uniform, before he became a detective, he had been in and out of all the prisons more times than he cared to remember. He had never got used to the locks, the noise, the smell. How would a man like Daniel Beckett cope, he wondered. He had watched the prison officers take him away after the trial. Somehow he was no longer the strong, handsome man that he had been that night at the house. His hair was unkempt and untidy, his clothes sagged from his body. The handcuffs around his wrists transformed and defined him. He was a prisoner now. Plain and simple.

Jack looked at his watch. It was nearly two in the morning. It had been a long day. He turned back towards the sea again. Where was Rachel Beckett now, he wondered. Somewhere out there, he supposed, beyond the Kish bank. There wasn't much chance of finding her body, not after all this time. She had loved the sea, so she had told him. Perhaps it was fitting that she should have ended up there. He hoped that she hadn't suffered too much. But there would have been that moment when she must have realized. There was no way out of this. There was no one to save her.

He turned away from the water and started walking again, and this time he didn't stop until he got home. The apartment was dark and silent. He undressed quickly and slid into bed, slipping his arms around Alison's shoulders, pulling her head over on to his chest. He closed his eyes. He slept.

The wind blew from the east through the trees that surrounded Elizabeth Hill's cottage. It smelt of resin and grass and the scent of the hops ripening on their bines. Rachel curled herself up on the sofa, a glass of wine in her hand. She listened to the music coming from the CD player. And she listened to the phone conversation that Elizabeth was having with the guard from Dublin. She waited until Elizabeth put down the phone.

'Well,' she said, 'tell me.'

She remembered the way it was the first time she ever saw the prison. It was through the mesh that covered the windows of the van which brought her from the Four Courts that day all those years ago. It was winter. It was late afternoon, early evening. Rush hour in Dublin. It was dark, or it should have been dark. Except for the bright white lights everywhere, flooding the tarmacadam when they stopped at the gate. The first gate. Behind which was another gate, and behind that another, and finally the door of her cell.

She knew the way it would be the first time he saw the prison. Through the mesh that covered the windows of the van which brought him from the courts too. The chain from his handcuffs would tug at his wrist as he tried to move away from the prison officer and the other prisoners crowded into their seats all around him. The bright lights would catch his eyes, making him blink and wince as he climbed out into the yard. The noise from all the hard surfaces would assail his ears. Stone and brick. Tile and metal. And there would be the card stuck into the slot on the door of his cell. Form P30 with his name, his number, his religion, date of committal and sentence. But because he was a lifer no date for his release. Nothing to look forward to. Until the time when his sentence came up for review. And they might eventually say to him, we think it's time, Daniel. It's time.

Who would be waiting for him then? His children would have grown up. They would know little of him. And what of his wife? She smiled when she thought of Ursula, her manner, her voice, her demeanour. Ursula would move on, get a divorce, a financial settlement. Not for her the indignity of prison visiting, the embarrassment of ringing the bell at the huge metal door, sitting on the benches in the dirty, crowded waiting room with the other wives and girlfriends.

And how would he survive in prison? What kind of resources would he need to get him through the long days and the even longer nights? Banged up in a tiny crowded cell, smelling the stench of other men's piss and shit. Hearing the screams and cries of other men's dreams and nightmares. Wondering how had it happened that he had ended up like this. Wondering how she had pulled it off.

She would be tempted to tell him. That it had begun a long time ago, when she was in prison and she saw the photographs in a magazine. His house and his wife. She had time then, all the time in the world, to work out what she would do, and who would help her. And then she had met Judith, and begun to write to Judith's mother. And continued to write to Judith's mother when she came out of prison. And when the day came to go out on the boat, she had brought with her everything she needed. Daniel had commented on the weight of her bag. He wasn't to know what was inside it. A change of clothes, a pile of letters and a large envelope containing most of her mother's money. She left some of it behind. Just enough to confuse anyone who came looking for her. And as she walked away from Daniel afterwards a small white van stopped on the sea road beside her. A van driven by Elizabeth Hill. She got into the back and lay down on a mattress, undressed and covered herself with a blanket. And took the sleeping pills that Elizabeth gave her. And slept. Right through the trip on the ferry from the port at the North Wall. Slept while Elizabeth took her blood-ied clothes, stabbed at her blouse with a knife, then put them in a plastic bag and dropped them over the side when they were far enough out, past the Kish lighthouse, where there were no tides to sweep them away from the fishing boats' path. Slept most of the way as Elizabeth drove her from Holyhead to Chester, then on to the M6 motorway, and the M40 travelling south, the van rocked and shaken by the backdraught from the lorries that roared past them, as the pain from her hand spread up along her forearm.

Not much further, Elizabeth shouted, passing back a bottle of water and a cheese sandwich as they skirted around London on the M25. And she slept again, hearing through her dreams the rattle of the rigging and the sharp snap of the sails as they shook and filled with wind. Felt the speed of the van slacken as they turned off the main road, saw greenness all around her as they stopped and Elizabeth carried her out and into the house. Put her to bed. Peeled off the bandages, sticky and brown with dried blood. Swabbed the cut with disinfectant as Rachel cried out in pain. Told her that it was too late for stitches, that it would have to heal by itself. It would leave a scar. A big one.

'I don't care,' Rachel said. 'It was worth it. It's only my hand, not my face.'

Cradling it with her other hand as Elizabeth told her that she would bathe it every day with a solution made from yarrow steeped in hot water. The way her mother had always treated cuts, when she was a child, Elizabeth said. Swore by it, said it was as good as any treatment the doctor could give you.

She nursed her through the next couple of weeks, watching the wound close from the inside out, a thick ridge of new skin growing over the cut. She sat by her bed and watched her sleep, and waited until she was ready to face the world again. Then told her what she had read in the Irish papers on the Internet. A woman called Rachel Beckett who had served a life sentence for murder was missing. There were fears for her safety. A man had been questioned by the guards. And a few days later more news that the woman's daughter was also missing. Her foster-parents were distraught. They couldn't understand where she might be.

Rachel knew then what Daniel had done. He had taken her trap and he had turned it back on her. Baited it with Amy. And she knew what she had to do.

Where would he keep her, Elizabeth asked. Rachel knew. He would bring her home. The same way he brought Rachel home. He felt safe there. He would be in control. He would be able to do whatever he wanted, in his house with the big garden that ran down to the cliff edge, and the high granite walls and wrought-iron gates. The house that Rachel knew inside out. The garden she had explored. She held out the bunch of keys. They jingled together, musically.

'Look,' she said to Elizabeth. 'Look what I have.'

That night was special. The garden was even more beautiful than she had remembered. There was a half-moon, a silver slice of light in the sky. She could name off its seas. Mare Serenitatis, Mare Tranquillitatis, Mare Fecunditatis. Martin had shown her, Martin had told her. She sat with her back to the huge oak beneath the children's tree house and watched it. She felt at peace. She stroked the ridged scar on her hand. It still felt tender, different from the rest of her palm. She held it up in the moonlight and looked at it. It was just what she needed.

She stood up and walked towards the house. The lights were on, the windows were open. She unlocked the glass door to the kitchen. She heard him upstairs, heard Amy's cries for help, and Daniel's shouted responses. She lifted the key from its hook and put it in her pocket. Then she walked outside again and locked the door. Everything was prepared, everything was ready. She had removed the boards from the inspection pit in the garage. She had planned her route through the garden, the places she would hide. The children had shown her. The children had been her allies. She waited in the shadows until she saw him in the kitchen, then she stepped forward into the light and held up her hand. She pressed it against the glass. It was cold on her skin, except for the place where the scar tissue touched it. There was no sensation there. No feeling at all. He moved towards her. They stood facing each other with only the glass between them. She took the cloth from her pocket. She wiped away the palm and fingerprints. She stepped back into the darkness. She heard him scream with rage. She heard the bang of his fists on the door.

Such pleasure to be had from the chase. She had played hide-and-seek with his children and blind man's buff too, feeling her way through the garden with her eyes covered. He sounded so big and clumsy as he followed her. She could hear his breath, gasping for air as he ran. And his shriek of rage as he fell into the inspection pit, and his grunts of pain as he tried to get out. And then the final triumph as she led him back into the house. She called out to him.

'Come and get me, I'm here, I'm waiting.'

She could hear Amy's cries again. She wanted to unlock the door to the attic room and free her. But she knew she couldn't. Only the guards who were outside the gate, watching, could do that. She knew he would call them. He thought he had her trapped. But he didn't realize that she knew more than he did. He didn't know that she had learned all about how to hold her nerve, how to wait, how to hang on right to the end. That she had learnt it all from him.

And when he left the house again, when he gave up and ran towards the gate to let the policemen in, she ran too. Back down the cliff path, across the beach to the car park at the DART station where Elizabeth was waiting.

Now she cried as she huddled again on her mattress. She thought of her daughter and how she had suffered. 'Forgive me,' she said out loud. 'Please forgive me. I had to do it. It was the only way. And now I've let you go. To live your own life. Easier for you to think that I've gone too. So please, my beloved, remember me with love as you grow older, as you too make mistakes, as you realize how easy it is to slip and fall.'

They went back to England the way they had come. She could think no further into the future. Not now. She felt like Clare Bowen. Helpless and lost. She had seen Clare's death notice in the paper. Peacefully, it said. Deeply regretted by her loving husband, Andrew. She was glad for Clare that it was all over. And grateful to her. She had told Clare too what she was doing. And Clare had promised. She would say what needed to be said, at the right time.

Now she lay beside Elizabeth every night and listened to her gentle breathing. From time to time she cried out in her sleep, the way her daughter, Judith, once had done. And Rachel turned to her and held her closely, and thought no longer of revenge and retribution but only of love and forgiveness. Perhaps one day Amy would speak of her kindly. Show her own children her photograph and say, 'She was your grandmother. She is gone now. But I will never forget her. And neither must you.'

And she smiled as her eyes closed and sleep finally overcame her.